DARK REAPER

DARK REAPER

HOWARD CHILVERS

First published in 2018 by
Redshank Books

Redshank Books is an imprint of Libri Publishing

Copyright © Howard Chilvers

The right of Howard Chilvers to be identified as the author
of this work has been asserted in accordance with the
Copyright, Designs and Patents Act, 1988.

ISBN 978-0-9954834-2-2

A CIP catalogue record for this book is
available from The British Library

Typesetting by Carnegie Publishing

Cover design by Felix Chilvers

Printed in the UK by Lightning Source

Libri Publishing
Brunel House
Volunteer Way
Faringdon
Oxfordshire
SN7 7YR

Tel: +44 (0)845 873 3837

www.libripublishing.co.uk

Dedication

For my wife Sarah and our eight beautiful children...
follow your dreams.

Massive thanks to my many early readers for their time and
feedback and especially to David Thomson who worked tirelessly
reading and editing many versions of this book.

Howard Chilvers

Howard Chilvers was born and grew up in Ilford, Essex. Initially trained as a classical musician, Howard went on to major in Art Education before taking an advanced degree in the History of Design, having a particular interest in the transference of American values into British culture. After fourteen years teaching in secondary schools, Howard moved on to work in London at the Design Council before moving on to work in higher education at Middlesex University, where he led the MA Professional Practice and MA Design Leadership programmes before becoming an Associate Dean Business.

When working at the Design Council, Howard took a lead role in both writing and producing a full range of teaching resources for schools, including the drama-based videos, *Quiche, Keys and Roller Skates* — a New York Film Festival award winner— and *Brilliant or What!* He subsequently wrote a feature film script, *Sacred Betrayal*.

Howard's first novel, **Dark Reaper**, a deep, psychological crime-thriller, set in Los Angeles, draws on his intense interest in and observation of US culture.

Howard lived in Devon with his wife and family until February 2018 when he sadly died, from a brain tumour.

1

(Sunday, 1.54 a.m.)

MY CELL PHONE SHRILLS, jolting me awake. I look at the screen. It's Dee.

"Where've you been?" she asks, breathlessly, without any introduction. "The lieutenant's looking all over for you. Left messages and everything ... He's got your neck in the wringer." She lets the last syllable ring out with a long *errrr*.

I quickly look at my watch and realize I've been asleep for three hours.

"He wants to meet you at six ... after we're clear."

"Why? What's up?" I say as I lower the phone and scroll through my calls. Three have gone to message – still nothing from Lena.

"It's another body, Oskar."

A chill surfaces in my brain as I put the cell phone back to my ear. I breathe in deeply through the silence.

"You there, Oskar?"

"Yes, I'm here."

"It's him."

I'm not surprised to hear the words. The only certainties we've been running with these last few weeks are that he's murdered two people already, and that he'll most likely strike again.

It sounds as if he has.

"He's left the signature ..." Dee adds.

I say nothing. Waiting.

"Broken right arm this time ..."

Dee pauses for a few seconds as if expecting me to say something in the space she's leaving.

1

"You still there, Oskar?"

"Yes. I'm here."

There's another pause.

"Oskar," she finally says. "It's personal."

2

(Sunday, 2.28 a.m.)

DEE MEETS ME AS arranged in a company Caprice near the entrance to the 101 Freeway. I can see her waiting on the hard shoulder as I park up behind Chang's in a side alley. We'll probably be meeting back at the restaurant for breakfast and I know Chang won't mind me leaving my car until I collect it later. I leave my ignition key on top of the front nearside tire, just in case I'm in his way. Chang knows to move it round the corner if necessary.

I leave the alley on foot and look across the street to where Dee is waiting. I can tell she's seen me because she tosses a half-smoked cigarette out the window – her concession to help me with my own nicotine addiction.

I get in beside her and we set off.

Heading west, Dee brings me up to speed. She can drive a car better than most cops and doesn't hold back on making her way through the early morning traffic, towards the suburbs, as she talks.

"The com center says the caller lives in the block. He apparently heard her come in late on Thursday, two nights ago. He says it was around ten-thirty and he thought nothing more of it. He phoned saying there had been the usual sound of her walking across the floor after she closed her front door. Says she was a good tenant. Played her music quietly when she came home late at nights. He says he hadn't seen the body but he knew she'd been murdered."

This makes me wonder. How does the caller know she's been murdered if he hasn't seen her body?

"He said that she was usually alone ... and hear this ... 'cause she's a *'woman of the night'*," Dee says, rocking her head with incredulity. "Whatever world does he come from, Oskar? ... A woman of the night ... Huh?"

Dee is not an in-your-face feminist, but she dislikes the way men portray prostitutes as if it's the prostitutes who have the problem. I look across at her as she has her little rant. She's dressed in trademark combat trousers with a black zip-up jacket. The reflection from our flashing lights hits her face, casting a greenish glow onto her black skin as we speed along.

"Why did the caller phone in a murder, Dee?" I ask. "If he hadn't seen the body?"

"He didn't say. He just said there's been a murder. Apparently hung up before anyone could ask him that question."

We're soon on the elevated section of the freeway and pick up more speed as Dee's foot goes flat to the floor.

"He didn't hear no struggle," Dee continues. "But the mess at the crime scene apparently defies that bit of his story. A beat cop got there first, around twelve-twenty. Took a quick look, saw she was dead and immediately sealed up the place."

I'm thinking Dee's got the same killer in the frame, but I want to see for myself before deciding or saying anything. It looks as if I'll not have to wait long because I can see the turn-off for South Normandie coming up.

3

(Sunday, 2.39 a.m.)

W E PULL UP BEHIND the emergency vehicles at the scene. Their flashing lights reminding everyone in the neighborhood that something's not right with their world and they're the lucky ones to still be alive.

At the entrance to the apartment block, I notice the usual, surreal mix of inquisitive onlookers. They're trying to sneak a glimpse of a corpse to claim a macabre association with the unacceptable.

State professionals lean against their vehicles waiting for the word to kick into action. They're pissed off because they've arrived before the detective team. I watch them go through the usual pantomime of checking their watches, working out how long it'll be before they're called upon to perform their well-engineered duty.

As I pass through the onlookers, I notice Emmerson's Jaguar parked at the curb and sigh with relief. He did the cut on the other victims. If it's the same killer he should get the job done quickly and let me have his official report soon.

The cop at the plastic tape checks our badges and lets us through.

Already, I can sense the stench of death but nothing's reached my nostrils yet.

It's a five-floor apartment block and I'm guessing it was renovated from a derelict warehouse. This district is beginning to be in demand for busy professionals working downtown, and I'm estimating twenty minutes from the action dictates a minimum fifteen-hundred-dollars-a-month rental.

The front door is reached by climbing eight steps, making it feel grander than it really is. Passing through two columns, we reach it. It's wide open on this occasion, but the security locks and the steel that strengthens the doorframe reminds me nowhere is safe in this city.

Looking at the array of bell pushes – I count twenty or so tenants – Dee gives me a look that says *"that's my night ruined"*. She knows it'll be her knocking on all those doors throughout the early hours asking the questions only the police ask at times like these.

"It's on the third floor," Dee says. "The caller's on the floor below."

I know from experience that perpetrators themselves call in a high proportion of murders, so I'm interested to meet our caller as soon as possible. Caller-perps often feel they can hide behind the good deed of reporting the crime and escape detection.

Dee and I get to the second-floor landing.

"The caller's on this floor somewhere," Dee says, as she heads straight on up the third flight of stairs.

I'm still on the second-floor landing, looking around, when I see a door open and then close silently.

"The vic's on the next one," Dee calls down, not noticing what I took to be the caller giving me the once-over.

I nod towards the patrol officer waiting on this landing. Seeing him there gives me some confidence our caller won't be a runner before I've had a chance to speak to him.

I follow Dee up the stairs. She's climbing them two at a time, because she wants me to know that she's fitter than me. For some reason she needs me to know this. She's fitter all right, but not smarter – not yet, anyway.

Halfway up the flight, I'm able to stop and look at both the second- and third-floors simultaneously. I can see all the way across the upper landing and in through an open door to where

Emmerson is crouching over a body. Looking down, I notice the caller's apartment is directly below. This might explain why the caller heard everything. But why had there been a delay of two days before he called it in?

I eventually join Dee at the doorway of the victim's apartment. Glancing in, I see the body lying sprawled in a mess of blood on the bare wooden floor, partially wrapped in what looks to be curtain material. I can't help noticing that one of the victim's arms is broken. It's sickeningly pointing in the wrong direction. The signature.

4

(Sunday, 2.43 a.m.)

EMMERSON LOOKS UP ON my arrival, hearing me snap on a pair of latex gloves, and then emits a long puff of air from his lungs. Dead bodies, blood, crime scenes are nothing new to either of us, but something's not right here, and Emmerson's exhalation is his way of communicating this to me.

My respect for Emmerson has grown over the years. He's always prepared to give me the heads-up at any crime scene. He knows that, if he ends up being wrong and I act in good faith on his first impressions, I'll never implicate him or mention any error of judgment on his part. It's an unspoken understanding between us. Although, of course, I'll always expect him to stand by his official reports which come later.

I join him beside the body to watch him in action. He's instructing the photographer to take various shots of the vicious wounds and blood trails. Emmerson is a smoker like me, and I can see the familiar stain of nicotine running up the right side of his mouth and onto his cheek. He has a habit of leaving a cigarette to burn its way down whilst holding it in his mouth. It's common knowledge he does this whilst working at his desk late at night when he does his paperwork. His colleagues turn a blind eye to his old-school transgressions. He's well respected and few want to rock the boat for him when he's just three years away from his pension.

At five-feet-seven and weighing in at over two hundred pounds, Emmerson comes across as a roly-poly, no-nonsense character. I like his straight talking and forgive all his foibles so long as he gives me what I want.

He's wearing his beige linen suit this morning with its customary series of body fluid splatters that mark out his trade. I can see his pajamas peeking out of his pants, despite his best attempt to disguise this fact by stuffing them into his paper bootees.

I crouch down close. He looks up with his right eye open and his left eye closed as if he's still got a cigarette perched on one side of his mouth. I immediately switch weight from one knee to the other on the unforgiving wooden floor, letting out a loud click, further prompting him to answer the first question that's on my mind.

"Liver says about forty-eight to sixty hours." Emmerson lifts up the victim's unbroken arm to show me the extent of rigor mortis.

It's been fairly hot these last two days and nights and this is what has speeded up the decomposition. The foul odor is clinging to everything in the apartment, including the inside of my nostrils.

"Twenty-year-old female, I'd say, but who can really say these days, Oskar? They keep lowering the age of puberty don't they?"

Emmerson looks across to the floor, drawing my attention away from the body.

"Sexually active, going by the contents of her purse."

It's not his job to point these things out, but I can instantly see the foil strips.

"And, good at her job, I'd say, judging by that roll of notes."

I can see a thick bundle of bills, tied with a rubber band, amongst the condoms strewn across the floor. I notice a bankcard amongst them and lean across for a closer look.

"Jane Chandler," I say out loud after turning it around with my gloved finger.

"Well, our Ms. Chandler seems to have been living the life of Riley. No expense spared, I'd say. And the décor in this joint? ...

that's a genuine limited-edition Hockney print, for starters," he says, nodding towards the turquoise expanse of sea and sky above the mantelpiece. "Fifty grand's worth of decent toil lying on your back to stick that sort of stuff on your wall. What say you, Oskar? What say you?"

I say nothing, knowing he often leaves rhetorical questions hanging in the air.

"Knife-wound to the neck coming after the limb had been broken, I'd say. Just one this time. The right arm. Artery bleed to death," he continues. "Probably five minutes start to finish. She's lost a lot of blood. Five pints I'd say."

Emmerson gently turns the head of the victim and shows me where the killer has pushed a sharp implement into the neck and then severed the carotid artery. He raises his eyebrows to me indicating he knows what I'm thinking. He then points to the victim's forearm to show a fierce contusion where both the radius and ulna have been broken. Splintered bone protrudes through the soft brown skin.

"See, that's pretty nasty, but if you know what you're doing it's quite easy to do really." Emmerson's heavily nicotined fingers now move delicately around the damaged arm. "Slight bruising, here and here, seems to indicate it was done by hand, before she died, possibly with a knee behind. It snapped like a green stick."

I can see faint bluish-black marks each side of the wound. These show finger bruising where the killer had gripped firmly. Emmerson then imitates how the attacker might have broken the young girl's arm using one, swift, knee-jerking action.

I look across to Dee. She's holding her hand to her face as if she's attempting to ward off the evil that delivered this violent death. But I think she's just displaying a rookie's instinct for keeping the foul smell of the decomposing body from her nostrils to prevent herself retching. *Decomposition is as natural as birdsong. If you're bothered by the smell, either learn to live with it or get yourself another job*", Emmerson would often say when new recruits threw up in his presence.

I had learned to live with it, but Dee hasn't. Not yet, anyway.

I look back at the corpse and think about how this twenty-year-old prostitute had died. Like Dee, Emmerson seems to hear my questions before I ask them.

"Yes, she was probably conscious throughout. Interestingly, though, there seem to be fragments of cloth and skin trapped underneath her broken fingernails. She put up a fight, I'd say. Anyway, that's what it looks like to me. I'll need to take a closer look back at H.Q. and, if we're lucky, we'll get some DNA off this little lot. But, if this were *you-know-who*, I'd say we'd be frigging lucky don't you? That would be a real piece of luck. What say you, Oskar? What say you?"

Emmerson lifts up his finger to hold my attention and then picks up the curtain material from the body, showing me the victim is wearing the briefest of panties. Then he points to some faint, dried-up deposits.

"If that's semen, then we're going to have someone's DNA locked in. It could be work-related, I know, but it just might be your killer's."

I look up at Dee and see expectation etched into her eyes. We're both thinking that we might've struck it lucky this time. But I can see Emmerson is not so sure. There's something not quite right and he leans back, turning his attention back to the hands, keeping his thoughts to himself. After a short pause, he pulls the material back around the victim to cover as much of her legs as the material will allow. It's as if he's trying to bring some decency to the brutal scene that lies before us. With a final deep breath he starts to tidy away his bag.

5

(Sunday, 2.55 a.m.)

I LOOK OVER AT Dee. This is my sign to tell her to move carefully around the crime scene and look for any clues the photographer won't easily find through his lens. Geoff Hinton is taking the shots today and he steps forward with his kit, on cue, looking to me for direction.

I'm glad he's on duty. As with Emmerson, he and I know how to work together, and I give him a slight nod of acknowledgement before getting started. He's the expert with the lens – that's a given – but he also never lets his professional pride get in the way, so he's happy for me to point out things I think he might miss.

I take a look at the curtains down off the rail and entangled around the corpse. I imagine the victim pulled it across her body in a vain attempt to protect herself from her attacker, or, perhaps, from the eyes of her attacker? She was after all, very beautiful. She may have been a *woman of the night,* but she may also have wanted some dignity in front of an unexpected or unwanted visitor.

I notice a broken wine glass on the floor by the balcony and what looks to be red wine spillage on the carpet and walls. Looking further around, I see another glass, intact this time and full of white wine, sitting on the work surface in the kitchen area. At this end of the room the sofa is splattered with what looks to be blood but may be the red wine. I point this out to Hinton.

I notice the stereo is still switched on and press play. The room is immediately filled with choral music. I recognize the piece immediately. It's Morten Lauridsen's *O Magnum Mysterium,* something Lena had been playing recently that I liked. She'd said the piece helped her connect to her spiritual side.

Whilst the music plays, I try to imagine what happened here.

The victim comes home tired after a hard day's work. She runs a bath and listens to some music and then pours herself some wine. Did she have the red or the white? She emerges from the bathroom to find her visitor. Is it a customer? Was he here all the time? She offers him a glass of wine – is it the red or the white? – but he doesn't take it. She realizes something's wrong and gets scared, so she retreats towards the kitchen. Once more she offers him a glass – yes it was the red – but he refuses and smashes it out of her proffered hand, sending the glass over towards the balcony and into the wall.

She's really frightened now and, feeling exposed by her nakedness, she makes a measured retreat behind the sofa, wrapping herself in the only thing she can find, one of the curtains blowing in the warm breeze that's coming in through the open balcony doors.

It's in these moments of imagining that pieces of the jigsaw can sometimes come together. I often rely on this instinctive, intuitive approach and so does Dee. I can see her keeping a watchful eye on me whilst she goes through a similar mental exercise.

Dee often arrives at an alternative version of events – another "story" – and this is what makes us good partners. I'm convinced we'll be arguing over this one at Chang's later on, because there are clues here that leave much open to the free-ranging gaze of our imaginations and the influence of our differing experiences.

Mine have been honed by working the murder-beat in L.A. for twenty years. Dee's, on the other hand, have been crafted by doing a law enforcement bachelors straight from school, followed by an intensive masters at California Baptist University. Dee has solved many crimes, I grant her that, but most were simulated in the classroom. I know she's also read many case histories because – as she keeps reminding me – I'm written into many of them.

More importantly, though, Dee is younger. She's also had a different upbringing and her experiences in life bring another perspective to our joint thinking. I can hear what she'll be saying over a coffee, *"Just 'cause you been around the block six times before I was outta diapers, Oskar, doesn't make you no expert on what a woman thinks at times like these."*

The more Dee and I work together, the more respect I give her, because her experiences are growing day-by-day. She's a dedicated learner, and her insights are improving with each case we take on, so I'll be listening to her very carefully today, especially if she disagrees with me.

Lauridsen's choral piece reaches a beautiful climax and I feel it jar with the brutality delivered in this room, so I eject the disk before moving across to the bathroom. The bathtub is filled to the brim. The fingerprint team will lift any prints off the taps because the killer may have ended up turning them off. The water is cold now and there's a faint smell of bath-oil in the air, fighting its way through the stench of drying blood and the decomposing body in the next room. It's fighting a losing battle.

In the bedroom, the victim's clothes lie on the floor, seemingly where they've been dropped. The designer labels suggest our victim didn't stint on paying for the best. I point these out to Dee knowing she'll be able to identify the designers and possibly know where the clothes have been purchased. Dee immediately pouts her lips at the Gucci shoes that I do recognize, nodding slowly, indicating she thinks they're genuine and not street-market fakes.

I see an oriental screen in one corner of the room. It looks antique. It's made up of six wooden panels depicting hand-painted erotic scenes that I'm guessing are from the Kama Sutra. Bodies are intertwined with each other in various positions of sexual intercourse. I look behind the screen to find that a small chair has been placed there. I wonder why. I sit down in the chair and find it surprisingly comfortable, despite its size. That's when I notice a knothole, about the size of a dime, letting in a shaft of light from the other side. I soon realize that this hole will allow anyone sitting here a "convenient" opportunity to look through to the other side. I have to lean down a fraction, but when I put my eye up to the hole I can easily look out across the room. I can see Dee on the far side. She's on her knees now, still examining the shoes and clothes. I'm looking straight at her – voyeuristically I'm thinking – knowing she can't see me.

Feeling uncomfortable, I pull away and look further around the back of the screen, noticing another shaft of light higher up. I stand up, hearing my left knee click again with the effort. I take a peek through this knothole and get a sudden shock, because Dee is standing immediately behind the screen studying the images on the other side. She's no prude, but I can tell she doesn't approve. It's also clear that Dee is completely oblivious to the fact that I'm watching her, closely. This makes me feel distinctly uneasy, so I come out from behind the screen, saying nothing to her about what I've been doing or what I've found. Dee in turn moves quickly away, feigning uninterest in what she'd clearly been scrutinizing very carefully with a "what-fits-where" look on her face.

I look again at the screen from this side and try to find the holes I've been looking through. They are very hard to locate because they've been strategically placed within the erotic images themselves, making it very difficult to spot them amongst intertwined limbs.

I turn my attention next to the floor-to-ceiling, mirrored-glass panels that cover one wall of the bedroom. Guessing what lies behind, I place my fingers into recesses and slide them apart. Lights come on automatically, revealing a cavernous, walk-in wardrobe about the size of the bedroom itself.

There are numerous racks full of beautiful clothes. They're all hung neatly and sorted according to their different color ranges. The victim's preferences seem to focus on deep-reds, blues and purples. More designer-label shoes are stored in boxes placed high up on shelves. I start counting the boxes but end up having to estimate the number because there are so many – at least fifty pairs. An old-fashioned oak stool is positioned nearby and I'm guessing the victim used this when she was putting on her shoes and when she needed to reach up for the topmost boxes.

Dee joins me in here now and lets out a long, low whistle. I can see she's impressed, knowing her love of clothes, and suspect there's a little envy in there too. There's plenty of space to move around, select items and then try them on. To one side are floor-length mirrors positioned to enable a full 360-degree view. It feels decidedly like one of the upmarket boutiques in Beverly Hills.

Dee takes down a deep-red gown off a rail and drapes it against her body, looking, at herself in the mirror. This time, she sees I'm looking at her and gives me her best imitation of a model's pout and then sports an "if only" smile before placing the dress back on the rail. It's very clear that this was an important room for our victim. At one level, the care and dedication she's spent on accumulating the clothing and storing it marks out her trade, but it also marks out her desire for dressing in the most beautiful clothes and looking her very best. This woman had expensive tastes in the things she hung on her body as well as her walls.

I move back out into the bedroom and realize Hinton has moved into the bathroom because the flash from his camera is bouncing off the tiled surfaces and is finding its way onto the mirrors in here. This is enough of a distraction to make me realize I've seen enough for now. Dee looks across at me indicating she has as well. I can also hear the Scene of Crime Officers hovering near the door of the apartment and, following a nod from me, I decide to leave them to work with their sprays, brushes and plastic evidence bags.

I spend the next ten minutes pointing out the areas where I'd like them to pay particular attention: The wardrobe doors, the taps, the wineglasses, the blood and semen splatters, the screen, doing my best to say this sensitively and not try to teach grandmothers to suck eggs.

When they finish and the body has been strapped to a gurney and wheeled out to the waiting ambulance, it will be taken back to the morgue. Eventually, it will find its way onto Emmerson's stainless steel table for its final, humiliating demolition.

6

(Sunday, 3.20 a.m.)

EVEN THOUGH IT'S AFTER three in the morning, Frank Tomlinson, the caller, is waiting for us behind his door; I see his shadow in the spy-hole as Dee and I approach. I ring the bell and he opens up. Rather too quickly for my liking.

Entering his apartment is like visiting a retirement home. There's a faint smell of boiled fish, mingling with the odor of someone who spends a great deal of time in here.

"Please come in," he says, before we've had a chance to introduce ourselves.

He leads us down the hallway and into his sitting room. I estimate there's about six hundred square feet of space, and it looks the same shape and size as the victim's sitting room above. Everywhere is neat and tidy and all furniture and furnishings seem orientated towards the television, which is positioned in the corner next to a large bay window that looks out onto South Normandie Street. It suggests the TV screen and possibly this window are the main focal points for the room. I get the feeling he's someone who notices everything. Not only is he our caller, I think he's a *watcher*.

We both hold out our badges.

"I'm Detective Salo and this is my partner, Detective Chance," I say as he invites us to sit down opposite him at a large coffee table.

I sit, but Dee stands to the side, as instructed by me earlier.

Tomlinson, pale-skinned and thin, is wearing a maroon-plaid dressing gown over large check pajamas. He's also wearing a pair of worn carpet slippers. Studying him further, I guess he's about fifty, although he did appear older at first. He's clearly anxious and I consider this for a moment, deciding his general attire and demeanor is not surprising bearing in mind the time of day and what's happened upstairs. But I'm just wondering if his anxiety is also about wanting to please me too much.

"We're with LAPD, Mr. Tomlinson, and we'd like to—"

"Call me Frank," he interrupts, leaning forward.

"—ask you ... Yes, Frank. I'd like to ask you a few questions."

"Please—Please do," he says, eagerly.

Out of the corner of my eye, I notice Dee is doing what she does best. She's studying the room very carefully by thin-slicing, as she calls it. She's looking for the little things by dissecting – slice by slice – what's staring us in the face. She's looking for those small clues hidden in the bigger picture. At this moment she's looking at the large framed print on the wall – no Hockney here. I think it's an early-morning view of the palms in Echo Park. The view across the lake. We both know that, the more we digest in these first few hours, the better chance we'll have of solving the case. Statistics demonstrate the first twenty-four hours are the most crucial and Emmerson has already given us the heads-up that we're probably forty-eight hours behind. So, like me, Dee is impatient to keep things moving.

"Frank, tell me in your own words what happened here on Thursday night."

"Well, Detective Salo, I came home after my weekly game of bridge around ten. I play bridge with the Jenkinsons on Thursdays. I partner with Mr. Johnston. He's a good friend but not a fine player of bridge if the truth were known."

I feel myself shift uncomfortably in my seat and hope he'll pick up from this that I can do without minor details at this stage.

"I know it was ten," he continues, "because I always leave at nine-forty, so I can get back here for the ten o'clock news. I like the news you see. The ten o'clock news packs all the day's events into one bundle. It lets you have it all in thirty minutes. Just thirty minutes."

He sits back slightly, as if he's considering the comment he's just made. I remain silent, giving him the space to explain.

"The day's news in just thirty minutes. It doesn't seem fair some days does it? All that torment, death, destruction ..."

He glances upwards before returning his gaze quickly back to me, as if he's seen something of the torment, death and destruction above. I sit forward in my chair, wanting to spur him on with his story, and glance across at Dee. She raises an eyebrow, suggesting she's glad he's mine.

"That's what I like about the ten o'clock news, it can—"

"Tell me, Frank," I interrupt, recognizing my patience with him is wearing thin. "Just tell me what happened with your neighbor on Thursday? Pick it up from when she arrived back home. What time was that?"

"Around half-eleven I'd say. Yes, half-eleven. I know that because I'd switched channels and was watching Columbo. It's on every night at the moment? It's the repeat – well they're all repeats aren't they? It was the one about the millionaire who kills his wife with the fishing line he'd used to catch tuna off the back of his yacht, earlier in the—"

"Frank. Look. Please keep to the key facts about Thursday night, will you?" I hear the beginning of exasperation in my voice, and see surprise written on Tomlinson's face, so I decide to start again. I take another breath and lean forward, doing my best to smile. "Look Frank. Work with us here. We need to find out what's happened and the sooner we get on to it the better. Please just take us through the important main events. The timings are very helpful, but not with the episode of Columbo at this stage. We can verify all this later when, perhaps, Detective Chance here can return and interview you in more detail. She can cross-check the finer points of your story with what happened in Columbo."

Tomlinson turns and smiles at Dee, who gives a pleasant smile in return, but when he turns back she gives me one of her classic *up yours* expressions.

"Please continue, Frank," I say. He takes a deep breath.

"Well, around eleven-thirty, before Columbo ended, I heard Jane arrive back home. She came up the stairs past my front door. I often open my door and wish my fellow tenants a good evening, but not after ten."

He gives me a look that seems to enquire if I understand his reasoning. I just nod and sit further forward, urging him to continue. I also hold at bay any thoughts I have about him using the victim's first name.

"She went into her apartment. I heard the door close with its usual bang. It's straight above mine you see, so I can always hear her footsteps when she returns ... on the floor above. She wears high heels," he says, as if attempting to qualify his knowledge of her movements. "If I listen carefully, I can even hear her walk bare-foot across the floor sometimes." He pauses again, smiling, almost reflectively, as if picturing something in his mind's eye.

"Then, what happened Frank? Take me through what happened next."

"Well ... Well, I'm not sure I know anything more that can help you, Detective. The truth is, I never heard anything else. There was nothing."

"You didn't hear anything?"

"No. Not after that, not on Friday ... or Saturday. Nothing that I can remember, anyway. Jane just came home late Thursday night as I say, went into her apartment above, walked across the floor in her high heels, took them off ... and then, all was quiet."

"You said she took off her high heels. How do you know she took them off, Frank? How do you know she *actually* took her shoes off?"

"Because ... after Jane walked across the floor ... I ... I never heard her footsteps again."

Suddenly, he stares at me with astonishment etched into his face. His jaw drops and he sits back, realizing the enormity of what he's just said and what he's thinking now. He looks into my eyes, almost pleadingly.

"You mean ... she was killed then? ... at that moment ... after she walked across the floor above me."

He slumps even further back in his chair, seemingly answering the question for himself. I look at Dee and nod towards the kitchen. Whilst she goes to fetch some water, I give Tomlinson the best sympathetic smile I can muster.

"Well, we don't know that, Frank, but I wondered how you were so sure she took off her shoes? At that point?"

Dee comes back with a tumbler of water and passes it to Mr.Tomlinson who gulps it down as if it will ease the situation.

"I'm sorry, Detective, it's just that I've never ... never had to ... you know ... I never thought that ..."

"That's okay, Frank. I understand and I'm sorry, but let's go back. How do you know that was the moment she took off her shoes?"

"I don't, Detective. I don't know whether she took off her shoes at that point or not. It's just that every night I hear her come up the stairs. Go into her room. Close her door. Walk across the wooden floor in her high heels. Then, the noises stop. It's the same most nights, you see."

Tomlinson is looking hard at me now, checking I understand what he's saying.

"Okay, I've got that, Frank. Okay, thank you. Let's move on. Let's get to the moment you called the police tonight. It was you who dialed 911 tonight, wasn't it?"

"Yes. I dialed 911."

"Why Frank? I mean, why did you call 911 tonight? You know, two days later."

This time, he just looks up to the ceiling without saying a word and lets out a long breath. After a few agonizing seconds, whilst my patience with him begins to disappear, I look up myself. That's when I see the deep red stain on the plaster, about the size of a dinner plate. I hadn't noticed it before and I don't think Dee had either. It's a dull crimson color, turning a dusty orange at the outermost edges, where the blood has started to dry.

"I dialed 911 because I saw the blood on the ceiling tonight. It was only then that I realized that Jane had been murdered … I know that it was just after midnight because Saturday night's episode of Columbo had just finished. Columbo always finishes at twelve."

7

(Sunday, 4.07 a.m.)

WITH THE SOUND OF a media chopper hovering in the sky, I leave Dee with two uniforms to knock on doors. I'm heading back in Dee's Caprice to the PAB to prepare for my meeting with the lieutenant. It's a short drive back, but I'm hoping this will give me long enough to review what we know and help me prepare for his onslaught.

No doubt the lieutenant will have been on the phone to his superiors, preparing for how they'll quell the ravenous appetite of the public for all that *'torment, death and destruction'* Tomlinson spoke about earlier. He'll be demanding to know why we're no further forward in nailing this killer than we were ten weeks ago, when the first victim was laid on the floor.

The first victim was a forty-six-year-old factory worker, murdered in a campground beside a fishing lake in the mountains. Our second victim, a thirty-five-year-old businessman, had been slain in a back-alley behind a hotel, five weeks later. Both had been savagely attacked, and like Jane Chandler, both had had a limb broken in what seems to have been a macabre ritual before their carotid artery had been severed and they'd bled to death on the floor.

As is standard practice, certain elements of the killings were not revealed to the media in case we managed to grab a suspect. These included details about which artery had been targeted and which limb had been broken. We could then use this information to trick a potential suspect into exposing his guilt. Or, identify a copycat murderer if he stepped into the drama by attempting to imitate our killer. There've been notable exceptions, but copycats won't necessarily know the finer points of our killer's perversions and would only be able to mimic what had been reported in the press.

However, I'm sure these three murder cases will now be classified as a single, serial-murder investigation, even though Emmerson hasn't presented his report on today's victim. There'll be national media coverage and also interest from additional powerful forces including, of course, the FBI. Hence the importance of my meeting with the lieutenant this morning, because I'm thinking I can use this potential exposure as leverage to get from him what I want.

I've asked Dee to make a start by knocking on the doors of other apartments in the vicinity of South Normandie, starting with the block where the murder has taken place and then moving around the neighborhood. Dee's agreed to work with two of the assigned police officers at the scene and then grab a lift back with them to the PAB when she's finished.

Speaking to people on the doorstep is Dee's specialty – she gets them to both open up their doors and open up to her. She's always been able to extract more than I ever could, because she puts people at ease in ways I can't. She and the officers will probably spend three hours knocking on alternate doors keeping in sight of each other as they go. Given the signs that we're almost certainly dealing with the same violent, sadistic killer, Dee and the officers will take extra care, and look after each other. Despite the fact we're all assuming the killer's long gone, we can't rule out the possibility he's a local. And, there's always the chance they'll knock on the door of some hothead junkie, sleeping off his addiction, and he might not be best pleased to be woken at four in the morning to be asked dumbass questions by dumbass officers.

I know that Dee is not only careful and vigilant in these situations, she's also observant, spotting things that are unusual in an everyday scene. Things that others – including me – will often miss. This makes her a very special and much-needed member of my team.

Very early on in her career, she came to prominence in one case by noticing marks down a hallway carpet after someone had opened up their door to her. These turned out to be impressions left by a murder victim's shoes when his lifeless body had been dragged across the threshold. This happened in the macabre morgue that had been Harold Delaware's home and business premises. He had stored his victims' bodies in chest freezers out the back of his house in a car repair shop. By following up on her observant actions, Dee single-handedly broke open the case, leading to Delaware's arrest, and his later conviction of multiple murders.

I suddenly find myself on South Grand and wonder if I've subliminally chosen this route so that I can drive past *Geometrix*. I look up to the third floor, willing that I'll see a light left on. Deep down I suspect Lena's left me for good this time, but I find myself looking up to my apartment, expectantly, hoping she's come back in the night.

My apartment in *Geometrix* is worth more than my LAPD salary could ever afford, but I'd struck lucky a few years ago when I was working as a private investigator after being suspended as a detective. I'd stumbled on the $12.2M heist from the LAX gold bullion haul. I'd seen the brains behind the gang enter a lock-up dressed as a woman and, despite there being a multitude of private dicks working the case, I'd had the luckiest break in my life and received 10% of the haul as reward money. The $1.2M paid for the apartment outright and also paid off my debts at the time.

The apartment block, designed by Ottar Hakkinen in the 60s, was built in 2003, shortly after the famous architect had died. I live in the *Cube* – a glass-and-steel-constructed block built of four floors, taking its name from its form. It's connected to the other blocks in the development – the *Pyramid*, the Sphere, and the *Curve*. All twenty-two homes are interlinked asymmetrically around the gated entrance and turnaround in front of the glass-sided atrium and lobby. This unique structure is cradled between other, more traditional office blocks that make up this downtown area of L.A. It was erected alongside another building created by Hakkinen. Although this is more formal in design, one of the conditions laid down by the Hakkinen Foundation was that the architect's experimental set of apartments had to be built alongside his carbon-neutral commercial center. It was controversial at the time, but a narrow vote by the city council cleared the way for *Geometrix* to be built. Like many quirky innovations in L.A., it has now become a major landmark feature and even appears on tourist maps of the area.

Pulling up at the security gate, I look down into the lower ground-floor car park to see if I can spot Lena's Alfa. I'd managed to secure an additional bay for her because one of the guards is an ex-cop, but I can see immediately that her 'reserved' space is empty. I take one last look up to the third-floor and, after satisfying myself she's not there, bang the steering wheel with both palms. I then gun the accelerator and pull back out onto South Grand with a squeal of tires, drawing the attention of the attendant at the gate who looks up from his Sudoku.

He recognizes me and gives me a friendly-enough smile and wave, but doesn't get anything in return.

Frustrated and angry, I speed my way along through empty streets towards the PAB. I'm soon in sight of headquarters and pull up at the curb and switch off the ignition. I recognize immediately that I'm in need of a nicotine fix because, somewhere along the journey, I've put the end of a cigarette in my mouth.

Looking at my watch, I notice it's four-thirty and decide I'll start my preparations for the day out here rather than at my desk. I know I sometimes do my best thinking sitting in a car. I'm physically tired, yes, but my brain is jazzed up for the hunt and I want to use this energy straight away. But, most importantly, I can also smoke a cigarette out here without setting off those fucking alarms we have in every room in our new police headquarters.

I light up and crank the window, recognizing it's Dee's Caprice I'm sitting in. I get out my book and look at the notes I've already made about the latest victim and start to consider what connects her to the other victims. They've all seemingly been picked at random: David Henshaw found hacked to pieces by the lake, the family man out on a fishing trip with his young son; Eric Green, the businessman, happily married by all accounts, found butchered in a back alley; and now Jane Chandler, a high-class prostitute, slaughtered in her own home. I know that if I find out what connects them I might stand a chance of identifying the killer's motives and this might help me find the killer. So far, I've got nothing.

Until today, there's been no DNA evidence to work from, so I'm hoping what we've found under Chandler's fingernails and on her panties might give us the break we've been seeking. Some of my colleagues talk about victim's bodies 'speaking' to them – revealing things personally – but I don't go in for that mumbo-jumbo. Nonetheless, I can't deny that dead bodies sometimes reveal key information. So, I'm just hoping that today's find will assist. But what I need most of all is more resources. I need to free up my time so that I can chase this killer down the black hole where he's hiding. I want to know how he behaves, how he operates. I want to be one step ahead of him rather than one behind. I want to delve into his personality and get into the way he operates. The way he thinks.

This thought makes me realize how important my meeting with the lieutenant will be in an hour's time. I'm thinking it'll not be what I say to him that'll get me what I want, but how I say it. He's a long-in-the-tooth negotiator who won't bend easily to demands on his over-stretched budget. I'll have to warm him up gently and then strike.

I toss the cigarette butt onto the sidewalk and immediately put another to my lips, trying to work out when my new quota for the day will begin. I've allotted myself twenty cigarettes a day in this new regime and, as I try and kid myself the new day hasn't started, I notice the sun's rays are beginning to creep over the buildings and wonder who's kidding whom. I reluctantly decide this will have to be my first of the new day and start the count.

As I light up, headlights catch my eye in the mirror, and I notice the lieutenant's Oldsmobile Bravada. I look at my watch. It's five A.M. He's an hour early. Experience tells me he'll be aggressive and temperamental if he hasn't slept properly. Because of his rank, he doesn't share the benefits of overtime pay, so this morning's early rise is bound to make him extra tetchy. Experience also suggests he's more pliable when he hasn't had time to sit and fester on things at his desk, so I decide the best option is to get in there now and confront him, head on.

As I collect my things together, I hear his tires squeal over the speed bumps that lead down to the underground car park. This makes me alight from the car even quicker. I drop the half-smoked cigarette to the floor and grind it into the dirt with my heel.

8

(Sunday, 4.54 a.m.)

THE REAPER LOOKS TO the horizon feeling reborn. He'd listened to the news of the slaying of the prostitute and liked the newscaster's reference to the murderer being a Grim Reaper. He's taken part of this moniker and used it to rededicate himself to the mission he started ten weeks ago.

Dawn is about to break and, with his new name emblazoned in his heart, he climbs into his pickup and heads off to his workshop in the mountains.

One part of him relishes this early light, beckoning him forward. It makes him feel good to be alive. It gives him a purpose. But the other part of him wants to retreat into the darkness.

Where he truly belongs.

9

(Sunday, 5.05 a.m.)

I MAKE MY WAY into the PAB and walk past the front desk. Joe Sifionios, a small rotund man with a grizzly face and stubby mustache, is on duty. No matter what time of day, he always gives the impression he's got better things to be doing than dealing with visitors or staff. On this occasion he gives me the hard stare, the friendlier of the two greetings he has available. The other is his smile, which he uses only when he's really pissed off.

"Morning Joe. Lieutenant in?" I ask.

"Yes, he is and he's gagging to see you. 'Cause he asked for you personally this morning."

"Thanks Joe. Buzz him and say I'm on my way up, will you? And, by the way, I take two sugars in my coffee when you've got a moment," I call out as I make my way towards the elevator.

"Sure thing," he shouts back. "And then I'll come massage your shoulders ... Smartass."

The ride up gives me my last opportunity to gather my thoughts on what I'll say to the lieutenant. Although I haven't had the chance to prepare fully, I decide upon the basic strategy. I'll give him some slack at first and make him feel all-powerful, then I'll hit him with a late punch, hopefully catching him by surprise.

I've known the lieutenant for three years and, although he's difficult to work with, I've few complaints. My confrontations are bearable at the best of times and frustrating at their worst. But, most importantly, I can usually predict what he'll say and this gives me the edge in the games we play.

The elevator arrives at the sixth floor and the doors open.

Although it's now a little after five, and my meeting has been scheduled for six, I can see the lieutenant in the tank waiting for me as I come through the swing doors. I suspect he struck a deal with Sifonios on his way in and got him to buzz as soon as I arrived.

"You're late!" he barks from inside his office as I walk across the empty squad room towards my cubicle. Colleagues are not in yet and anyone working a night shift is probably into a second stack of pancakes at Mickeys by now. The lieutenant is standing in the doorway of his office and he's got one arm up against the pillar. This is his, *I'm-pissed-with-you-and-you're-gonna-fucking-pay* stance – maybe his wife has chucked him out for good this time. I'm also guessing he's dressed quickly this morning and ended up stuffing himself into the first shirt he could find; it's too small, and he's not been able to do up the top button. He's attempted to disguise this by wearing a large, flower-patterned tie, dating back to the 60s, making me suspect it's genuine and not a retro-design. Although powerful and strong in his prime, the lieutenant's put on at least twenty pounds in the last three years – his physique may have changed, but his wardrobe hasn't.

He looks at me long and hard, prompting me to get on with my report. But I'll not roll over on this one. I need more backup to nail this killer, so I'll take this conversation at my own pace. I want to be in control, even though I'll have to play the victim at times.

"Sorry Boss, I've been following up on a few leads," I lie, as I sit down low in my chair. The lieutenant comes across, clearly agitated. He has to look down at me and I see this helps him gain a sense of physical superiority before we start.

"Well, whaddaya got then?" he asks, bluntly.

"Same crude tactics. Same telltale signature. Inflicting brutal pain before draining the victim of blood ... another innocent victim by all accounts. It's him all right."

I refer to my notebook.

"A Ms. Jane Chandler is the vic. The perp crept in, crept out. No one's seen him come or go. Dee's on the doors and floors now

31

and she'll be on the streets around the block, asking questions. She's not reported anything significant yet," I say, suggesting I've been in regular contact since I left the scene an hour ago.

"What's the time of death?" he barks back. "Not confirmed. Emmerson's doing the cut."

The lieutenant nods slowly, so I decide to continue.

"He suggests it's around midnight, Thursday. The caller's said he heard her come back, slam her door, walk across the floor above, then, zilch. He eventually calls 911 last night, when he notices a red patch on his ceiling. It's apparently only then that he suspects she's been murdered. We reckon it's taken forty-eight hours for the blood to soak its way through from the floor above. He didn't notice it till last night."

"Why'd he call in a murder and not anything else? Why didn't he call in and just say that he thinks she may have injured herself or something? Or, that he was just concerned for her? Why call in that she'd been murdered? Why did he use the word 'murder' if he hadn't seen her body?"

It often takes the lieutenant four or five attempts to get to the real question.

"Good point, Lieutenant, but I'm not sure I can answer that yet. I'm gonna haul him in and grill him more thoroughly, A-S-A-P."

I write something down in my notebook because I want the lieutenant to feel he's contributed something positively to the investigation. He immediately steps back, nodding his head a few times, and taking up a less aggressive stance. I sense he's *warming*.

"The real issue here, Lieutenant, is that we'll have to nail this case before the Feds come sniffing around ..."

I see this statement ignite a fire that's possibly been smoldering. I know the lieutenant will not be prepared to kowtow to the FBI – no one in his position will want to do that, especially in LAPD where animosity between the two organizations is high.

"... If they haven't done so already," I add, putting more fuel on the fire. "The tally's three now, Lieutenant, and that makes this guy a serial murderer. Unless we solve this case quickly, the powers-that-be will be making the decisions for us both," I say, pointing a finger upwards to the ceiling. All the way to the tenth floor.

The chief has his suite on the tenth and his deputy on the seventh, and I know that either is capable of getting under his skin should there be a whiff of the FBI muscling in. Like him, the chief and his deputy know that the FBI is always interested in serial murder cases, especially ones with salacious overtones.

"Perhaps the best way would be to go straight to the NCAVC and ask for their support rather than wait around for the Bureau to come forcing its way in. We could then maintain the upper hand but still give the FBI some minor involvement. They'll have some personality profilers to help us identify who we're chasing."

He knows that the National Center for the Analysis of Violent Crime provides behavioral-based support on request. Nonetheless, it still has the tag of being FBI, so I'm guessing he won't want them either.

I press on towards my goal.

"They could bring in the expertise to help us here, Lieutenant. If you're prepared to ask for it, that is. It's either that route ... or, you could agree to buy in an expert yourself ... go to a private contractor."

"What ... What do you mean?"

He's nibbling at the bait, so I sit back. I want to give him space to bite.

"Well, you could hire a private profiler for a few days, someone who specializes in serial murders ... an expert of your own choosing. There are excellent ones working freelance. We've used them before, haven't we? Very successfully in my opinion. And, if you want to keep the momentum going, you'll need more people on this. We need more feet on the ground ... people watching suspects, following leads, scrutinizing witness statements, doing the legwork, analyzing data ... In fact, we need people to do the work the Bureau guys would do if they came waltzing in with their sharp suits and sharp haircuts ... and their *own* fancy experts."

The lieutenant starts to stroke the top of his balding head, a sure sign he's trying to make up his mind. He then moves away and starts pacing the floor – another sign – and then starts tapping out a staccato rhythm on his leg with his pen – I think he's doing the math. He finally rubs his hand over his balding head again before moving back to his office – to check his budget forecasts, I'm thinking.

"Wait there," he shouts over his shoulder as he disappears inside the tank. "Give me a minute, will you?"

I think he's taken the bait. Hook, line and sinker.

10

(Sunday, 7.15 a.m.)

I MEET DEE AT Chang's with a renewed sense of enthusiasm after my big win with the lieutenant. I see Dee's already arrived and made a start on breakfast. She gives me a dejected look suggesting it's been a long slog pressing on those doorbells and asking questions. I slide along the bench-seat opposite her and order an orange juice and toast from one of Chang's cousins. I see from Dee's demeanor that she thinks her work has gone unrewarded.

"What's up?" I say in an attempt to rouse a response.

"One guy says he's seen some short Hispanic come into the block around eleven on the evening in question, Thursday. Said he looked *'suspicious',*" she quotes, sarcastically, wiggling two fingers in the air. "He apparently turned his head away to hide his face when he came up the stairs ... But, Oskar, don't mortgage your house on it. He was one of those creeps more interested in my knowing how I should spell his name rather than helping me catch the killer. Anyways, I've put out a BOLO and sent Cerillo to get an artist's impression for the early morning news."

Cerillo is our resident artist with the knack of getting very good likenesses from witnesses' verbal descriptions. Like the FBI, LAPD continues to rely on artists' sketches rather than use computer-based, facial-composite systems preferred elsewhere. I nod to Dee, letting her know I'm pleased with her actions, especially the Be-On-Look-Out call to patrolling officers. Even though it might not lead to anything, it will alert officers to the developing investigation. Dee knows I like all major decisions run past me but she also knows when she can act without my approval.

Fuelled up with food, Dee now buries her face into a large Americano. Chang makes a special early-morning 5-shot coffee in a large double-handled cup that takes a pint of his best brew. He promotes it for hard-core coffee-drinkers like Dee who need their systems rebooted at the start of the day.

When Dee sees me looking towards her expecting more feedback, she shakes her head. A silence follows coinciding with traffic stopping outside. Dee looks at her watch and smiles at me over the top of her cup. She's telling me it's seven-twenty. Dee has a theory that lulls in conversation often appear at twenty minutes past the hour. Knowing I don't go in for that kind of nonsense, Dee relishes any opportunity to rub my nose in it when she's right.

"Nothing else, Oskar. Sorry," she says, ending the interlude.

I decide this is my moment to bring Dee up to speed on my conversation with the lieutenant. I know I'll have to take great care with how I release some of the news, because of her sensitivity to any changes I make to the way we both work together.

"To give us the extra support, the lieutenant's pulling Beavis and Butthead off the Gentiles case and bringing them over to this one, under my command."

Dee raises an eyebrow at this news. I don't know much about the newcomer, Jordan Treviss, but I do know enough about Geoff Buttle. We have 'history', and Dee is aware of the antagonism we share for each other. But I'm hoping she'll know we need support from wherever we can get it and having these two on our team is one step in the right direction.

"I'll brief them both this afternoon ... before the press conference at four," I add.

This news brings up the other eyebrow and a sarcastic smile spreads across her face.

After my meeting with the lieutenant earlier, he and I had gone straight down to Media Relations to find out what's being planned. It had been agreed that LAPD would set up the conference on the steps of the PAB this afternoon. It's quite rare to hold one on a Sunday but such is the interest in the Chandler murder this morning that the decision had been made without too much discussion. I tell Dee that the Chief of Police, David Kramer, is bound to haul in the top brass to stand up there with him. I sense Dee's waiting to hear if she'll be called up to stand in the back row.

"As you can imagine Dee, the press is all over this like a rash and most of the news channels have it as their lead story this morning. It'll go beyond state boundaries this time."

This will make the conference a frenzy. The media pack will want everything we know to help them write their stories. As always, they'll be asking the same questions we're asking. But they're working a different angle; they want to sell papers and blocks of broadcast news whilst we just want to catch the killer.

The chief and his deputy, Eugene Garner, are both masters at dealing with the press and rarely miss an opportunity to get in front of cameras. Garner – a hard-liner republican – will want the lens of the Fox news camera in his sights if he's called into action, whilst Kramer will want to please everyone and maintain the political momentum he needs to ensure the Police Board will re-elect him for another five years.

I tell Dee she'll not be needed for the press conference, and this pleases her. Most cops hate the public showcasing that goes on at these events, especially ones that capture the fear and imagination of the public. Nonetheless, I do know in cases like these that there's work to be done gaining public support.

As my orange juice and toast arrive I see Chang at the main counter on the other side of the restaurant. He gives me a brief wave and holds up my car keys to show me he's leaving them at the till. He then points out towards the main street, telling me the car's been moved around to the front.

Dee finishes her coffee and looks better for it. Reboot complete. She places her hand behind her head and stretches out her shoulders and neck muscles and then leans forward, expectantly.

"What's next?" she asks.

"We'll work the first two cases again with Beavis and Butthead's help this time. This will mean re-examining statements and re-interviewing some of the key witnesses again. We have to do this whilst driving forward our investigation of the Chandler murder at the same time. Perhaps, you'll let me have your thoughts on this?" I ask.

Dee just nods, seemingly accepting the request, but I see she's still waiting to hear what I've got in store for her.

I decide to drop the bombshell.

"One more thing ..." Dee sits back. "The lieutenant has also agreed for us to have a psychological profiler and serial killer expert on hand ... For five days ... He's given me the budget."

I'm not sure how Dee will take this news, because I've often used her developing skills in this role. She has an intuitive psychological approach when identifying and profiling potential killers' personalities and I've certainly benefited from her insightful observations in the past. We've even discussed her specializing in this area and going back to school on it.

Although Dee's good, I want the best. I want Sam Callan.

I used her once before on the 'B-Movie case' as it became known. Sam helped me get inside the mind of a killer who'd stalked moderate film celebrities and then brutally murdered them. Sam's insight was that the killer was probably a minor celebrity himself, and was jealous of his victims' status as his own career faded. She felt that he would take intense pleasure in their complete demise.

Her advice led me to trawl a long list of actors that eventually put Duncan Alleyne in the frame. He was a forty-four-year-old member of the Actors' Guild. He'd had a few film-credits to his name but was disappearing rapidly from view as he got older. After getting approval to have him followed, we caught him outside a minor film celebrity's home. This got us our warrant and we searched his apartment. We found everything we needed to have him convicted. The walls of his basement studio were covered in photographs, film memorabilia and press cuttings, parading his victims together with detailed surveillance of their whereabouts and movements before he killed them.

I look across at Dee. She's sitting back in her chair now, stony faced, arms folded.

"How the hell are we going to fit all of this together? How will we work as a team?"

"I'll get Buttle to do the legwork, chasing down witnesses and checking statements. Treviss will sit at a desk, cross-checking crime scenes, you know, the measurements, blood-splatters, details like that ... checking to see if we missed something first time around."

This news immediately seems to lift Dee's spirits because she wants to break free from that role and take more responsibility.

"What about the profiler?" she adds, getting to the nitty-gritty of her concerns.

"I've decided that you'll work with her."

"Who is it then? What's her name?" she asks, as I suddenly realize I've mentioned it's a woman.

"I'd like you to work with Sam Callan. If she'll take the commission."

I take a quick look at my cell phone to see if Sam's replied to my text invitation and, when I look back up, Dee's grinning from ear to ear.

Although not public knowledge at the time, Sam and I got it together on the case – a little B-movie of our own – and whilst it didn't lead to anything significant, we both knew a bit more about each other than what coffee we liked to drink. This was well before Dee joined up as a police officer, so I'm guessing she's heard about the relationship from gossip around the drinks station. Notwithstanding, this is her moment to let me know she knows without having to say a word.

I don't really care what people say or think about my private life, so long as it doesn't affect my capacity to do my job – and this includes Dee – so I see no reason to apologize or respond. I think Sam and Dee will make a good pairing, that's the important thing.

Sam will benefit by having someone working with her who'll know the three cases intimately, and Dee will have the bonus of working alongside a serious profiler.

I also want Dee to keep an eye on Treviss with the deskwork. He's an unknown so I want to be sure the information we work with is accurate, up-to-date and reliable.

I suggest to Dee that we go straight back to the PAB and make a start on digging out the records that'll need processing again. I also ask her if she'll brief Treviss once he gets on board this afternoon, hoping this will give her the authority she needs to feel she's taking a lead. However, I tell her that I'll liaise with Buttle, because we both know this will not necessarily be straightforward.

Buttle has a year or two on me and we've never hit it off. Dee says I bristle when he gets close. This is mainly because of the run-in we had in the old Parker Center, ten years ago, when I'd suspected he'd short-changed Felix Capelli, an ex-partner of mine. I'd always cut Capelli a bit of slack getting to work in the mornings because he lived out in Cypress with his new wife and baby. Unfortunately, his home situation became an excuse for lateness and some of his colleagues came to resent it. When he got transferred across to work with Buttle, things came to a head. Buttle expected Capelli to be there on time. Period.

Issues exploded when the lieutenant we had at the time picked up on this and disciplined Felix for lateness, threatening to dock his pay the next time it happened. I knew Buttle had shopped him and I told him so in the stairwell one evening. He didn't take too kindly to this, and frankly things got out of hand. It ended with Buttle falling into a glass panel and cutting his arm. He needed sutures and a dose of injections in his ass for a week. There was a moment when it looked like Buttle was going to follow this up with an accusation of assault, but the lieutenant persuaded him to drop it, if I took a course in anger management – which I did, reluctantly. Needless to say, Buttle was none too pleased with the whole episode and deep down I believe he's never let it go. Apparently, he tells a different story about what happened on the stairs when it comes up in the squad room, and I don't look so good in it. The animosity between us is still pretty palpable, it seems. *'Get your horns in Oskar'* is usually Dee's response when she notices that Buttle and me are about to cross paths.

As we finish up in Chang's, I make a change of plan and ask Dee to bring in Tomlinson, our caller, first of all. I tell her this'll not be a read-his-rights interview but a lets-see-if-his-story-hangs-together discussion. Dee nods at me, fully understanding the situation and the delicacy that is needed, especially with a character like Tomlinson, who's still an unknown. We definitely don't want him to lawyer up. Not yet. We need to finesse our way with him to see what more we can get him to reveal without him feeling the threat of being a suspect. I have the press conference to deal with this afternoon, but I still want to maintain momentum and get Tomlinson's story together as soon as possible. As Dee has spent some time with him already, I tell her I'd like her to take the lead. This lifts her mood, immediately.

We go through a list of questions she'll ask Tomlinson and agree a strategy. Dee suggests that we watch him through the one-way mirror before starting. This is a good idea and I ask her to remind me to tell Treviss and Buttle to sit in, because this will be an opportunity to start building the now-enlarged team.

"You never know, one of them might just see an angle we've missed, especially Buttle," I suggest, thinking he's a wily old dog when it comes to these situations

My cell phone suddenly vibrates. I grab it quickly, thinking it's a text from Lena.

It's from Sam Callan:

> Sure thing partner. Be with
> you tomorrow @ 10.20.
> Flight AA 27. X

11

(Sunday, 8.30 a.m.)

LENA LIES IN DARKNESS, unaware of where she is, or why she's there. She can't move any of her limbs and can't make sense of what has happened to her.

She thinks she catches the distant glimpse of light coming from somewhere, but can't move her head.

The surroundings seem familiar but she doesn't know why. She wants to scream but that's not possible either.

It isn't a dream.

She's sure of that.

12

(Sunday, 10.00 a.m.)

I ARRIVE BACK AT the PAB after my summit meeting with Dee, feeling pretty fired up. Dee's gone back to South Normandie to bring in our caller, Frank Tomlinson, leaving me to pull in the paperwork and make the start on the Chandler murder investigation.

As I arrive in the busy squad room, I see the lieutenant out of the corner of my eye. He's over by the tank, having seen me arrive as soon as I came through the swing doors – this really does make me wonder if he has a 'hotline' to the front desk. He's using expansive hand gestures attempting to redirect me over to his office. I can hardly miss him doing this, and neither can anyone else in the squad room, because all eyes are on me. The lieutenant wants me in there now and he doesn't seem to mind who knows it.

He shuts the door behind me as I enter, and immediately offers me the seat by his desk. The lieutenant closing the door like this always suggests a confrontation of some kind, and through the windows of his office I can see everyone's ears prick up, expectantly they're hoping for some office fireworks to brighten up their morning.

Like a male lion warning off competitors, the lieutenant gives anyone still looking in, a long, lingering stare as he fumbles with a hand-held remote and closes the blinds that separate his office from the rest of the squad room. Satisfied, the lieutenant sidesteps his way to his chair and sits down, thrusting a piece of paper in my direction with one hand and tossing the remote into his desk drawer with the other.

"Whaddaya think?" he barks as I notice a glint in his eyes that I've not seen before.

I start reading:

PRESS RELEASE

MURDER SUSPECT SOUGHT

On Saturday June 15 2013, around midnight, Los Angeles Police Department responded to a call for assistance in the South Normandie district. On arrival, they discovered the victim, identified as Jane Chandler, on the floor of her apartment. She was pronounced dead at the scene, the result of a brutal murder. Her body was transported to the morgue for examination and an autopsy.

The exact time of death is not yet known, but investigators believe Chandler may have died sometime between Thursday June 13 and Saturday June 16. This will be confirmed once the post-mortem examination is complete.

An intensive search of the area, followed by an equally intensive investigation by this Department's police officers and detectives assigned to Robbery-Homicide Division, has been taking place since this tragic incident was uncovered. Additional resources have been supplied, and the strengthened team will be working full time to find the perpetrator of this vicious crime.

With the help and co-operation from countless community members who have provided crucial information to our officers and detectives, we have learned the identity of one person we would like to speak to. He may be able to assist police with their lines of enquiry. He is male, Hispanic and about 20 years of age. He was seen in the South Normandie district on the night of the 13 June.

It is not yet clear whether this case is related to two other recent murders currently under investigation, namely the deaths of David Henshaw and Eric Green, although the department is keeping this possibility constantly under review.

We want to express our most sincere gratitude to all who have contributed to this investigation so far, and call on anyone who feels they may know something in connection with this crime to come forward immediately.

For Release 16.00 p.m. PST June 16, 2013

Attached is another sheet of paper with Cerillo's impression of the Hispanic we're looking for. There's also a list of phone numbers to a LAPD hotline for members of the public to phone in to if they have information.

There are no real surprises in the press release itself and I just give the lieutenant a non-committal *uh-huh* expression. In fact, I consider it to be the usual gibberish. It will possibly satisfy the appetite of the media and it definitely tells a story – the story that LAPD top-brass want to be out there on the screens and in the press copy going to print – but it doesn't say enough, in my opinion. And, certainly not enough if we're to get the help from the public that we really need. Nonetheless, I suspect the press release will help calm the city and convince most citizens that the Los Angeles Police Department is on the case, pressing forward to *'Protect and Serve'* as it says on the tin.

I think the lieutenant can read my thoughts, but there's still a strange look in his eyes. It looks as if he's scared of something.

"It'll keep them quiet for the moment," he eventually says, "until we know more."

He emphasizes the word, *'know'*, and I suspect it's his way of telling me we mustn't let any hounds go running off in the wrong direction. I also suspect the deputy chief – or perhaps it's the chief on this occasion – will have instructed Media Relations to keep things on a need-to-know basis, so we don't have too much quoted back in our faces later on if things get out of hand.

"Remember, the press conference is out front this afternoon. At four o'clock. Be there. Here's the plan."

He brings out another piece of paper and passes it across to me. It's one side of A4 identifying the choreography for this afternoon's pony show. It details where everyone is going to stand, and in what order we'll descend the steps of the PAB. As I suspected, Kramer will head up the event, and Deputy Chief Garner will also be in attendance. It's not often we get both guns firing at once.

"I don't expect you'll be called upon to say anything, Salo. So, bite your tongue if you feel inclined to speak."

"Is that advice, Lieutenant?" I speculatively ask.

"No. It's an order, d'yer hear?" he says, giving me those eyes again. "Any more questions?" he then asks, not giving me the impression he wants any. But, I need to know what's happening about the extra support he promised.

"What about Beavis and Butthead, Lieutenant?" I ask and realize my mistake immediately.

"For chrissakes, Salo. It's Treviss and Buttle. You drop that crap," he orders, continuing to hold my eyes for a few more seconds, daring me to say something else I'll regret. "I've informed them both of their move across to your command, forthwith. I've only

46

been able to leave a message for Buttle, but I've spoken personally to Treviss. He's across the other side of the squad room awaiting your instructions as we speak – Anything else?"

"No, that's it from me, Lieutenant." I reply, wanting to get out of here as soon as possible.

"Okay ... Okay ..." he says, as I suddenly see his aggressive stance recede in a matter of seconds. He then swivels on his chair and faces towards the squad room, attempting to look out of the window to the men under his command. But the blinds are still drawn and he ends up staring at these instead. Something is troubling him, I can tell, and faint alarm bells start ringing in my ears telling me it really is time to leave.

"I'm taking you into my confidence here, Detective ..." – alarm bells start ringing even louder – "I know we've had our run-ins in the past, but we're at a watershed moment in the department ... Things are being said ... in corridors and in the boardroom. Do you follow me, Oskar? I need you to watch your step ... We *all* need to watch our step ... above all, I need you to work with me here."

He's still staring at nothing in particular, and then I see the glint again. I'm suddenly reminded of the killers I've interrogated in the past that go into a trance-like state like this. They end up starting to spill the beans by confessing their crimes. I often feel it's as if they've got the key to their own redemption, and they're fumbling at the keyhole, desperately trying to turn the lock that'll open the floodgates. I've heard colleagues call this the 'golden door moment'.

"I need your help with this, Oskar," the lieutenant eventually says. "We need to find this killer quickly and not get—"

The phone on his desk suddenly starts ringing and we both jerk our gaze towards the handset. It's his private line. The one reserved for personal calls and those from his superiors. The lieutenant is seemingly undecided about what to do. Surreally, it feels as though he's looking to me to decide for him. As we get to the sixth ring, the lieutenant's eyes suddenly seem to refocus on the here-and-now and he sits up straight, snatching up the handset and giving me one of his bulletproof stares. He puts the receiver up to his ear, still holding my eyes to his. I hear someone on the other end of the line start talking, immediately. I can't recognize the voice or what's being said.

"Yes ... It's here," the lieutenant eventually says as he picks up the press release. "I have it right here in front of—" There are some more rapid-fire instructions and then the lieutenant looks directly at me again. "Yes ... I will ... Yes ... I'm—"

The line goes dead, but the handset is still to the lieutenant's ear. After a few seconds the lieutenant returns it to the cradle, seemingly contemplating his next move.

"You're to report here at three forty-five, Detective Salo," he suddenly says "The press conference will start at four and we'll go down together. I'll brief you more fully then. That's all."

He doesn't say, *'dismissed'*, but it's implied by the military tone in his voice.

I stand up and make my way out of his office and across to my cubicle. As I descend in my chair I'm aware of colleagues' eyes staring into mine. Like me, they're all wondering what the hell is going on.

13

(Sunday 10.52 a.m.)

THE WORKSHOP IS ANY craftsman's dream, and the Reaper is proud that he has these facilities at his disposal. It has taken him many years to build up his collection of tools, equipment and materials. There is a range of saws, planers, routers, benches, cramps, vacuum-forming tables, oxy-acetylene and plasma cutting equipment, and he has a hearth for forming metal and various multimedia machines to cut, fabricate and to join materials together. His supply includes all kinds of timbers, plastics and metals.

The Reaper's most recent purchase – and his pride and joy – is a computer-controlled lathe. It is capable of machining materials to very high tolerances. He used it recently to produce a precision pump that he modeled on one that he had taken to pieces in the place where he works as a volunteer handyman.

Feeling elated and revitalized by the rededication of his mission, and by his new name, the Reaper sets about assembling his most recent project. He takes great delight selecting everything he needs, just like his Master had taught him. *'Rule number one: Always remember to choose the best materials and the best tools for the job'.*

He keeps all his wood stored away out back, seasoning in stacks against the north wall of the workshop. There is a mixture of hardwoods and softwoods and certain planks are extremely rare, coming from a time when his Master had sourced them for a special commission. The Reaper felled some of the trees himself, having hauled them onto the back of an ancient flatbed truck with a winch he'd renovated and bringing them back to the farmstead down the winding mountain-paths.

He always enjoys selecting pine and today is no exception. It's the smell and touch that he particularly likes. He loves the way the scent from the resin races up his nostrils as he runs the timber through the saw. It excites his senses and emotions, reminding him of happier times. Sometimes, he thinks he's the only person in the world who can tell the age of a particular piece of wood just by the smell as it passes through the revolving blade. He wonders if Stradivarius had that same, highly developed sense of smell, because the revered violinmaker would select different trees for their different sound qualities when he made violins for his clients.

After half an hour, the Reaper has the wood cut and prepared the way he wants, so he begins to rout out the grooves.

His design is following the exact measurements set down by the State of California, so he occasionally crosschecks these with the masterplan. He makes sure of this because it matters. It matters to him that the rules are being followed. Precisely.

Once the framework is erected he starts sliding in the plywood sheets into the grooves. His Master had taught him the art of cutting panels slightly smaller, to allow for expansion. *'Only an eighth of an inch,'* he thinks to himself as he taps them into position with a soft mallet. *'Easy does it. Let it all come together. Naturally'*.

14

(Sunday, 2.10 p.m.)

I MEET UP WITH Dee on our side of the one-way glass as arranged. She's brought in Mr. Tomlinson, our caller, who's sitting on the other. She's had him warming up nicely in the interview room for an hour and a half. I'd taken a quick look at the thermostat on the way in and noticed it had been set to a slightly uncomfortable 75 degrees – enough for him to feel quite warm but not too hot. She's hoping this will unsettle him enough so that he'll end up saying things he might want to hide. Of course, she doesn't want to freak him out by leaving him waiting in the heat for too long, as this might have the opposite effect and make him clam up. I know that she'll have been watching him very closely and looking for the signs that'll tell her he's ready for her questions.

Dee's heard me arrive, but remains silent. She's giving me some time to acclimatize myself to what's going on here. Through the window I can see Tomlinson sitting upright on a chair. He's positioned under bright fluorescent lighting that's not doing him any favors. I take a step closer to get a better look and see that he's mumbling quietly to himself. He then gets up and walks towards the window, almost as if he knows I've arrived. I know he can't see me, but I find this kind of spooky, because it appears as if he's looking directly into my eyes. If he's really into detective stories like Columbo, he'll know this is no ordinary mirror, yet he gives no impression he really knows we're in here watching him. His face is quite flushed and I can see he's loosened his tie and undone his top collar button. I can also see he's taken off a woolen cardigan and left it hanging behind the chair.

Dee turns and smiles towards me.

"Nicely roasted don't you think? Ready for me to lead him up my garden path?"

I exchange a quick smile and then turn my attention back to Tomlinson.

He's beginning to study himself in the reflection of the glass, checking his clothing for general tidiness. Satisfied, he then licks his hand and attempts to smooth down a section of hair on one side of his head that's sticking up. Each time he presses it down it just pops back up, again. It looks like a well-practiced maneuver. Dissatisfied on this occasion, he turns his attention to his face. Using a neatly pressed handkerchief, he starts by wiping away something he's seen in the corner of his mouth.

"Have Beavis and Butthead showed up yet?" I ask, because I'm expecting them to be here by now.

"Yes. Treviss stuck his head round the door, saying that Buttle's on sick-leave today."

She says this with a straight face knowing that's Buttle's way of saying to me, *'Up yours, fuckhead'*.

'Treviss should be back here in a minute, though," she continues. "He's gone for a coffee."

I'm still looking at Tomlinson who's only a foot or so away from the glass. He appears to be reciting something to himself, occasionally putting his finger to his mouth as if he's trying to remember a sequence or some fact or other.

The door opens behind me and I turn to see Treviss come into the room. He takes up a position near to the door.

"He hasn't shown any signs of anything really, Oskar," Dee says, without acknowledging Treviss's entrance. "He's been doing a lot of this. Looks like he's rehearsing how he's going to say things. There've been no tells ... no sweats, no panics ... in fact nothing that suggests he's guilty of anything ..." Dee then turns to Treviss, smiling broadly. "In fact," she continues, "if he's our guy Oskar, he deserves an Oscar ..."

That's not the first time this has been said in my presence, and I attempt to ignore it the best I can.

"What's up with Buttle?" I ask Treviss.

"Uh? ... Dunno, Sunday fever, I guess."

It's well known around the department that many cops who pull a Sunday shift will take sick leave, especially those that like to drink on a Saturday evening.

I give Treviss a nod of acknowledgement and move nearer to Dee, leaving some space for him to join us at the window when he's ready.

I refocus my attention back on what's about to take place in the interview room, thinking that all we have in there is a lonely do-gooder, who's only sin in this world is to be nosey and bored, and that possibly this murder is gonna be the most exciting thing that's ever happened to him in his life.

Tomlinson is standing even closer to the window now, but he's moved across to Dee's side of the glass. He starts to check himself out all over again. I can see that Dee's very uncomfortable with this, because she takes one pace backwards, nearly knocking into Treviss who's moved across silently and is standing behind her. Treviss backs off quickly, spilling his coffee in the process. I know Dee has issues about anyone standing in her space, and being crowded out on both sides of the glass like this is clearly getting her rattled.

It's my turn to smile.

"He's just looking for someone who'll listen to him, Dee ... That's all. And, you know what? I'm glad it's you leading him up *your* garden path!"

15

(Sunday 3.10 p.m.)

BY MID-AFTERNOON THE REAPER has completed his wooden frame. It's ready for the cladding. Whilst the inside is to be made of wood, the outside will be made of something much stronger, hence his need to secure the frame firmly to the dirt floor of the barn on cement foundations, four feet deep.

The main conduit for electricity comes through the floor, along a previously excavated and then back-filled trench. The Reaper has also designed in an emergency diesel generator should the mains fail for any reason.

He stands back and admires his creation. He thinks again about how he will record all of this for posterity.

He picks up an 'imaginary' camera and enacts taking a close-up of something he can see through the imaginary lens. Then, quite dramatically, he sweeps his arms away from the structure and ends with a broad panoramic shot of the inside of the barn, including the row of chairs he has set out along one side.

He attempts this three times, improving the choreography on each occasion. He knows that he wants to capture the best images possible and he makes a mental note to himself to ensure the floor is clear of any hazards when he does this for real.

He *must* get this right.

He smiles to himself at a thought. A distant thought. He thinks of the irony: He detested drama lessons at school but here he is embracing the theatrical with a relish and a passion that would have pleased his teachers significantly.

16

(Sunday, 4.45 p.m.)

THE PRESS CONFERENCE ENDED twenty minutes ago, and I'm making my way down the stairs of the PAB. I've decided to head home to freshen up, whilst I leave the tail-end of Tomlinson's interview in Dee's safe hands. Arrangements are in place for Dee, Treviss and me to meet up at Chang's later on to discuss the implications of what Tomlinson has revealed, and to make a plan for tomorrow.

Buttle is still a no-show, and as I step out into the late afternoon sunshine, I have a bad taste in my mouth realizing I've got to waste valuable time dealing with him, rather than getting on with the job of finding the killer.

I'm using the back stairs, hoping I'll not meet anyone, especially the lieutenant. I don't want him slowing me down with another of his gut-wrenching monologues, or forcing my hand to make a declaration that Tomlinson is in the frame for something. I'd met up with him at three forty-five, as arranged, before going down to the press conference. We travelled down in the lift together and joined the party outside on the steps. Interestingly, at no time on that journey did the lieutenant refer to anything he'd said to me when he freaked me with his personal ramblings. I took this as a sign to approach the issue with caution and not to raise it myself until I work out what's bugging him. Or, perhaps, *who* is bugging him.

At the press conference, I was more interested in who turned up on both sides of the lectern – rather than what had been said. Chief Kramer, had brought along an assortment of captains and other senior colleagues. I counted fifteen members of his senior team in total, no mean feat for a Sunday afternoon, but overkill in my opinion. This may have been the chief's tactic for diluting the presence of his deputy, who was standing by his side.

There were several TV stations represented, including CBS, Fox and NBC, plus a number of independents that would be selling their news onto other channels, statewide. There were some familiar faces behind notepads, and below the voice recorders held aloft, including reporters I know from the LA Times and USA Today. Some tried to catch my eye with a friendly nod or a smile, in an attempt to ingratiate themselves to me. All were hoping that this might lead to me giving them the heads-up on something, or an 'exclusive' one-off quote. On this occasion, I made sure my eyes didn't connect or acknowledge anyone in particular. I don't want to get drawn into anything like that. Not now. Not yet!

The chief spoke for seven minutes to a prepared speech that pretty much followed the outline of the press release circulated beforehand. He did his best to make the city's inhabitants believe they were safe to walk the streets, and, most importantly, that he was the man to be in charge of LAPD for another five years.

"My brave and loyal officers are on this case 24/7," he said at one point. "And the full force of the law is well on its way to bringing this killer to justice."

When it came to questions, the chief made a fair attempt to sidestep anything that would confirm we had a serial killer on our hands. But he didn't rule out that possibility either. This was to prevent any of his answers coming back to bite him on the ass, later on. As soon as the press conference ended, I'd shot upstairs to check on how things were going with the interview. I found Treviss sitting on his side of the one-way glass, manning the video recorder and watching Tomlinson, who was sitting by himself on the other. Treviss told me that Dee had just slipped away for a 'comfort break' and he reported she had managed to get a great deal of information out of Tomlinson whilst I'd been downstairs. There were intricate details about what he'd seen in the apartment block and along South Normandie on the days leading up to the murder. It's appearing as though our caller really is the 'watcher' as I'd predicted when I first saw the layout of his apartment.

Once out of the PAB, it's a welcome sight to see my car. I think of it as a kind of refuge on occasions, like these. And, like my apartment, it's somewhere where I can rest up for a while and think. And, of course, it's where I can smoke another cigarette.

I open the rear door and hang up my jacket. It's quite warm and I know I'll enjoy the drive home with the window down. I'll get some air to blow around inside the car and hopefully it'll loosen up my thinking.

I climb in and start up the engine, and then attempt to pull out into the slow-moving traffic. As I'm checking for anything coming up from behind, I notice the spider that lives in my mirror. He's laid out another one of his sticky webs, which is glistening in the late afternoon sunshine. I can just see the spider curled up in the corner with his legs tucked up beneath its body. I'm thinking he's patiently waiting to catch some hapless fly or bug that'll drift by on the breeze.

As my eyes focus back on the traffic, I spot a gap coming up and pull out and make my way down South Los Angeles Street. I make my way towards West Fifth, where I'll take the right towards my apartment.

Just as I'm about to light up, my cell phone rings. It's Dee, breathless.

"Get your ass back here!" she demands. "All hell's broken loose!"

*

I'm back on our side of the one-way glass, again, and I've rewound the video recorder to the point where Tomlinson actually flips. I've asked Dee and Treviss to step out of the room, go grab a coffee and smarten up. I want to look at what actually happened. By myself.

I'd arrived back just as the pair were coming up from the holding cell. Although they looked disheveled, it was the blood-splatters that really caught my attention. They were both smiling and decidedly upbeat about how things had gone, looking like the proverbial cats that had gotten the cream – and had the catfight as well.

Dee told me how she'd challenged Tomlinson about his true identity and how he'd suddenly *'lashed out'*. She said it was as if someone had *'lit the blue touch-paper'*. Understandably, she thinks the case has been blown wide open by Tomlinson's actions and by her find. But I'm never sure until I'm sure. That's why I want to study this tape carefully. Very carefully indeed. I want to see what it might reveal about Tomlinson – if that really is his name.

I press play and take a look at my watch at the same time. I've started the tape at the moment when Dee asks the question: *'Is Frank Tomlinson your real name?'* He explodes immediately and, within a fraction of a second, comes flying across the table. From the camera angle I can't work out if he's attempting to make his way to the door and Dee just happens to be in his way, or if he's going directly for her. It's clear his sudden advance catches Dee by surprise, but she quickly gets into action once he starts to push his way through.

There's a great deal of noise, and it's difficult to work out what's being said, but I can make out Tomlinson's voice above the hubbub, declaring his innocence, over and over again. I can also see that Treviss – who's now arrived in the room – and Dee are having difficulty restraining him. He appears unusually strong for his size, and both of them do very well to avoid his flailing limbs. He certainly puts up a fight and resists their attempts to contain him. It's not until Officer Garland comes bursting through the door to help out that all three of them eventually pin him to the floor.

Looking at the video, I sense that Tomlinson felt like a trapped animal – an animal that just might have a chance to escape, if only he could break free from the room. Of course, it was a futile impulse because, even if he'd made it past Dee and Treviss, he'd never have gotten through the security gates down the corridor. And certainly he'd not have gotten past the two guards stationed on the other side. But more importantly, on tape, I can see that he *believes* he can do it. This is what's driving him on; the belief that he can break free from the net that surrounds him. And, even though the camera is high up on the wall, I see this belief in his eyes and wonder what this is telling me.

All along, he's appeared timid in many ways but I can see, as the events unfold, that he has the resolve and determination to do things violently if he chooses to. The trouble for him now is that, if he's really innocent, he's not done himself any favors. On the other hand, if he really is the killer, we'll not have to look any further than this video recording to convince any jury in the land that he has the physical power necessary to deliver the violent deaths we're investigating.

As the fracas ends, I look at my watch and work out the violence lasted no more than eighty seconds, start to finish. It seems longer, but so do some of the minutes in a boxing contest when a fighter is trapped in the corner of the ring, fighting for his life. I'm always amazed by the strength some people find when they're minded to, especially frail-looking souls like Tomlinson.

Fortunately, no one has been badly hurt trying to restrain him, but there's embarrassment all round, because Garland tumbled awkwardly onto the edge of the table, knocking into Treviss in the process. This left them both sprawled across the floor on top of Tomlinson with blood pouring from a two-inch gash on Garland's forehead. I'm sure he'll get ribbed by his colleagues, but I'm not sure whether it'll be the embarrassment about tripping up that'll be worrying him or the fact that we have it all on camera.

I'm still considering how to handle all this when the door opens and I turn to see Dee and Treviss return with their coffees. Dee has her hair tied back up now; it's impeccable, just as she likes it. I can see she's washed off the blood from her face and it looks as if she's been to her locker for a change of shirt. Treviss, on the other hand, has still got Garland's blood on his clothes. He's wearing it like a warrior. Understandably, I can sense elation in the room as we sit down around a table. Dee has the biggest of grins and looks at me with one of her *I-told-you-so* faces. She'll be thinking we have Tomlinson – or whatever his real name is – boxed up, for sure. She's hoping I'll be straight on the phone to the DA after this. That's the adrenalin talking, of course, so we'll take this at my pace. We'll go to the DA when I'm ready. Dee knows this but she's not afraid to let me know what she thinks as we stare at each other across the table.

As far as Tomlinson is concerned, I'm pleased we have something positive to work with. But I'm realizing, if I'm to keep both Dee and Treviss on board, I'll have to handle how we move forward from here very carefully. Forty minutes ago I had him for a hanger-on, a nosey parker, but if this episode tells me anything it's not to jump to conclusions too quickly.

What is in no doubt, though, is that Dee well and truly led Tomlinson up that garden path of hers. And she knows it. That's another reason why she's smiling so much. It had been her show. And she got a result.

17

(Sunday, 7.30 p.m.)

I CLIMB INTO MY car and pull away from the curb, catching a glimpse of myself in the rear-view mirror. My eyes are staring back at me like two black marbles and there are dark rings etched into the skin underneath. I realize I'm extremely tired, having not slept properly for two days now, but I'm hoping a couple of hours' rest will do the trick before Dee and I search Tomlinson's apartment. The streets are quiet, and I'm able to thread my way through the early evening traffic fairly easily.

Thankfully, I've been able to give the lieutenant an update on where things stand and I'm hoping I've done enough to stop him contacting anyone about the incident until we've undertaken the search.

Tomlinson has been read his rights and is now locked up in the department's padded cell with a 24/7 guard. He's also lawyered up and we're grilling him first thing tomorrow morning, or earlier, if the search of his apartment tells us he's our killer.

I soon get to *Geometrix* and make my way through the security gates and down into the lower ground-floor car park. Instinctively, I look across to see if I can spot Lena's car parked up in her bay, but it's not there. I then climb out of the car and make my way across to the main entrance. I push open the door and walk past reception and straight into a waiting elevator without meeting anybody. I reflect that, unlike Tomlinson, I don't know anybody who lives around me. I rarely meet anyone and hardly know a person by name except for a couple of the security guards.

As the glass-sided elevator starts its ascent through the glass-and steel-walled atrium, I look out onto all the other floors in the *Cube,* knowing all the apartments are identical in layout. This makes me think back to South Normandie, when I was halfway up the flight of stairs and realized that Tomlinson's apartment would probably be identical in design to Chandler's, and it was.

As the elevator rises, I'm able to look across to my apartment and the one that's directly below mine. I can't remember ever seeing anyone come or go in there. I know it was up for lease recently, and a new tenant has moved in, but the only acknowledgement I've received that someone actually lives there is the occasional sound of a door opening and closing onto the garden terrace below.

The elevator reaches the third floor and the doors open. I exit onto the corridor and walk along to my apartment hearing the sound of my shoes whispering on the carpet. As I open my front door and switch on the lights, I go into each room looking for any sign that Lena has returned since I was last here. But the more I look the more I realize that nothing has been moved, touched or taken. I consider whether this is a good sign or not and end up deciding it's good, but I'm not sure why. Surprised by this abstract thought, I conclude that Lena's possibly not made up her mind what she's gonna do and will come back in her own time.

I need fuel and go into the kitchen. I look inside the fridge and bring out a bottle of beer. I notice it's one Lena brought back with her from Brats Brothers, a restaurant serving a German specialty she wants me to try. I open it and drink half standing in the kitchen. It hits the spot. I look back inside and notice there's another bottle and decide I'll possibly drink it too. I then take out a cooked burger covered in food wrap and a pot of coleslaw – Lena's coleslaw – and take them both out to the garden with the beer.

A setting sun greets me, lighting up the sky with its deep ochre glow. I make a start eating the cold burger, holding it between my fingers. I don't eat it elegantly, and even end up using the burger itself to spoon the coleslaw out of the pot and into my mouth.

Refueled, I light a cigarette, counting those remaining in the pack. I'm still on quota for the day and get some satisfaction from the count. I direct a jet of blue smoke high up into the air and realize I can't shake off the frustration of not knowing where Lena is. I also realize I haven't given much time to finding her today and, suddenly, this hits hard. It's been three days now since she left and I wonder if she's made her way back to her parents' home in San Francisco. I think about contacting them but quickly decide against it. They're both elderly and frail, and my call might worry them unnecessarily if she's not there.

I'm brought out of my thoughts by the sound of sprinklers clicking into action in the flowerbeds, and find myself walking across the garden. I run my hand across some jasmine billowing in the breeze, releasing a pungent scent into the air as I sit down on the garden bench. I generally get early evening warmth here and today is no exception. I feel the sun's rays on my face and close my eyes for a moment, enjoying the warming effect. I hear the sound of the traffic out front. It's still fairly dense, but at this time of night the sound is different. It has a softer, mellower tone to it, as if the drivers are more at ease with themselves than during the day.

I send up another column of smoke and find myself looking along the bench to the statue at the far end. It's an abstract, wire-framed design of a full-size man sitting down. His legs are outstretched and crossed at the ankles. He's leaning back with his face turned slightly upwards as if he's looking towards the horizon. I smile to myself, because I realize I'm sitting in the same position, only I'm holding a bottle of beer and smoking a cigarette. Each apartment has its own individual and unique sculpture, representing a different stage in the 'Progression of Man', as the artist's catalogue explained it. The statues trace life's journey in a sequence, from conception through to death and then into the spirit world. I'd had a chance to view all of the sculptures

63

before they were erected in the apartments when they went on show in a local gallery. They had been commissioned from a young Finnish artist, fresh out of college, who had known Hakkinen, the architect. The show received much publicity at the time and this was one of the reasons I ended up coming to view the apartments in the first place.

I chose the apartment with the sculpture of a man reaching the end of his middle age by happenstance. He's contemplating the life he's about to leave behind as he considers impending old age. It wasn't the reason I bought this apartment, but I did like this statue for some reason. I still do.

The gardens have their own particular water feature. Mine is a pond with a stream that flows around the raised beds. I often find the sound of the gently burbling water comforting. And feeling more relaxed now I stand up and walk across to the pond. I can see the shoal of eight golden carp and go through my familiar routine of feeding them and counting they're all there.

I finish the first bottle of beer and consider going back to the fridge for the second, but I choose not to, suddenly thinking what I'll be doing later tonight. Dee's writing up the warrant and Treviss is researching the best judge to take it to for signature. Actually, I don't think Dee will encounter any difficulties getting it signed off, even on a Sunday evening, because she can sweet-talk *any* cat down a tree if she has to.

My thoughts stay with Tomlinson and what I learned from Dee's interview and my viewing of the video recording. Dee pretty much followed the plan we'd agreed in Chang's. For the first twenty minutes, Tomlinson gave the clear impression he'd seen a great deal from his bay window and out on the stairwell that goes up past his front door. He projected the image of someone who has the ability to recall images, sounds and objects with complete precision. He certainly appeared to remember visual details with a rare clarity.

He even claimed he could identify people by *'the tread of their step on the stair'*. At one point, he said self-assuredly, *'I'm rarely wrong*'. He also told Dee that he could tell when someone came up the stairs who was unknown to him, a visitor for example. Dee and Treviss are planning to check out all the people he's listed, to see if their movements tallied with the schedule that he laid out so clearly.

He's definitely convincing. And, therefore, if he is fooling with us, he's being cunning and manipulative; two qualities that would make him a prime suspect. When Dee went for her *'comfort break'*, Treviss left the video recorder running, and I could see that Tomlinson was feeling relaxed, possibly thinking the interview was over and he'd be heading for home soon. Dee said it was on her return from the restroom that she had her *'brainwave moment'*, as she's now called it, deciding to go straight to the squad room instead of going back to finish off with Tomlinson. She ran the name Franklyn J. Tomkins through her computer. She'd got a direct hit, which led to the explosive moment.

Treviss and I quizzed her on why she'd had this idea and she said that Tomlinson mentioned that he collected scenic photographs. This had apparently jogged her memory of a renewal notice for National Geographic magazine she'd seen lying on his coffee table when we were there on Sunday morning – doing her *'thin-slicing'*. The envelope was addressed to a Franklyn J. Tomkins, not Frank Tomlinson.

At the time, she'd thought it was just the usual sort of error a mail-out company would make but, at that moment, on her way back from the restroom, she decided to give it a run through her computer, before sending him home – to *'tidy up a loose end,'* she said.

Dee found that a Franklyn J. Tomkins had been arrested and charged for attacking a prostitute in 1997, after the prostitute had apparently attempted to steal some money out of Tomkins' wallet. Although it was sixteen years ago, the picture Dee found on the file was definitely that of a younger Tomlinson. He was staring into the lens with that same frustrated expression she'd seen in the interview room. Dee said the case against Tomkins had eventually been dropped but he'd received an official warning about his over-aggressive behavior and that was the reason it was still on file.

Dee had then gone back down and discussed what she'd found with Treviss and they decided the best option was for her to go straight back in and confront Tomlinson with this information before phoning me, to see what reaction she would get. They agreed that, if he owned up to the name, she would immediately back out and contact me before going further. But Dee didn't get that chance and the rest is history.

I find myself focusing back to the present as a small rainbow over one of the sprinklers catches my eye. This is showing up clearly against the backdrop of a rapidly darkening sky. The sight of a plane reminds me Sam Callan is flying into LAX tomorrow morning and I realize I haven't heard from her since I emailed across my report this afternoon. I had been minded to delay her arrival until things become clearer with Tomlinson, but something makes me want to leave things as they are.

I rise from the bench, yawning, and make my way inside. I want to rest for a while before heading across to South Normandie for the search. As I lie down on the couch, I catch a faint smell of Lena's perfume but it soon disappears and I realize I'm too tired to find it again. I place my cell phone onto the glass-topped table, knowing Dee will ring as soon as she receives the green light. I pull a throw over my shoulders, feeling my eyelids become heavy. My last image, as my eyes start to close, is of a dark and empty sky, slashed by contrails and perfectly framed in the panoramic window.

18

(Monday, 7.30 a.m.)

I'M STANDING WITH DEE on our side of the one-way glass, once again, and take another long look at the same man we had in here yesterday. Only this time we know his real name. It's Franklyn Tomkins, not Frank Tomlinson.

It's been confirmed.

He's looking anxious and worried; a different show to yesterday's incessant preening. He's sitting down for a start, bolt upright in his seat, tight lipped, arms folded, deep in thought – deep in shit is what I'm thinking.

He has a lawyer with him this time. It's Harold Asnick, a well-known counselor to those of us who've worked out of LAPD for years. He seems to come around on rotation every four or five years. I'm not sure Dee has come across him before, so I'm thinking this will be a good opportunity for her to learn something new. The plus side is he'll sit at the table and play the same game as me. The negative, is that he knows how I shuffle the cards, so I'll not have a chance to sneak any aces from the bottom of the pack.

I'm thinking Dee's using the same ploy as yesterday, because Asnick is sweating profusely in that expensive silk suit. He won't like that and I'm sure he'll not fall for it. As if on cue, he brings out a thermometer from his calfskin briefcase and takes a reading.

"That's the third time," Dee says, giving me one of her white teeth smiles. I immediately go into the corridor and look at the thermostat. It's set to seventy-two degrees. This surprises me and it must show, because Dee's smile is even broader as I come back in.

"Don't worry, I've turned it back down … just before you arrived. It should be bearable soon."

Asnick checks the time against his Rolex, and makes a note in a small book he's set out on the table with his Mont Blanc pen. He then turns and stares through the one-way glass, registering his frustration at being kept waiting and letting me know that he knows we're watching him.

"You ready?" Dee asks.

I see that, underneath his calm and stoic appearance, Tomkins is holding on to a deep-set anger. But it's not necessarily the anger of a guilty man, I'm thinking, it's possibly anger about the unfairness of the situation he finds himself in.

"How we going to play this, Oskar?" Dee asks, pointedly.

We'd put a list of questions together after successfully searching Tomkins' apartment a few hours ago. We didn't finalize who'd ask what, and when, because I wanted to give it further thought, so, what Dee's really asking is: *'Alright, Oskar. Who's leading?'* She wants it to be her.

After Dee had the warrant signed by Judge James Hilton, out in Lincoln Heights last night, she phoned me and Treviss and we'd all made our way over to Tomkins' apartment. We went through everything; every room, cupboard and drawer we could find. This first trawl took us four hours. Nothing stood out as being unusual or unexpected – not initially that is. Yes, there were eccentric possessions – three pairs of long-range binoculars, a pair of dueling pistols, a collection of military medals – but there was nothing that shouted out it was related to the murder. That was until Dee stumbled on 'Pandora's Box'.

Just as we were about to come back to the PAB and leave the SOCO techs to mop up, Dee noticed a few wooden floorboards were loose under a rug in Tomkins' photography studio. Treviss and I watched as she prized up one of the boards, using her neatly clipped fingernails. We all looked in and saw an old wooden box – about the size of a standard shoebox – tucked in between some joists. Dee smiled and, with eager apprehension, lifted it out, placing it on the floor gently, as if it were a treasure chest. There was silence as she opened it up and we all gazed inside.

At the top were photographs of Jane Chandler's comings and goings along South Normandie – photographs of her walking along the sidewalk and up the steps to her apartment. These were shots indicating Chandler wouldn't necessarily have known the photographs were being taken. Treviss thought a telephoto lens had been used because of the grainy images in some of the prints and the flattened perspective, but, never mind how they were taken, it was clear to me these had all been shot from Tomkins' bay window.

Below the prints was a piece of paper recording Chandler's comings and goings, and these were meticulously set out in neat handwriting. All were catalogued and coded against the photographs: Times, dates, places. The works. In fact, the *full works,* if we were looking for any evidence to implicate him.

Next were rather more revealing photographs. These were glossy eight by tens, and it was clear Chandler must have known a camera was being used, because in each she's looking right into the eye of the lens – almost teasingly at times. These were highly explicit photos. Poses of her either performing various acts on her own with sex aids or of her having sexual intercourse with different men. Throughout, it was difficult to work out who the men were, because their faces were not always visible. We counted at least seven different clients and judging by the range of bizarre positions on display, all appeared to be strong and agile. Nothing was said at the time between us but I think we were both remembering the paintings we'd seen on the oriental screen in Chandler's apartment.

Finally, clipped in a card folder and lying at the bottom of the box, were photocopies of hand-written letters that we presumed Chandler had sent to her clients; these promoted the full range of sexual delectations to suit personal tastes. Clearly, she not only promoted a private and personal service, she also offered a bespoke one.

Why Tomkins had this little horde we've yet to find out but it definitely ties him to Chandler. It isn't proof that he murdered her, of course, but it is evidence that connects him in ways I think he'll have great difficulty explaining.

Tomkins doesn't yet know we've found his stash, but he may suspect we do, so if we're to make any arrest warrant stick, we'll have to play this next interview with him very carefully indeed. Having Asnick in there with him won't make our job any easier, that's for sure, so we'll definitely need to finesse our way through this, big time.

"I'll lead this time and bring you in as needed," I say, looking directly at Dee. I can see she's disappointed but she just nods, affirming what she's possibly suspected all along: She'll be riding shotgun on this one today.

Satisfied we're both in the right frame of mind, I take a deep breath. Dee picks up on this and moves towards the door, opening it up. We make our way into the corridor to be met by Police Officer Shadwell – some muscle I've brought along in case Tomkins decides to make a run for the door again. I walk into the interview room and Dee and Shadwell follow in my wake.

Before we've sat down, Asnick's in my face.

"Detective Salo, would you please adjust the heating in this room. I've taken readings every ten minutes for the last three quarters of an hour you've kept us waiting and I've recorded temperatures of over eighty degrees. This is completely unacceptable and I will be making an official complaint."

Dee immediately moves out and leaves the room, making a show of checking the thermostat. Wrong move.

"It says it's seventy-two out here, Mr. Asnick," she shouts back. "You can come and see for yourself if you like," she adds with a hint of sarcasm in her voice.

"That's neither here nor there. My records show something different," Asnick retorts, thrusting his notebook across the table towards me, ignoring Dee. "You can see for yourself if you like," he says, imitating Dee's tone of voice.

Asnick has trumped Dee and she knows it. As she comes back into the room, I just stare at her with a look that says, *'Sit down. Keep quiet. Leave this to me.'*

Message delivered, Dee sits down.

"I'm sorry about this, Mr. Asnick," I say as I turn back to face him. "I've made a note of your concerns and I'll get the system checked out thoroughly as soon as we finish up in here. Is there anything I can get you or your client? Some more water, or is there something else you need at this stage?"

Asnick knows this is all bullshit but he acknowledges me anyway with a quick nod of his head and a feigned mopping of his brow with a silk handkerchief for effect.

"No, thank you Detective," he adds. "Can we just get on with this, please?"

I go through the preliminaries swiftly, starting with my list of questions about the false name Tomkins gave us yesterday. Tomkins readily admits he used this subterfuge to hide his real identity from us because of what happened to him in 1997. He lays out his reasons very carefully and methodically, continually checking with Asnick that what he's saying is in the script they've clearly discussed, beforehand.

I have my own garden path that I want to lead him up, and everything goes according to plan for the first twenty minutes. I get the details I need that can be matched with others' testimonies and might catch him out as a liar.

Tomkins also mentions that much attention was brought to him through media coverage in 1997, when he'd first been charged with attacking the prostitute. He says that, even though the prosecution had dropped the case, there had been a great deal of embarrassment, hence his defense at using a different name at the time and his use of it since then.

I'd also carried the burden of being accused of a crime I didn't commit for eight, long months, having been blamed for the death of a colleague whilst on duty. Fortunately, an internal enquiry eventually found there was no case to answer, but I don't need lectures from this jerk about what that might feel like. But I just nod and smile as reassuringly as I can, not wanting to challenge him on this point. I just need him to feel comfortable about speaking to me. I see Asnick sit forward as if he's registered my subterfuge here, but he says nothing and I suddenly wonder if Asnick has already done his homework and knows about my suspension and subsequent return to work.

Knowing Tomkins wants to convince us he's got a memory as long as his arm, I go on to spend another forty minutes asking him about his whereabouts at the time of all three murders. He tells us, yet again, how he lives alone and spends many nights on his own or playing bridge with friends, but we also learn that he works part-time at a local charity cooperative selling furniture.

I get details of the names of people he says he works with and an extended list of his colleagues, friends and acquaintances that I know we can crosscheck later with his previous interviews. He's confident and clear with his answers, even recalling who'd come into the store, what items they'd purchased and how much they paid. Even Asnick allows a slight smile to trace on his lips, thinking he's got Tomkins' defense sewn up and his invoice will be in the post this evening.

What we've definitely had from Tomkins today are his assurances that he does indeed have a photographic memory. This makes me consider the possibility that Tomkins is a copycat killer, because of the attention to detail he shows. I know we've held back certain information of each murder from the media, but I've learnt from personal experience that copycats can sometimes circumvent all this by obtaining the information they need by other means. So, Tomkins is not in the clear yet.

I remember the serial killer, Lee Craven, who I'd chased for nine months in 2003. I eventually brought him to trial, accusing him of killing seven women, only to find out afterwards that someone else, a random opportunist, Mark Tempest, had committed one of the murders. Tempest had studied the serial killer's technique so carefully that he killed his wife with the same precision and intricacy that convinced me, initially, that it was the work of Craven. Tempest had been dating an intern working at the morgue and this had given him both the idea and the opportunity. He managed to get sight of the autopsy report of one of Craven's victims and then he found out the full extent of Craven's vicious attacks on women. It was only when we had Craven under lock and key that I worked it all out. The only positive thing coming from this piece of shit was that he had an *integrity* streak. He was only willing to admit to six of the murders, but not the seventh.

Tempest had a meticulous brain and was very focused and determined, just like Tomkins. So, perhaps there is a copycat type and perhaps Tomkins is a copycat killer and he's running rings around us here. I look up at the clock, deciding it's time to ask him my first curved-ball question. I lean forward and ask him straight if he has ever hired prostitutes for the purposes of having sex since he was last accused of assaulting a prostitute in 1997.

He looks flummoxed at first, possibly indignant that I should dare ask him such a question, then I see the anger return to his eyes. I look across to Shadwell at this point, checking he's still awake. I also see Asnick pick up on this and see him put a hand on Tomkins' arm. Like me, he's obviously realized this could be another blue touch-paper moment. They immediately get into a huddle and have a *sotto voce* conversation. I ask Asnick if he would like to be left alone with Tomkins for a few moments but he holds up a hand, indicating he'd like us to stay. He continues to talk quietly to Tomkins, and Dee and I exchange a quick smile, wondering where this is going.

Eventually, after a final flurry of whisperings, Tomkins leans forward.

"No. I have not," he says, quite emphatically. "I've *never* hired prostitutes for sex, Detective."

At this point I slide the eight pictures of Jane Chandler I'd selected from the box across the table towards Tomkins. I think everyone in the room picks up on the electricity generated by this action. I even hear the metal and plastic in Shadwell's chair groan under his weight as he sits up, expectantly. I keep my eyes fixed on Tomkins' gaze.

Both Tomkins and Asnick flinch as they look through the pile. Tomkins gradually looks more and more stunned as he realizes we now have his box. Asnick, on the other hand, is completely confused or that's the way he's making it appear. He immediately advises Tomkins not to answer any more questions and asks that we leave until he's had a chance to speak with his client. Tomkins sits back in his chair at this point and folds his arms with a frustrated and angry expression – the 1997 mug shot coming to mind immediately. He then looks at me and shakes his head, almost pleadingly.

I have enough to charge Tomkins for the murder of Chandler – and Asnick will know this – but I tell them we'll pause for the time being. I'm gonna let them both stew in their own juice and resume the interview later. I also know the SOCO techs will have finished their scrutiny of Tomkins' apartment by then, and this may give me all I need to take him to the DA.

I know that Dee thinks we have the killer on the rack, but everything's falling into place too easily, in my opinion. Since finding the photos, Dee's convinced we've got Tomkins 'boxed up' for the Chandler murder but, given what we know about the other related murders, I still have reservations about it all. It doesn't fit together the way I like. There's something about Tomkins' defense that feels genuine, and I can't quite shake it down. He's certainly desperate, and he's certainly boxed himself into some deep shit, but is he the killer? I'm still not sure, despite all we've learned about his character, his behavior, his temper … and his strength.

I'm still not sure.

As I leave the room my cell phone vibrates. I take a quick peek. It's from Sam Callan:

> Caught earlier flight.
> Be with you around 2.
> Sam x

19

(Monday, 12.15 p.m.)

THE REAPER SURVEYS THE wooden framework he's spent the morning erecting, feeling proud of his achievement. He examines the various jigs he's just attached, checking each one against his master-planning sheet and making sure he's got them in the correct position. Satisfied, he cross-references the work to date against a time-line, realizing that his volunteering job is making it difficult to fit in everything he needs to do. It's a busy time, but the Reaper enjoys the planning. He's feeling particularly pleased this morning, because, despite the pressures, everything is on schedule.

He knows his Master would be proud of him, and he glows with pride at the thought.

He sets about his next tasks by bringing out a new planning sheet from a wooden file chest. This includes a detailed cutting list and itinerary. He spends the next ten minutes going round the barn checking he has everything ready for the final assembly.

Some months ago, the Reaper bought an old bullion lorry. He'd paid $17,000 for it from a collector who'd reclaimed it from one of the film studios in L.A., twenty years ago. It had been in full working order when he'd bought it, and the owner had told him of its *'glorious heritage.'* It was used in Hollywood films in the forties and fifties and the owner had waxed lyrical about the famous names who had held the steering wheel. The Reaper had not told him that it was his intention to dismantle the lorry. Piece by piece.

Over the last month, he had carefully removed the steel panels from the vehicle and cut them to size using a plasma-arc cutter. All he was left with at the end was the running chassis. He parked this in one of the adjacent barns alongside other redundant vehicles and farm equipment.

The steel sheets are now leaning on the walls in the workshop. He has chalked a code number on the side of each panel, representing the order of construction, and also identifying their unique positions in the overall structure.

As the Reaper lifts the first panel into place with a portable hoist, he sees the wooden frame strain under the weight, but he knows the structure is strong enough. He's done the math. Everything *will* work. Perfectly.

He knows he'll have everything in place in four hours and then he can make a start on welding the panels together into one seamless skin.

Ready for inserting the bulletproof glass.

20

(Monday 2.07 p.m.)

HEADS TURN AS WE walk into the squad room. It's not often we get a head-turner like Sam come through the PAB, let alone someone who's going to set up shop for a few days. Someone's brought in a box of donuts and colleagues are standing around brushing sugar off their clothes and wiping fingers on paper napkins. Conversations dip in volume as they all take a look at their new visitor. I suspect Sam's noticed this behavior too, but she doesn't show it.

Plastic crates obstruct us as we walk between the cubicles. The lieutenant had reminded us we'd have sixty per cent less storage space in this new building but many colleagues packed up everything, intending to have a good clear out once they'd arrived and hadn't got round to it yet.

I can see the lieutenant across in the tank. He's also giving Sam the once-over. He rubs one hand over his balding head, then strokes his tie with one of the 'is-my-erection-showing' mannerisms he reserves for these occasions.

I've agreed with the lieutenant that Sam will spend five days – Monday through Friday – with the team and me then return to Denver. She'll clock up further time as needed, each additional day needing to be signed off by him. He'll be keeping a watchful eye on how we all work together, making sure he gets his money's worth.

Sam will stay at the Marriott Hotel on South Figueroa Street, a mile or so from the PAB, but a crazy seven-mile taxi ride because of the one-way system the drivers use. I wanted her to stay at the

Hilton Checkers. It has a higher spec, but the lieutenant insists we get an extra 20% discount at the Marriott. I think I know the real reason.

Occasionally, the lieutenant will swing by the Marriott bar on his way home and I'm darn sure his tab never gets paid. I've always kept this to myself on the off chance I can use it against him one day, if push came to shove. I did wonder if this was the occasion, but decided to save it for a bigger battle.

Keen to get started, I point out where the room is that Sam will be using and follow Sam through the cubicles. I watch the male detectives smile ingratiatingly towards her, moving crates out of her way. I follow in her wake, knowing they wouldn't do this for me. If I'd been leading, they'd be nudging them in my direction, hoping to trip me up. I can see Dee, on the phone, smiling at this little charade as we make our way across.

Behind Dee is Buttle. He's drilling his eyes into me over the top of his computer in an attempt to stare me down. I'm guessing the lieutenant has spoken with him about his re-assignment and he wants to show me what he thinks about it. I stare directly back until he feels obliged to look away. One nil. Dee spots this and gives me a parental shake of her head. She thinks this old-guard rivalry stuff is something of the past. She's right of course, but Buttle and me are schooled in this past so it's a language we both understand.

When Sam reaches the entrance of the room she pauses momentarily before entering, slumping her shoulders in the process. When I catch up and look inside, I realize why. My request for the room to be fully equipped meant someone has to unpack all the items from their packing crates because they're brand new. Fortunately, the desk and chair are out of their wrappings, but everything else is still in its box.

"Same old, same old," Sam says matter-of-factly, as she turns and gives me a sarcastic smile. This turns into a full-face grin as she acknowledges the smirking of male colleagues in the background, hiding behind their donuts and napkins. The tension is suddenly broken as she blows them a kiss and they fall about laughing. She knows how to handle the boys.

We spend the next fifteen minutes getting the basics unpacked and assembled to Sam's liking. She has her own desk phone and she can key in a four-digit code to send and receive calls. There's an answer-phone and forward-calling function to direct calls to her cell phone should she wish. She also has use of a small, portable, two-drawer filing cabinet.

I feel slightly embarrassed explaining all this to her because it's a million miles from the take-it-or-leave-it culture at the old Parker Center when she was last here. Sam jokes she was fully prepared to play stone, scissors, paper for 'first dibs' on the department's typewriter but hadn't expected all this.

Gradually the room begins to take shape and, as Sam reaches into her briefcase for the copy of my report, I start to pace the room. I'm eager to hear what she thinks. My hand goes to my jacket pocket.

"Look, I'll be five minutes ... ten max," Sam responds, having seen me reach for my cigarettes. "Then I'll be ready. Honest. Why don't you go outside for a smoke, or make us coffee or something? It'll probably be quicker without you prowling around in the background."

Breathing deeply, I look at the clock and then at my watch, suddenly thinking about Tomkins. I realize I haven't made my planned trip down to the basement lock-ups, because Sam arrived early.

"Okay. Ten minutes," I say, looking back at the clock, as if to reinforce my decision.

I slide out of the room, leaving Sam to make her preparations, undisturbed. Catching Dee's eye I hold up both hands and flash ten minutes as I walk towards the swing doors. She's standing up in her cubicle, phone perched under her chin and rummaging through paperwork on her desk. She gives me a cursory nod before continuing her conversation. Treviss is sitting beside her, deep in thought, looking intently at her screen. I can see from the concentration etched into his face that he's definitely on board with this investigation. This feels good but, when I look for Buttle, he's nowhere to be seen.

*

I enter the elevator. As it descends, I find myself rummaging in my pocket again but know I'm going straight to the jail cells to look in on Tomkins. There's no time for a smoke.

As I arrive, I make my way past the security desk and along the cell corridor. I find an officer, Earl Costello, looking at a screen that shows him the inside of Tomkins' padded cell. He has the job of looking after Tomkins today and it looks as though he's having difficulty staying awake.

Knowing he's a smoker, I offer him a five-minute break and he accepts this without question. Before leaving, he checks there's enough tape in the videocassette without my needing to switch cassettes whilst he's gone. Satisfied, he heads off for the shelter with a smile on his face.

After interviewing Tomkins earlier this morning, I'd sent him to his cell to ponder his options because I wanted to hear what Sam thinks about the killer's personality before confronting him again. But I also wanted to look at him like this, on my own, just to see if anything shakes loose.

I sit in Costello's chair and take a long, hard look at Tomkins on the screen. The room looks completely white, almost sterile and bleached out like some art-house movie. Tomkins is sitting on a simple bed that cantilevers out from one of the walls. I want to see what sort of expression he has on his face, but that's not possible from here, so I stand up and go across to the cell-door and silently slide open the peephole and take a look inside. Tomkins is only six feet away from me now, leaning forward, elbows on knees, holding his head in his hands. He doesn't move. He doesn't even blink. In fact he's completely motionless, like the statue in my garden, contemplative, distant, otherworldly.

After a minute or so, Tomkins suddenly turns his head and looks across at the peephole, as if he's realized someone's watching him. He gazes straight at me, holding my stare for what seems like an eternity, before standing up abruptly and moving across towards the cell-door. He can't know it's me, of course, because all he can see is my eye looking in through a hole about the size of a dime. I continue to hold his stare as he moves in closer. I can see him focus on my eye. Eventually, when he's standing two feet away from me, he smiles.

"Oh, it's you, Detective Salo. Have you come to gloat?" he says.

I find the fact he's recognized me, alarming, but try not to show it. If he can identify me through this hole, what else can he see, for chrissakes? Can he see what I'm thinking?

"I recognized you by your eye, Detective Salo ... Don't worry, it's not a trick." He moves back a fraction, as if he's picked up from my reaction that his move was possibly threatening. "It wasn't a guess either. Your eyes, you see, are very dark ... and slightly bloodshot, I'm afraid. You're right-eyed and it's more bloodshot than the left. Did you know that? ... I recognized the red capillary traces. That's all ... No tricks."

He smiles, but there's no humor.

"Now, your partner, Detective Chance, her eyes are a lighter brown, and the whites are crystal clear ... perfectly white in fact ... No alcohol ... and anyway she'd have to stand on tip-toe, wouldn't she, and that would have been a complete give-away?"

It's humor this time, and I end up smiling. He must notice this, because he smiles back, connecting with me.

"I see things, Detective. That's all. There are no tricks," he says, getting serious again.

This is freaking me, because Tomkins seems to be taking control. That's not how I'd planned it. My intention had been to flush him out, not the other way round. I was hoping that, by looking in on him like this, I might end up 'believing' he was the killer or not. And, most importantly, if I did, this might be all the fuel I'd need to take him to trial and then all the way to San Quentin.

I'm realizing I'll only get one chance at this so I decide it's my turn to take control.

"Why'd you kill her, Tomkins? Why did you kill Jane Chandler?" I say back to him.

Tomkins just stares at me for a few seconds and then takes a deep breath. I wonder if it's anger building. After a beat, he turns and walks down his cell towards the far wall. And, knowing his temper and volatility, I find myself getting ready to snap the peephole closed.

We once had an officer blinded through a cell door at the old Parker Center, after a local gangbanger had managed to smuggle in a small screwdriver when he was arrested. He'd been holed up two days and apparently flipped when he was told his bail-bond hadn't been paid. He contained his anger just long enough to call over the guard and then he rammed the screwdriver blade into the officer's eyeball, leaving him blinded in one eye and with brain damage.

Tomkins reaches the far side of the cell and taps the wall with the end of his fingers on his right hand, counting quietly to himself.

"One, two, three, four, five, six, seven, eight, nine, ten."

He then turns and walks back towards me, stopping about four feet from the door this time and looking at me with strong, piercing eyes.

"You've got me wrong, Detective. But then, deep down, I think you know this."

Tomkins leans forward holding out both hands, palms forward, showing me he's no threat.

"I'm sure you know this," he reiterates. "I'm no killer. I don't kill. I would never kill anyone. And, most importantly, I would never have done anything to harm Jane Chandler. You're wasting your time with me, Detective, when you could be out there hunting down the real killer. I can help you, you know."

"Tell me about her, then? Why did you have those pictures of her in that box? Look, Tomkins, you really need to help yourself here. I've already got enough to take you all the way to prison."

Tomkins turns and walks back down the cell again and goes through the same routine, tapping the wall ten times with the ends of his fingers. He then walks back towards me, returning to the same spot in the cell, seemingly checking his feet are in the right position.

"I was very close to Jane, Detective, as you'll no doubt find out when this whole, sorry tragedy is out of the way and your mistake with me is history. Yes, I was infatuated with her, I won't deny that, but I didn't kill her. She liked me Detective. We were good friends. Close friends. We had a unique relationship. You probably won't understand … It was special, very special indeed … for both of us."

"In what way, Tomkins?"

He stops to think about this question, raising his eyebrows, slightly.

"Well, I looked after her. I'd make sure she was okay when she was ill. Go to the drugstore. Errands mostly. I'd check her things were safe when she wasn't around." He smiles at this memory. "She liked me doing things for her. She used to leave messages around, shopping lists, things for me to do. She'd hide them for me sometimes, knowing I'd find them in the end. She loved playing these secret games. She loved me looking through her things. It was the secrecy that turned her on. I liked helping and watching over her. That's the truth."

I'm sensing that Tomkins is opening up but know that I ought to be doing this by the book, with his lawyer present, however, I decide it's too good an opportunity to miss, so I remain silent, willing him to continue.

"It was a symbiotic relationship. It worked well for us both, you see."

Tomkins looks directly at me, assessing how much of this I believe. How much I understand.

"We both got what we wanted. We both enjoyed doing things for each other, Detective."

Thinking about the photographs and Chandler's profession, I decide to push him further.

"And what was it that you got from this relationship, Tomkins? What did she give you?"

Tomkins turns and walks down the cell and goes through the same habitual routine and returns to the same position. However, this time, he assumes a more confident pose. He straightens himself up, raises his shoulders and sticks out his chest.

"She allowed me to photograph her, Detective. Whenever I wanted."

"Where would this happen, Tomkins? Where would you photograph her?"

"In her apartment, mainly, although I took shots of her in other places, as you know. She'd let me set up my camera and take photographs of her in different situations. It was all consensual, Detective. Believe me, she enjoyed being photographed this way. This was all part of the deal ... I told you it was a very special relationship."

"Tell me more. How did it develop?"

"Well, as our relationship grew, we found new ways to please each other. She'd ask me to take photographs of her behind the screen in her bedroom or from inside her wardrobe. It was the secrecy, you see ... that's the way she liked it. I would sometimes just take photographs of her as she moved around ... as she got dressed, took a bath, cooked a meal, or chilled out on the couch ... And then, after she'd gone to bed I'd let myself out and make my way down the stairs." He pauses at this point, seemingly reminiscing about something.

"Sometimes I would photograph her when she was asleep, lying in her bed. Those were the most beautiful photographs I ever took of her, Detective. She was so beautiful when she had her eyes closed. She was just like a baby. An angel. She was so peaceful ... so contented when she was asleep."

I'm still trying to work out if Tomkins is in a dream world of his own or if he's telling me the truth. I've seen the pictures of Chandler in erotic poses, but I hadn't seen these more sensitive and touching portraits he's describing.

"When did it all start? Your relationship with her?"

He seems to change tack, having to think back a long way.

"Well … after she moved in … let me see, March twenty-fifth, two years ago, we spoke a little, on the stairs mainly, and then I ended up talking to her about my love of photography. She'd come into my apartment for a coffee and we were looking at some of my photographs. She especially liked the photos I'd taken of people walking up and down the street and she was particularly pleased with a candid shot I'd taken of her. She then asked me if I would take a photograph of her. I did and then one thing led to another. The first photographs I took were headshots, straight-forward shots, fully clothed. I then went up to her apartment and took photographs of her posing in her bedroom the way she wanted, for her website." Again, he looks at me to see whether his fantastical tale is being believed. "She wanted me to photograph her and I was happy to oblige, that's the truth of it. It was after about the fifth session that we realized it was the experience of taking the photographs that was exciting for us both."

"Did you love her?" I ask, wanting to push his story towards his personal emotions, to see where this might lead.

"I was infatuated with her at first," he admits. "And she knew this, but then it grew into a love. A deep love."

Tomkins looks at me, searchingly, wondering if I really believe him, but this time he's not really caring if I don't. I see his eyes moisten.

"She was a very beautiful woman, Detective Salo … very beautiful indeed. I miss her very much."

Thinking her profession might have enraged Tomkins into killing her through jealousy, I decide to push him a little harder.

"Tell me a bit more, Tomkins. You know we've got the photographs of her having sex with other men, did you take those as well?"

"Yes. I did," he answers, proudly. "Jane and I would set it up carefully. This happened mostly in the hotel bedrooms she used downtown, when she met up with clients. I'd have to hide away with my camera. We would choreograph the sessions beforehand."

"Did this upset you, Tomkins? Seeing her with other men."

"No. Not at all. What I got was more than I could ever expect."

"What do you mean, 'more than you could expect?'"

"Mmm ... I'm just saying I was grateful to be there. That's all."

"But, why did she want you to be there, Tomkins. For what purpose?"

Tomkins looks at me now, with a slightly confused expression on his face, as if he can't work out why I would ask such a question.

"Well, she enjoyed being a prostitute, if that's what you mean. She really enjoyed her work," he replies, as if it should be obvious. "She would often discuss the routines she would go through to please her clients, and we would choreograph this together beforehand. She loved sex and I enjoyed watching her is the truth of it. That's what drew us together. She was highly prized by her clients. Some would ask for photographs of them having sex with her and Jane always shared the extra money she charged for this service with me fifty-fifty, down the line. She was always scrupulously fair. Even if she got an extra tip on top of her fee for this service, she'd always share that with me too."

"Did you have sex with her, Frank?" I ask, hoping this will flush out the demon if it's hiding in there somewhere.

"No, Detective, we *never* had sex," he says, quite emphatically. "She did ask me once, but as soon as she found out about me, she never offered again."

"Why didn't you have sex with her if you were so infatuated with her ... If you loved her so much? Why didn't you have sex?"

Tomkins smiles, rather sadly this time, and he shrugs. Then I think I see the beginnings of annoyance come across his face.

He turns and walks away down the cell again. I'm not sure what's gonna happen next.

Suddenly, he starts to rummage around at the front of his pants, as if he's decided on something. I can't see what's going on from here, and think about going across to the monitor to see if I can get a better view but decide against it.

After about five seconds he lowers his pants to his knees and pauses for a beat. As I stare at this incongruous sight, he turns around slowly, lifting up his shirt, to face me.

I hear myself gasp involuntarily.

"This is why, Detective."

21

(Monday, 3.45 p.m.)

"NO SHIT! WHAT THE hell do you mean?" Dee announces as I begin to tell her and Sam about what's just happened.

"Well, when he lowered his pants," I repeat, still trying to get my own head around it, "he turned towards me, and then lifted up his shirt. I could see he had both male and female genitalia."

Dee lets a burst of air escape from her lungs as she starts to pace around the room. "What kinda freak show you got down there, Oskar?"

Dee and Sam had both been ready to make a start on the afternoon's session when I came back up, but I started to tell them straightaway about Tomkins' deformity.

Whilst Dee is pacing the floor with that incredulous look of hers, Sam goes to her laptop, deep into something. I decide to let my disclosure settle in our minds for a minute or two, before telling them what Tomkins said about his loving – but weirdly voyeuristic – relationship with Chandler.

After about thirty seconds, Sam suddenly sits up, drawing our attention her way.

"Got it," she announces. "I think I know what this is all about."

I join her at her computer. She adjusts the screen so I can obtain a better view. Dee's still pacing the floor.

"It's Five-Alpha Reductase Deficiency," she announces. "It's a condition brought on by the body's failure ... here it is ... '*to convert testosterone into dihydrotestosterone that's responsible for the development of external genitalia*'," she reads.

Sam looks at me to see if I'm catching the gist of what she's saying. "I know a little bit about this condition, because of this particular case."

Dee stops pacing and joins us at the computer.

"It's from a collection of synopses for a conference I went to in Chicago, entitled Personality Disorders and Physical Deformity."

"It's basically about some guy who had been brought up as a girl, only to find out that he was a man—"

"No shit. Is Tomkins a man or what?" Dee asks, interrupting.

"From what I know about this condition, and what you've said about Tomkins, it sounds as if he's probably a 'he'," Sam replies. "But, he was quite possibly raised as a girl."

Sam goes onto her search engine and brings up pictures of people with this condition and scrolls through various images. I look at them, closely.

"Yes. That just about sums up what I've seen," I say.

"No shit," Dee exhorts, once again. "I knew he was a mixed-up son-of-a-bitch, but I didn't expect this."

"You see, the mix-up in the sexing of a child born with this condition makes any classification difficult," Sam continues, reading from the screen. "Mainly because they don't yet have a recognizable penis or a scrotum. That's why they're initially brought up as a girl."

"So, Tomkins was a girl before becoming a man. Is that what you're saying?"

"It's not as easy as that. His voice probably deepened and he grew characteristics of a man as he became a teenager. But, he probably had all the usual testosterone-driven stuff that normal boys have. In fact, he probably developed in ways you would expect a teenager to develop, going through puberty, etcetera, etcetera. You know, stronger muscles, deeper voice, if you will. It was probably then that he developed what could pass as a functional penis and this grew out of what may have been understood previously as his clitoris."

Dee is wide-eyed listening to this, both shocked and amazed. She starts pacing the room again.

"No shit," she says, one more time, as if we haven't got her message. "No wonder he's so strange ... Some way to grow up as a teenager, huh? We had spots and greasy hair to worry about and this kid had to deal with all that crap."

Dee shakes her head and then stops pacing, looking down at the floor as if she's piecing together another thought.

"Could all this have turned him into a predatory sexual killer?" Dee asks. "A rapist?" she suddenly adds, looking across to us both. She's thinking about the semen we found, and her view that Chandler's attack was sexually motivated.

"A murderer? Yes. He could probably develop murderous tendencies, like any man," Sam says, looking towards me with that half-smile of hers. "Because it's mainly men that exhibit the violence we associate with murders, and Tomkins has already shown you he has a testosterone-fueled rage – a violent streak, if you will – so, to all intents and purposes, I think Tomkins is probably capable of murdering someone. But, rape? No. I don't think so. Sexual desires? Yes, quite possibly. But, sex, penetrative sex? I think not. It's probably out of the question for Tomkins, because his penis will not be fully formed."

There's a lull in conversation now as we all take Sam's prognosis on board. I'm already coming to the conclusion that Tomkins may be some crazy, mixed-up-guy, but he's not our murderer. I think Sam is coming to that opinion as well, but I'm not sure about Dee. I start to wonder if I'll have my work cut out persuading Dee to shift her mind from Tomkins, because I want to put all our energies into looking at other factors, other ideas, other potential perpetrators, and not spin our wheels just focusing on him for the moment. And I want to hear back from Sam on what she thinks about all three murder cases and what this will say about the personality of the murderer.

I decide to put some breathing space between the two sessions and my suggestion to go across to the kitchen to make some hot drinks meets with everyone's approval, even Dee, who's still wrapped in her thoughts. I look out across the squad room as I go to the drinks-station, and see Treviss working away in his cubicle. But there's still no sign of Buttle. I'm thinking he's made his way over to Billy's for an extended liquid-lunch. I make coffees for Dee and me and a black tea for Sam remembering the enormous quantities she drank when we'd first met at the Minneapolis conference.

As I make my way back with the drinks, I catch sight of the lieutenant. He's looking across at me from the tank, checking the time on the clock. Checking we're on schedule ... On the money.

*

Sam pats the paperwork that's piled up on the table.

"What about I give you a summary of my thoughts at this stage. Will that work for you?" she asks looking mainly in my direction, possibly wanting to get approval from me that we're on the right course.

"Yeah, let's get this rolling," I say.

"These are just my initial thoughts," Sam continues. "You know, the ideas I've put together after reading this little lot last night, and on the flight across this morning."

She turns towards Dee, now.

"Okay, let's also see if I can help you find out whether Tomlinson, Tomlins, or whatever this jerk calls—"

"It's Tomkins," Dee interrupts, correcting Sam.

"Okay, thanks Dee ... Yes, let's see if Tomkins is up for this or not, and also whether this new revelation fits the personality profile of the murderer I'm developing."

Sam takes a step back and then looks down at her notes for a few seconds.

"So, what we know about this unsub is that he has little respect for people," she starts off by saying. "I think it's people, *per se* ... *All* people. On a fundamental level, he's got no respect for anyone, and I'm beginning to think this is what he's showing in his treatment of the victims. He's also possibly detached from what he's doing and yet he's sequencing things, you know, going through the moves, quite methodically."

"Yes, but, there's something else, in this mix," Dee adds, bringing her hands out from under the table. "I think he's quite meticulous, as if he can't help himself. As if it's his 'thing'."

"Yes. You're right about that, Dee, and there's the final frenzied attack that's part of his methodical plan, despite appearing to be out of control. He brutally inflicts pain in an orderly way as well, doesn't he? You know, breaking limbs before killing his victims. It's quite common for people who act in this way to have been dominated by a strict disciplinarian sometime in their life. Someone, who has had a major impact on their upbringing."

"What about a parent, or a teacher? Someone in authority?" Dee asks, giving me every impression she's suddenly settled into this introspective approach.

"Yeah, could be. Or a father-type figure, an uncle maybe ... or a close family friend."

"He's maybe missing that dominating influence in his life now," Dee asserts. "His sequencing of the murders feeds his desires, enabling him to retain control of his emotions and the meanings in his life ... the ones he wants to hang on to."

It sounds as if Dee has been reading up from one of her college readers overnight because of the language she's using. Never mind Sam, she's got theories of her own!

I feel my cell phone vibrate.

"Yes, quite probably," Sam responds, not appearing to notice my surreptitious peek at my phone – still nothing from Lena – "He might want to hold on to an existence he doesn't quite understand," Sam replies, eye to eye with Dee.

"So, Sam, perhaps he re-enacts in the murders some of the things he's not been able to process for himself ... you know, things personally. He may have been hurt both physically and emotionally sometime in his past, and he's playing out the

92

sequence of events ... victim, pain, death ... by bloodletting, giving himself the relief he needs until his inner torment drives him to want to kill again."

"You know what, Dee?" Sam says, holding up the copy of my report. "The timeline here shows that the instances are getting more frequent, which is often the—"

"And, more importantly," Dee interrupts, leaning forward, "I think he's cleverer than he wants us to believe."

"Yes, Dee, I agree. He's clever and manipulative. Remember Ted Bundy? That son-of-a-bitch fooled so many people with his good-looking face ... Have a look on Youtube ..."

There's a sudden lull in our conversation and I remember something that Dee mentioned to me yesterday.

"Why did you say it was personal, Dee?" I ask. "Early Sunday morning, you used the word 'personal' ... when you first called."

She thinks about this for a beat, seemingly trying to find the words to help her explain.

"Well ... It's just a gut feeling, Oskar, that's all. Up until yesterday it felt as if the perp was getting a kick out of knowing we were no further forward than we were ten weeks ago. Yesterday, I felt he was playing us as well as his victims."

I'm still not convinced and it must show, because Dee sits back and folds her arms.

"It's just a feeling Oskar, that's all. Ignore it if you want. It's just a feeling I have."

I know I've been wrong about Dee's intuition in the past, and remember the *Hallowed Case,* six months ago. She convinced me to search a young priest's rooms where SOCOs found traces of cocaine hidden behind a panel in an oak dresser. Suddenly, we had a case involving a street gang, the priest himself and dealers from Mexico. All were involved in smuggling drugs across the border under the guise of doing church charity work. Remembering this, I soften a little and ask Dee to explain her feelings further.

"Well, our perp seems to know how we work, Oskar, because he does things that take us in all directions. In directions we can't resource properly. I think he selects certain elements in a random way to confuse us. He seems to know how we'll work, what directions we'll go in. And, as I said, it feels like he's playing with us ... He's leading *us* up that garden path, for chrissakes"

"Well, maybe he just wants us to respect him." Sam says, moving the thinking along. "He's clever, and despite the fact he's unhinged in many dimensions, he most probably has normal desires like all of us. Or, maybe, like many other serial murderers, he wants to communicate with his pursuers. Perhaps he wants to be respected by them. He may even crave love and affection ... and friendship and respect ... Does this sound like Tomkins, then?" Sam asks directly, tapping into what Dee must be thinking.

Dee looks back and forth between Sam and me and then opens up both palms, raising her shoulders a little.

"Well, sometimes, serial killers want this dialogue with their pursuers," Sam continues. "You know, they want to communicate with the detective team. Aren't the switchboards always jammed with would-be-doers phoning in and saying they're the killer? Sometimes, there's something obsessive about it."

I think about Tomkins' obsessive tapping on the wall but say nothing, wanting to keep things moving.

Sam picks up on this and moves across to a folder at the end of the table. I think she's about to change direction.

"There appears to be no sign of an assassin at work in any of the murders, don't you agree?" Sam asks, turning to the first page.

Saying things that are controversial has always been one of Sam's ploys to awaken fresh thinking. Unfortunately, for Dee, she won't have experienced this before, and I see her shake her head in disbelief, mouth wide open.

"Look, all the evidence so far suggests we're dealing with a lone killer who's getting a hard-on from his exploits," Sam continues. "There appears to be no involvement of organized crime, whatsoever. No hallmarks of a contract killing or a gang in sight. So, why am I bringing this up?"

Dee's still gobsmacked. I remain silent. Sam's about answer herself.

"Well, just because the evidence so far tells us this is the work of a lone killer, doesn't mean it is. Have you any evidence it isn't an assassin? Because, this really could be the work of someone who *is* leading you up your garden path."

Dee and I smile at each other at this point.

"You've said all along that you have little evidence to go on to help you identify a motive or a profile of a murderer, so why dismiss a contract killing? These murders just might be the work of someone who is engendering a belief that we do indeed have a lone, mad, sadistic, serial killer on the loose, when in fact it's something more sinister."

"*More* sinister?" Dee exhorts. "What's more sinister than a lone, mad, sadistic, maniacal, cruel, serial killer?" almost flabbergasted by her own question, not seeming to notice she's added words to Sam's list.

"Well, it could be a cold, calculating, professional hit-man, obeying the orders of his client."

This statement brings things to a full stop.

Dee sits back with another of her incredulous looks, then, much in the way a yawn becomes infectious, we all take a long pull on our drinks. Thinking the room's suddenly gotten hotter, I lean across and rejig the thermostat.

"We have assassins around the world that'll do anything, as instructed, at the right price," Sam continues, bringing up details on her laptop screen that I'm guessing she's been itching to show us.

Dee and I lean forward to look.

"In Sweden, eighteen months ago, there was a series of killings that led Swedish police to think they were dealing with a lone killer, when in fact the murderer had been a professional assassin working for a drugs baron who'd been attempting to protect his patch from a rival."

Sam has put up extracts from *Sydsvenkian*, a Swedish daily.

"The gang leader, a recent Russian émigré, hired an assassin to kill distant relatives and friends of his new rival in a macabre set of ritualistic assassinations. It was only when the assassin had been seriously injured in a freak traffic accident that he apparently pleaded out for remission and the police managed to unpack the full, sorry saga. "

Sam scrolls forward to some gory images.

"One of the bizarre rituals was to brand each victim on the forehead with a key before setting fire to them using lighter fluid. The gang leader insisted on this as a way of demonstrating to his enemies in the criminal underworld that, above all else, he was a person to be feared ... It was the gang leader's 'calling card', if you will."

"His *signature*?" Dee asks, looking across at me, eyebrows raised. "Yes, his signature," Sam replies, quickly. "So, please, let's not rule out others' involvement in this murder gig of yours. Not at this stage, anyway. There could be a vendetta being played out here. After all, there may indeed be a connection between the victims that you haven't identified yet. So, I suggest we consider *all* options ... Until we're sure."

A long silence follows whilst we grapple with our thoughts.

"What in fuck's name have we got here then?" Dee eventually retorts.

No one is expecting to give her an answer, and none is offered. I just reach for my cigarettes.

22

(Monday, 5.05 p.m.)

I MAKE MY WAY upstairs from the smoking shelter, having had a two-cigarette opportunity to review my thinking about Sam's evaluation. I was right to anticipate she'd bring some unexpected angles.

"Okay guys," she says, as I take my seat. "I'm here to help you develop the personality profile of this murderer. That's what you're paying me for, and that's what you're gonna get."

I couldn't have put it better.

Sam turns away and brings up a list of words on the screen:

Random – Anybody? – Confusion? – Intimidation?

Invisible – Hiding? – Teasing?

Signature – Reenactment? – Communication?

"I've made a start on listing what you know about your killer and what this might mean for his personality. This may help you either put Tomkins in the frame or eliminate him from your enquiries," Sam says, looking towards Dee, who gives her a quick assertive nod in return.

"You've found nothing so far to connect the victims. They're from different backgrounds, different economic groupings and they're different genders. The only thing they have in common is that they're all *victims*. And, all except for our last one, they don't fall into the traditional category of being a serial killer's victim;

they're not *all* prostitutes, for example, which is what you might have expected."

Dee and I already know from experience that serial killers will often attack a particular section of society, like prostitutes or down-and-outs, because they're a category of people which society will readily dismiss, making them easier targets.

"No, we have to consider that our murderer is probably choosing 'random' people on purpose. He may, indeed, clearly enjoy the intimidating nature of his power, by hiding himself more carefully behind this random selection."

"That's great," Dee asserts. "I'll go tell all the whores on Sunset or down at Angels' Flight that they're in the clear now. He's not going there, 'cause he's already notched up his hooker."

I shift uncomfortably, knowing Dee's getting prickly around Sam's mention of prostitutes like she did with me yesterday. Again, I decide today's not the day to find out why.

"Why the signature?" I ask.

"I've given a great deal of thought to this," Sam replies. "If this were the work of a lone serial murderer, why would he do that? Perhaps the murder gives him an opportunity to release a pent up inner-frustration. Perhaps it's got something to do with a childhood trauma ... an overbearing parent or an attack by a school bully. Any of these could be driving his murderous ambitions. The signature ends up being his personal mark to physically stamp his authority on the crime scene, to make it *his* own."

"Are you trying to make me feel sorry for this son-of-a-bitch?" Dee exhorts impetuously, lifting herself out of her seat for a moment. "Because I can't see where this—"

"No, I'm not," Sam says calmly, interrupting Dee in full flow. "Addressing these desires and getting close to an understanding of where our killer is coming from is why I'm here. It's my belief that unlocking the reasons why he operates this way will allow us to unlock the whole case. I am not asking you to have pity on him, I am just asking you to seek an understanding of his motives

– his make up, if you will – and then you'll stand a much better chance of catching him before he strikes again."

Suitably chided, Dee hunkers back down in her seat. Arms folded. Sam turns and points to some images from my report.

"Look, here. It shows the breaks of the radius and the ulna. Why do it? For what purpose? How does he benefit from it?"

"Maybe, it's pure sadism," Dee says. "Perhaps he takes sadistic pleasure in inflicting the pain on the victim. It's a power thing. He's showing us he's in control. He's in charge. Maybe, he's telling us, *This crime scene is mine. I did this. Be scared of me. This is what I can do. This is what I could do to you!*"

"But, the autopsies seem to suggest that the victims are not conscious at the time," I add.

"I think this is a key point," Sam says. "Because I don't believe he's necessarily doing this to cause pain. It's a ritual thing. He's making it his *hallmark*. It's the same with the bloodletting. He cuts a main artery, always the carotid, using a sharp bladed knife. A small craft knife is your M.E.'s suggestion. That's why I brought up the Swedish killings. If it's not a lone killer, it could be a gang-ritual thing."

Sam now puts a picture of the victim's neck wound onto the screen.

"He made a careful incision here," she says, pointing at the three-quarter-inch slit in the skin. "Despite the frenzied nature of the attack that followed, the victim bled to death through this cut."

There's a pause as the shock of this fact sinks in.

"Let's move on for now and consider the three murders in sequence. The first victim was a blue-collar service-industry worker living with his family out in Arcadia. Apparently, he went to the mountains most summers to hike and fish with one of his children in tow. On this occasion, he went with his ten-year-old son, to fish on a reservoir-lake up in the Angeles National Forest."

Sam pulls up a Google Earth shot of the location showing where the two had pitched for the night, near a reservoir. I remember it clearly.

"They'd made camp on the Friday and erected their tent, here, and had one night's sleeping under the stars. Another hiker had seen them on the Saturday around 11:00 A.M. and shared a mug of coffee. They'd chatted about rods and bait. The hiker remembers seeing smoke rising from a few fires along the shore where other campers had based themselves. The nearest was two hundred yards away. The hiker left them after twenty minutes or so, passing the other camps on the shoreline, but not stopping to speak to anyone else. A forensic search of the murder site and all the campsites didn't tell you anything else, either. And, across the lake, around the dam, where a road comes down, there's a toilet block. Here you found tire marks identical to those left by a vehicle identified at the murder scene. That's right, isn't it?" Sam asks.

"Yes, that's correct," I say. "There had been no transfer en route. None that we could discover, anyway, and there was nothing that our techs could find in the toilet block, either."

Next up are pictures of the murder site itself. This scene shows all the horribly familiar hallmarks of the killer's brutality.

"Most interestingly, the boy was spared in two ways," Sam says, turning to a page in my report. "Firstly, and most importantly, he was left unharmed. And, secondly, he was spared the sight of seeing his father being killed."

"Yes, the boy said he'd been fishing by the lake when he thought it was his father coming up behind him," Dee says.

"You say here, Oskar, that SOCOs found traces of chloroform inside the sack and they believe it was this that rendered him docile and manageable throughout. He was taken by car and dumped on the San Gabriel Canyon Road, seven miles away, and a passing motorist found him about twenty minutes later. The killer then retraced his journey back to the campsite – a round trip of about twenty-five minutes – and then murdered the father."

"That's correct," Dee says. "The father had also been anesthetized with the same substance."

"Of course, your main question remains unanswered, Oskar," Sam says, turning to me and holding up the copy of my report. "Why didn't he murder the boy as well? Why select this victim and complicate the mission by dealing with him the way he did? Why take that risk? Why do it?"

I've given this a great deal of thought over the last six weeks, and had some ideas, but I don't want to voice them now because I want to hear what Sam thinks.

"Your report suggests that the killer might have only noticed the boy after going for the father. But I think not. I think he knew about him. And, most importantly, I think he possibly relished the challenge."

There's a pause here whilst we all consider this.

"Why do it, though? Why make all those plans? Why take the risk?" Sam asks, again.

"Maybe this was a paid hit, and the assassin's client had given him precise instructions to only murder the father. Not the boy," Dee suggests, picking up on Sam's assassination theme.

"Let's see ... Let's see where this takes us," Sam responds, turning a page of my report and pressing a key on her laptop.

"Anyway, when he returns to the site, he sets about the father."

Sam points to some photos of the scene. We pause, looking at the brutal images of the battered and bloodied body.

Sam glances at the clock again and then across to me. She's looking for my agreement to press on. I just nod.

"Okay. The second murder was more sophisticated in my view. Eric Green, the wealthy banker. He was attacked in a back alley after a business meeting. His car was incapacitated by someone with the skills of a skilled mechanic, you seem to be suggesting, Oskar."

I nod again.

"SOCOs suggest the killer slid a piece of metal up inside the engine compartment and disengaged the locking mechanism. He also attached another device that kept the alarm from sounding – it was a Beemer so it must have been sophisticated. Your guys suggested that anyone with solid engineering know-how could have designed this. Someone with access to a work bench and a full range of tools."

I remembered the technician had proposed this by studying the scratch marks inside the engine compartment and on the locking mechanism.

"Your report goes on to say that, once the hood was raised, the killer made sure the engine turned over but didn't start. This made the victim go off to find a cab. He was brought down in an alley behind the hotel using chloroform as an anesthetic. This incapacitated him enough so that he could be dragged to a porch area behind a shop unit that was being refitted, next to a dumpster."

Sam brings up a picture of the doorway in question. I remember it very well.

"Here, the killer could go through his ritual, breaking of a limb – a leg this time – and then cutting the victim's artery. He then rained down a series of blows using a standard claw hammer … Again, no traces."

Sam now brings up a DVD recording.

"This is the CCTV footage from the scene that Dee passed to me this morning. This camera gives you a good view along the main street and up to the end of the alley, but not much else. You think the killer was responsible for incapacitating the other camera, the one that looks down on the actual alley itself."

Sam points at the screen as we see the victim come into view. "Here he is … this is Eric Green isn't it?"

"It sure is, poor sucker," Dee retorts.

"This is when he's making his way along the street towards the camera after he left his meeting at the hotel. Look, the digital read out tells us this was eleven-forty. It's quite late for this family man, so that's the reason I'm guessing he's in such a hurry. His car is a couple of blocks away, parked up at the back of the practice where he worked ... No CCTV there, unfortunately. I suspect the killer knew this, otherwise he would have incapacitated that camera as well, I'm thinking. Now, if I speed up the footage to twelve-ten, we get him returning back the way he's just come. Back to get a taxi at the hotel rank."

We all watch Green walk back up the street, only he's moving even faster this time, almost at a trot.

"Now, look, he appears to hesitate at the entrance to the alley ... There you go ... It looks as if he's contemplating the long way round, doesn't it? ... A route that would be better lit ... and look ... we see him turn into the alley ... and that's the last time he's seen alive."

"Except by the murderer?" Dee adds.

"Yes. Except by the murderer," Sam replies.

We all look at the screen, transfixed by the enormity of the victim's decision, poignantly realizing that his choice at taking the short cut sealed his fate and left a young wife and family without a husband and father.

"You state Oskar that from this point on through to seven o'clock in the morning, no one sees anything in the alley. Cars drive by, but no one stops. A couple of drunks walk past, but no one enters or leaves the alley at all. No one sees anything."

"No one *reports* anything," Dee says, giving Sam a righteous look.

"Okay, Dee. You're right, no one *reports* anything. But, we must all ask ourselves, how did the killer keep himself from view even though we suspect he tampered with the camera?"

I replay in my mind all the permutations that Dee and I have considered. I'm not going to repeat them all here now and say nothing, hoping that Sam may have something new for us. Only, she remains silent as well, eyebrows raised.

Dee suddenly sits up with the start of a smile on her face.

"I know. That's easy," she says, breaking into the tension. "The scene's not covered by CCTV. Right? The perp knew that. Right? He just plotted his path away from the scene by avoiding all the routes that were covered by cameras. So, maybe, just maybe, he travelled over the rooftops." Her smile is even broader, this time. "You know, like Dick van Fucking Dyke, in Mary Poppins. Gee, I loved that movie as a kid."

Dee gets out of her chair and stands like Van Dyke did in the scene, looking as though she's about to give us a rendition.

"'Never was there a more happier crew, than them what sings Chim Chim Chiroo,'" she sings in her best Cockney accent.

Sam and I look at each other and then across to Dee and we all start laughing, and I recognize the benefit of having some light relief.

There's a further lull in the conversation as we settle back down, and then, as if on a roll, Dee picks up on another thought, but she's not smiling this time.

"Well, seriously, perhaps he's done a David Copperfield on us?"

I know she's referring to the professional entertainer's famous trick when he appeared to remove the Statue of Liberty from his audience's view. Dee had mentioned this on another case where we had been misled – or to be precise, misdirected. A suspect had sought to convince us the murder weapon we were seeking was nowhere to be seen, when it was there, right in front of us the whole time. Dee had gone straight across to a didgeridoo displayed in an alcove and pulled it down. She immediately guessed by its weight that it contained the disassembled parts of the gun we were looking for; I've always remembered the look of horror on the doer's face as she held up the instrument in her hands.

"You know, Oskar, the Statue of Liberty was there all the time, you'll remember," Dee says, interrupting my thoughts and turning towards Sam. "Copperfield made the audience believe it had disappeared, before their very eyes. Check it out for yourself on *YouTube*, Sam—Hey, perhaps, the sucker's still there. Come on, Oskar, let's get down there and pick him up, shall we?"

We all laugh again, but I make a mental note to think about this further. I've always wondered how our killer has managed to stay out of sight for so long. Perhaps there really is an illusion taking place. Before our very eyes.

There's complete silence for a moment and I see Dee look at the clock. She turns to me with a slight smile, wanting me to notice the time. I look up. It's five-twenty.

"What about Chandler?" I ask, wanting to press on.

"Yes. Let's consider what we know about the recent murder. Our third victim," Sam says. "She was a prostitute earning top rates. This all suggests she had many satisfied customers and would—"

"Why did you say that?" Dee suddenly interrupts. Sam turns to her with a confused look on her face. "You know, that bit about her having satisfied customers," Dee explains.

Here we go again. Dee's short fuse on this point is not a surprise to me but I'm just wondering how Sam will deal with it.

"Let me explain," Sam says, turning toward Dee. "If you charge upwards of $500 for a blow job in that part of L.A., you've got to be good at it. The rent she was paying, the original Hockney print on the wall and her fancy lifestyle, lead me to suggest she was a high-class hooker. Someone in demand, someone who was good at her job ... unless you know something I don't," she says, looking assertively at Dee. "Are you happy with that for the moment? We can always come back to it later if you want."

Dee nods assent – nice retrieve Sam, I'm thinking.

"Chandler comes home and finds someone's there. She may know him but we're not sure. I think not, because indications suggest she doesn't take customers home. Is it her pimp? Possibly, but you state you've yet to find him or ascertain if she even had one in the first place. This sets her apart from other prostitutes working Sunset, don't you think? She's something 'special'. Different."

"Although a pimp wouldn't frequent the woman's home unless they had something going," Dee suggests.

"Is it a partner then?" Sam asks.

"I think not, because the evidence so far suggests she lives alone, with very few visitors."

Sam looks back to her notes, turning a page.

"She's incapacitated, probably chloroform again, and then the killer goes through the same ritual. Breaking an arm this time before he goes for the carotid. The killer takes a kitchen knife and cuts, cuts, cuts. Two days later, blood is seen seeping through the ceiling and your man phones in the murder. Bingo! Victim number three makes her way to the morgue."

Sam sits down, suggesting she's finished for the moment.

My cell phone suddenly vibrates and I take a quick look. It's not from Lena. It's from the lieutenant. He wants me in the tank. Now!

I look across the squad room and see him standing in his doorway, looking straight at me. He's got his cell phone in one hand and he's tapping his pen furiously on his leg with the other.

I ignore this and turn back to Dee and Sam. I've decided to wrap things up anyway and I ask them if we can all meet back here tomorrow morning at eleven.

Before going our separate ways we agree various tasks: Sam wants to focus her attention overnight on researching the ritualistic aspect of the three murders, wanting to find out what this might mean for describing the killer's personality; Dee agrees to do some further research online with the LAPD archives looking for evidence of similar ritualistic approaches in the past; so far, we've only had time to research the *unsolved* murders in the hope we could build a case from an existing investigation or one that's been put on hold, but now I want to widen our search to include *solved* cases as well. I'm thinking that, by studying similar past crimes, we might gain a better handle on our guy's motives.

As Dee leaves the room, I start collecting my papers together and then look across at Sam. She's closing down her computer, looking as though she's preparing to leave as well.

"Nice work today, Sam," I say. "You too, partner,"

"Mind if I give the lieutenant the heads up on what we're thinking so far?"

"Sure. Go ahead. I'm just packing up. I'm going back to my hotel for a shower and then I'll—" Sam stops mid-thought, looking upward, as if she's relishing something special. "No, it's a bath. A long soak I think, with lots of bubbles. It's been a long day. I deserve it … What about you?"

"I'm heading home, but I thought we could get a drink before you go to your hotel. Maybe sketch out a plan for the week at the same time?"

Sam stops what she's doing and looks at me directly.

"Good idea Oskar, but I don't know how much fun I'll be … And, anyway, you look as though you've a date or something. The way you've been checking that phone of yours all day."

"No, that's not what it's about," I say, flustering a bit. "We could find someplace on South Figueroa for a drink … Or, would you prefer something else? Some food?"

Sam thinks about this for a moment and looks at the clock.

"Okay. I know what. Let's meet in the bar at the Marriott at eight, after I've washed up. We can decide what to do then. But I wanna be tucked up in bed by nine-thirty at the latest … Deal?"

"Deal."

23

(Monday, 6.10 p.m.)

THE LIEUTENANT IS IN his room as I make my way across to meet him. He's back to fumbling with the top button of another of his ill-fitting shirts. The same tie he wore yesterday is draped over his arm and he's looking at himself in a small hand-mirror lodged on top of his filing cabinet. I step into his office and he sees me arrive in the reflection.

"You finished five minutes ago. Sit down. Whaddaya got?" he blurts out, staccato fashion, continuing to struggle with his button.

"Sorry Lieutenant, I couldn't come straight across, because—"

"Bullshit! You were smooching. Get on with it, will you. You got that caller in the frame? What's his name? ... Tomlinson? ... Tomlins?"

"It's Tomkins, Lieutenant. Tom-kins," I say, repeating Dee's reproach to Sam. "And, no, we don't have anything on him. Not yet anyway."

I see this doesn't meet with his approval because he immediately slumps his shoulders and loses grip on the button. I'm sure he'd been hoping he could have gone straight upstairs to report we've got the killer under arrest.

"Whaddaya mean, not yet? There's talk he smashed the place up, attacked officers. Fuckin' hell, Salo. There's even evidence linking that creepy piece of shit to the victim for chrissakes. What else d'yer need?"

"Something that will stick, Lieutenant. That's what we need. We don't want to lose him on a technicality because we didn't

108

take care at this stage—Look, Lieutenant, Tomkins *is* linked to this somehow and we'll get to the bottom of it but for now we need to work out in what ways. We need to tread carefully. I'll let him stew one more night. And once we've got official news from forensics on the apartment we'll get him interviewed again. It's a delicate situation now that he's lawyered up."

"Who's the counselor?"

"Asnick."

The lieutenant gives me a disdainful grimace. He knows all about him.

"Hopefully, forensics will either tie him into the story he's telling us or it will put him in the frame ... for something."

This news seems to placate him and he returns to work on the button.

"I'm also getting the team to dig out and review all CCTV footage," I add, in an attempt to steer this conversation away from Tomkins. "There didn't seem to be any visuals from Dee's first trawl but another look might bring up something."

"What about that fancy professor of yours? She come up with anything? And before you start, don't give me any of your *it's-early-days* bullshit."

"Yes, she has, but I'd rather wait until tomorrow or the day after, because—"

"Tomorrow! Or the day after!" the lieutenant suddenly explodes. "What in hell's name do you take me for? I've got everyone on the third floor crawling over the budget for this already, and now I've got someone on the tenth waiting for me to tell him how it's all shaking down—Oh fuck!" he suddenly shouts, as I see the shirt button fly across the room. Completely frustrated now, he turns and drills his eyes into mine. "And, now you're expecting me to hang on till fuckin' tomorrow ... or the day after—Get real, Oskar. I need you to work with me here!"

This is the second time he's used this phrase in as many days and I suspect it's an expression someone's been using with him. More importantly, I'm realizing it's possibly the chief because of his mention of the tenth floor. This revelation surprises me. Not least because it's extremely rare for the chief – or any senior member of staff come to that – to circumvent line management protocols this way.

The lieutenant can see my confusion with this in his mirror.

"Yes, it *is* the fuckin' chief, for chrissakes," he says, as he straightens his collar the best he can without the button and starts to put on his tie. "Why do you think I'm going through all this?" he adds, pointing both hands at his tie to emphasize his dilemma. He makes one final adjustment and sits down in his chair, facing me.

"Look, Oskar, work with me here," he tries one more time, also trying to remain calm. "What direction are we going? What have you learnt? And if you can convince me you're in a better place now than when I signed that paperwork to fly that fancy lady of yours over from Denver, so much the better," he says, almost running out of breath in the process.

"For me. For you. For my relationship with the chief of police. And, for his fuckin' relationship with the city council ... In fact, for every goddamn person's relationship up and down the line. Do you follow my drift here, Salo? Do you? Have you got my message?"

His attempt to remain calm has failed but I'm wondering if something else is going on here. He's looking at me as if I don't believe him. I remain silent.

After a few seconds, I see his eyes flicker back and forth as if he's deciding on something. Then he looks down at his desk, sees something and then grimaces in pain, holding his side. He swivels his chair and reaches for the 'pills' he keeps in his desk drawer. They're in a nondescript brown jar and he unscrews the top with dramatic flourish.

I've experienced this little act before, and this time I look for something on his desk straightaway. I see the memo lying on his blotter, realizing this is what all the theatricals are about.

He wants me to read it.

The lieutenant stands up, still holding his side, and goes with his jar to the water fountain on the far side of the squad room.

I lean in to read the hand-written memo:

Lieutenant

STRICTLY CONFIDENTIAL – FOR YOUR EYES ONLY.
Case 234/11 – Suspected murder of Jane Chandler.

We need a quick result on this. The FBI is watching and I doubt I can hold them off for much longer. I need to keep them out <u>for the reasons we've discussed</u>. This has all the makings of being a serial killer case now and it's bound to take its grip on the city.

<u>Keep Salo focused. No distractions. Remember the important issue we discussed. No grandstanding of any kind.</u>

I want confidential daily reports on progress – in person.

Remember, this affects <u>all our careers</u>, and the good name of the department, so take great care!

My mind starts to race every-which-way as I try to work out the memo's significance: No one wants the FBI muscling in but what are the 'reasons' he's discussed with the lieutenant? What's the 'important issue' he refers to? It's apparently a confidential memo, so has his deputy been informed? If not, why not? What does he mean by suggesting it affects everyone's careers? Is this a threat?

All these questions flood into my brain, confirming my suspicion that the lieutenant's drama has all been about the chief. I can understand the chief will be extra-sensitive around any suggestion the FBI might seek to trump his leadership – especially now that his re-election campaign is well underway – but why is the chief spooking the lieutenant so much? Sure, he'll want to maintain his authority with the mayor, the Police Commission and all the members the City Council and I can also understand he'll not want to show anything that could be taken as a sign of weakness. But why hound the lieutenant this way? That's a big risk.

Maybe he fears his nearest rival, Deputy Chief Eugene Garner, will steal his thunder over this case. Everyone knows Garner has a gung-ho, army-style approach that makes him popular in certain FBI quarters and with right-wing members of the city council, so he really could be a threat when it comes to the vote for the chief's second five-year term.

But all this doesn't fully explain why the lieutenant is behaving this way? It's that glint in his eye. Almost as if he's running scared. Has the chief got something on him? Something that is making him take professional risks in showing me the chief's confidential memo?

I look across to the lieutenant at the water fountain and see him toss his head back three times in quick succession as he swallows his 'pills'. I've often wondered if they're just tic tacs and he's able to kid himself they're doing him good.

I turn back to read the memo one more time, committing the contents to memory, as I hear the lieutenant return. He comes back in and sits down, banging his fist against his sternum, continuing the drama. After a moment's pause, he leans across and picks up the memo, rather deliberately – much in the way Oliver Hardy would if he were looking to camera. He then slides it into his desk drawer, nodding towards me at the same time, affirming that I've read it and received *his* message, loud and clear. Job done.

Now's not the moment to ask him anything, so I realize I'll have to find answers to my questions another way. I sit perfectly still not giving him any sign that I've read it. He closes the drawer and smiles, knowing he could say with a clear conscience that he'd not personally divulged or leaked any of confidential information to anyone. He knows it will be my call to explain how I came upon the information revealed. Not his.

"So what progress can I report, Detective Salo?" he asks with a downward swoop of his breath. As if we're all clear on the situation confronting him.

I recognize the lieutenant will need to be able to pump himself up in front of the chief with some fine words and decide to give him phrases he can repeat.

"Tell him it's the same murderer alright and you are developing a clear profile. Tell him that your decision to bring in Sam Callan, a world-renowned serial killer expert and personality profiler, has enabled you to identify things that have put renewed energy into the investigation. Tell him the doer's very smart, very skilled at what he does and that you think we're looking for an obsessive individual, someone who's screwed up, possibly by his family—"

"Great!" the lieutenant interrupts, "That puts sixty per cent of the population of L.A. in the frame for this. I'll need more than that, goddammit."

"Yes, I agree. But you'll have to give Callan more time to work up a personality profile that we can use. The cut takes place tomorrow and we'll get tox results soon after. And, don't forget, forensics will have leads they're following as we speak … It takes time. You know that, surely," I say, choosing my words carefully, and also thinking what the chief will want to hear, I decide to add more repeatable phrases. "You've got this case well and truly under control, Lieutenant. The people of Los Angeles have nothing to fear," I add, for extra effect.

He seems to be contented by this bullshit and sits back, appearing more relaxed. Sensing the meeting might be coming to a close, I lean forward.

"Stay where you are. I'm not finished. If you're to hang on to this case, you'll need to work quickly—And, no, I don't want you to cut corners, before you come back at me with that. I've given you the resources. Now do the job. Get it done. Quickly. Just remember who's on my back with this, and what may be around the corner." I think he's inferring it's the FBI but, after his performance today, I'm not so sure.

"Any more questions?" he barks, not really inviting any. "Good. Let me have another update tomorrow. You know to contact me at any time, day or night, should anything break that's important." He pierces me with his eyes again. "That's an order, Salo. You get the evidence that nails Tomkins, I want to be the first person to hear. Do you understand? I don't want surprises. Keep me updated. Good or bad … preferably good. We'll speak again tomorrow. That's all."

He looks away from me and then up to the clock. There's a slight pause before he suddenly retreats into himself. His eyes seem to be gazing off to a distant thought. But then, just as quickly, they come back into focus again.

"Okay, that's it. Let's get back to work, shall we?" he snaps, raising one arm and pointing towards the door.

24

(Monday, 7.34 p.m.)

As I MAKE MY way to my cubicle and drop into my chair, I feel energized and angry at the same time. I've learnt a little of what's going on between the chief and the lieutenant, but, frustratingly, I don't know much, or why.

I soon hear the lieutenant lock his office before making his way to the tenth floor for one of his 'confidential' meetings and keep my head down, not wanting any more stare-downs. After I hear the doors swing to, I look across to the Special Meetings Room and notice Sam has already left for that long, hot soak in her bath. Looking further around, I see that most detectives have either left for home or made their way over to a bar somewhere to see out the rush of traffic for an hour or so. A few are still here, and some are still looking in my direction wondering what on earth's just happened in the tank. Despite attempts to sound proof rooms, booths and meeting pods, it's still possible to listen into conversations if minded to, especially when you've got your lieutenant bellowing at full volume.

It takes a few moments to stare down anyone looking at me and, in doing so, I catch sight of Buttle. He's back at his desk with his head down, appearing oblivious to anything that's going on around him. I decide now's as good a time as any to square up to him. I rehearse in my mind how I'll play this, and then make my way across. I've caught a few river trout in my life and fly-fishing skills can come in handy at times like these. If you want to catch one cleanly, you need to know what the fish you're targeting is thinking and how it's going to react when it's faced with the bait.

So, knowing Buttle's a smoker like me, I go across with a cigarette in my mouth.

When I get to his desk he doesn't look up but knows I'm here.

"Do you want to step outside for a smoke, Buttle, so we can talk about this?"

I'm thinking the neutral territory of the smoking shelter might enable us to agree terms. It may also prevent the animosity we share for each other escalating before we've even got started.

Without saying a word, Buttle pushes back his chair, nearly banging into me. I take this as a sign he's in agreement, so make my own way out of the swing doors and down the stairs. After a couple of flights, I hear him following, matching his pace with mine. As I exit into the yard, I realize I'm in luck. We'll be alone. As soon as I get to the shelter, I light my cigarette and wait for him to join me. I see he's decided to smoke one of his own rather than accept one of mine.

"Look, Buttle," I say, when he settles down on the bench. "I don't like this any more than you, but we're stuck with each other, so let's make the best of it, shall we?"

Buttle draws on his cigarette and blows out the smoke, sending it in all directions. Whilst he doesn't aim any towards me, directly, it's close enough to be intimidating.

"What I want to suggest is that I slice up what needs to be done in ways that give you the autonomy you'll want, so that you and Beavis can work to—"

"It's Treviss, for fuck's sake. It's Treviss—If we're to work together you've got to drop this Beavis and Butthead crap."

I immediately realize this was a poor start, but I'm not gonna apologize.

"Whatever … Treviss … If we all work together on discrete elements, we can make sure we don't get in each other's way." I'm hoping this approach appeals to Buttle, because I'm thinking that, if I give him some latitude, he can carry out the business I want him to do without appearing to kowtow to my demands in front of other colleagues.

"We can stay in touch by phone and meet here if you like, or we can meet in Billy's ... What do you think?"

"What do I think? ... What do I think? ... I think it stinks, I think everything fucking stinks, but I'm five years short of a full pension and I don't need any fucking aggravation at this time in my life. Just tell me what you want me to do, will you?"

Despite his reputation for being a shirker, I know Buttle can be a good detective. Yes, he's long-in-the-tooth and needs to update his approach, but, at heart, he's a good, solid, down-to-earth detective.

I outline that I want him to interview Tomkins and see if he can get anything more out of him, especially if forensics ends up supporting Tomkins' story that he's not the murderer. I know Buttle can get people to talk.

Like Buttle, I know from personal experience how difficult it's been to change approaches to detective work, post-Rodney King. Before that debacle, a surreptitious elbow in the face or a threat out of sight of a lawyer often turned cases around and brought villains to justice. But it's a different world now. The accountability and professionalism of all those working for LAPD has been challenged since Rodney King was beaten by law enforcement officers in ninety-two. The media spotlight, public enquiries, intrusive do-gooders and cell phone images changed everything. Buttle's bitterness over the years has accelerated, and his beef with me in the stairwell was probably down to inner frustration at knowing he should have left LAPD when he was on top – ten years ago – well before he descended into this half-glass-empty rut of his. Despite these inadequacies, I know Buttle can still be perceptive and scrupulous, often seeing openings where other, younger colleagues don't.

We smoke two more of our own cigarettes, whilst discussing ground rules. I even make sure that I put up a few for him to shoot down, because I need him to go away from this with the sense he's scored a few important points over me. Nonetheless, the wry smile he gives suggests he knows full well the manipulative nature of my strategy. Yes, he's an old dog that isn't gonna learn new tricks, but he'll also not roll over and have his belly rubbed. For anyone.

I spend a further ten minutes giving him background on Tomkins and a summary of all the cases, leaving out, for the moment, some of the speculative work that Sam, Dee and I discussed earlier. I agree to send him a copy of my report on the interview with Tomkins and a copy of the case file I'd prepared for Sam. He nods and I take this as a good sign that we've struck a deal.

Feeling things are coming to a natural conclusion, I stand up and throw my cigarette butt onto the floor, treading it into the dirt and prepare to make my way back up the stairs. At this point, Buttle brings his own head up and turns to face me. I realize this is the first time he's looked my way in our thirty-minute conversation.

"Remember that case you and I worked way back?" he suddenly says. "...You know ... *waaay* back? When both of us got hauled in to help with an investigation that had stalled ... just like this one?" This catches me by surprise. "Back in the early nineties. When we more or less started out in RHD. I had a coupla years on you, but we were both a bit raw ... and you were definitely wet behind the ears." In other settings, I might have taken this as an insult, but it's not meant that way. "We were brought in to assist with the Peacemaker Case. It was going nowhere ... Remember?"

I nod, because I could certainly remember it. How could I forget? It was the first case I worked in RHD. We had both been reassigned across to support Detective O'Connell and Detective Jardine.

"It started then, didn't it? You and me? All this fucking animosity?" Buttle says, laughing to himself at the thought.

I remembered that Buttle and me indeed crossed paths for the first time on that case, and a string of lieutenants after that point always thought twice before putting us together. Most kept us apart, and, as we got older and our careers developed, we basically learnt to keep out of each other's way.

"We worked on that case together, but we didn't hit it off, did we? And, a whole career down the line, we're still at each other's throats." He laughs again. "Pathetic, really, isn't it?"

I'm sure Buttle isn't looking for a reply, because he stares off into the past – wide-eyed and still.

I'm not even sure what to say, so I choose to say nothing.

I take a look at my watch, and suddenly realize I need to prepare for my meeting with Sam at the Marriott. I move towards the stairs and Buttle looks up for the second time.

"What was the doer's name?" he calls out.

"Gargailis … John Gargailis," I say, stopping in my tracks.

"Yeah. Gargailis, that's the one. Some fucking Russian immigrant or something, wasn't he? Into religion in a big way."

"Yes, he was Latvian by birth. A prominent member of the Latvian Orthodox Church."

"Yeah, that's the guy." He looks back to the floor once again. "The son-of-a-bitch had the whole department running around like headless chickens. Trying to find his wife's killer. Then O'Connell and Jardine worked out he'd been the doer all along. The pair take him to trial, only to find he nearly gets off on a technicality. We all think he's about to walk and then the son-of-a-bitch confesses … The little fucker deserved the needle, in my opinion. All that running around …"

He turns towards me now and looks into my eyes for the second time. "You knew what was going down though, didn't you … you righteous motherfucker?" he says, attempting a smile to take the sting out of his expletive. "You couldn't leave it alone could you? … Hmm? … Nearly got yourself suspended I seem to remember."

I smile back, not really knowing why.

He looks down to the same patch of dirt. The smile has gone. He looks dejected. I notice he's managed to build up a small pile of cigarette butts with his feet whilst we've been talking. As I look at him I realize he looks empty, lost … almost uncared for. I can even see pet hairs stuck to his clothes making me think he's stroked a cat or a dog and couldn't even be bothered to brush them away.

I wonder what his ramblings are really about and what he means by saying I *knew* what was going down but decide to leave these questions to another time. I have bigger fish to fry at the moment. And I have Sam waiting.

I leave Buttle to finish his cigarette and make my way upstairs. When I reach the sixth-floor lobby, I stop at the men's room to rinse my face. I'm immediately surprised by my pallid reflection in the mirror. I lean in for a closer look. Tomkins was right. My eyes are definitely bloodshot. I end up telling myself the fluorescent lighting isn't helping me in here but I know the truth. I need some rest.

As I continue to stare into the mirror, I can't help but think again about Buttle's speech. I know he's carried venom towards me over the years but, deep down, I also know he's right. We've both wasted negative energy on each other for too long. It was indeed pathetic, as Buttle had suggested.

I hear the clock tick on the wall and I'm reminded I need to hurry if I'm to make my appointment on time. I lean forward again and tousle my hair. I rinse my face and rub my chin with my hand, feeling two day's growth breaking through the skin.

Why am I thinking about my appearance so much when I'm only going for a quick drink with Sam? I need to square this circle in my mind because I think it's getting in the way. It's obstructing my work and my relationship with Lena.

25

(Monday, 5.05 p.m.)

SWINGING HIS ARMS AROUND one at a time, the Reaper stretches his aching muscles, recognizing that manhandling the steel panels into position has given him a full-body workout. He takes a long drink from a quart bottle of water and wipes his mouth with the back of his hand. With immense satisfaction he admires his creation, thinking it's all coming together, nicely. Just as he'd planned.

Then, using the same hoist as earlier, he brings the reinforced glass panes into position. He'd ended up designing the structure around the stock size of glass that he could buy from the factory. Although the glass panels are not exactly the same size as those set down by the State of California, he's satisfied it's close enough, and certainly within the tolerances he'd set for the project.

Most importantly, he'd checked the panes could withstand bullets fired from close range, and they will certainly remain shatterproof from a determined attack with a hammer or pick. After all, this was the main brief he'd set for the salesman when he contacted the company. He'd picked up the delivery himself from the factory gate, without having to convince anybody what his real reasons were for buying it. The company was happy to take his cash and load the glass onto the back of his flatbed truck.

After the glass is secured, he begins fitting the specially designed door into place, checking that the door's lock works to his satisfaction. As he's doing this, he's reminded of the peerless skill his Master had shown when he crafted his own original locks. He glows with pride remembering how he'd helped him take this ancient craft of the locksmith one step further in evolution. This was when his Master had designed and made an ingenious lock for a chest that he explained would hold something more valuable *'than you could ever imagine'*.

26

(Monday, 8.10 p.m.)

I DON'T WANT SAM to see me the way the mirror did, so I park a couple of blocks from the Marriott, hoping the walk to the hotel will revitalize my body. The evening is clear and cool and I enjoy its soothing effect as I step out of my car. Traffic is light and moving more slowly than it was earlier in the day. This makes it easy for me to cross the street. A few people walk to and fro as I make my way along the sidewalk. Most are clearly going home after work but some look as though they've come out for the evening. For a meal, perhaps. One or two couples walk lazily by without any apparent care in the world.

I walk along West Fifth and past the famous landmark library where Lena had given one of her art-history presentations a few months ago. I remember the meal we had afterwards at Café Pinot, next door, and the fun we had spending her fee in one fell swoop.

I turn onto South Figueroa and the Marriott comes up on my left. I cross the street and make my way into reception. As I move towards the bar the woman behind the desk greets me politely. I look at my watch and realize I'm early, so I decide to give Lena a call, using one of the payphones in the lobby rather than my cell phone. I'm thinking that, if Lena is choosing to ignore my calls, she might just pickup on this line, believing it's someone else. I punch in the number and am transferred to message straightaway. I hang up feeling embarrassed about this subterfuge and try not to think any more about it as I walk straight into the bar.

I'm surprised to see Sam sitting on a stool with a drink in her hand, as if she's been there a while. She's chatting to a barman. They seem to be enjoying a story because they're laughing.

I'm sure she hasn't seen me arrive yet, so I stand and look at her before approaching. A deep purple pashmina is draped over the bar stool and I see her black dress is cut low at the back. She clearly works out, because I see her trim body and the definition of her muscles. There's something about her style that sets her apart. She suddenly sees me in the reflection of the mirror behind the bar and gives me a mock look of annoyance.

"Am I late?" I ask by way of an apology in case I've made a mistake with the timing.

"Yes, one hour, actually," she says, tapping her watch and continuing to give me her fake, stern look. This is immediately followed by a broad smile. "But don't panic. I'd forgotten to reset my watch from Denver time and came down here an hour early. I've tried to make two drinks last all this time. Raymond here has been looking after me." This starts them both laughing again.

I order a Bushmills and water as a small threesome starts playing headline numbers. Sam takes this as a cue to jump off her stool and collect her things, spotting a suitable table. I follow in her wake bringing her drink with me. It's turquoise-blue in color and I can smell rum. Sam is always adventurous in everything, so I'm guessing it's a cocktail she's never tried before.

"So, who's the unlucky girl you've stood up to be with me this evening?" she says, before we've sat down.

I know Sam's a straight talker, and it's something I've come to expect, but I'm caught out by her frankness on this occasion and can't think of a suitable response.

"You didn't really answer my question earlier, did you? So, what I'm really asking is why I'm honored with your company tonight and not the woman you were watching out for on your cell phone?"

Fortunately, Raymond delivers my drink and I have a moment to compose myself as we sit down.

"It's not a date, but it did have something to do with another woman," I freely admit, matching Sam's frankness.

"Oh, I see. Tell me about it before I embarrass myself even further," Sam says, adjusting her shawl around her shoulders and placing her purse on the bench seat beside her.

I don't do 'private', so I take a long pull of my drink and feel the whisky slide into my body giving me some courage. I had been expecting to choose the moment myself to tell Sam about Lena but it seems the moment has been chosen for me.

"Well, Lena and I go back eighteen months, she's a critic and lives her life around the arts, writing articles, visiting theatre, opera, and the like. She moved into my apartment about three months ago but left last week ... It didn't work out, that's all," I say, suddenly convincing myself that our relationship must be over. "She couldn't deal with what I do. That seemed to be the problem. I'm a detective. I do detective work. I hunt down criminals. I bring them to justice. I send them to jail. That's what I do ... She didn't like it, that's all."

I know it's not as straightforward as that but I'm surprised by the words I've used to explain her leaving.

"She must have known all about that before she moved in. What brought things to a head?"

I think carefully about what to say and the 'crunch moment' comes to mind.

"Well ... last week, I came back with the case file for the David Henshaw murder ... the guy on the lake. I'm sitting at my desk when Lena comes in and asks me to show her the file and explain what it's all about. You see, she's always been squeamish about my work, so I didn't make a spectacle of showing her any case files that I bring back. But on this occasion, I laid out the whole case for her, possibly thinking she was genuinely interested. Well, that's how it appeared to me at the time. Lena showed no sign of any sensitivity to hearing the full story and even looked carefully at the photographs, which, as you know, are tough to look at for someone unused to seeing dead bodies. In fact, she asked to see them all. Each one. Separately."

I pull out a pack of cigarettes from my jacket pocket and turn it over between my fingers.

"To cut a long story short, she looked at everything in the file. She asked questions ... good questions, actually ... Intelligent questions. She wanted to know the details of how Henshaw had died, the boy, the sack, the murder scene itself, my investigation techniques, etcetera, etcetera ... Every goddamn thing."

I take another long pull at my drink and finish the glass. I notice Sam is still cradling her cocktail, so I look up towards Raymond and indicate I'd like another.

"Then, Lena packed up her things and left. There and then. I haven't heard from her since. In fact, the more I think about it, the more I suspect she'd packed her bags before this whole charade took place, well before she set me up like that." I remain silent as Raymond arrives with my drink and turns back for the bar. "There've been no texts, no messages. Nothing. I just want to know she's all right. That's the text I'm waiting for, the one saying she's safe and I don't need to worry about her."

I pause and look at Sam, realizing it's all come out in a gush. She pulls her pashmina further around her shoulders, as if a chilly breeze has entered the room, but I can also see a churlish smile on her lips.

"Well, that's certainly got the evening off on a high, hasn't it?" she says, as I make my best attempt to smile back.

I know my professional work has come between me and other women in the past and realize what I've blurted out to Sam is shorthand for saying I've screwed up, once again.

"But you're a special type of detective, aren't you Oskar?" Sam says, seemingly picking up on my thinking. "This is what sets you apart from other detectives. It's your life. If you're not on a case you sit and wait for the phone to ring. You need to work as a detective ... It's your lifeblood."

My lifeblood? It's not the first time I've heard that said about me, but it surprises me nonetheless.

"Look, have you ever worked out why that's the case?"

"You going all 'psychiatrist' on me, Sam?" I ask, really wanting her to move away from this level of introspection.

"Yes. You know it's what I do best," she replies, sitting back and smiling over the top of her cocktail glass, waiting for an answer.

I don't have one and look for an escape. I find it and reach across the table for the menu.

"Shall we take a break from all this self-analysis, and come back to it at another time? I feel hungry. And, anyway, I've done enough purging of the soul for one day."

Thankfully, Sam doesn't push any further but she does snatch the menu out of my hands.

"That's all crap in there anyway," she says as she stands up to leave. "Raymond's confirmed it. Everything is with French fries. Let's go to the restaurant he recommends two blocks down. I can tell you more about my life since the B-Movie case. It's been far more exciting and challenging than anything you've had to deal with in this sleepy town."

I realize I'm about to go to Café Pinot but say nothing about it as I follow Sam towards the exit.

27

(Tuesday, 5.30 a.m.)

THE REAPER ENJOYS HIS volunteering work at a hospice. He's employed to do odd jobs around the place and he's cleaning floors this morning – a job he particularly likes doing. He finds it humbling.

He joined the staff team a month ago and usually takes on three or four early-morning shifts each week. Although it's been a tight schedule recently, he's been able to maintain his other important work without becoming distracted.

He likes to please and often undertakes small jobs for people, such as putting up shelves and completing small pieces of carpentry. Recently, on his way downtown, he called in to put another coat of varnish on the wooden sign he'd erected at the front entrance. He's also just finished racking-out a new cupboard in the storeroom for his mops, cloths and buckets. Everything can now be accessed easily and all items are stored in their rightful places. He also has a space where he can keep his chemicals, hiding them alongside the cleaning products he uses to keep the floors and surfaces spotlessly clean.

He particularly enjoys mopping the corridor that runs the full length of the building. In fact, he gets great pleasure seeing the outcome from this work. He really gets satisfaction looking at the shining surface.

He applies the same technique to mopping floors as he does to sanding wooden surfaces in his workshop. To ease monotony and repetition, his Master taught him to divide large areas into discrete, manageable ones, so that he could work on each in turn.

'Just focus on what you're doing, not on what you've got to do, and the job will soon be done,' his Master said to him on many occasions.

So this morning, as usual, he's divided the floor into practicable areas. Using the square tiles as a guide, he moves the mop head first one way, then the other, and finally, with a swish of the mop head in a bucket of detergent, he moves across to another section of the floor.

He always enjoys the praise which comes his way. Today, the pretty Filipino nurse commented on the impeccably pristine floors. His supervisor often thanks him too, and occasionally patients will say nice things, even though he knows most have more important things on their minds than whether the floors are clean or not – like their impending deaths.

One patient has always had his very special attention, though. This was his reason for taking the job in the first place. In fact, it was the *only* reason.

28

(Tuesday, 10.56 a.m.)

A S I MAKE MY way to the sixth floor, refreshed after a good
night's sleep, I wonder how much work Dee and Sam have
been able to do overnight, especially Sam. She and I did end up
going to Cafe Pinot and didn't return to her hotel until after
eleven, well past the curfew she'd set for that evening.

I'd intended to plan out her five-day stay and to discuss
the personality profile she was developing but, in the end, we
talked about her flourishing career and expanding international
stature as a keynote speaker on the conferencing circuit. She also
mentioned her recent work supporting legal cases across the U.S.
where her professional fees more than paid for her 'life in the fast
lane', as she put it.

Thankfully, Sam didn't refer once to my stream-of-consciousness
blast about Lena. Why I spoke out about her like that in the bar
I've yet to work out but it's clear my worry is fast turning into
anger; an anger that might impede my chances of catching this
killer if I'm not careful.

By the time I'd escorted Sam back to the Marriott, it was clear
we were both ready for sleep. We'd lingered slightly at the hotel
entrance and then parted company. I went with my thoughts
about what might have happened if she'd invited me inside and
suspect Sam had as well, but she just kissed me on the cheek
and disappeared through the front entrance without looking back.

As I come through the swing doors into the squad room, I see
her standing in the Special Meetings Room as if she's been waiting
for me to arrive since the crack of dawn.

"Hey, let's make a start shall we?" Sam says, without a *'good-morning'* or a *'how-are-you?'* and before I've even had an opportunity to take off my jacket. "My research overnight suggests this guy is most probably a loner ..." Dee is sitting in a chair with her feet on the desk and immediately licks the end of a finger, making the sign of a tick in the air – one nil to Tomkins, I'm thinking. "Or," Sam continues, "that's just the way it's been made to appear. All evidence suggests this is a single-minded individual with single-minded ambition. But I'm not ruling out other angles until I'm sure. Really sure."

Sam switches position, parking that thought for the moment. Good move.

"Let's go with the percentages for the moment and look at the loner scenario. Firstly, there are implications this guy derives satisfaction from his exploits. Immense satisfaction. That's my top belief and it'll take a lot to shift me from that proposition. These loner-killer guys don't have much to cheer themselves up with, except a pride in what they do. Secondly, I'd say these killings are going to become more frequent. But you've probably guessed that already, hence your need to spend money on me. Thirdly, there's precision in his actions; we've seen this before with lone killers. Despite the frenzied nature of his attacks, everything else is organized and carried out in a methodical manner – almost obsessively."

I don't look across at Dee, but I sense it's two nil.

"Number four, he's possibly enjoying playing with you – teasing you, if you will. He's juiced by the need to mock you provocatively with what he sees as his dominating power. Remember Bundy. Have you had a look at those clips, yet? Remember that arrogance. That son-of-a-bitch played to the media, the court, any goddamned person who would listen. Yet, he was a determined and vicious killer underneath, with a deep and dark mind. And, most intriguingly, my fifth point, our guy seems to be showing us a gentler side to his personality."

Dee sits back, arms crossed, eyebrows raised, mouth ajar, completely disbelieving what's Sam's just suggested.

"By not killing the boy?" I ask quickly, in an attempt to stop Dee stepping in and stalling things.

"Yes. By not killing the boy he's showing us a gentler side to his character. Why would he do that, you know, save the boy? Why would he bother? Why would he show us this act of kindness alongside his most violent, obsessive and sadistic behavior? It's because ... he ... it's ..." Sam looks upward in an attempt to collect her thoughts. Dee leans forward, as if she's about to answer the question for her, so I raise my hand, stopping Dee in her tracks.

"I think ... I think this killer may have mixed, multiple personalities. One that's destructive and murderous, the other, kind and gentle. The inner tension between these two competing psyches is possibly being played out in his mind ... in his 'minds', if you will. Constantly. One side of his personality may have a deep, inner despair that drives him on to kill – and, of course, his lust for violence and retribution satisfies this need. The other, his softer, more passive side, is calmer and kinder, possibly wanting to seek redemption and forgiveness for what his alter ego is doing. It's possible it was this side to his personality that snatched the boy away from the lake."

We all remain silent for a while. "Find this kind and considerate man and you may also be facing your cold, sadistic killer. So, you'll need to take great care because his murderous side will be waiting for that moment. This side of his personality will want to break your limbs, drain you of blood and rain blows to your body until he sees you die. Don't be fooled by him."

We sit in silence again as we let Sam's soliloquy sink in.

Eventually, Sam sits back in her chair and Dee picks up that it's her turn. She pulls out some paperwork and lays it down on the table.

"I agreed to look out cases we haven't considered so far. Cases where the villains are either locked up or have been dispatched with the needle, gas or 2,000 volts of the state's cleanest electricity.

Dee turns over the front page of her notes and puts on a pair of reading glasses. I'm sure I've never seen her wear these before and my surprise at this must be showing because she stares at me with an expression that says, *'Go on, make my day. Say something and I'll give you a forty-five-caliber mouthful straight back!'* "These are cases where murder victims have been savagely attacked," Dee continues, still holding my stare. "Where limbs have been broken, pre- or post-mortem and where there has been a great deal of blood at the scene."

She looks back down at her notes, content that I'll not say anything, but I notice she self-consciously moves her head, trying to place things in focus.

"I've found ... here it is ... I've found two cases that fitted all three points and both are worth considering. First up, John DeBurgh. He was juiced at San Quentin in 1997 for his crimes."

I remember this case and the public disgust and outcry but I don't know about Sam. If she does, she's not showing it.

"DeBurgh had been the leader of a gang," Dee continues. "He had mutilated the bodies of his victims, often girls enticed into the gang and groomed for their 'sacrifice', including, breaking their limbs, and stabbing the bodies, repeatedly. It was never clear whether DeBurgh had acted alone or whether it was all part of a gang ritual. After brutally killing the women, he masturbated into the open wounds, dismembered parts of their bodies and ate some of the remains."

There's a pause here whilst we take on board the sickening aspects of this crime. Dee then looks over the top of her spectacles and a dry smile appears on her lips.

"It's usually dinner *then* sex," she quips. "But, hey, there's no tellin' with some people, is there?"

I ignore her jest and lean forward to speak.

"The Unsolved Unit have had a look at this case recently."

"Yes, they have," Dee responds. "That's why I brought it up; spoke to someone in the unit, this morning, he's looking into it. Much of the evidence suggests he acted alone but the detective team was convinced at the time that he had one or two accomplices. I wonder if it's one of his accomplices who's resurfaced here. The main problem was that DeBurgh remained completely silent in custody and throughout his trial. Detectives had interviewed many members of the gang but they hung on to their view that DeBurgh was off his head, high on drugs – PCP I think – and they knew nothing about his actions, until the half-eaten bodies were found in a mass grave out in Antelope Park."

I remember the time. There'd been a plea of diminished responsibility by his attorneys but this was overturned following independent psychiatric reports. It was Detectives Patrick O'Halloran and his partner, David Clements, who worked the case. I remember they were both deeply affected. O'Halloran had to deal with the aftermath of the killings and liaise with parents and relatives.

Dee holds up a photograph and Sam takes a close look. It's a mugshot of DeBurgh after his arrest. He's got a defiant and grizzly expression on his face. One that's taking no prisoners.

"Whoooa!" Sam says. "He looks to be a mean son-of-a-bitch, doesn't he, Oskar ... Relation?"

I'm still not in the mood for smiling.

"He finally got the justice he deserved," Dee adds, rescuing me, quickly. "Despite the do-gooders camped outside his jail, pleading to have his sentence commuted to life without."

Dee shakes her head a few times, holding up a printout of a newspaper article. I can't read the headline from here, but Dee's got 'disgust' written right across her face. Dee's always been sickened by the campaigns of many citizens in California who petition to have all death sentences commuted to life without parole.

"There's an L.A. Times piece here about thousands of names being—"

"Look," Sam suddenly interjects, making sure she's got Dee's full attention and mine. "None of them is our guy, if you want my opinion. This DeBurgh case is about a sexually motivated attack.

Our guy is not into that group-macho stuff. All that let's-get-our-dicks-out kind of junk. Our guy's into dominating power with all people. Male or female. He's disconnected sexually, in my opinion. He's possibly asexual, despite the semen we found on Sunday and what we know about Tomkins.

I'm thinking where the hell is that SOCO report on the DNA.

"Okay Dee," I say, choosing my moment. "Let's have the other case you've got for us."

Dee mechanically closes one file and opens another, spreading out photographs of a mutilated body on the desk. I lean forward and take a look. A surge of electricity travels through me.

"The other is in 1993," Dee says. As if I needed reminding.

The images hit me like a sucker punch and I let out a long breath as it lands, then wonder if Dee and Sam have heard me.

"John Gargailis," Dee says.

This is the second time in two days the memory of this case has come to hit me square between the eyes. It's not the grotesque nature of the barbarity on display that shocks me. It's just the coincidence. Months, possibly years, go by when I don't think about the case and suddenly it comes up twice in as many days.

I stand up and go across to the window and stare across the squad room. I find Buttle, who mentioned this case to me yesterday. He's with Treviss. They're huddled together in a cubicle talking animatedly to each other. I think back to what Buttle had said, remembering how he'd asserted that I 'knew what was going down'. Buttle must be the only person in the squad room who will remember the case. He'll know about my problem with the outcome, with John Gargailis being sentenced to death. Was he referring to that? Did he think I was right to protest Gargailis's innocence the way I did?

I turn back to look at the table. I can see images of the victim, Sylvia Gargailis, lying on the kitchen floor in a pool of her own blood. Although it happened such a long time ago, I'm surprised I've made no connection with this killing in terms of the similarity with the recent murders. There's the same battered body, the broken contorted limbs, hideously misshapen. I ponder for a moment. Could there really be a connection between this case from 1993 and the ones I'm investigating now?

Isn't this what coincidences are about? I ask myself. Isn't it your subconscious jogging your conscious into a realization that something's happening around here, and you're just not noticing it?'

"He killed his wife in a fit of rage. Didn't he, Oskar?" Dee asks, interrupting my thoughts, eyes still focused on the images spread out on the table.

I say nothing.

"Says here, he broke her arms with an iron bar first of all ... before battering her body."

Yes, that's correct, I say to myself.

"That's right isn't it, Oskar?" Dee prompts, wanting to hear my answer.

Still I say nothing.

Dee and Sam continue to pore over the scenes of violence and mayhem.

"It was the breaking of the arms first of all that drew my attention," Dee continues. "There were no suggestions that he cut her carotid artery with a blade, or any other artery come to that, but because of the ferocious attack there was much blood at the scene. That was another important sign ... Do you remember that, Oskar?"

Dee turns around this time and looks at me, expecting me to say something, but I remain silent. Dee eventually turns back, thumbing her way through the images, seemingly content with my silence. I take a look across to Sam and see she thinks differently. She's studying me intently, having noticed my discomfort. I try to hide my emotion by shifting position and moving in closer to the photographs.

"You're mentioned in this case, Oskar," Dee continues. "You're listed as one of the detective support acts. Is that right? ... You're mentioned quite late on in the investigation. I know it was a long time ago but I'm surprised you've not mentioned anything about it before, because of the similar nature of the attacks."

"Erm ... Yes ... I was involved," I hear myself suddenly say, coughing slightly as I find my voice. "I ... I'd just started out in RHD. It was my very first case as a detective at Parker Center. I'd been brought in to support the detective team near the end of its investigation, as you've just said. I assisted the detective pairing of O'Connell and Jardine. I helped them conclude the case, just before it went to the DA."

I pause and lean forward to look more closely at the photos on the desk, remaining silent once again.

"He was sentenced to death by lethal injection in the now converted gas chamber at San Q," Dee continues. "Four years later, he apparently had this overturned at the last minute. It was reported that he'd even been strapped to the gurney and taken to the chamber. Is that right, Oskar?"

"Yes, that's right," I say.

"The sentence was commuted to life imprisonment by the Governor at literally the last minute, making it a three-versus-two Board vote. That's what happened, wasn't it?" Dee asks.

"Yes, that's right," I say again.

"There'd been a vociferous campaign by the Orthodox Christian Church movement to have the death sentence commuted. Say's here that Gargailis was a *devout Christian and witnesses testified to his peaceful nature*. He confessed to the killing of his wife in the end, though. At the trial."

Dee turns a few pages of the report.

"Look, here this folks, whilst in prison awaiting sentence he was known as the 'Peacemaker' by prison guards and fellow inmates. Such was their *'respect'* ... Son-of-a-bitch."

Dee holds up her report, folded back to the page concerned, and is clearly disgusted by the insinuation that a convicted murderer could be called a Peacemaker.

Sam leans in.

"I don't understand, Dee. Where is he now? Are you suggesting he's our guy?"

"No. No, that's not what I'm saying. No way. He's locked up in San Quentin. I checked that. He's out of sight and out of mind so far as we're concerned. He's not our guy. Anyway, he's got to be seventy years old now."

I walk across to the window again, hands deep in my pockets this time, and look out to Buttle. What was it that was 'going down' for chrissakes? I think back to the trial and remember the dramatic conclusion. The way it ended with the prosecution's case seemingly blown apart, leaving us thinking Gargailis was gonna walk anyway. And then came the confession. Gargailis's damn confession. The confession that got him his fucking death sentence. Is this what Buttle is referring to? Is this what he meant by saying I *knew* what was going down?

I turn around and look at Dee and Sam, not quite able to work out why I'm holding back from saying something to them about it. Is it because of my shame at not doing more about these concerns back in 1993? Is my silence now my attempt to protect myself from having to admit I fucked up?

I suddenly realize how deeply affected I've been by the mention of the Gargailis case again today. And, more importantly, how long I've allowed my concerns with the outcome of the trial to sit and fester inside. Yes, there's been a coincidence, and yes, there's some unfinished business for me to deal with but, if these cases are related, I have to find out what the glue is that joins them together.

As I conjecture further, I wonder if I might end up settling all my concerns with Gargailis in one fell swoop. I quickly throw together a plan in my head, looking at the clock at the same time, trying to work out if it's doable in the time available.

Thinking it's all possible, I tune back in to what Dee and Sam are doing. It sounds as if they're bringing their discussions to a close so I turn around and see Dee pulling all her papers together but Sam is staring straight back at me.

Why am I not surprised?

"Let's wrap it up here and return to work," I say, ignoring Sam's stare, and breaking into the silence. "You sure, Oskar? Don't you want to discuss this Gargailis case further?" Sam asks, still holding my eyes. "You look as though you've got something you need to share."

Dee looks up as well. Goddammit, they're both staring at me now. "Yes, I'm sure," I say, impatiently. "And no, I don't want to say anything. Let's proceed with our jobs at hand, shall we? What are we all gonna be doing. Dee, you first?"

Dee starts looking between Sam and me, unsettled by the sudden change in mood.

"Me? Oh ... I'm going to liaise with Treviss and see how things are shaping up with the CCTV footage he's looking out for."

"Well, I'm particularly anxious to see any video images from the back of the shop where Henshaw was killed. Check to see if there's anything worth investigating or following up after LAPD cleared the scene? You know, for a couple of days. Perhaps the perp came back to have a look," I instruct, as I start collecting my things together.

"Yeah, sure ... Why? Where you going, Oskar?" Dee asks, looking between Sam and me again, clearly concerned about something.

"Don't know. Probably a quick bite to eat ... and a smoke ... in reverse order," I say in an attempt to lighten the situation. "Let's all meet here after lunch and we'll hear from Treviss and Buttle on what they've found. We can ink in a plan for how we move forward. How's that sounding?"

"Yeah ... That'll work, I guess. But ..."

"But, what?" I ask.

"Oh ... Nothing. I'll ... I'll talk to you later," Dee replies, looking between Sam and me again, before moving out into the squad room, continuing to shake her head.

I turn to look at Sam. She has her head down, busy pulling her own things together.

"What about you?" I ask, as I put on my jacket. "What are you gonna do?"

"I'll head back to my hotel and work on a few things there if that's okay—Hey, what's all this with Gargailis?" she suddenly asks, taking me aback with her abruptness.

"Uh ... Can I hold on to that for now?" I hear myself say, almost apologetically. "I want to check out something first, then I'll come back and lay it all out for you ... if anything's there. Okay?"

"Yeah, sure thing ... When you're ready, Partner ... When you're ready."

29

(Tuesday, 12.24 p.m.)

I MAKE MY WAY out into the busy squad room, feeling uncomfortable with the way the meeting ended and look across at Dee and Sam as I go. They're both working on their respective 'jobs at hand'. I even see the lieutenant in his office shouting his mouth off to someone on the phone. So everything's back to normal, I'm thinking, as I drop into my chair. I don't want the lieutenant to come barging across asking me questions I can't answer, so I keep low in my chair. In fact, I don't want to be distracted by anyone at the moment. I need to figure out what to do now the Gargailis murder case has raised its ugly head.

I reach for my notebook, find a fresh page and break the spine. This is my ritual at moments like these. It's a private, personal sign. When I hear the spine crack, I sense new energy being released – a fresh page, a fresh direction, possibly a new beginning.

First, I write the name, *Gargailis*, at the top, and underline it. Then I list the words, *Orthodox Church* and *Buttle*, underneath. I'm realizing I'm against the clock, so I decide to deal with one item before heading off on my lunchtime *mission*.

I go online, look up a telephone number and punch it into my keypad. Whilst waiting, I take another look across the squad room, checking on Buttle this time. He's still at his desk. I try and work out when would be best to corner him, because I want to talk some more about his memories of the Gargailis case and, more importantly, I want to find out what is that was '*going down*'. Just as I'm wondering if Buttle's memories will be as strong, someone answers the phone on the second ring.

"St. Catherine's Cathedral," a woman announces. I ask to speak to someone who might know the history of the cathedral and its congregation in 1993. I'm put on hold, expecting to wait or be asked to phone back later.

"Father Peter speaking. How may I help you?" someone asks almost immediately, catching me by surprise.

"Um ... Father, I'm Detective Salo. I work for the Los Angeles Police Department."

"Yes, Detective, how can I help?"

"I'm investigating a case, and I wondered if you would help by answering a few questions."

"Of course. Please go ahead."

"Back in 1993, there was a case of some notoriety—"

"The John Gargailis case."

"Yes, the John Gargailis case. I'm doing background research."

"Go ahead; however, I was interviewed at the time by one of your colleagues a Detective ..."

"A Detective O'Connell, I should think."

"Yes. That's right. What do you want to know?"

"You knew John Gargailis, Father?"

"Yes, I knew John Gargailis very well. In fact, I still know him, because I visit him up in San Quentin Prison."

I pause at this point, not so much out of curiosity, but because I wasn't sure what this might mean or where it might lead.

"Is that a problem, Detective?" Father Peter asks, seemingly picking up on my hesitation.

"No ... No, Father. It's not a problem."

I want to follow with, *'Should it be?'* but just leave a space for him to respond further.

"Well, I take the holy sacraments to him, Detective. Once a month. I drive to San Francisco and meet him. We share in the sacrament of bread and wine."

Trusting my instinct, and realizing I'm up against it for time, I decide to step out further with him.

"You see, up until the point of John Gargailis's confession there was every indication the prosecution's case was collapsing and he'd be released from custody. Do you remember the occasion?"

"Yes, I do. I remember it very well indeed."

"Was the confession a shock to you?"

It's Father Peter's turn to hesitate.

"I'm ... I'm not sure I understand what you're asking, Detective," he eventually replies.

"I'm asking, if you were surprised the confession came in when it did?"

Surprised? Surprised? It was a big surprise, Detective. Believe me, it was the biggest surprise I'd ever had in my life. It still is. John was a loyal member of the church's congregation. He was a quiet, softly spoken, peaceful man – he still is come to that – and he gave so much of his life to the church community. Yes, Detective, it was a surprise, very much so. It was a surprise to all here in the cathedral that he went to trial in the first place. It still is for any of us who care to remember."

I put in another pause here, knowing people often fill in gaps with crucial information.

"I remember your name," Father Peter says, eventually "You were one of the detectives at the time, weren't you?"

"Yes, I was, Father, but can I just—"

"Then, why are you asking me these questions now?" he interrupts. "For what purpose? John is due for a parole hearing in a few weeks. Does it have anything to do with that?" he asks, tetchily.

The statement that John Gargailis is about to have a parole hearing is news to me but I don't want to reveal to Father Peter I'm not up-to-date with the situation.

"No, that's not the reason I'm asking, Father."

"Then, what *is* it, Detective? Because we have great plans for his homecoming and I wouldn't want them spoilt now."

"As I said at the outset, I'm investigating another case at the moment and the Gargailis murder has—"

"What case is that, Detective?"

"I'm sorry I can't go into that with you. I'd just like you to—"

"Has it got anything to do with the Jane Chandler murder?"

"I'm afraid I cannot comment on that," I say, wanting to ask the questions myself. "John Gargailis's family, do you know what happened to them after he went to prison? I remember a brother and a son."

"Yes ... Well ... No—John's brother, Mikelis, is presumed dead. He went missing on a hiking trip in the mountains, about ten years ago. His body was never found. And, yes, there's John's son, Danil. He was thirteen at the time of the murder. I don't know what's happened to him. He initially moved in with Mikelis, after his father went to prison. The last I heard he'd moved away. But I can't tell you much more because I've lost touch."

"That's fine, Father. Thank you—You mentioned there are plans for John's homecoming. What plans are these?"

"Well, we have many fine pieces of John's craftsmanship in the church and we are planning a very special ceremony indeed for one item. I could show you if you're interested.

"Thank you, Father, you've been most helpful." I find myself saying, wanting to end the conversation and think about all of this. I add the words *San Quentin* to my list.

As I hang up, I continue thinking about the fall-out from the trial, and imagine the impact the outcome and the event itself must have had on Gargailis's family.

I zone in on the son. What must it have been like for him? He was only thirteen at the time, for chrissakes. A recluse, Father Peter had said. No wonder. I find myself wincing at this thought.

I stare at the list in my notebook, reworking a schedule in my head. It's not just for today, I suddenly realize.

This gives me an idea and I snatch up my cell phone, tapping in a message, sending it immediately. I look at Buttle again and wait. After a few moments I see him reach for his phone. He stares at the screen for a few seconds before finally looking up and giving me an imperceptible nod before returning to his work.

I bring out my cigarettes and put one in my mouth – almost robotically – and prepare to leave. I see Dee's still linked up with Treviss, deep in conversation. I also see Sam in her room. She looks about to leave herself but is held back by something on her computer screen.

Seeing my team working like this makes me realize it's the right decision to leave them in the dark for now. I'm running on gut instinct, but I do know that to enroll them into what I'm about to do would require fine words. Words I don't have in my vocabulary right now.

I put on my sport coat and start moving towards the exit. I catch Dee's attention by making rapid hand movements near my mouth. I'm letting her know I'm about to grab that early lunch but she's seen the cigarette. So, whilst she continues to talk to Treviss, she takes an imaginary pull from an imaginary cigarette and blows the imaginary smoke back in my direction. At the same time, I hear an office door close and we both turn to see Sam make her way across the squad room towards the exit, ahead of me.

I turn back to Dee. The smile has gone. She's looking between Sam and me, clearly putting two and two together and making five.

*

I make good time and reach my destination in twenty minutes. I look at this giant slab of a building and think about grabbing a coffee and a sandwich from Denny's next door, before going inside. The normal procedure is to file a request on the telephone and arrange for the file to be couriered over to the PAB, but I don't want to waste any time. I want the Gargailis Murder Book now and that's why I'm turning up in person.

You can't miss the place once you're in the vicinity because LAPD choppers are serviced and stored here. I often see them parked on the site from the highway that runs past, so, occasionally, I'll hear the *whop, whop, whop,* of rotor blades as I drive past, but not today. All is quiet. There aren't many cars parked in the visitors' area either, so I'm hoping I'll be in and out quickly.

The LAPD archive is looked after by dutiful people, mainly women, who've always implied they've better things to do than serve customers who come knocking on their door. Have a bad start with them and they'll keep you waiting, unnecessarily. My advice to anybody turning up on spec is to go with the flow. It's the best service on offer until everything is stored away on an electronic database, which is still years away. Dee tells me they're more customer-focused these days, but as I make my way up the stairs it still feels like the same old place.

A young woman badged as Marcia Grande is in reception. She's dressed smartly in light blue overalls and smiles willingly when I approach the counter – perhaps this is my lucky day and she'll go that extra mile. She's wearing heavy-duty gloves and I work out she's been heaving boxes of papers from the reception area over to a cart on her side of the counter.

I flip my badge.

"Detective Oskar Salo," she says, looking at it carefully, flushed from her exertions. "How may I help you?"

I think she's been on that customer-facing training course. "I'm looking to take away a case file, Marcia."

I emphasize the words *'take away'* in the hope she'll know I'm not interested in having it dispatched through internal mail.

Marcia pauses, looks across at the pile of boxes on my side of the counter and starts pulling off her gloves.

"Sure thing. If we've got it, I'll find it. What's the case number?" I refer to my notebook.

"93–639," I say.

"Nineteen ninety three, huh? Quite a good year for the Dodgers."

I don't think she's old enough to have been following their form at the time, but I can't resist correcting her. "I think you'll find 1988 was the best year around that period."

Marcia thinks about this long and hard, as if she's remembering back.

"Yeah, I think you're right. It was my grandpappy who used to tell me about those glory days. Never could trust that fella."

With that quip, she turns on her heels and exits into the vast repository, leaving the door swinging to and fro on its hinges. I smile to myself at being caught out this way and settle back in a chair.

I hear the faint sound of Bach 'muzak' coming from speakers somewhere, and remember Lena saying Bach used whatever loyal instrumentalists turned up to his church on any given Sunday to play his compositions, but what his reaction would have been to hearing his pieces played on an electronic synthesizer is anyone's guess.

This makes me reflect on Father Peter's cathedral, and his assertion that John Gargailis was a loyal member of the congregation in 1993. Father Peter also alluded to the fact that Gargailis's son, Danil, was a worshipper at the same time. I have a strong memory of the boy sitting behind Gargailis at the trial. He always looked so stunned and shocked by the whole affair, like the proverbial rabbit caught in headlights. Who could blame him? He'd sat through the shocking spectacle of seeing his father sentenced to death for his stepmother's killing, and of course he'd seen her lying brutally murdered on the kitchen floor of his home.

That murder scene. I can see it in my mind's eye now and I notice again the similarities to the current cases. Why hadn't I recalled this memory before?

I consider again what Buttle had said about my knowing what was going down. What did he mean? Why did he use the phrase, *'going down'*?

I find myself standing up at this point, as a pulse of energy pumps its way through my body. I look at the clock, work out Marcia's been gone for a few minutes and consider slipping outside for a quick smoke when I hear the swing doors open suddenly.

"Here she is!" Marcia announces cheerfully, holding up the book, obviously pleased with herself. She looks at the clock.

"Four minutes flat. My record for the day."

I go across to the counter and watch as Marcia attempts to pull off the rubber band around the file, breaking it in the process. With a cloth she wipes away the dust along one edge and passes the file across to me, together with a pen.

"Would you sign here, and put your ID in the box, please?" she asks, pointing at the next available space on a form attached to the front of the book.

I take my time signing because I'm always interested in seeing who's reclaimed the file before. I see there are two names, one in 1994, the other in 1995. The first is O'Connell but I'm having difficulty reading the second because the writing is faded. I can just make out the initials, 'P.' and 'O.' and then a name. It takes me a second or two to compute before I work out the initials stand for 'Police Officer'. I turn the form towards the light for a better sight of the name without having to strain my eyes. I re-read it, catching a few of the letters and wonder if my eyes are deceiving me. I look at the signature and a hammer blow hits my brain in realization. It doesn't have the professional flourish I see in it nowadays but it's his signature all right. What's written on the form is *P.O. Kramer*. He wasn't the chief of police in 1995 but I do know he was working his way up the greasy ladder. From the bottom rung.

I'm stunned and shocked and realize I must be showing this to Marcia.

"Know these guys then, Detective? Or do you want to borrow these?" she asks, holding up a pair of reading glasses hanging from a colorful braid around her neck. "It comes to us all in the end."

I'm not really paying attention because my brain is running in all directions trying to work out what all this means.

Why would Kramer take out the Gargailis Murder Book? What interest would he have in looking at it in 1995, two years after the end of the trial? Has this got anything to do with why he's been hassling the lieutenant so much recently? Does this link the Gargailis murders to the ones I'm investigating now?

I eventually look up and realize I've withdrawn into myself and haven't answered Marcia's question, because she's still holding out her glasses.

"Uh, no thank you, and, yes ... they both work for LAPD," I stammer, falteringly.

Despite the blood thumping in my head, I do my best not to register any more interest and write my name and details in the space provided.

"The PAB, then?" Marcia adds, having watched me intently, but giving no indication she's noticed anything untoward.

"Yes, Marcia. The PAB."

"I know what I'd rather be doing, any day," she says, leaning over the counter and looking straight at me. I catch the smell of her perfume and this reminds me of something Lena had said. She stated that men only notice the scent of a woman once their subconscious minds have become attracted to the person.

"What's that, Marcia?" I say as I pass back her pen, recognizing the theory was accurate on this occasion.

"I'd much rather be catching criminals, like you, than lugging these old files around. Most of them will never see the light of day anyway."

I smile at this, wanting to leave here straightaway.

"Thank you, Marcia. You've been most helpful," I say, backing towards the door with the murder book clutched in my hands.

"Call by anytime, Detective Salo, I'm always here to help," she says, as the door swings shut and I start descending the stairs.

I haven't even opened up the front cover yet but I'm now connecting Gargailis to Kramer, and Kramer to the lieutenant, and I don't like what this is telling me.

I reach for my cigarettes.

30

(Tuesday, 1.43 p.m.)

A S I SETTLE INTO the driver's seat, I reflect the drive back will give me fifteen minutes to think all this through and decide on what, if anything, I'll say to my team. My dilemma is that, by tying them in 'officially' to my suspicions about the chief, I'll expose them to the same risks I'm exposing myself to. They'll know that connecting the chief to a murder investigation will be potentially suicidal for their police careers. This is because the 'pack' will always close ranks around the alpha-male. Any whiff of controversy will be deflected downwards by senior management to rank and file colleagues like us. We'll end up being sacrificed for the 'good' of the department. I decide I'll not expose my team unnecessarily to those risks. Not yet anyway.

Feeling frustrated, I look at the murder book lying on the seat next to me and wonder if the evidence will be there. I even think about pulling over and reading the book now but know this is neither the time nor the place. I need to return to the PAB as soon as possible and not raise any more suspicions that I'm flying solo on something.

I pull forward in the traffic, waiting to turn right onto East 1st and look in my mirror. There's no sign of the web or the spider. For some reason, I reach for my cell phone and ring Lena. It goes straight to message. I say nothing and end up staring out of the windshield, looking to the clear blue sky above, frozen with my thoughts about what our relationship might have been. After about ten seconds, I hang up and stare at the phone instead, letting my thoughts drift away. It suddenly starts vibrating in my hand, bringing me out of my trance with a jolt.

It's Dee. I pick up the call as the driver behind leans on his horn, giving me the finger in my rear-view. The lights have changed and a large gap has opened up as cars have pulled forward. I adjust my mirror to give the guy behind a long, cold stare, but he's not looking at me now. He's busy tapping his steering wheel and jiggling in his seat to the beat of loud music that I can hear coming at me from behind. Jerk!

"What's up?" I say into my cell phone, rather too aggressively.

"Whoa ... Easy Tiger. What's eating you?"

"Oh, nothing. I'm on my way back." There's silence for a moment.

"We're making progress and I wondered when you'll be here, that's all. Buttle has been grilling Tomkins and says he thinks Buttle's seen so much it's difficult to know where to start."

I'm not surprised to hear this but say nothing, thinking there's something else on Dee's mind. "He says you'll be interested in some of it and he wants to speak with you about it as soon as possible ... Not me. Just you!"

"Oh, yeah, I understand, leave Buttle to me," I say, not rising to the bait. "But will you make sure that he and Treviss are available for a team meeting? Say, fifteen minutes?"

"Sure thing. I'll also open your mail and pour that afternoon tea. Darjeeling, isn't it?"

I sense we're moving ever closer to what's really pissing her off, so I remain silent.

"Where you at, Oskar?" Dee finally asks after a long pause. "I'm in my car on my way back to the PAB. I've said that."

"You didn't say anything about your car—because I thought you were just going for a smoke, a quick bite to eat."

That's code for fifteen minutes, I'm thinking, and looking at my watch realize I've been gone for nearly an hour.

"I did," I lie. "But I also took a ride to clear my head, that's all. I've ended up being snarled up in too much—"

"Where's Sam then, Oskar?" Dee asks, much in the way she could have substituted the word 'dickhead' for my name.

"She told me she was going back to the Marriott—Look Dee, what's this all about?"

There's silence on the line for a few seconds and all I hear is incessant thumping coming from the bass woofer in the car behind.

"Well..." she eventually says, above the din, "it's none of my business, but—"

"No. It's not, is it Dee?" I interrupt. "So don't give it a thought. Just do your job and I'll do mine."

"That's the trouble, part-ner. My job is to work *with* you. In a part-ner-ship," she asserts, pumping out the last three syllables, almost matching the bass beat.

"Whoa, Dee, don't go off on this now, for chrissakes. It's not what you—"

"How do you know what I think?" she almost shouts. "Ever since Sam arrived yesterday I've felt you cutting me out. First, there's your clandestine rendezvous at the Marriott Bar last night, then there's all that eye-to-eye crap at the meeting this morning. And now, you've both gone off without telling me what you're up to—I was expecting you to be back here over an hour ago. You said you were going for a smoke and a quick bite, that's all. What in hell's name is going on, Oskar?"

"I can't discuss this right now. Let me deal with this particular issue and then I'll—"

"What issue is *this* issue, Oskar? We're supposed to know what each other is doing. That's why we're called part-ners."

"Look, we'll talk later. I'll be back soon," I say, hanging up before Dee has a chance to take her rant with me further. I make a snap decision and punch in Sam's number on speed-dial. She picks up after the first ring.

"It's Oskar. Can I come by your hotel? I want to bring you up to speed on something I've just found out and would rather talk to you face-to-face before sharing it with others."

"Yeah. Sure thing."

"Where can I meet you? In the bar at the Marriott, or the lobby?"

"No. Room 706," Sam says, before cutting me off.

I turn right at the lights and make my way towards the Marriott. As I'm working out how much of the story I should reveal to Sam, I nearly miss the pull in lane for the hotel. I end up hitting the brakes at the last minute and the junkie that gave me the finger nearly rams into my trunk.

"Crazy fucker!" he yells, after sliding down his window and sharing his particular taste in music with the rest of L.A.

I gather the murder book and make my way inside, still wondering if my theories about Gargailis and the chief will stack up under Sam's close scrutiny.

"Yeah, some crazy fucker," I say to myself.

*

Sam is waiting for me at her hotel room door. She's dressed in a light-blue oxford shirt and indigo jeans. As I step into the main room I smell flowers and guess Sam's got a candle burning somewhere. The balcony door is open and the curtains are swaying in the breeze. I almost find myself looking for a broken wine glass and splatter marks on the wall – so real is that image from Sunday morning.

Back in the present, I sit down in a low chair that Sam proffers. She smiles warmly and slides a black coffee across the glass-topped table towards me. She tucks up one leg and, with a simple, silent gesture, invites me to begin at the beginning.

I place the Gargailis Murder Book on the table and prepare to make a start. Sam doesn't look at it but I can tell she knows it's there and that this is what all the fuss is about.

"It was Dee's mention of the case today that made me drive across to the city archive and take out the Gargailis Murder Book,"

I say, patting it with my hand. "I don't have any theories yet, just a gut feeling that maybe there's a link with the ones we're investigating now."

"Tell me what you're thinking."

I'm caught between the devil and the deep blue sea and wonder how much I should reveal. There are my suspicions about Kramer but there's also my 'guilt' over Gargailis's conviction. And, of course, there are now my fears that both are about to collide like a couple of express trains.

"Well ... the thing that sticks in my throat – the personal bit – is that I let something ride," I find myself saying first of all. "Deep down, I should have done something about it in 1993. That's the deal there. Memories of the case have cropped up, and yes there's unfinished business, but maybe, just maybe, there's also a link to the cases we're investigating now. That's what I'm thinking. That's why I've gotten this book."

"You want to kill two birds with one stone," Sam says matter-of-factly, more as a statement than a question.

I find myself staring through the glass-topped table to the floor, remembering the emotion from 1993. I suddenly realize this is the first time I've voiced my concerns about the Gargailis case since then.

"What was the drama for you?"

"Well, at the trial, the evidence against Gargailis wasn't stacking up. We could all see that. We all thought he was about to walk. But the next thing was he wanted to confess face-to-face with O'Connell, the lead detective on the case. The defense team shuts up shop. Slam dunk. One nil to the prosecution and O'Connell cracks open a case of beers in the squad room. But it does nothing for me except leave a bad taste in my mouth."

I try to smile but it doesn't come out that way.

"What made you think Gargailis was going to get off?"

"Well, first, one of the key prosecution witnesses backed off with his testimony. He'd supposedly seen Gargailis arguing and fighting with his wife the day before the murder – it was a major plank in O'Connell's case – but he changed his story on the stand under cross-examination. And a vital piece of damning evidence – Gargailis's fingerprints on the knife – was challenged successfully by a legal expert the defense team brought in from Colorado. Anyway, on about the fourth day, the prosecution's case was crumbling before our very eyes, when—"

"Gargailis makes his confession?"

"Yes, Gargailis makes his confession," I reply.

I pick up the murder book and start flicking through the pages. "It didn't make sense at the time and it still doesn't now."

I put the book down and take a drink of coffee. I look across at Sam. She's looking at me intently, clearly wanting to hear more, but I stare back because I have nothing more to say. I wait her out.

"I can go along with all that stuff about his confession," Sam says, breaking into the silence. "But why did you go across to the archive the way you did? You know, just now. Why do it on your own? Secretly?"

I just shrug, leaving the question unanswered, because I know I don't have a satisfactory reply.

"Why do you think Gargailis was innocent?" Sam asks, changing gear.

"Well, a number of factors. He'd played the distraught husband, very well in my opinion and, even when O'Connell and Jardine had him boxed up, he was still desperate to find the real killer."

"Come on, Oskar, there have been plenty of instances where the husband plays the role of an innocent victim. You've come across some pretty decent acting skills from grieving husbands in the past, haven't you?"

"Yes I have, but this was different."

"What was different?"

"Well, the confession, it felt so contrived. And then everything stopped dead in its tracks."

"That's often the situation following confessions, isn't it?"

"Yes, that's true, but it was the manner of it. It was as if O'Connell, Jardine and, to a lesser extent, Buttle just went—"

"Buttle?" Sam blurts out. "The Buttle as in Beavis and Butthead? – That jerk who's supposed to be helping you with this case now?"

"Yes, Buttle. Detective Buttle. He and I were brought in to the Gargailis case in 1993, much in the way he and Treviss have been reassigned to me now."

"That's a bit of a coincidence, isn't it?' Sam asks, smiling ruefully. "Yes it is." I reply. "And, as you know, I don't like—"

"Coincidences," we both say in unison, bringing some welcome relief from Sam's interrogation.

"And there was another coincidence yesterday," I add.

"What do you mean?"

"Well, yesterday, I met Buttle, down at the smoking shelter, to discuss how we could work together, and he also mentions the Gargailis case to me. He and I bandied thoughts about how we'd been at each other's throats ever since that case, and, of course, Dee then mentions it—"

"Synchronicity," Sam interrupts. "That's what it's all about, Oskar. So don't give me any of your detective hocus-pocus about coincidences. It's at times like these they will often appear." Sam gives me one of her 'surely you get this' expressions. "It's like when you find a new word for your vocabulary and then recognize it the following day in a newspaper article. The word is internalized first time around for some reason and then it crops up the next day and you notice it. You're 'tuned-in', if you will ... Perhaps you're engineering the situation with Gargailis so you can convince yourself to do something about it... like rushing off at a crucial stage in a murder investigation to obtain a murder book that's twenty-years old without telling anyone what you're up to."

Sam directs her gaze right at me now, wanting an answer this time.

"Why *did* you do that, Oskar?" Why go off by yourself like that?"

I remain silent and sit back in my chair, realizing Sam's about to answer her own question.

"I can see why it's possibly related to the current case you're investigating. I can even see why you'd want to look for possible connections. And I can also see why it came up in Dee's search, because of the similarities in the way the murders were committed. So all that makes sense. But why go off on your own without saying anything? To anyone?"

I still remain silent.

"You see, I'm thinking it's possibly related to what's happening to *you* at the moment. You know, what's happening in your professional *and* your personal life."

My hackles start to rise at this new trajectory of Sam's and I start to feel distinctly uncomfortable.

"We had that outpouring in the Marriott Bar, and now, for some reason, you have a heightened sensitivity around the Gargailis case. And there are these 'coincidences' you keep noticing. What's that all about? ... And ... there's something else. Something is missing here." Sam pauses making me wonder if she's on a fishing expedition, "Because I think you're still holding something back." She is. But I decide I've heard enough. I want to keep Sam away from Kramer at this stage and I'm feeling particularly uncomfortable about Sam's idea that I'm mixing my professional life with my personal one. I haven't time for this. Not now.

"Any-which-ways, Sam, I don't like coincidences," I say. "Most detectives don't, and that's the long and short of it. And how in hell's name did synchronous actions yesterday make Buttle mention the Gargailis case, for chrissakes?"

Sam stands up, walks to the balcony window and peers out to the city beyond, cradling her cup in her hands.

"Perhaps it was your subconscious pondering on the past that allowed him to express his feelings that way. He just picked up on it, that's all. It came up on his radar. Just because he's a thick-skinned bigot doesn't make him any less sensitive than any other thick-skinned bigot," she says, attempting some humor.

"Bullshit, Sam!" I say, feeling my pulse quicken.

"Maybe, but your meeting with Buttle possibly raised issues for him as well. I picked up on all that bad crap yesterday when we walked across the squad room. Perhaps down at the smoking shelter you allowed him the space to express what a couple of pricks you've been for twenty years."

"That *is* bullshit Sam and you know it."

Feeling the adrenalin really start to pump, I take a deep breath, trying to calm myself down before I say something I'll regret.

"It might be," Sam says. "But, hey, we're all giving off weird signals. You included, partner."

I take another deep breath as Sam returns to her chair and sits down. She leans forward, picks up the murder book and starts to leaf her way through the pages, letting things cool down for a beat.

"Let me get this clear. O'Connell had him in the frame with enough evidence to take him to trial and win the case. Correct?"

"Correct."

"But, initially, Gargailis pleaded not guilty?" "Yes, that's correct as well."

"How many days into the trial did the confession arrive?"

"Four."

"Four days in ... and then Gargailis confesses?"

"Yes. That's right."

"And you can't think why he would suddenly do that?"

"I don't know. I've never known. It just happened when I arrived at court one morning."

Sam stands up again and paces across the room, deep in thought. "What about the boy? How old was he?"

She's firing off random questions now, like a true detective. Perhaps she's hoping to trip me up.

"He was thirteen years old at the time." "What do you know about the boy's mother?"

"By all accounts a strict disciplinarian, someone who ruled the roost. A tough cookie. She was Gargailis's second wife and was therefore the boy's stepmother. His actual mother died when he was born."

Sam takes a few more paces down the room.

"After the confession, how did Gargailis appear to you? You know, what was he like ... his demeanor?"

"In my opinion, Gargailis got the sentence he was wanting. That's how it appeared to me. Strange as it may seem, he seemed quite content to be found guilty as charged. Even with his death sentence he never contested the verdict... refused, apparently. That's why he went to the death chamber so quickly. There's normally years of legal wrangling and appeals; he refused all that."

I suddenly remember a moment in the trial. The last time I saw Gargailis before he was led away.

"When he was sentenced, he turned and looked me in the eye, almost warmly. And thinking about it now, I think he knew that I knew ... if you know what I mean. He knew that I knew he was innocent. He just smiled at me as if to say, *'It's okay, Detective Salo. Don't worry yourself. It'll be all right in the end.'* ... It wasn't though, was it?"

There's silence from us both now, allowing my thoughts of the moment to fill the vacuum.

"I also remember looking at the boy when his father was led away," I say. "He just stared after him and he looked across at each member of the detective team in turn ... There's something about that expression of hurt on his face which haunts me to this day."

There's silence again.

"What were the victim's injuries? Tell me about them, will you?" Sam eventually asks.

I pick up the murder book and flip through the pages to the relevant section. I read:

"'The victim, Mrs. Sylvia Gargailis, was found on the kitchen floor, lying in a pool of her own blood. She had injuries to her limbs following an attack with an iron bar found at the scene. There had also been a sustained and frenzied attack with a carving knife after she had fallen. This had left her with over fifty cuts to her body.'"

As I read the statement, I see the connections to the current spate of murders. It's clear they're not identical but there are many similarities – broken limbs, a battered body, bleeding. Sam looks at me with a wide-eyed expression, suggesting she agrees.

"So, are you trying to tell me we have the same murderer from 1993 committing the current murders now? Is that what you're proposing? Perhaps you're seeing things that are just not there."

"Maybe, I just don't know."

That's the truth but thoughts are coming together quickly in my mind as I take the enormity of the suggestion into consideration.

"All I know is that the current investigation has brought up the memory of the Gargailis case, whether I like it or not. And there are similarities worth investigating in my view—Look, Sam, enough of this introspection, just leave me to read this murder book tonight. Let's see if I can lay it all out. Because, if it's there I'll find it," I say, optimistically.

Sam slowly nods her head at this proposal but I see she's not completely satisfied.

"I want to suggest you focus on the prize, Oskar, and not let yourself become distracted with side issues. Gargailis is possibly a side issue. An important one for you, I grant you. He's either good for that murder in 1993 or he's not. So, the sooner you find out if it is connected the better but don't dwell on it."

Sam paces the room, again. There's more.

"This guilt thing you have. You think that you might've let Gargailis and his family down, so why not follow this up at another time. Go find the boy and make sure he's okay. Or go see Gargailis if you have to. But do it later. Don't do it now. Not at this crucial time in the current investigation."

I've been feeling distinctly uncomfortable with her diagnosis so far and stand up to signal I'm out of here. But Sam has her back to me.

"You want to hear what I really think?" she asks.

"What?" I say, feeling my radiator start to boil over.

"Well, I think this is all about *you*. It's about that bust up you've had with Lena. It's about those reasons you cited for her shutting that door. It's about you and that guilt you now feel for Butthead, Buttle, whatever that creep's name is. You're possibly reevaluating your relationship with every goddamn person you've ever met. And now you realize what a son-of-a-bitch you've been and you can't work out what to do about it."

Sam turns and gives me a long stare, checking I can take her punch. I just stare back, unblinking, wondering what planet she's on but deciding to let her have her say and be done with it. I sit back down, hardly managing to contain my frustration.

"And, unsurprisingly, you're dealing with the guilt you've buried for twenty years with the Gargailis family—Jeez, Oskar, you're mixing everything up and losing sight of the—"

The radiator gasket blows.

"This is no fucking mid-life crisis," I explode. "Listen up, will you? This is about the fundamental concern that I have a killer out there taking down innocent victims in cold blood. He's doing it for no apparent reason or logic other than he's fucking playing with me ... and fucking enjoying it. With me, goddammit! He's getting a hard-on from it. GODDAMM-THIS-MOTHERFUCKING-SON-OF-A-BITCH!" I shout.

It comes out in a bile-driven stream-of-consciousness torrent, and, as the words explode from my mouth, I hear the point that Sam had so expertly made.

It's all about *me*.

31

(Tuesday, 2.47 p.m.)

I'VE LEFT SAM AT the hotel to make the short journey back to the PAB on her own. Sam said she wanted to walk and give herself the chance to prepare her thoughts for this afternoon's session. But we both know the real reason: She wants a bit of separation to help clear the air between us.

Surprisingly, despite the verbal workout, I'm not feeling too bruised or battered. I'm thinking that most of what Sam said was psychobabble bullshit but her assertion about me flying solo was well made. So, before leaving the Marriott, I resolved to keep all my colleagues on board with this investigation, wherever it'll be safe to do so. Unfortunately, that's the rock and hard place I'm faced with.

As I reach the PAB, I park and make my way inside, disguising the murder book between some freebie magazines I found in the Marriott lobby. The last thing I need now is for someone to notice it before I'm ready.

Dee doesn't give me her usual friendly welcome when I walk back into the squad room. I turn to the clock and realize my 'quick lunch break' lasted over two hours, and know this is adding to my problems. I sit down and put the Gargailis Murder Book in my desk drawer before moving round to the other side. I can see that Dee is continuing the work of looking at the security camera footage. Out of the corner of my eye I can see Buttle with Treviss doing the same.

Dee doesn't look up, but she knows I'm here.

"Anything back from forensics?" I ask, attempting to start building some bridges.

"No. Not yet," Dee replies, punching out each syllable on a monotone.

The swing doors open and we both look up to see Sam walk in with a spring in her step, as if she's just enjoyed a brisk walk in the sunshine – a different picture to Dee.

"We should get something by late afternoon … part-ner," Dee continues, emphasizing the word 'partner' in a disdainful manner, whilst staring across at Sam – I can do without this.

"Have you spoken to Hargreaves?" I ask, ignoring her jibe.

"Because you weren't here, I called in on the third floor about forty minutes ago. They're not giving me the heads up on anything. Hargreaves told me to wait until they're finished … said around four."

Like Dee, I'm impatient for news on the forensic search of Tomkins' apartment. I'm hoping the SOCO update will determine whether he's up for the murder or not.

"Are we meeting now?" Dee asks, looking at the clock, impatiently.

"Give Sam a minute or two and then round everybody up, will you?" I ask.

"Yes, sir. And how many sugars is that you'd—"

"I'll get the drinks," I say, interrupting quickly. "You finish off what you're doing here. I'll call everybody together."

I walk away before Dee has a chance to fire off another quip. I just don't want a fight with her at this stage.

"Five minutes," I say in a loud enough voice to be heard by Treviss and Buttle. Even Sam looks up from inside the meeting room as I make my way across to the drinks station. She gives me a warm enough smile in acknowledgement, and I take this as a positive sign that at least she and I are getting our mojos together again.

As I pour out four coffees and a black tea for Sam, I realize I'll have to tactfully steer through the next hour or two, especially if I'm to bring my now-extended team fully onboard.

As I carry the drinks through the squad room, I feel a fresh spring in my step and wonder if this is a sign things are about to come together.

Once we're all settled, I ask Buttle to be first up. I ask him to tell us what he has extracted from Tomkins and whether Tomkins' story is holding up.

"Whoooaa!" he exclaims. "Where do I start? This guy freaks me out. He's just one weird son-of-a-bitch. Isn't he? What doesn't he know? If it turns out he's not the murderer, he'll be one helluva witness because what hasn't he seen?"

"His balls," Dee quips without smiling. Others start laughing but I don't.

"Give us the headlines, Buttle," I demand, keeping my eyes on him and away from Dee. I want to maintain momentum and remain focused.

"He says he's seen a lot on the streets and in the area, leading up to the murder. It would be worth putting up any suspects in a beauty parade, because if they came by at any time he'd have seen them, for sure."

"What makes you think he'd be such a solid witness?" I ask, knowing from experience that any defense lawyer worth his salt could shoot down one who's unreliable at trial.

"Well, I tested this out." Buttle says, smirking good-naturedly. "I had Cerillo do a quick sketch from one of Tomkins' verbal descriptions. You see, I asked him to explain to me in words someone we'd all know. Someone we'd recognize straight away, to see if his verbal reporting was accurate and could be a sign his recollections could be trusted."

Buttle is continuing to hold his smirk as he passes round one of Cerillo's pencil portraits. I'm the last to see it and soon realize why everyone's grinning. It's a sketch of me. I can't help smiling myself because the likeness is very good.

"Oh, look at those cold, bloodshot eyes," Sam says, looking over my shoulder at the portrait. "Now ain't he a mean lookin' son-of-a-bitch? Reckon this guy needs trackin' down an' shootin' up a bit, don't he?" she says in her best cowgirl accent and flicking an imaginary hat of her brow.

There's more laughter and no escape this time. I join in.

Buttle spends the next ten minutes taking us quickly through his interview, giving a succinct account of what Tomkins said he'd seen in and around his apartment on South Normandie over the past week. Buttle also shows us how it ties in perfectly with Tomkins' previous accounts. Dee is still looking sullen. I suspect Buttle's report is testing out her own theories about Tomkins' guilt and is moving things in the wrong direction for her.

"After this meeting, will you run through his story again with a fine-toothed comb, Buttle? I want to make sure we triple check all the alibis he's offering."

"Let's hope it doesn't come to that," Dee says, looking at the clock. "We might just nail this fucking jerk with that lab report at four. We can then book him before leaving tonight. I'm looking forward to taking him to the DA in the morning."

Dee knows, as do the others in the room, that we have until this evening to either pin a charge on Tomkins or let him go.

Buttle passes across a detailed summary of his interview, and a quick glance suggests he's done some good work. I thank him and ask Dee and Treviss to tell us what they have. They've been working the screens, especially the video images of the Henshaw murder, the second killing, and the images from the second camera that Sam hasn't yet seen.

Treviss already has a monitor set up on the desk. Once he sets the video rolling, we see that the camera is mounted quite high and looks down onto the back alley. We see all the way across to the rear door of the hotel where we think Henshaw was heading before he was struck down. It shows clearly where the murder took place.

"You can see here," Treviss says, pointing at the screen. "This is where Henshaw makes his way from the hotel the first time, when he was on his way back to his car."

We see a grainy image giving the familiar two-second interval frame-shots. Henshaw is moving quickly and turns at the corner, walking off to the camera's left and then out of sight.

Treviss cuts to another shot taken from the camera further up the street – the images we looked at earlier – and we see Henshaw walk towards camera, still at his familiar brisk pace. He crosses the street at one point and disappears from view.

Treviss now switches back to the first camera and brings up another image.

"Look, this follows immediately. It's the moment before this unit is shut down ... see the time. The security company thinks that someone put a plastic container over the lens. Our guys think it was held in place with duct tape. You've not had any luck finding it because the guy who came to fix it in the middle of the night tossed it into a trash bin on his way back to base but couldn't remember which one. I've worked on him some more and identified a possible location so we might strike lucky. We suspect it may have been placed over the camera with a fruit picker or some such implement. We think the perp lifted the pot into position and then attached it over the lens. We've tried it. It's possible. As you know, this prevented anything being seen until the guys came across to rectify the fault, two hours later."

"Perhaps it was lowered into position. From a window above," Buttle suggests. "We might get prints—"

The camera is still running and Treviss is keen for us to see something coming up, so he holds up his hand towards Buttle.

"Look ... Look, this is the moment someone lifts the pot onto the lens."

The screen suddenly goes blank.

Treviss looks towards Buttle and then plays this scene once again, but much slower this time. We see the image darken gradually, but, more importantly, we can see also that something comes down from above, not up from below.

"Yes. You're right." Treviss says, excitedly, looking across towards Buttle. "Nice noticing."

"Have the window above dusted, will you?" I ask. "You never know, even after six weeks, there might be a print left somewhere."

"Okay, will do," Treviss answers. "Now, if I fast forward, we see the moment the two guys from the security company come by to check on things."

Treviss taps commands into his laptop and we suddenly see one of the security staff take the plastic pot off the camera. He gives a generous smile and a friendly wave into the lens. It's wide-angle, so the picture's distorted and his smile seems to fill the screen for a second or two. We then see him talk to someone below before dropping down the pot. With one final wave to camera, he disappears from view and makes his way down the ladder.

"Lookee here, we can now see directly into the alley again," Treviss states, matter-of-factly. "And notice, this time it's now two thirty-nine on the digital clock."

In the silence that follows, I think we all take on board what we're looking at. We know that Henshaw's battered body is lying out of sight, behind that dumpster. After a while, I ask Treviss to slow everything down and then I ask everybody to look closely at the screen, hoping someone will spot something new. But there's nothing. No movements. We continue to sit in silence, realizing the deed has been done. The victim is lying in a pool of blood, out of sight of the camera, with his limbs broken, having bled to death on the floor.

"Can you get in closer for me, Treviss?" I ask, wanting to see for myself if anything's there. He zooms in but the grainy image reveals nothing more. "Can you tidy it up?"

"I've done that already. It won't go any further. Sorry."

"And following your instructions, Oskar," Dee suddenly interjects, "Treviss and me have analyzed the recordings from this point onwards. You asked us to see if the perp returned to the scene, or if anything happened that's worth investigating ... or following up ... That's what you said, wasn't it? ... That's *two* whole days' worth of recording," Dee finally emphasizes.

I see where this is going and look across to Dee and Treviss. They both hold my stare, expectantly. They want an answer to their unsaid question, *'What in hell's name was the purpose of doing all that?'*

"What did you get?" I finally ask, knowing already what their answer will be.

"Nothing, Oskar," Dee says, barely able to contain her frustration. "That's what we got. Nothing ... Zilch. What were you expecting, for chrissakes? The killer had long gone. They don't come back. You know that. Surely. They never do!"

There's an embarrassing silence as Dee's rant peters out. I move in closer to the screen.

"Do you have the recordings for the third day?" I eventually ask.

Dee stands up, nearly knocking over her chair, clearly past caring whether she's showing her feelings or not.

"Let me get this clear, Oskar. You want us to look at the third day's recordings, as well?"

"No, that's not what I'm asking," I say, turning my head to face her. "I want to know if you have them. I'll do the looking. Myself."

Dee sits back down in her chair.

"Help me here, Oskar. Please! What, for chrissakes, are we looking for?"

I turn towards the screen and point out a section of the image I'm interested in.

"This area, here. It's the doorway at the back of this shop unit, behind the dumpster." I'm thinking on my feet now, trying to remember the exact layout in my mind's eye. "Perhaps the killer used this unit here as a hideout both before and after the event."

"After the event?" Dee asks, incredulously.

"Yes, afterwards."

"Why would our killer hang around after a murder? Surely he'd have hightailed it out of the way, as soon as he'd gotten the chance? No killer hangs around at the murder scene any longer than he has to."

This is starting to feel like the film, *Groundhog Day*, but Treviss and Buttle won't know about the discussion of this point yesterday, so I decide to repeat my explanation for their benefit.

"That's what we'd all expect, of course. But, with all these killings, the perp has seemingly vanished every time. I'm just wondering whether he's so confident he feels he can hide out at the murder scene and move off later. Perhaps *we* are the ones creating the illusion for ourselves. Perhaps we're thinking he's long gone when he's there all the time," I say, pointing at the screen.

Treviss and Buttle won't know about Dee's mention of David Copperfield's stage act, either, but I can see that Dee picks up on this straightaway. So does Sam, because she raises her eyebrows with an acceptance of this as a possibility. I decide to press on.

"Just, perhaps, he waited around here for three days ... Or, maybe, four?" I add.

Silence follows as we think about this. Even Dee sits back, arms folded, giving it some thought.

"What about Jane Chandler?" I ask, looking towards Treviss, wanting to move attention away from Henshaw – and Dee – for the time being. "Did you find any CCTV images at that scene?"

"Uh? ... Yeah ..." Treviss mumbles, not expecting to be called up to speak so suddenly. "But I didn't get anything else from any of the cameras, except the ones set up near a string of stores, a block down from South Normandie. It's on the main route into the area. So, there's a great deal of traffic, both on the street and on the sidewalk."

"What about the time in question, last Friday, around midnight?"

"Yes. I've seen people turn onto South Normandie but there's nothing conclusive, nothing we can use, although we have people working on it as we speak."

"What about the victim? Did you catch sight of her?" I ask.

"Yes. We caught sight of Chandler's cab bringing her back around twelve." Treviss refers to his notebook. "It was eleven fifty-three, to be precise, and I've spoken to the cab company concerned. I've also interviewed the driver. He doesn't remember anything of note but he does remember the tip. It was twenty dollars. That's high for a twenty-two dollar cab fare at that time of night, so I'm guessing this made him remember ... *'Apart from her being a hooker, she was a looker'*, is what he said to me ... Pointed her out on the sheet straightaway."

"Where did he pick her up?"

"West Olympic Boulevard. I've been to all the hotels in the area but no one's prepared to say definitely whether she was there on Friday evening. One staff member did say she'd been seen in the last few weeks. She's apparently not a regular but, when she's around, the same man accompanies her for a few days at a time. She didn't exactly report to the desk. As you'll know, most prostitutes will be discreet about their entry and exit into high-class hotels. They'll keep clear of cameras if they can but I'm still following up on this, checking a stack of hotel lobby tapes," Treviss says, pointing to his own cubicle where I see a pile of plastic boxes. "That's about it from me ... For now," he ends.

I thank Treviss and ask if anyone has anything else to say.

Dee looks up at this point and mentions, almost obliquely, that she bumped into the lieutenant in the elevator when she went down to meet Hargreaves earlier.

"What did he say?" I ask noncommittally.

"He asked me how things were going with my work digging out other cases. Apparently, you'd told him I was doing this overnight, so I ended up running past him what we discussed. You know, the work I'd been doing digging out information about that skunk, DeBurgh, and then the Gargailis case we looked at afterwards."

I feel heat prick under my collar.

"What did he say to that?" I ask, rather too quickly, suddenly wondering if the Gargailis case is the 'important issue' referred to in the chief's confidential memo.

"Why? What's the problem?' Dee asks, picking up on my concern. "He only asked if any of this research was relevant. I just said we're not dismissing anything—Why, what's this about, Oskar?"

"Nothing. There's no problem. I just wanted to know." Conveniently, I suddenly feel my cell phone vibrate in my pocket, breaking my concentration from Dee's interrogation. I take a quick look. It's from Hargreaves:

Drop by when you're ready.

32

(Tuesday, 4.30 p.m.)

"COME IN, COME IN, Oskar. Whaddaya got?" the lieutenant asks before I've had a chance to sit down. He's behind his desk, stroking the top of his head with one hand and beating out a rhythm with a pen on his desk with the other. For once, he's left the door open – and the blinds. Since receiving Hargreaves' verbal report, half an hour ago, the lieutenant's been watching my every move, clearly willing me to come across and make his day. Of course, he's hoping I have Tomkins in the frame and I'm about to book him.

Initially, Dee thought the forensics didn't clear Tomkins but, when I revealed the full extent of what he'd told me through that peephole of his, especially his secret liaisons with Chandler in her apartment, she had to sit back and accept he was now possibly innocent.

I also realized – and I'm regretting this now – that I was telling Dee old news. She was hearing most of this for the first time. She kept her fury in check in front of Hargreaves but let rip on the way back up the elevator.

"How do you expect us to operate as fucking partners if you don't fucking trust me with the information you're getting hold of?" she said. "Can you imagine what it feels like to learn the full details about your little tête-à-tête with Tomkins at the same time Hargreaves is hearing about it?'

I told her she was right to be angry but said I'd not revealed it to her because I'd been so busy with other things. It was a weak and feeble excuse and we both knew it.

"Yeah, you're so busy you can take a two-hour lunch break whilst the rest of us run around like headless chickens," she added, pointedly.

Not surprisingly, my apology fell on deaf ears and, when we'd gotten back to the squad room, Buttle further hammered the nail home for Dee by reporting that Tomkins' alibis were definitely holding up. This was the clincher. Tomkins was in the clear and we had to release him.

As I look across the lieutenant's desk now, staring into the eyes of a man who's clearly unsettled and anxious, I'm working out the best way to tell him, hoping I can make a better job of reporting the facts this time around.

"You don't think he's the doer, then?" he asks, reading my face before I've had a chance to say a word.

"No, Lieutenant. I don't." I lower myself into my seat, taking a less dominant position, watching him carefully.

"Jesus Christ, you sure? He looks as though he's up for it to me. I thought you'd be booking him today? What's the news from forensics?"

"He's in the clear, Lieutenant. Forensics put him in the vicinity of Chandler but that's to be expected, bearing in mind the relationship he had with her. It turns out they were friends, very good friends. But he's in the clear for the murder. There's no DNA – and no fingerprints – to tie him in to the actual murder."

"Does he have rock-solid alibis?" he asks, with a hint of desperation in his voice.

I see what looks like a draft press release sitting on his blotter – awaiting his signature no doubt – and I'm guessing it's been drafted to suggest that Tomkins is our suspect killer and we have him under lock and key.

"Yes, all his alibis check out. Everything hangs together. Buttle has grade one evidence that puts him elsewhere at the time of the Henshaw and Green murders, so there's—"

"What about Chandler? It doesn't take him off the suspect list for that one, does it? You'd better be sure of your facts, Salo."

"I am, Lieutenant. I'm sure. We'll have to release Tomkins this evening."

It's the lieutenant's turn to slump in his chair, clearly disappointed with this news. No, it's more than that, he seems resigned to something ... something I can't quite put my finger on.

I sit up, deciding to change tack, hoping I can give him something to take upstairs.

"On the positive front, we've managed to get some security camera footage further reviewed by Treviss and Dee. This has helped to clarify the timings of the Henshaw killing, and I now have Treviss and Buttle scouring South Normandie and in the hotels and areas Chandler frequented."

I look across at the lieutenant and notice he's switched off completely. I'm feeling decidedly uncomfortable and wonder if he's about to reach into his drawer for the remote and close those fucking blinds.

"What's all this with John Gargailis?" he suddenly asks, looking at a yellow post-it note on his desk next to the press release.

I try to remain calm.

"It came up in the search that Dee was doing, that's all. There were similarities with the murders, so it obviously showed up when Dee punched in the right keywords into the database."

The lieutenant nods once but I can tell he's still troubled. There's that hint of 'fear' in his eyes, again.

"What's your interest in this guy?" I ask, hoping he might reveal something of his fear to me. "Why did you raise it?"

"No reason ... No reason at all ... Other than Detective Chance mentioned it to me when we met in the elevator today. It's ... It's just that I don't want you spinning your wheels unnecessarily, that's all."

"What do you mean, spinning my wheels, Lieutenant? I'm just taking the case wherever it leads. That's my job, isn't it? To ask questions and to follow leads?"

He runs a finger around the inside of his collar and I notice his face start to turn red.

"Yes ... Yes, that's right. But it's just that we need to take care how we proceed. We don't have time on our side, do we? We must get a result," he barks, ramming his finger onto the blotter this time. "I see no reason to follow a path that's as old as Gargailis. It'll just waste yours and your colleagues' time. It was fucking 1993 for chrissakes, so what's this latest trio of murders got to do with that son-of-a-bitch?"

The conversation has clearly heated up too quickly, so I decide it's time to back off.

"Yes. You're probably right, Lieutenant—"

"Probably? PROBABLY?" he explodes. "Leave that fucker alone, Salo. That's an order," he shouts, as he stands up, pushing his chair back in the process. It crashes into the wall, drawing the attention of a few detectives out in the squad room. I notice his hands are shaking and he sees me staring at them, so he takes a look himself. Not quite believing what he's seeing, he balls them up into fists before snatching up a plastic bottle of water and taking a long pull, emptying it in one go. He then tosses the bottle across to a waste paper basket, missing it completely.

"For fuck's sake, Salo. Let's keep focused here," he says, turning back to me. "I don't want to hear anything more about Gargailis, d'yer hear?"

I see his eyes start to twitch back and forth, as if he's searching for something. Something to ease an inner pain ... an inner torment, I'm thinking.

He suddenly moves across to the window and looks out over the squad room, rubbing the back of his neck and twisting his head around a few times.

"I have a duty to us all here," he says, quieter this time, as he stares across at all of *his* detectives working away in the squad room. "Just stay away, that's all." His voice tails off as he remains stock-still.

Eventually, after what must be thirty seconds, I rise out of my chair and leave the room. Leaving the lieutenant to his dark thoughts.

As I reach my cubicle and sit down, I turn back to see him still standing at his window, but he's staring way out beyond the squad room. He's looking to a distant place where his demons are sitting – deciding his fate, I'm thinking.

I turn back to my desk and spot a handwritten message attached to the top of my screen. It's in Dee's writing:

> Marcia Grand phoned.
> Wants you to call back.
> No message, but says
> it's URGENT.

*

I slip out of the PAB, unnoticed, to meet up with Marcia at Maxi's Wine Bar – a local waterhole. She refused to discuss on the phone exactly what made her contact me and said she wanted to meet me personally. I immediately went to the photocopier to make a duplicate of the Gargailis Murder Book. I sensed this might be the time to have my own copy. It took me over thirty minutes to make it, as the file contained many different-sized pieces of paper; some were handwritten and others were double-sided, so I ended up having to photocopy each page manually.

Before going to the copier I'd asked Dee to go downstairs and smooth through Tomkins' release papers. She mentioned she'd offered Tomkins a lift to his apartment but he'd declined. I don't blame him. Having been put through his ordeal over the last three days, and knowing his sensitivity, I'm sure the last thing he'd want would be to arrive at his South Normandie neighborhood in a patrol car. Dee reported that all the legalities would be completed by eight and he'd be back in time for another episode of Columbo.

I soon reach South Grand and see the wine bar coming up. As I approach, I think through how I'll play this, deciding I don't want to predispose myself to any thoughts about what the chief has been up to, until I've heard Marcia's account.

As I walk in, I see she's sitting with her back towards me, in the far corner. She's wearing a simple purple dress under a classic black jacket. I'm guessing she's heading out for the evening and that's her reason for suggesting Maxi's for our meeting. It's convenient.

Marcia sees me approach the table in the reflection on the mirrored walls and turns to greet me. We shake hands and I notice her palm is clammy and I see she's extremely nervous. As I settle in my seat she looks around the room, as if she's checking we'll not be overheard.

A waitress arrives at the table immediately. I order a coffee. Marcia declines, saying she'll stick with the spritzer she has.

"Thanks for coming, Marcia. I appreciate it," I start off by saying.

"No problem, Detective Salo."

"Call me Oskar."

"Okay. No problem, Oskar."

I don't want to waste time but feel the best way to proceed is to let her take this at her own speed. I've one eye on the clock and only one thought in my mind, to find out what took place at the archive which scared Marcia so much that she couldn't talk about it on the phone.

"Okay, Marcia, tell me what happened?"

She leans forward over her drink, checking one more time that no one will hear what she's about to say.

"I was working at reception, this afternoon, after you left – finishing off moving the files actually – when someone comes in. I later worked out this was Mr. Kramer's chauffeur but I didn't know that at the time. He just walked in casually and asked me for the Gargailis Murder Book. Well, you can imagine, I remembered that you'd taken it away a few hours earlier, so I just said it's not here because someone's got it already."

Marcia looks around the wine bar again, checking she can't be overheard, and takes a sip of her spritzer.

"What happened next?" I ask.

"Well, he looked annoyed by this and immediately asked me who had it ... Thinking on my feet ... I said I couldn't reveal that to him because it was confidential. I don't know whether that's true or not but it was the only thing I could think of at the time ..." I can see Marcia's looking for approval, but I show nothing. "That's okay isn't it? ... Isn't it?"

I end up nodding, willing her to keep her story moving.

"Well, he just seemed to accept this and then turned on his heels and left the room. Just like that. No 'thank-yous' or anything. I went to the window and watched him go outside to a large black car sitting on the tarmac."

The waitress arrives with my coffee and we wait for her to put it down and move back towards the counter.

"I thought you said on the phone that it was the chief of police that—?"

"I did—Look, hold on. I haven't finished yet."

"Sorry, carry on."

"Well, in a matter of minutes the door opens again, and in walks Mr. Kramer this time – although, again, I didn't know who it was at first – followed by this same guy, the chauffeur. And Mr. Kramer asks me directly, *'Who has the Gargailis Murder Book?'* Again, I say, *'I'm sorry that's confidential information, sir'.* He then says, *'Do you know who I am?'* Well, that really scared me, because I didn't know but he was very forceful, almost aggressive. I was flummoxed by all this and ended up stepping back from the counter and blurting out, *'I'm sorry, sir. It's just that I cannot reveal information of that kind, not without authority,'* or words to that effect."

Marcia takes another sip of her drink, as if she needs it for courage to say what's coming next.

"*'Well'*, he says, staring at me with cold, angry eyes, *'I'm giving you that authority. Please release that information. I am David Kramer, the Chief of Police of the Los Angeles Police Department'.*"

There's silence and Marcia takes a long gulp of her drink, finishing it in one go and placing her empty glass on the table, fingering the stem with both hands.

"What happened next?" I ask.

"Well. I just froze for a second or two, and then, thinking on my feet, I said, *'I'll have to go out back and check the name from the files, sir'*. So I went out and tried to phone you first of all. I got through to one of your colleagues. She said she'd take a message and be sure you received it."

"Then what did you do, Marcia?"

"I went straightaway to my in-tray where the paperwork had been placed, along with a few others from customers earlier in the day. I found the one for the Gargailis Murder Book in the pile, the one you signed."

Marcia sits back, as if she's nervous to say what she did next. "And for some reason ... I put it in my desk drawer and locked it."

"Why did you do that, Marcia? Why didn't you just tell him it was me?"

Marcia goes bright red with embarrassment and starts running her hand through her hair.

"Oh dear ... Well ... I noticed your reaction today, when you saw the names of the two people who had taken the case file out in the 1990s, and I ... kind of thought ... you'd rather I didn't reveal your identity."

Marcia's looking searchingly at me now, seeking approval. She doesn't get any.

"Heaven knows why I did this," she adds. "Have I done something terribly wrong? I'm so sorry, I really am. I've done something wrong haven't I?"

"I just don't understand why you went to all the bother of not telling him it was me. That's all."

"Well, it's the same name, isn't it? David Kramer? He was the guy who took out the case file in 1995 and now he comes storming in, the same day as you, first demanding the book and then demanding I release your name to him."

"Okay, let's leave that for the moment. What did you do next?" I ask.

"Well, I went out to reception and said to Mr. Kramer that the paperwork has already gone through to my supervisor, Mr. Johnston, along with the others for the day. I also say my supervisor is not available because he's gone home – which he had – and that I think the paperwork is locked up in his personal filing cabinet—Oh dear, I shouldn't have lied like that, should I?"

"What happened next?"

"Okay ... He looks annoyed and just asks me, *'Was it Detective Salo? Yes or no?'* Well, I did my best to appear as if I didn't remember or even know your name but then I said I'll be able to let him have the name tomorrow, when my supervisor gets in ... I thought I'd be able to speak to you first of all, you see ... Well, he calms down a little when I say this. Then he gives me his card with a telephone number on it, saying I can contact him through his P.A. at any time." She passes the card across to show me. "He then stares at my badge and says, *'First thing tomorrow if you please, Ms. Grande'*, and with that he turns on his heels and storms out with his chauffeur following close behind."

Marcia goes to take another drink from her glass, realizing it's empty when she tips it up against her lips. She lets out a long sigh, appearing slightly flustered.

"Anything else?" I ask, ignoring her embarrassment.

"No. Not really. I watched them both go to the car and that's when I realized the other guy's the chauffeur, because he opens the door of this shiny black limo for Mr. Kramer—Have I done anything wrong, Oskar?" Marcia suddenly blurts out. "I have, haven't I? I'm really sorry. Is there anything I can do to put it right?"

"No. You've done nothing wrong," I find myself saying. "However, it would be best to cover your tracks tomorrow. I suggest that, in future, if anyone comes asking again you just tell them the truth."

I'm desperately trying not to dig any more holes for Marcia to jump into.

"Hey. Well done, Marcia. You did great," I find myself saying, wanting to close this conversation and get out of here.

Her cheeks flare at this comment and she sits back in her chair, looking a bit more relaxed. I take a drink from my coffee cup and look at my watch, wanting to signal I'm about to wrap things up.

"Then what happened?" I ask. "After you stashed the Gargailis paperwork in your drawer?"

"Well, I took the other forms over to Mr. Johnston's in-tray and piled them up there, as I normally do. I was just a little bit behind with my filing, that's all – because of the delivery – and hadn't got round to it. I've been extremely busy these last few days, loading stuff from one cart to the other and then filing it away in the archive."

I don't want to get into the trivia of her workload and just nod as though I empathize with her work situation but I see that Marcia has rumbled my attempt to be sympathetic.

"My life's quite dull really, isn't it, so please excuse my inability to deal with all this excitement ... I've probably screwed up real good, haven't I?" she adds rather despondently.

"No, you haven't, but you mustn't put yourself in a firing situation on my account – or anyone else's, come to that. You don't want the sack, do you?" I ask, remembering her little speech about the boring nature of her work and the fact that she'd much rather be 'hunting criminals' like me.

"...Unless, that's what you really want?" I add.

Marcia smiles at this but doesn't answer, leaving me to only guess at the mind-numbing monotony of her work.

I look at my watch again, wanting to escape as soon as possible and work out what Marcia's revelation might mean to the investigation. I'm now thinking that, even if I don't find anything in the murder book to implicate the chief, I have him for something over this episode. I just need to work out what it is.

"Thanks for coming all this way to tell me," I say, as I stand up and look around the bar. "Are you heading downtown for the evening? Is that why you suggested this place?"

"No," she says, looking up at me with a hint of embarrassment on her face. "I came down here just to see you, Oskar."

Her make-up suddenly looks like stage-paint as I recognize her dilemma. She's gotten dressed up for me tonight and I'm thinking she was expecting a little bit more from our meeting than I'm prepared to offer.

"I've screwed up on all fronts, haven't I?" she adds. "From the very start to the very finish."

I'm feeling a little embarrassed by all this now and feel my own cheeks start to flare. I look down at Marcia thinking that, had things been different, we might indeed have got it together for the evening.

All I manage is to thank her once again and make my way outside and start heading back to the PAB.

33

(Tuesday 6.17 p.m.)

M Y WALK BACK DOES nothing to calm me down. In fact, as I come through the main doors of the PAB, an overwhelming feeling of frustration creeps over me, because I'm connecting the chief to everything I'm doing at the moment. First, I have him muscling in on my current investigation, and now I have him linked into Gargailis. But the most disabling aspect of it is that I'm feeling neutered by rank. My frustration is starting to bubble up into anger – no, a deep-seated rage – that I feel powerless to stop. *'Unless, of course,'* I hear myself suddenly reason, *'I take direct action.'*

When the elevator doors open I step inside with Gladstone, one of the SOCO techs I've worked with in the past.

"Which floor for you, Oskar?" he asks, pleasantly enough. I'm still deciding.

"Which floor ... five?" he prompts, trying me again. "No ..." I suddenly hear myself say. "Ten."

As the doors close, a red mist descends and I realize it's my fury driving me forward towards this confrontation with the chief. I start trying to breathe steadily and deeply, attempting to turn the red to blue.

Gladstone leaves at the third and, when the doors open on the tenth, I see an administrator at a desk this side of the glass security door that leads to the chief's suite. He's badged as Peter Walters and I can see Daphne Marchant, Kramer's P.A., sitting behind her desk at the far end.

"I've got an appointment, Walters. Let me through," I say assertively, showing him my badge and letting him know I'll not take no for an answer.

He checks my name carefully, writes it on a sheet on a clipboard and presses a four-digit code into a keypad, opening the door and letting me through.

I see Marchant ahead. She's looking at me over the top of her reading glasses, holding my stare as I make my way down the corridor.

When I'm close enough, she looks me up and down and presses a button on her desk that opens the door, the entrance to the chief's suite.

I hold out my badge as I walk in, making sure I have my fingers over my name. I want to keep her on her toes if I'm to bluff my way through.

"Good afternoon, Diana. Is the chief in?" I ask.

"No, he's not. I didn't catch your name, Detective—"

"That's a shame." I say, faking annoyance.

I look across to the chief's door and see it's wide open. His office is empty. There's nothing on the enormous desk on the far side of the room and there's nothing hanging on the coat-stand against the far wall.

I turn back to Marchant and see she still has a confused look on her face, as though there's a mistake somewhere and it's got nothing to do with her.

"I didn't know you had an appointment. Let me see," she says, as she thumbs her way through a large desk diary.

"There's nothing in here. Do you have the right day, Detective?" she asks, turning over the page to tomorrow's schedule.

"I don't have an appointment," I say. "I just called in on the off-chance."

Marchant gives me a quizzical look, as if she's a tennis umpire about to enforce her own line-court decision.

"The Chief does not meet with anyone unless they have an appointment," she announces, emphatically.

"I know that, Daphne, it's just that he asked me to call by whenever I needed to discuss things," I lied. "And this is one of those occasions."

"He's never told me anything about that arrangement."

"Well, would you tell him I called in, when you get a moment?" I ask, turning around to leave.

"Your name, please, Detective?—"

"He'll know who I am, Daphne," I call back over my shoulder, as I hear the door swing closed.

When I reach the lift I glance back. Daphne is on the phone. I suspect she's letting the chief know I just called by to see him – 'as arranged'.

*

The fresh air greets me like a friend as I walk out of the PAB into the late-evening sunshine. This calms me down after my near-miss with the chief. With the benefit of hindsight – and the three cigarettes I've just smoked back-to-back – I tell myself I've probably had a career-saving lucky break. Who knows what might have happened had I squared up to him in his office just now? I might not have been walking out with my badge, that's for sure.

When I think about it sensibly, I had very little evidence to back up any accusation I might have thrown at him anyway, and I realize that, if I really am to confront him, I'll have to go in fully loaded next time, rather than with some half-baked theory up my sleeve.

I reach my car and open the passenger door, tossing the copy of the Gargailis Murder Book into the front. I feel the heat radiate off the seats so I take a few minutes to cool down the interior. As I walk around to the other side, I notice a black Lincoln parked up the street, about one hundred yards away. I'm really spooked now, because I'm sure it's Kramer's car.

I can't see if anyone's inside, because of the reflection of the sun on the windows, but it definitely looks like the chief's. I open

185

my driver's door and swing it to and fro, affording me a further chance to give the Lincoln another lookover. I'm sure I see the silhouette of someone in there this time.

A pulse of adrenaline finds its way into my bloodstream, making me want to walk straight over and confront him, but this time I decide to take notice of the alarm bells ringing inside my head. I just take a deep breath and slip into the driver's seat as nonchalantly as I can, putting on my dark glasses as I go. This gives me a further opportunity to direct my eyes towards the Lincoln without it appearing too obvious. The more I stare, the more I convince myself this case definitely has 'conspiracy' written all over it.

I start the engine and pull away from the curb, making my way down North Los Angeles Street. I soon come alongside the Lincoln and ease off the gas. There's no chance to read the plate but I can definitely make out a driver sitting behind the wheel. An arm is drawn up across the face – a give-away maneuver in my book, and one of the official disguises listed in the department's stakeout manual. Before I start believing in the incongruous spectacle of the city's chief of police spying on one of his employees, I decide I'll need more evidence that it's him, or even his car, before doing anything about it. And anyway, wasn't it Sam who said I was seeing things that just weren't there?

As I drive away, leaving the Lincoln parked up at the curb and giving no sign it's about to follow, I begin to think it was all a false alarm and my imagination was working overtime – just like Marcia's but I still find myself grabbing one final look in my rear-view, to make sure. All I see this time are my own eyes staring back, like black pebbles in a stream – dark and distant.

Earlier, I'd been thinking about the lieutenant's state of mind but now I'm beginning to worry about my own. I even hold out my hand, to see if it'll shake like his. It doesn't, it's rock solid and I take some comfort from this.

As I start my curving turn onto the Santa Anna Freeway, the murder book slides across the passenger seat towards me, making me think about something else Sam had said. *'Focus on the prize, Oskar'*. She's right, of course, but, if I find anything to incriminate Kramer in the book tonight and can add it to the drama enacted in the archive this afternoon, this will be a 'prize' indeed.

This thought makes me drive even faster along the 101 and I soon reach West Sunset, where the traffic slows down. Sensing I may have a long night ahead, I pull over at a liquor store and buy an above-quota pack of Marlboros. I don't particularly want to stop but I know I'll not get through the night without them.

The store is busy with early evening shoppers buying their groceries on their way home from work. As well as the cigarettes, I select a bottle of Rioja and a pack of ground coffee, Ethiopian mocha. All will help me stay focused for my night's work.

As I wait in the queue to pay, I see today's newspapers spread out on a newsstand. Many lead with the Chandler murder, and most have a picture of Kramer on the front, standing on the steps of the PAB, like some Emperor God. One banner headline pronounces, *'Police Chief manages to Calm City.'* Another boasts, *"'Our Streets are Safe."* In each photo I can see Deputy Chief Garner as well. He's sitting behind Kramer, looking just as resolute and determined.

Of course, this whole media circus – the LAPD top brass, the reporters, the copy editors and the photographers – is operating like a well-oiled machine. All performers and choreographers in their own right, working together to perform their intricate dance to their waiting and willing audience which wants to be excited and titillated on one hand and comforted and made to feel safe on the other. A delicate balance.

The Chinese woman at the checkout sees me looking at the papers and smiles, showing me her brown and disfigured teeth.

"You want paper?" she asks.

I decline and pay for my shopping, giving her my best smile back. She sees my cigarettes and throws a couple of books of matches into the bag as well.

Back in my car, I notice my cell phone flashing. It's a text from Sam. She's asking how things went with the lieutenant. I'd promised to let her know the outcome from my meeting with him earlier but I've forgotten to give her a call back. I decide to contact her later after I've read the book. Perhaps I'll be able to unpack everything for her then and *'lay it all out'*, as I'd promised.

I easily pull back into the slow-moving traffic and soon hit a slight downhill stretch leading up to a right hand filter lane. As I pull up at the lights, I have a chance to look in my rear-view and suddenly catch a glimpse of a black Lincoln cresting the hill behind me, about twenty cars back.

I feel a buzz in my blood again and put my foot on the gas as the lights change. Not in an attempt to escape from my tail but wanting to reach my apartment as soon as possible, without any further distractions. I'm more confident than ever I'll find out what's troubling the chief between the pages of the Gargailis Murder Book.

As I reach *Geometrix*, I drive swiftly under the security barrier and straight into the dark recesses of the lower ground floor car park. Not wanting to give away my position by flaring brake lights, I use my handbrake to come to a standstill in a parking bay that gives me a good view of the street outside.

I watch the Lincoln approach and, when it reaches the entrance, it slows down considerably. Then, almost threateningly, a telephoto lens appears out of the driver's window, like a sniper's rifle, searching out the full extent of the site. After about ten seconds, and two attempts by a following car to move him on by leaning on the horn, the driver lowers the camera and does one final visual check before racing off up the street with a squeal of tires. That's when I catch a brief glimpse of the driver. I'm convinced it's Rodriguez, Kramer's chauffeur.

I get out of the car, lock up, and quickly make my way up the back stairs, carrying my bag of supplies in one hand and the photocopy of the Gargailis Murder Book in the other. I'm also carrying the full belief that I now have the chief locked into all of this.

Big time.

34

(Tuesday, 7.10 p.m.)

'IS IT ALL A dream?' Lena asks herself.

She can't always tell in this half-asleep, half-awake state she sometimes arrives at. But gradually, she works out she's definitely waking up because it all begins to feel real.

It's also familiar. She knows this room. She recognizes it from somewhere ... the proportions ... the background sounds. All familiar.

'Am I dead, then?' she asks herself, confused by her own feelings.

There's movement to her left and she sees someone come to her side.

'Is it Oskar? Surely, he should be here by now.'

It's a man who leans over but it's not Oskar. It's the same man as before. He's dressed in white, as usual. He's wearing a mask, a hood, gloves. Everything he's wearing is white.

'Where's Oskar?' she asks herself, getting agitated once more. *'He should be here.'*

She tries to scream but there's nothing.

Behind the mask, the man is smiling. He leans over and injects Lena one more time, making soothing noises towards her as she drifts off.

Into another deep sleep.

35

(Tuesday, 9.42 p.m.)

AFTER TWO HOURS OF intense reading, I have the 'connection' that ties David Kramer, LAPD Chief of Police, to the Gargailis case in 1993 but I don't have his 'crime'.

I've found out he'd been the first patrol officer who arrived at the Gargailis household after the murder had been called in. There's a statement in the murder book, signed by him, that sets out his account of what he'd found at the scene and what he'd done to facilitate due process. Nonetheless, no matter how many times I've read it, all seems correct and proper to me: Standard procedure in 1993 and standard procedure now. He'd checked on the condition of the victim, sealed up the scene and waited for the ambulance and police backup to arrive. Textbook police work from the man starting out on his police career, and well before his meteoric rise through the ranks to becoming LAPD's top dog.

What's also worrying is I can find nothing that can help me understand why he'd want to take out the murder book two years after the trial. And there's nothing to help me understand why he's been spooking the lieutenant so much in recent days, or why he's having me followed by his chauffeur, Rodriguez.

I decide to put my concerns with the chief aside for the time being and consider the case itself.

The Gargailis house is referred to as a farmstead but I do remember it being quite close to Pasadena, in the north of the city. It would have been on a farm during the late 19th century. Since then, the area has been in-filled with other houses and factory units that spread as quickly as the population grew in California. By the 1980s this urban growth was nearly complete. I'm thinking this area of the city must have been Kramer's patch when he first started out as a patrol officer in 1993.

I remember rumors circulating at the time that much of the building work after the 2nd World War had been controlled by a single group of investors. They'd apparently cashed in on the gullibility of smallholders in the region who'd been encouraged to sell off parcels of land at a low price. The new owners had seen their investments return hefty profits once properties had been sold on to willing buyers moving in from the east.

This was nothing new, of course, and was the way of the world since money had been invented, especially in California. And after all, Los Angeles itself was built on a mixture of greed, avarice and favor. I remember city councilors being indicted for taking bribes at the time parcels of land were sold on to these investors. I also remember an LA Times exposé in the late eighties that suggested illicit wealth had made its way into the region following the collapse of communist regimes in Europe.

What is clear, having read the murder book from cover to cover this evening, is that Detective O'Connell, who led the murder investigation, seems to have followed the protocols in place at the time. On this read through, I have no problem with the investigation techniques he employed. My beef is still with the confession, Gargailis's confession. It comes out of the blue and then everything slows down. All lines of enquiry stop dead in their tracks. That's not the protocol. Not now. Not in 1993.

The murder book becomes very thin on substance from this point. No checks on Gargailis's story seem to have been made. No further interviews with the major players.

'Why this sudden abandonment of due process?' I ask myself.

I turn the pages and begin to read Gargailis's confession once again. There's a signed copy in the book:

September 24, 1993

STATEMENT BY JOHN GARGAILIS

On Monday May 10, 1993, my wife brazenly admitted to me that she had been having affairs with other men and started to berate me about my own inadequacies, both as a husband and a father to my son, Danil.

On Tuesday May 11, I came home from work and murdered her. I arrived with an iron bar I'd brought with me from my workshop. I lashed out, raining down blows to her body in a fury, until she fell to the ground. I then went over to the kitchen work surface, picked up a kitchen knife and stabbed her repeatedly, striking her all over her body. I did this until she stopped moving. Until I was sure she was dead.

Later, I concocted my initial story about finding her there, on the floor, when I got home.

I'm the one responsible for my wife's death. So help me God.

I re-read the penultimate sentence, *'I'm the one responsible for my wife's death'*. It doesn't sound like a resounding claim to have committed the murder itself, does it? You could still feel responsible for a murder even though you hadn't actually committed it. I remember his use of these words at the time but I hadn't noticed their significance until now.

Of course, I remember O'Connell being cock-a-hoop at wringing this confession out of Gargailis, because it backed up the initial accusation he'd taken to the DA in the first place – almost to the letter. In fact, as I think about it now, all the pointers and evidence he'd accumulated were backed up in the words Gargailis had used. It's almost as if Gargailis had scripted his confession to fit O'Connell's accusations.

It came on the fourth day of his murder trial, when the prosecution's case had seemingly been falling apart. All prior reports and statements documented in the murder book indicate Gargailis had pleaded his innocence throughout. He'd always stated that he just came back from work and found her lying dead on the kitchen floor. I do remember it had been difficult for Gargailis to explain the blood on his body and his fingerprints on the weapons, but he'd stated that he'd handled these items when he'd returned and found his wife on the floor. He'd even said he ended up transferring blood onto his son's clothes when he cradled and comforted him, after finding him cowering in the corner.

I turn the pages back to the first interview with Gargailis, on the day of the murder itself. O'Connell's report explains that Gargailis said he'd come back to the house around 5:00 p.m. and, after realizing his wife was dead, called 911 immediately.

There's no recording of the phone call that he made but there is a transcript:

Case No. 93–366 Comms Center Record 5/11/93 — 5:04 p.m.

CALLER: There's been a terrible accident. My wife, she's dead. She's lying on the floor. It looks as if she's been attacked and killed.

COMMS CENTER: Are you in any danger, sir?
CALLER: No, I'm not. I don't think so, anyway.

COMMS CENTER: Then please wait outside your house. The ambulance and police have been mobilized and someone will be with you shortly. Please remain outside at all times and be clearly visible to approaching police officers and ambulance crews when they arrive.

CALLER: Please come quickly

COMMS CENTER: We will, sir. Someone is already on the way.

Kramer's report follows, and it details his own involvement immediately afterwards.

I reread it:

STATEMENT: P.O. Kramer

At 5.06 p.m. on Tuesday May 11, 1993, together with P.O. Jenkins, I was in the vicinity of E Orange Grove Boulevard on patrol when we were called out to a suspected death of a woman on N Altadena Drive. I was met at the household by John Gargailis. He was standing out on the front path with his son, who was wrapped in a blanket.

John informed me that his wife was lying on the kitchen floor. He was clear in his mind his wife was dead and that she had been killed violently, but he could give me no clear indication at the time exactly how this had occurred.

For their safety, I asked both of them to sit in the back of the patrol car whilst I went into the house to investigate further. P.O. Jenkins stayed with them whilst I did this.

I eventually made my way to the kitchen and found a woman I recognized as Sylvia Gargailis lying on the floor. I went across to her and found she was dead.

There was a great deal of blood at the scene and I had to carefully work my way around this. There was also the debris lying around on the floor and on the work surfaces – broken crockery, glasses, etc.

At 5.11 p.m., I radioed in to control to be told that the ambulance would be arriving shortly. I was also told Detective O'Connell was on his way. I left the scene and went back outside to await their arrival and the paramedics.

It's textbook stuff I'm still thinking. Things were done slightly differently in those days, because I notice Kramer's use of people's first names, but, in general, Kramer has definitely captured the *'when, what, where, who, how and why'* principle in police reporting. I also notice, for the first time, the familiarity shown by Kramer in mentioning he recognized the victim as Sylvia Gargailis and wonder what this signifies.

I try to recall my own memories of the time, to see if something will shake loose. First, I concentrate on when I was called out to the farmstead, a week or so after the murder, wanting to connect with my initial meeting with Gargailis and the crime scene itself. But there's nothing. It's as if the disk has been wiped clean.

I feel slightly disturbed by this, because case memories normally come easily to me. Why have I managed to shut out these memories? Is it because of my sensitivities to the case that I've carried all these years? Is it my inner concern about an injustice being served on John Gargailis?

I think further about this, and consider employing a technique I picked up on a training course. The program focused on tapping into past memories that, for whatever reason, have been locked away. I was taught to visualize past crime scenes and re-enact in my mind what my usual professional movements would have been at the time.

The theory goes that, by applying my own *Detective Protocol Routine*, I could dislodge past memories stored away deep in my subconscious. I don't normally go in for this touchy-feely stuff but I do remember being surprised by what the DPR program revealed, and decide to give it a try.

I rise from the table, go across to the recliner and sit down, adjusting the chair until I'm nearly horizontal. I start by trying to relax by closing my eyes and breathing slowly, noticing each breath I take. It takes me a bit of time to switch off and I have to keep telling myself this is not surprising, bearing in mind all that's been happening. I persevere until I reach a physical and mental state where I think I can go a little further.

I now concentrate on my hands, imagining they are becoming more relaxed and heavy with each outtake of breath. When I think I've relaxed them fully, I move to my arms and then across to my shoulders, softening my muscles as I go. I work my way up my neck to my head and then relax my face, feeling each region unwind and loosen. I turn to my torso, and then my legs, eventually reaching my feet and toes.

When I'm convinced this is about as relaxed as I'll ever be, I start to visualize my time arriving in the squad car at the Gargailis house for the first time, in 1993. I'm immediately struck by the realization I'm not alone, because Buttle is sitting here with me, in the passenger seat. When I gaze out of the windshield to the scene in front of me, I'm surprised, because I see everything in my mind clearly. It's a wooden frame house, painted dark green. There are hibiscus plants in bloom in the flowerbeds, along with a mass of evergreen bushes out front. I also see mature trees extending above the roofline, growing out back.

I'm surprised to see another police car parked in the drive. There's a patrol officer standing at the open driver's door, leaning against the car, one foot on the sill. A pair of wire-framed Ray Bans dangles from one hand as if he's about to put them on. He's talking with Gargailis. Could this be Kramer?

I climb out of my car and walk up the drive, hearing Buttle alight and close his door behind me. The patrol officer waves to Gargailis before climbing back into his patrol car. I study him carefully and realize it *is* Kramer. I'm sure of that. He's much younger, of course, but he has the same fresh-faced vitality he carries with him now. I look to the passenger seat and see he's alone and wonder what this means, because uniforms normally travel in pairs.

I approach Gargailis, recognizing his face and small stature immediately. He doesn't look the sort of man who could pick up, let alone wield, the iron bar the way it was reported at the trial. I approach with my arm outstretched in greeting, but I'm suddenly disturbed by the sound of a bell ringing. Gargailis doesn't seem to hear this, because he steps forward good-naturedly, seemingly unaware of this rasping, ringing sound in the background. I shake his hand, introducing myself above the din. I'm immediately surprised by Gargailis's firm grip – the grip of a manual worker. I suddenly start considering that perhaps my initial thoughts about Gargailis's inner-core strength have been misplaced but I'm distracted by the persistent ringing of the bell in the background.

Where the hell is it coming from?

I come out of my self-imposed trance with a jolt. Someone's ringing the front door bell!

36

(Tuesday 11.23 p.m.)

I MAKE MY WAY towards the front door, trying to piece together what I've just heard. I look at my watch. It's late, nearly eleven-thirty. There's no sound of the bell now and, just as I'm starting to wonder if it was my imagination, someone raps loudly on the front door, not taking no for an answer.

I approach the door cautiously, making sure I stay the brick-wall side of the doorframe for protection. I take out my gun and sneak a peek through the spyhole.

I'm taken aback and pleased at the same time. It's Sam.

"C'mon partner, open up," she yells. "I gotta bottle of chilled Marriott getting warm and some warm Chinese getting chilled out here. And besides, it's ungentlemanly to keep a girl waiting at your door for more than fifteen seconds. Heaven knows what your respectable neighbors might think."

I replace my gun in its holster and open up.

"Hey, Partner, you should improve security in this fortress of yours," Sam asserts as she breezes in, making her way past me down the hallway towards the living area. She walks her way through as if she's been here before and all I can do is follow in her wake, tidying up as I go. When she disappears into the kitchen, I take the opportunity to throw everything I've collected so far into the spare bedroom.

"It took me two minutes to convince your security guard at the gate I was a legit guest," she calls out, as I hear her bringing crockery and cutlery from cupboards and drawers.

"Oh, by the way, he asked me to wish you a happy birthday."

"But it's not my birthday," I reply.

"Got him!" she screeches, really pleased with her 'win'. She sticks her head out from the kitchen doorway and strikes down *one point* with her finger. I remember this being one of the games Sam used to play when I first met her in Minneapolis. There's a pause now and I'm thinking Sam is about to set me up again. I'll be ready this time.

"He thinks I'm your birthday strip-o-gram," she suddenly states, quite boldly.

I remain silent and carry on tidying up. Eventually, Sam sticks her head out again.

"Only joking," she says. "I just assured him I'm your date for the evening, so there's nothing to affect your impeccable reputation around this classy joint of yours ... and, of course, your status with the Residents' Committee," she continues. "I took a look at those beautiful flower beds out front and all that potpourri on the landing. I guess your committee is fairly active around here."

Satisfied the place is now tidier, I join Sam in the kitchen.

"Let's eat before it gets cold," she announces.

I can see the food comes from Yang Chow and the smell reminds me I haven't eaten since midday.

"You take the glasses and cutlery and set that table of yours in that fancy garden. I'll bring out the food and we can eat and talk at the same time. I can show you what I've found, which is my real reason for coming over."

I must be looking surprised at this comment because Sam gives me a wry smile.

"Well," she says, "what do you expect if you don't return a lady's call?"

I remembered Sam had phoned me earlier and I hadn't returned to her but, deep down, I was hoping her surprise visit wasn't just work related. It must show in my face because Sam's still smiling.

"Don't look so disappointed, I was keen to meet up with you as well."

I don't know how to respond to this and feel my cheeks flare.

"Me too," I find myself saying, knowing this sounds rather pathetic as the words leave my mouth.

"Whoa, partner, don't start gushing on me," she says, looking out to the garden, urging me to set the table. This also provides an opportunity to escape my embarrassment, so I quickly pick up chopsticks and glasses and take them outside. When I arrive there, I realize the table is strewn with my papers and, of course, the copy of the Gargailis Murder Book. I'm not sure I want Sam to know I have it here, so I collect everything and bring it inside, putting it in the spare bedroom on my writing desk.

When I return to the garden, I see that Sam has laid the table herself. Job done. She's even set out a candle that's burning in a holder. Where on earth that came from I'll never know.

I'm amazed at the speed with which Sam has managed to find everything, plates, cutlery, glasses, candle ... and even my corkscrew, which I reflect I can never find myself.

I make my way into the kitchen to join her again and she looks up, seeing me staring at her.

"Read these, they're for you," she says, passing across two photocopied newspaper clips she's taken from her purse. I scan each page quickly as she goes back to putting the finishing touches to the plates of food.

The cuttings are dated Thursday June 17 and Friday June 18, 1993. The first has a 5 x 3 black and white photo attached of Gargailis being escorted into LAPD, after his initial arrest. He's cuffed with his hands at the front. O'Connell, wearing his trademark 'gangster' hat, and Jardine are steering him through the mêlée of reporters and onlookers outside the old Parker Center. A police officer stands on the other side holding up his arm, appearing to shield Gargailis from the press intrusion. Buttle and me are walking behind, following in their wake. The flash from the camera has captured the energy of the moment and I can't help but be drawn back to the drama of his arrest and the intense public interest shown at the time. I remember O'Connell waiting with Gargailis in his car and choosing the moment to exit when he thought as many people as possible were thronging the entrance to Parker Center. Such was O'Connell's love of the limelight.

I'm brought out of this reverie by the delicious smell of Yang Chow's food. I look across and see that Sam is serving out portions of Slippery Shrimp, Yang Chow's premier dish. She suddenly looks up expectantly, as if anticipating I have read both articles and wanting my opinion. I hold up my hand and start reading the copy. The first one is written by the legendary, and now deceased, LA Times' crime reporter, Dean Jacobs.

BRUTAL MURDER, HUSBAND ARRESTED.

Yesterday, at 11.00 p.m., John Gargailis of North Altadena Drive, Los Angeles, was taken to Parker Center where he is currently being held and questioned. The brutal murder has shocked the community and it was not until yesterday that any suspicion fell on the husband. Detective O'Connell, who has been leading the investigation, later said, "John Gargailis is being questioned in connection with the murder of Sylvia Gargailis, his wife."

O'Connell said, "The murder took place ten days ago at the family home in Pasadena, opposite Victory Park. This is a quiet neighborhood and not used to sordid crimes of this nature." Details of the murder itself have been scant, however a police statement reveals Sylvia Gargailis suffered multiple injuries to her body from an iron bar and also with a knife.

I look at Sam. She's finished serving the food and looks as though she's about to pick up the plates and take them out to the garden.

I walk out ahead of her, holding the second article, and, when I reach the table, I sit down and start reading:

HOUSE OF HORROR – SECRET REVEALED.
Dean Jacobs

Following his arrest yesterday, John Gargailis was formerly charged today with the murder of his wife, Sylvia Gargailis. A police statement reveals that a further search of the property, where Mr. and Mrs. Gargailis lived with their thirteen-year-old son, Danil, is still going ahead.

Neighbors are shocked by the news. Angelina Bedlow, who lives next door, said to me today that she had always known Mr Gargailis to be a quiet and gentle man. On two occasions she had called on the family to babysit for her young daughter. She said, "The whole community is in complete shock."

Sam has followed me out into the garden. I watch as she puts two plates of food and three side dishes on the table with a professional flourish. I'm guessing she's waited at tables in her life and that's why she's managed to put everything together so effortlessly, with such aplomb. I immediately want to dive in but see Sam wants my opinion on the cuttings first.

"Come on Detective, haven't you noticed anything yet?"

I lean across the table, helping myself to something that's fallen off one of the dishes. I bite into the sumptuous batter coating. Sam gives me a teasing glare and points at the second cutting. I look closely at the photograph above the copy and continue eating the delicious battered oyster. It's a photograph of the Gargailis farmstead.

"He's in both and, remember, every picture tells a story," Sam says, trying to prompt me into an answer.

I look more closely this time and that's when I spot what she's on about. He wasn't so muscled in those days, and he's definitely thirty pounds lighter, but it's Kramer all right. Rather unbelievably, I recognize him from my little DPR session earlier. He's standing to attention underneath the front porch in this photograph, looking like an army guard on duty. In the other, he's the police officer protecting Gargailis from the press onslaught.

"You see, I reckoned you must have been on to something, otherwise you wouldn't have been acting so much like a prick today."

We both smile and Sam leans across the table to wipe away some grease that's spilt down my chin.

"So, what have you got? And don't hold back on me this time. Tell me everything."

Feeling cornered, I stand up, go back inside and fetch the Gargailis Murder Book and bring it back into the garden.

After taking a deep breath, I let Sam know what I've found out about Kramer and what my developing conspiracy theories are. To her credit, she listens and doesn't interrupt. No quips. No cutting commentary. She just listens as if she's willing to believe everything I'm saying is worthy of consideration.

When I've finished, I sit back and hold out both of my hands, inviting Sam to respond.

"I can see that Kramer's the symptom of something, and he's got a lot of answering to do," she starts off by saying. "But we don't know there's a high-level conspiracy going on, do we? So, until we get some answers from him – or find them on his behalf – we're swimming in the dark if you ask me."

Sam looks out across the garden, as if she's surveying the horizon, but I think she's just trying to place her thoughts into the right order.

"O'Connell's the key to all this, in my opinion," she continues. "If we're not careful, we could end up getting trapped into thinking it's all to do with Kramer because of his seniority now, but O'Connell was the lead detective back then and he took the book out as well."

Sam looks directly at me at this point, asking by her expression if I'm ready to receive her next point. I just nod.

"But I have to say I'm really struggling to find a connection between the Gargailis case in ninety-three and the cases we're investigating now ... Surely you don't think we're dealing with the same killer? Do you? Is this what you're suggesting?" she asks, quite pointedly, demanding an answer.

I shrug, because I just don't know.

"Anyway, where is O'Connell in all this? We've got to speak to him first—Is he still alive for chrissakes?"

"I think I would've heard through the grapevine if he'd passed away—and, anyway, I've got him in my sights," I say, remembering my schedule set out in my notebook. "He's on my list for tomorrow."

"Good. Whilst you're doing that, I'll look into some of the history you've talked about. You know, all that corruption with the city councilors at the time, and all the stories of eastern European gang-money finding its way over here. Perhaps it's all connected ... You did say Gargailis was a Latvian, didn't you?"

Sam's brought up the gangland angle again and I immediately recall our discussions yesterday, thinking it doesn't sound so far-fetched now.

I look out across the flowerbeds and notice all remnants of the day have disappeared from the horizon. The sky is tinged with the glow from the city's lights. Sam rubs her bare shoulders with her palms as a cool breeze finds its way into the garden, gently rocking some of the longer-stemmed flowers. I'm sure we've both noticed we're moving towards a make-or-break situation. I want her to stay and I think she knows it, even though Lena's shadow lies heavy in the background.

"Let's get this tidied away and I'll be off," Sam suggests.

We collect the plates, glasses and cutlery and make our way back into the kitchen area. Sam starts by discarding the takeaway boxes into the various recycling bins and, when she's finished, joins me in loading the dishwasher. She makes a better job of scraping the plates than me before positioning them neatly in the racks.

When we've finished, we both stand looking at each other for a second or two. Sam suddenly steps forward and kisses me on the cheek, before taking a step back and collecting up her purse.

"I'm pleased you decided to talk things through, Oskar. You should always trust your instincts but I suggest you should try trusting your friends a bit more."

I'm not gonna land in another conversation about this now, so I don't say anything. I just put my hands on her shoulders and gently pull her closer.

We stand looking at each other.

I feel her breath on my face and I also smell her perfume. We both smile, knowing what's about to happen next, but we stand for an extra second or two seeking reassurance from each other that this really is what we want.

Our smiles suddenly broaden as we both realize it is.

We come closer together and I see Sam's eyes have dilated. I gently place my hand behind her neck and pull her head towards mine. Our lips touch gently at first, then we lock onto each other in a passionate embrace. This lasts a minute or more as we both sense an unburdening of pretense and an unbridled passion to make love.

Now.

We continue kissing whilst we attempt to undress each other but soon realize the futility of this. Without saying a word, we decide it'll be easier if we do this ourselves. There's laughter at first as we take off our own clothes as quickly as possible.

Very soon we're standing naked in the kitchen, kissing passionately again and feeling each other's bodies with our hands. It's as if we have to declare our desires as quickly as possible, in case we miss this opportunity, or think rationally about what we're doing.

We both know that everything will change after this moment. And neither of us knows in what ways, and neither of us seems to care. The desire to make love in this moment is overwhelming.

I lift Sam onto the kitchen work surface and she leans all the way back, her legs dangling over the edge. I kiss her neck and breasts and work my way across her torso, enjoying the smell and excitement of her body. Sam gives me encouraging moans, and directs my head this way and that, so I can explore her body the way she wants. My tongue finds its way across her belly and down into the soft region below. I seek her out with my face, resting in the soft hair – that sweet smell again – and explore her luxuriantly. I'm guided by her moans of delight as she encourages me to find ways to excite her even more.

Eventually, sensing Sam's restlessness, I lift myself up. She draws my face into a long, hard and passionate kiss – almost primitive. Our tongues are strong and raw, penetrating each other eagerly. Sam's body pulsates with joy as she presses against me, rocking exultantly to an ancient and instinctive rhythm. Before I've had time to enter her, and with her legs wrapped tightly around my body, Sam's orgasm vibrates through us as she grips me in her four-limbed embrace. Her uninhibited shrieks of joy bring her the release she's so clearly wanting. I feel Sam's mouth exploring and kissing my ear as she joyously expels her pent up sexual energy in a pulsating thrill of ecstasy.

As her orgasm gradually subsides, Sam stays entwined and her moans in my ear turn into unintelligible whispers, then into words.

"... I... I've... I've wanted to do this from the first moment I saw you on Monday ... You know that don't you." This is not said as a question, but as a statement.

Sam's grip on me has ceased and her legs are hanging down the sides of my body but she still has her arms around my neck, wrapped loosely this time. Her cheeks are flushed and I see a bead of moisture on her top lip, which I wipe away gently with the tip of my finger. She smiles like the proverbial Cheshire Cat before letting out a deep breath of satisfaction and returning to the land of the living.

Pulling herself away from me, she looks down between our bodies. Her smile broadens.

She leans in closer.

"It's your turn now, Oskar," she whispers in my ear, realizing I'm not yet finished. "Where would you like to take me?"

*

I wake up and look at the bedside clock. It's nearly three-thirty in the morning. Sam is lying beside me, breathing deeply, having fallen asleep as soon as her head hit the pillow, three hours ago.

Light filters in from the windows and I watch her for a minute or two. I study her face, realizing it's not often I have a chance to look at someone as closely as this – particularly someone usually so active and never still. The smile on her face has gone but her lips are turned up slightly at the corners, as if she's dreaming pleasant thoughts and, deep down, is contented and happy.

For some reason, I think back to what Tomkins said about watching Jane Chandler whilst she was asleep. I consider that what I'm doing here is no different, except Sam is completely unaware of what's happening and Chandler probably knew Tomkins was staring at her voyeuristically.

I wonder what all this says about me. Am I being voyeuristic too?

Sam starts to mumble something in her sleep, as if she's answering the question for me. She then turns over, pulling the bed-sheet with her. This reveals her bare back, reminding me of the view when I arrived at the Marriott bar on Monday evening.

I run my hand over her skin, feeling its warmth and smoothness and remember our extended – and passionate – lovemaking last night.

After our session in the kitchen, I was feeling slightly bemused and disappointed. I'd even wondered if Sam had selfishly pursued her own orgasm at my expense but, when she led me by the hand into the garden, I knew this view of her had been misplaced. Under the stars, her sole purpose had been to make my sexual pleasure the center of her attention.

The rising scent of orange blossom from the garden below enveloped us as we made love on the grass and in various other places around the garden. We found positions that gave us an opportunity to enjoy each other's bodies and our moments of lovemaking. It was a little clumsy at first but there was no embarrassment. It was no less passionate either. It was more focused and less frenetic, less carnal and raw. Every time I opened up my eyes, Sam seemed to have her eyes open as well. At key moments she smiled opulently, making me feel purposeful and worthy of her attention.

At one point, we heard soft music coming from another apartment and, when the saxophone started to wail out its lonely call, we ended up moving gently to the rhythm. Our need to be desired and wanted seemed to be summed up by that saxophone's solo. We both felt safe and secure, entwined in a moment of personal pleasure we craved and wanted.

It seemed obvious to me that, no matter what might follow and what might end up happening to us, the moment could never be taken away.

It was a celebration. Nobody could see us. Nobody could hear us. It was *our* moment.

Beneath the stars.

Suddenly, back in the present, my eye is drawn to the small red light flashing on my cell phone. I have a text. I grab for it and notice it came in at eight-thirty last night. It's from Dee:

> Paperwork complete.
> Lieutenant's taken Tomkins
> back to South Normandie.

37

(Wednesday, 4.23 a.m.)

I FEEL STRANGELY NUMB as I look at the scene before me. The makeshift noose around Tomkins' neck has been made from interlinked plastic cable ties and the one around his neck must have formed a tourniquet as it snapped shut under his body weight, leaving him hanging from the hook on his wall.

I've seen dead men's eyes many times before but I've never seen anything quite like this. There's the usual milky caul but they also look as though they're about to explode from his head. His tongue is protruding from his mouth and has started to swell and his face is a deep red color, turning blue in places. I reckon he's been dead for at least three hours.

Next to the scuffmarks left by Tomkins' flailing feet I see a large photograph of Jane Chandler. I decide the hook on the wall had originally been used to hang the print. I don't remember seeing it when Dee and I came here on Sunday morning, or when we searched the place, Monday, so I take a closer look. I soon work out why. There's a different photograph on each side. The one on the other side is the view of the palms in Echo Park that I remember from Sunday.

I look closely at the Chandler pose. She's sitting on a chair that's back to front, her legs wide apart, staring resolutely into the eye of the lens. She's set against a backdrop of white curtains blowing in the breeze. I work out this was taken in her apartment, directly above where I'm standing.

As I stare at her naked body, I try and figure out why this woman would want to lead her life the way she did. She was young and beautiful and clearly confident with herself, her looks and her lifestyle, so why did she expose herself to so much risk?

I surmise that, like so many of L.A.'s 'beautiful people', Chandler wanted more from life and this ended up costing her everything. I know from experience that crime scenes often expose the broken dreams of people, drawn to a city full of lies and false hopes.

My thoughts are interrupted by the sound of a clock ticking on the mantelpiece, and I realize I've been here nearly fifteen minutes. I wonder why no one's arrived and go across to the bay window that looks down onto South Normandie. I'd phoned for medics and backup as soon as I arrived and then I'd phoned Dee. Where the hell are they? Surely they should be here by now?

Once Dee worked out where I was, she bombarded me with silence, letting my sentences hang out in the air, without comment or reply. I'd clearly broken the 'partnership' rule – yet again – and she was letting me know what she thought about it. Eventually, she just spoke to say she was on her way and hung up.

I realize I mustn't let my mistake with Dee affect my judgments now. I have to stay focused. But, alarmingly, I'm beginning to question my own abilities to run an investigation in the first place if all I seem to be doing is pissing off my partner.

I turn back from the window with a heavy heart, realizing I've far more questions than answers. I'm also struggling to work out how everything fits together, especially my thoughts about the lieutenant's involvement. Did he say something to Tomkins in the car on his way over? Something that pushed him over the edge? Forcing him to take his own life? Or, is it far worse than that? I've seen many murderers dress up their crimes to look like a suicide. Surely not. I can't believe I'm even considering this so I move across to the kitchen to look for more evidence of what's happened here, before jumping to any conclusions.

On the work surface there's a pack of assorted cable ties, seemingly tipped out and scattered as if someone's sorted through them all. There are also different designs of nooses in various stages of construction. They're set out on a table nearby and I surmise that Tomkins – or the killer – tried out various versions until he was satisfied with the one to use. I pick out one of the ties from the pack and slide the end through the ratchet, pulling it closed with my fingers. It's easy to work out that, once the tie had snapped shut, Tomkins would have had no means of escape. The noose would have been impossible to loosen as it stopped oxygen reaching his brain. The scuffmarks on the wall suggest he tried to fight against the pull of gravity. I've seen this before with other suicides and it doesn't necessarily indicate it wasn't his choice to take his life. It just demonstrates nature's way of fighting against the decision to go through with it.

I haven't found a suicide note, so I move across to the bedroom and have a look there. Again, there's no note and nothing untoward that I can see on this first trawl. Everything seems to be back in its proper place following SOCO's intrusive search on Monday, so I presume Tomkins must have tidied up as soon as he arrived here tonight.

Why would he do that? Why would he spend time clearing things away before killing himself so violently?

Unable to answer my questions, I continue my search and consider the arrangement of rooms. I suddenly look up, because I find myself remembering the layout of Chandler's apartment directly above. I calculate the only difference between the two apartments is that, where Chandler had her walk-in dressing room, Tomkins had his office-cum-darkroom. I decide to look in there next, so move across to the door and turn the handle with my gloved hand. I switch on the light and look around. Again, everything seems to have been put back in its rightful place.

I remember we had taken this particular room apart, opening up and emptying all of Tomkins' cupboards and drawers. We also pulled out his photographic equipment, looking for anything that might incriminate him. We opened up boxes of prints and contact sheets that Tomkins had filed away so meticulously. Even the floorboards, initially lifted by Dee when she first found the Pandora's Box, have been repositioned now, making it difficult for me to work out where it had been secreted. I look across the work surfaces, anxiously seeking a final note or any clue that might reveal answers to this mystery, but there's nothing.

I look at my watch, wanting to start another of SOCO's forensic searches, and wonder, again, why no one's arrived. Frustrated, I move out to the sitting room and across to the bay window, and look down onto South Normandie. I'm half expecting to see a squad car parked this time, but there's nothing.

All is quiet.

I think about what brought me over here tonight and suddenly panic, fearing it might be the lieutenant who'll be first to arrive this morning. How the hell will I react? What if he comes barging in thinking he's in charge? What will I do? He's been treading over this case, and me, for too long and I'm seriously worried I might push him through this fucking bay window!

I breathe in deeply at this wild thought, trying to calm myself down, realizing I'll have to confront him soon enough. I'm just hoping it'll not be tonight, that's all.

As my thoughts settle, I continue staring out of the window and find my eyes traveling to the buildings on the far side, realizing Tomkins could see into these apartments as well. In fact, it would be easy for him to see all of life on South Normandie from here, just like James Stewart could see into those apartments in that tenement block thriller. However, the scene I'm looking at now is far removed from Hitchcock's film set; everywhere is quiet and still. People are sleeping behind their drawn curtains, completely unaware of what's about to hit them again when all of LAPD's paraphernalia shows up on the street.

For some reason, my eyes are suddenly drawn to one apartment in particular. It's directly opposite. Although it's faintly lit on the outside by distant street lighting, I see in through a bay window, just like the one I'm standing in, because the curtains are not drawn.

The more I stare, the more I begin to see further into the dark recesses of the room. I move closer to the window and cup my hands, cutting out as much of the reflective glare as I can. I immediately work out why the curtains aren't drawn. The room is devoid of any furniture or furnishings. It's completely empty. Just as I'm about to pull away, I think I catch a glimpse of something in the shadows. I can't work out what it is and have to focus in, concentrating hard. Gradually, I discern it's a silhouette of someone standing up against the far wall. A silhouette of someone staring directly at me.

As I consider this and wonder if it's just a reflection, or a shadow cast by some distant light, I'm suddenly distracted by the sound and sight of an approaching squad car coming up the street, lights flashing, siren blaring. I also see a maroon Mark 1 Jaguar coming up behind, noticing how Emmerson grips the steering wheel of this mighty beast as it judders its way around the corner.

I turn back to look at the apartment opposite and realize the image of the person has gone. I think about this for a moment and then make a snap decision.

I race out of the room, past the two patrol officers who have made their way up the stairs and are standing in the doorway, scratching their heads, as they look at the grotesque sight of Tomkins body, hanging on the wall. I move swiftly down the hall, out of the front door and down the stairs. As I run down the front steps, I slide past Emmerson, catching the smell of his smoky breath, and make my way across to the apartment block opposite. I look up at the bay window protruding out, to get my bearings, and then I head inside through the front lobby. Fortunately, the door has been left off the latch and I'm able to make my way inside unimpeded.

I take out my gun as I climb the stairs, two at a time, and soon reach the second floor landing and work out which is the apartment I'm looking for. I move to the front door, standing to one side. I lean across and rap on the door, three times.

"Police! Open up. Open up it's the police!" I shout. No response.

I suddenly hear a door open behind me and turn to see an old man in his pajamas stick his head out gingerly, with his wife standing behind him, holding the crook of his arm.

"I'm with LAPD, sir," I say, flipping my badge. "Please remain inside and keep your door closed." The man shuts the door immediately and I turn back and set to work with my picks. I have the door open within two minutes – it's a straightforward, five-pin tumbler deadlock. I prepare to move in and consider that, if things go pear-shaped now, I'll be reprimanded for not awaiting backup. But I'm not gonna wait. I've reasons to go in quickly I tell myself, if my instincts are correct.

With my gun out front I push the door open and sweep the hallway as I make my way inside. There are no lights on but I manage to work out which way to go by using the faint light coming in behind me from the landing. I can see four doors leading off, just like Tomkins' apartment – and Chandler's I suddenly realize.

"This is the Police," I shout once again, keeping my ears keenly tuned. "Please make yourself known."

There's no answer and I continue to listen for any sign of movement. There's none.

I start by checking each room. The place seems empty and, except for fitted cupboards and wardrobes, there's no furniture to be seen.

I eventually reach what I believe is the main room, the sitting room with the bay window where I caught the glimpse of someone just now. I step to the side of the door with my gun raised.

"Open up. This is the Police. Make yourself known. Come out with your hands raised. This is the Police!" I shout for the last time.

With my senses heightened and my breathing shallow, I gently turn the door handle and take a look into the room over the barrel of my gun. It's devoid of furniture, just like all the other rooms in the apartment. I can easily scan the full extent of the room because of the flashing lights coming up from the street below, casting an eerie glow over the whole scene. I notice there's a section leading off into a kitchen area, just as in Tomkins' and Chandlers' apartments. I make my way across the room checking carefully as I go. I open up all the kitchen cupboards and a walk in larder, but find nothing.

I finally decide the whole apartment is empty and lower my gun to my side.

After a moment's reflection, I move across to the spot where I thought I'd seen someone standing, moments ago, to see what made me think I was looking into the eyes of the murderer.

Yes, I can identify a half-light leeching in from a distant street lamp but there's nothing here that I could have mistaken for a person. I'm not sure whether I'm feeling relieved or frustrated by this realization. I finally decide I'm fucking annoyed. Annoyed I've been unnecessarily spooked by a shadow, some fucking ghost of my imagination, willing the killer into my grasp for chrissakes!

I'm about to return to Tomkins' apartment when I'm suddenly aware of a slight scuffing noise, like a shoe scraping on the floor. I think it's coming from behind me, out in the hallway, but it's difficult to tell from here. I stand still and listen, raising my gun once again.

After about thirty seconds of silence, I hear a similar noise, followed by a floorboard creak this time. I remain quite still, gun in hand, pointing the barrel towards the doorway. I feel my finger tighten around the trigger, as the adrenaline starts to pump fiercely around my body.

After what must be a minute's silence this time, the floorboards creak again and I work out it's under the tread of someone's footsteps. I'm certain this time.

I'm in an excellent position to see anyone enter the room. So, without moving my feet, I crouch and prepare to confront them, with a volley of bullets if necessary.

Again, there's silence and I feel the tension build. A minute ticks by, then another. Finally, I hear a movement in the hallway and see the beginnings of a shadow creep out from under the door. I brace myself for an assault by settling into an attack position, finger held firmly around the trigger.

"Hey ... Oskar ... Is that you in there? It's me, Dee. Is it clear to enter, or what?"

I take a deep breath and look to the heavens, recognizing the danger I've put us both in by my go-it-alone actions. I immediately replace my gun in its holster and breathe out, as my body starts demanding more oxygen.

"Yes," I shout back. "I'm in the room straight ahead. Down the hallway."

I move to the bay window and look out across the roofs of the patrol cars and ambulances, now assembled below. I hear Dee enter the room behind me. She finds a switch and floods the room with light, maintaining a silence, hopefully unaware of the danger she was in just now.

The light coming on has seemingly caught Emmerson's attention. He's standing across in Tomkins' bay window, looking in my direction, tapping his watch. He's telling me, in his inimitable fashion, to get my ass across there.

'Pronto, if you please. We've got work to do!'

38

(Wednesday, 6.30 a.m.)

Dee AND I HAVE left the SOCOs to finish off in Tomkins' apartment whilst we head to the PAB in my Caprice. I've asked a uniform to take Dee's car off her hands for the time being, so that she can travel up front with me. I want to see if we can pull our partnership back on track. I need to start dealing with the aftermath of Tomkins' death and having this standoff is not helping me. She's remained resolutely silent throughout. Yes, there've been a few grunts and the occasional nod of her head to a question but there's been nothing that could be construed as cooperative discussion or partner-to-partner analysis.

I'm also keen to square up to the lieutenant when he arrives first thing, so I don't want my disagreement with Dee snarling up my attempt to defuse that potential time bomb. I want to find out where he is along the sliding scale of involvement in Tomkins' death, from innocent bystander to up-to-his-neck-in-it.

Out of the corner of my eye, I see Dee sitting low in her seat, looking out of the side window, still giving me the 'silent' treatment. We both know I've broken the golden rule by not contacting her before driving across to South Normandie in the early hours. In my defense, it was just gut instinct that led me to Tomkins' front door. Nonetheless, when she blows, she'll know she's right. I *should* have phoned her first. And, of course, there's the incident with my gun. I feel myself stretching out my trigger finger as I consider the possible consequences if Dee hadn't announced her arrival from the other side of the door.

When we'd returned to Tomkins' apartment, Emmerson had already made a start on his examination of the body. He was still puffing from his exertions up the stairs and, initially, kept mumbling things to himself and writing things in his notebook, in that illegible, fountain-pen scrawl of his. *'Tomkins leapt off his stool around ten'*, was the most significant thing I extracted from him. Although he did mention he'd seen a lot of suicides in his time but never one where the face of the person had been so contorted. He was clearly struggling for an explanation for the grotesque features, and wasn't afraid to admit it baffled him.

I took Dee around Tomkins' apartment, showing her what I'd found on the work surfaces in the kitchen and in the photography studio. I also showed her the double-sided print. She'd nodded when she saw the view of Echo Park, confirming this was the photograph we'd seen on the wall on Sunday morning. She gave the print of Chandler on the other side a long, lingering stare. I wondered what was going through her mind, because she seemed to make an uncharacteristic connection with the victim in that moment which made her pause. Is this the prostitute thing raising its head again?

We're soon speeding along the Harbor Freeway and, after ten minutes of silence, I take the opportunity to glance across at Dee, to see if she's starting to thaw. Fat chance. She looks resolute and determined. I've had these silent treatments before but never one that's been so focused, so lengthy. A guy behind taps his horn and Dee gives a slight shake of her head. I've crept into another lane.

"Keep your eyes on the road, please," she says.

This is the first thing she's said since we set off and I smile slightly. Unfortunately, Dee sees this and starts shaking her head, more vigorously this time.

"You don't get it, do you?"

"Get what, Dee? What don't I get?" I ask, encouraging her to speak. "You don't get ... what's happening to us, Oskar ... You don't, really ... You ..."

She pauses, seemingly exasperated. I wait, saying nothing, giving her space to gather her thoughts. Eventually, she turns to face me.

"I'm gonna put myself up for immediate transfer, Oskar," she announces, as if a great burden has been lifted. "I'll not work for a partner who's a one man army ... I can't do it anymore ... I'm not going to, so don't go all broody on me, Oskar. Don't spend the next ten minutes trying to figure out how to encourage me to think this all through again ... It's final ... I've decided. We've hit the end of the line this time—" I have to brake suddenly as traffic stops at a signal for West 1st. Dee puts up her hand on the dash. "Hey. Take it easy, will you?"

As we wait to turn, I feel released tension bouncing around inside the car. The lights change and we head towards the PAB which I see coming up in the distance.

I know Dee will have a strong case if she asks for a transfer and I doubt she'll have trouble ensuring the paperwork is signed off. But I also know what it will mean for her to be labeled a 'whiner' in the squad room. Yes, she'll receive immediate sympathy once the full story emerges, for sure, but, as to cutting and running from a partner like this, nobody will want to touch her.

"You need to think about this, Dee," I say. "Perhaps we can find a way that won't leave you hung out to dry in the squad room."

Dee will hopefully understand my reasoning so I pause to see if she'll give me room to expand my point.

She hunkers down in her seat and takes out a stick of gum from her top pocket. She starts to unwrap it methodically before placing it in her mouth, folding it between her perfect white teeth, seemingly going through the motions of releasing the intense flavor in those first few bites. She then starts to go through her familiar routine of folding up the wrapper into a little origami animal, just like Gaff in the film, *Bladerunner*. Dee normally does this when she's sitting round a table in meetings so I take this as a sign she'll listen.

"The guys on the floor will crucify you in the end," I continue. "You know that don't you? You'll have some sympathy from my enemies but don't be flattered; you know what happened to Callander?"

Dee shakes her head back and forth, still continuing to fold her gum-wrapper.

Jon Kruse kept putting his junior partner, Paul Callander, in the line of fire, unnecessarily. Things came to a head on a stakeout, when both had agreed a procedure they would follow to bring in a local gangbanger. Only Kruse changed plans, midway into the bust, without telling Callander. He ended up having his hair parted by a stray bullet. Needless to say, Callander was none too pleased and decided to pull the plug on Kruse, claiming it wasn't the first time he'd put his life at risk.

"Callander always gains the sympathy vote," I say. "You know that, you've heard it before, but the taint of being labeled a whiner lives on. Colleagues think he can't be trusted. That's the deal." Dee looks up as if what I'm saying is bullshit. "It's true, Dee. Ask around. Senior detectives can't be sure Callander will take the risks that are sometimes needed in those make-or-break situations when guns are out." Dee's still folding. "No one wants to work with Kruse I know, that's a given – that jackass is a fucking liability – but no one wants to work with Callander either. No one wants to work with a junior partner who might hold back when the chips are down. You need the trust. That bond. That belief. Every partnership needs that. It goes both ways. I know I've fucked up but you can trust me when it comes down to it, can't you? Partnerships need that assurance. You jump ship like this and colleagues will think you won't give them the trust they'll be wanting, especially the old guard."

We pull up at the PAB but stay sitting in the car, in silence. Dee's still folding but I can see she's nearly finished.

It's time for my main point.

"Anyway, I've a better route for you to follow, so you can avoid all that crap."

Dee sits up now but still doesn't say anything. She's holding her origami animal in the palm of her hand – it's a chicken.

"Just sit tight. Just for a while. Until we've cleared this case. Because I'm the one that's gonna do the walking."

Dee looks across, giving me a face that shows she's either confused or hasn't heard what I've just said.

"I've been thinking about my career," I say. "And I've decided it's about time that I quit anyway. It'll save you the embarrassment, because I'm the one that's gonna ask for the transfer. A transfer out of LAPD."

There's a pregnant pause and then Dee places her folded chicken on the dash, making sure it stands up properly before releasing it from her fingers. When she's satisfied with its position, she opens the passenger door and climbs out of the car, without saying a word. I alight and follow her up the steps and across to the entrance, then the inner lobby. We walk past the front desk, flashing our IDs to the duty officer. When we reach the elevators, Dee presses the up button and looks around, as if she's checking no one's in earshot.

"You know what?" she eventually says. "You're full of shit. You're no nearer leaving the squad than I am of giving up chocolate—Look Oskar, I've said my piece, but can I get one thing straight before you start laying your anger and frustration out on me? It's not just what's happened today that's driven me to this edge."

Dee holds my eyes for a second, making sure I've heard this, before I see a slight smile blossom on her lips.

"Look, I'll give you until tomorrow to come up with a more convincing reason for me to stay put, otherwise I'll put in for that transfer and face the consequences ... and, if necessary, be 'hung out to dry'."

There's a ping as the elevator arrives and the doors open.

"And, hey, do me a favor will you? Don't send me on no fucking guilt trip by making me think it's *me* that's pushing *you* out," Dee says, gesturing for me to enter the elevator first. I step inside, expecting her to follow but, as I turn, she's still standing in the lobby. "I'm taking the stairs and calling in on the third floor. I'll see if I can pick up anything from one of Hargreaves' goonies. See you back in the squad room in ten," she says into the closing doors, sealing the end of our conversation before I have a chance to respond.

39

(Wednesday, 7.24 a.m.)

I REACH MY DESK and sit down with an unburdening sense of relief at what I've just declared to Dee, nonetheless, I decide to put these thoughts aside and focus in on the here and now. I have a job to do.

The lieutenant is not in and neither are most detectives but there's the usual sprinkling of early-risers winding up their computers for the day ahead. I hear a conversation coming from two young male go-getters, exchanging battle stories about their sexual conquests last night. I also hear the gentle burbling of the coffee maker at the drinks station. Dee said we chose cubicles this side of the squad room so we'd be first for hot drinks. I start wondering if my partnership with Dee is irrevocably destined for the scrapheap but her little smile to me just now, as the elevator doors closed, suggests it's not over yet.

The squad room doors open noisily and, thinking it's the lieutenant, I look up, ready to confront him. It's the sixteen-stone figure of Roland 'Roly' Chasner, a grade three detective, as he comes bustling his way through the swing doors, muttering expletives about some son-of-a-bitch stealing his *'fuckin' parking place'*. He's one of the fifteen or so detectives who took up the offer of leasing an annual parking bay in the department's new multi-story, rather than struggle on the streets or in the public car parks. It saves ten minutes each day but I like the walk most times because it gives me time to think. And until the State of California bans smoking on the streets, I can have a much-needed shot of nicotine at the same time.

As Chasner settles down, I start thinking about how I will handle the lieutenant, when my phone suddenly vibrates. I pick it up after the first ring.

"Where are you?" No introduction. It's Sam. "Why didn't you wake me before you left?" she asks, clearly peeved.

I realize I've forgotten to let her know what's happened since I left her curled up asleep in my bed, in the middle of the night.

I do my best to apologize and tell her everything. Much of it comes out in a stream of consciousness torrent. And, thinking about her request that I trust my friends a bit more, I even tell her about the person I thought I'd seen in the room opposite Tomkins' apartment, despite my fears she'll start offering me a psychoanalytical explanation.

Once again, Sam just listens, without any interruptions or complaints; she just makes uh-huh noises as if she's deep in thought about something. I take this as a good sign that, unlike with Dee, she and I are on the same page.

"I've been considering things," Sam suddenly says, interrupting my flow. "Things that make me think Dee is actually right."

"What do you mean, *actually* right?"

"You know, about all this being personal ... personal to you. I've been digging into parts of the Gargailis Murder Book this morning, and now there's all this stuff about Tomkins and the lieutenant, and it all seems to be drawing you into the quagmire, irrevocably. I can't put my finger on it but the cogs are starting to line up. It's something important to the case, I think. But, crucially, everything keeps coming back to *you* ... and Gargailis— Hey, and who, for Christ's sake, is that phantom you saw last night?"

"Uh? ... Well, I've no idea, Sam. A phantom? – a good word – to tell you the truth, I'm not really convinced I saw anything, because—"

"Don't you believe it?" she interrupts. "You saw something whether it was real or not."

I can't work out what she's on about, so I remain silent, hoping things will become clear.

"Whether you saw something is not what's at stake here. Someone is *playing* with you, Oskar. Playing with your mind. I think the killer might be attempting to draw you in on purpose … It's even possible he wants to be caught … Caught by *you* … Think about it. Every-which-way you turn the killer's been there first – that's a given, I know – but I'm beginning to think that he wants to capture you in the process. He wants you to join him. In his lair. It's here if only we can find it."

I hear pages being turned in the copy of the murder book I left behind in my apartment this morning.

"If the Gargailis case is connected it'll be in here," Sam says. "I'll bring this in with me now and we can check it together if you like. Find the connection."

I then realize what I've got locked away in my desk drawer for safekeeping.

"Hey, wait up," I say. "I've got the original here—let's look at it together."

As Sam continues to expound her views before I'm ready, I quickly extract a key from my pocket and start unlocking the desk drawer but I soon realize it's not locked. As I start to slide it open, I know what's happened before I've looked inside.

I glance up and across to the tank and see the lieutenant. He's standing at his door, staring straight at me, with rage in his eyes. He has the Gargailis Murder Book in his hand and he's banging it gently against the side of his leg.

"Sorry Sam, something's come up. I'll have to call you back." I close the line before she has a chance to respond.

I know the lieutenant has oversight for security in the squad room and I now realize this includes being able to open up all the department's desk drawers.

As I make my way over to the tank, I feel the significance of what the lieutenant's done is driving me towards a line. A line I feel compelled to cross. But I also know it will probably mean the end of my career if I do.

I sense my anger building with each step I take, so I start counting my exhalations, keeping them long, as I'd been trained. —*One—two— three—four,* I go past the lieutenant and into the tank —*five—six,* I sit down in the chair next to his desk —*seven—eight,* I hold my hands firmly by my side, just in case I feel compelled to strike out before we've even made a start —*nine—ten—.*

The lieutenant moves around his desk and sits down opposite me. The situation is not helped because he's wearing small, brass rimmed reading glasses that he's perched on the end of his nose. For some reason, his arrogance makes me smile and I see him pick up on this.

"It's no laughing matter, Detective Salo," he says, looking at me over the top of those fucking glasses.

"No, it's not, Lieutenant, but then it's not every day you get your boss breaking into your desk drawer like a thief in the night is it? You're good with the rules, Lieutenant; what page in the procedural handbook describes how you do that?

I can feel my heartbeat start to rise —*eleven—twelve—.*

"I warned you, Detective Salo," the lieutenant suddenly declares, not flinching at my raised voice. "I said leave Gargailis alone. You've only got yourself to—"

"Oh. Really? I'm the one to blame here ... It's my fault, is it? It's my fault I'm going where my leads take me?"

I can see that our raised voices have drawn the attention of colleagues in the squad room. They're listening intently to what's going on but they're also making out they're busy working away at their desks.

"You and me, Lieutenant, we're playing different games in the different worlds we live in. Your fucking procedural handbook deals with covering your ass, mine deals with following leads, finding killers and bringing them to justice. In this case, there's a killer out there who's taking down innocent people who've done nothing other than be in the wrong place at the wrong time. What about them, Lieutenant? What responsibility do I have for them? Don't you have a duty to them as well, Lieutenant? To their sons and daughters? Their friends and loved ones? Or are they just collateral in the big game of chess you're playing with those fuckers upstairs?"

I see by his expression that he's got my message but his chin remains strong. He's not going down without a fight, so I decide to try a different approach.

"Do you really want to wake up every morning in the full knowledge that all you are doing is protecting and serving the fucking Chief of Police and his crazy minions, instead of the people of Los Angeles? Instead of all those victims out there?"

The chin remains resolute, rock solid, like the chins on Mount Rushmore.

After a second, he sits up straight in his chair, trying to gain more height on me, and then he gives one of his long withering stare-downs, as if his superiority out-trumps any moral issue a grade three detective might lay at his door. I can tell he's about to jump the wrong way because he sharpens his gaze as if about to choose his words very carefully. Or to be precise, to *read* his words. He's reached across for a card propped up on his desk and is holding it under his nose below those fucking glasses.

"Detective Salo, you are formally under orders to leave the Gargailis case alone. Completely alone," he says, reading. "Is that clear enough for you?"

I suspect all this has been run past the chief because, if it came to a grievance, he'd want to be sure he'd followed the correct protocols. And, of course, he'd need to produce the evidence to prove it, hence his 'prompt' card.

"Because of the publicity surrounding the current murders you're investigating," he continues reading, "I've been asked to give daily reports in person to the Chief of Police. These updates will include keeping him abreast of your investigation." There it was, his mention of the chief of police once again. Whilst the lieutenant's only the middleman here, he's trained to follow orders no matter where he is in the pecking order. "Like me, the chief has been perturbed by your actions in connection with a murder case in 1993," he continues. "The chief thinks your line of investigation is off beam, way off beam, Detective Salo."

The lieutenant frequently brings nautical phrases like this into his official communiqués, and we all know he hankers after owning his own boat. He'll often be seen scouring the small ads in boating magazines as he dreams of spending his pension check before it arrives.

He picks up the Gargailis Murder Book and holds it up as if it's an exhibit in a trial.

"This is going back to the archive, Detective, and I want your update on today's work before you leave this evening. You know you can phone me at any time, day or night, as well. Have you got all of this, Detective?"

I'm not really concentrating, because I've switched off, planning my next move.

"Detective?" he asks again, speaking louder. "Are you getting all this?"

I just nod.

Moderately satisfied, the lieutenant puts down the murder book, places the card on the corner of his desk and leans back in his chair.

I remain silent, making sure he's got nothing more to say and then I stand up. I want to give him the impression I'm about to leave but my ruse is to throw him a curved ball question and catch him unawares.

He nods, as if he's been in complete control of this concocted conversation. As I leave and approach the door, I turn around and see him place his prompt card into his own desk drawer for safekeeping.

"One last question, Lieutenant," I say. He looks up in my direction. "Why did you take Tomkins back to his apartment last night?"

My question has the desired effect because his eyes flicker and he appears confused.

"I just offered him a lift back to his apartment. That's all," he eventually replies.

"You ever done that before, Lieutenant? Give a suspect a lift home like that?"

"Well, I don't know ... No, I haven't actually, but ... what's—Why are you asking me this, Detective?"

"Because he's dead, Lieutenant. That's why. I found him in his apartment early this morning. Strung up like a fucking chicken on a hook—Did you know anything about that, Lieutenant?"

He looks astonished by this news, as if he knew nothing about it. So, if he's acting up, he's doing a fine job for the moment. I move back towards his desk, looking intently at his face for any clues that he's lying.

"*Did* you know anything about it, Lieutenant?" I ask again, but more assertively this time.

"No I didn't, Detective ... Why? ... What are you implying? ... Fuck ... What ... FUCK YOU DETECTIVE ... What are you saying? ... I resent your implication. What are you—"

"I'm saying a lieutenant, who's never taken home a suspect in a murder case before, suddenly does take one home and a few hours later the suspect's found dead, hanging from a hook on a wall. That's what I'm saying, Lieutenant—So, what time did you take him back? Straightforward question. Deserves a straightforward answer, don't you think?"

I want my questions to come at him from left field. Rapid fire, so that I might hopefully catch him out or make him stumble. I also don't want him thinking he can palm me off with throwaway answers so I sit back down in the chair, reasserting my authority as an interrogator. I want him to know I'm not leaving until I obtain some answers.

"Well, it was about ... nine ... ten ... No, nine-thirty ... Yes, around nine-thirty, I think. Last night—why are you asking me these questions? ... Surely ... Surely you don't think I—"

"I'm just following where my leads are taking me, Lieutenant. Just doing my job. That's what you pay me for, isn't it? Did you take him up to his apartment? You know, when you got to South Normandie, last night. Did you go upstairs with him? To his apartment?"

"NO ... NO, "he shouts. "Not at all. I just dropped him off outside and went home—Goddammit Detective I ... I—"

"What did you say to him in the car, Lieutenant? What did you talk about?"

"We ... We talked ... about ... we just talked—goddammit, what do you—"

"About what, Lieutenant? What did you talk about? Did you tell him what you think about disgusting perverts like him? Did you convince him you'd always be watching? That he shouldn't rest for one moment, because you would be coming after him one day? Did you? ... DID YOU?"

He doesn't answer me but I see I've hit a raw nerve, so I decide to take a risk and put on more pressure.

"Did you kill him, Lieutenant? Did you string him up with that concoction of plastic ties you made for him in his fucking kitchen? Did you string him up like a chicken and push him off that fucking stool?"

The lieutenant suddenly slumps in his chair and starts to 'disappear' from me. His eyes glaze over, like they have before, only it's deeper this time. He goes pale, then softens as if he's about to unburden himself in this trance-like state.

"I ... I ... I just wanted to get to the truth," he says, almost in a whisper, as he loosens his shirt collar. I want to fetch him water but know I mustn't break the flow, so I sit tight and wait for the door to open.

"I wanted to get to the truth, that's what I was after, Detective. The truth ... But, I didn't ... I ... didn't ..."

I'm kicking myself for not having my mini-recorder with me.

"You didn't what, Lieutenant?" I ask as calmly as possible, knowing that what I really want to do is reach over and throttle an answer out of him.

"You didn't what?" I prompt again.

He doesn't answer but, gradually, I see him start to break free from his trance. He suddenly grasps where he is, what he's been doing and, more importantly, what he's been saying. A fire seems to ignite behind his eyes and I sense danger. I put my feet firmly on the floor, ready to make an escape, but he suddenly explodes and lunges at me. I manage to push my chair backwards, just in time to see his arms grasp at nothing. This doesn't stop his momentum, though, and the top half of his body pivots over the desk and he ends up somersaulting into a heap on the floor.

"YOU FUCKER!" he yells, as he scrambles to his feet. I'm standing now and I see him prepare to make a charge. I don't have enough time to open the door and escape and can only look on as he comes at me like a raging animal, propelling me into one of his filing cabinets and sending a stack of trays high into the air. The contents rain down like confetti as we grapple with each other on the floor. I smell sweat and fear all over him as I try to break free. I eventually manage to stand up, avoiding his flailing limbs as he lashes out in all directions. I can only back off towards the corner, away from the door. I manage to dodge his first two attempts to land a punch but, when I suspect his third is going to catch me, I send in a short-arm jab to his solar plexus, with maximum power. This stops him dead in his tracks, like a bull that's run into a fence post. He grunts heavily, fighting for breath, and then slowly drops to his knees, still thrashing out weakly with his arms.

Thankfully, three guys have now come into the room and restrain him. They hold on to arms and fists that are still attempting to strike out. Gradually, they calm him down and sit him in a chair.

I now have an opportunity to deliver a verbal salvo if I want to, accusing him of dereliction of duty, sending Tomkins to his death, or worse still, murdering him, but decide it's not worth it. I'll hold my counsel for the time being until I've proof to say these things with authority. Anyway, I've bigger fish to fry, I say to myself, thinking of the chief of police upstairs.

The lieutenant is starting to regain his breath.

"You fucker, Salo ... You fucker ... You're dead meat, you hear? Dead meat," he manages to say through clenched teeth and with faltering breath.

I go across and pick up the Gargailis Murder Book lying on the floor and place it down carefully on his desk.

"So you say, Lieutenant. So you say."

"Fuck off ... you ... you MOTHERFUCKER," he manages to spit out, defiantly.

To me he looks like the dejected fighter beaten to the count and is sitting in the corner of the ring waiting for his opponent to be declared the winner.

For a fleeting moment, I think I catch him searching for some meaning to all of this and, finding none, he slumps back in his chair, head held low, looking at one of the detectives groveling around his feet and picking up the paperwork now strewn across the floor.

As I come out of the tank, I think I didn't exactly obtain the confession I needed but I'm more than one step nearer the heart of what this is about.

Everything is pointing towards the Chief ... and Gargailis.

As I return to my cubicle, I'm aware of various heads looking in my direction.

There's no smirking this time. No laughter, no smiling. Suddenly, Dee walks into the squad room, quite noisily. All heads turn.

She's back from the third floor with a SOCO report in her hand. She's confronted by a wall of silence.

"What?" she eventually says to everyone in the room, as she realizes all eyes are on her.

There's a pause whilst she gathers her thoughts and then she suddenly looks at her watch.

"Hey!" she says, doing her best impression of the Fonz, with thumbs tucked into the top of her cargo pants. She gestures towards something high up on the wall.

It's the clock.

It's exactly twenty minutes past eight.

40

(Wednesday, 8.20 a.m.)

I'VE DECIDED. IT'S TIME to give Dee the full story. No edits.
The incident with the lieutenant has brought things to a
head and, much as I wish I'd handled him differently now, I know
I can't change what's happened – there's no rewind button.

I direct Dee to the Special Meetings room and start by telling
her about my fight. She sits goggle-eyed throughout, looking
at me incredulously, not saying a word. As I'm speaking, I see
colleagues in the squad room doing the same. They're not exactly
goggle-eyed but they do have that disbelieving look, as if they
can't quite understand what they've witnessed.

Two of the guys who waded in to restrain the lieutenant,
Claude Doherty and Jerry Clark, are doing the rounds of the
cubicles, revealing their part in the drama. As more colleagues
arrive, I see their version of events being replayed with increased
actions each time. I've also seen the other guy who came in to pick
up the papers, Cal Metcalfe, take the lieutenant out of the squad
room a moment ago. Metcalfe's an appeaser by instinct so I'm
hoping he'll be smoothing the way to keep this fracas between the
lieutenant and me private. It will require a formal complaint from
one of us to activate an internal investigation, so he'll be trying
to persuade the lieutenant to sit tight and not go to IAD. Once
detectives from LAPD's Internal Affairs Division stick in their
snouts, there'll be no knowing what will happen. I could probably
say goodbye to at least three days of my time, possibly more,
whilst they go through their interminably arduous procedures.
Meanwhile, my killer escapes justice because nobody's on his case.

After ten minutes, I've given Dee the unedited highlights of the fight, then I decide to move to other things, starting with the chief. I tell her about my suspicions of his involvement and about the fact he had his chauffeur tail me last night. I tell her about the Gargailis Murder Book and my trip to the archive, explaining my reasons for keeping this a secret. I also give her the low-down on my follow-up meeting with Marcia Grande. I move on to mention my phoning Father Peter at St Catherine's Cathedral and my discussions with him about John Gargailis and his family. I tell her I want to track down Detective O'Connell, to see what he might reveal about the murder case in 1993. I even tell her what I saw – or thought I saw – in the apartment from Tomkins' bay window last night.

Dee sits impassively throughout, with an open expression, keeping her eyes focused on mine, and not displaying any sign that she's critical or frustrated by my behavior on this occasion.

After I think I've come to the end of my story, I sit down, realizing it's all come out in a seemingly never-ending surge. I wonder if it's been clear enough for Dee to digest in one sitting. More importantly, I'm speculating it'll be the make-or-break moment for our partnership because I guess the involvement of senior management in all this now has increased her problems with me exponentially.

Dee maintains her silence for a few seconds and then gives me a focused stare, as if deciding what to say. But just as suddenly, she stands and goes to the window overlooking the squad room, hands dug deep into her cargo pants.

I decide to sit tight and wait for her judgment.

In the silence that follows, I reflect on what I've blurted out, realizing some parts of my story are connecting in ways I hadn't noticed before. But I keep asking myself how do the chief, the lieutenant, Tomkins, Detective O'Connell, John Gargailis and the three recent murder victims all connect? And what about Father Peter? What links all of them into this investigation?

I go to my notebook and start writing down the list of names, just as Dee comes back to the table. She lets out a long sigh as she drops into the chair. I keep my hand on the page and look at her as she reaches for a stick of gum from her top pocket.

"I can see why you've been so secretive, Oskar ... and why you've been withholding so much from me ... Yes, it does all sound, so ... far-fetched ... almost unbelievable. But after what's happened in here today with the lieutenant, I'm beginning to think anything is believable ... anything's possible. I'm just sorry I've been so untrusting of your actions."

Dee sits back and raises one of her eyebrows.

"How can I help you then ... Partner?" she says, as she starts to fold up the gum-wrapper into one of her origami animals.

I'm relieved and must be showing it, because Dee smiles back, encouragingly. However, deciding I'm up against the clock, I turn back to my notebook to complete the list of people I think are now connected to the case.

Dee suddenly laughs.

"What?" I say, without looking up.

"Nothing ... It's just that ... It's nothing ..." she chuckles.

I finish writing my list, hearing Dee walk across the room to the window. There's another laugh. I look up to see Dee is staring out across to the tank. It's still empty.

"What?" I prompt, again.

"I know your game, Oskar," she says, turning back with an even bigger smile on her face. "You thought by taking out the lieutenant you'd have a sure-fire way of delaying me getting my transfer form signed off, didn't you?" She broadens her smile, showing me even more of her perfect teeth and, with a final nod in my direction, breezes out of the room and walks towards her cubicle. "Let me know when you're ready to talk," she says over her shoulder, continuing to chuckle to herself as she goes. "I've got plenty of things to tell you."

"Let's meet in ten," I call back.

"Whatever ... When you're ready ... Partner."

*

When I return to my cubicle, I rifle through my desk drawer and look for the old LAPD internal phone directory. I brought it with me from Parker Center when we moved. I keep it hidden from view because I don't want colleagues to know I have to rely on it at times like this, especially now we've entered the high-tech world of the new PAB. When I find it, I put it on the desk and turn the pages, looking for someone in the pensions department. Pension checks are paid at the end of every month, and most ex-employees have them transferred directly to their bank accounts. Others have them mailed to wherever they might be. I decide the best person to speak to will be a middle-ranking employee, someone hopefully not too busy.

I select Delia Carmichael, Pension Assistant, at LAFPP, and direct-dial the number. I look at the clock and realize she might not be at her desk this early but she picks up after two rings.

"Good morning, Los Angeles Fire and Police Pensions, Delia speaking. How may I help you?"

As I listen, I see Dee over the top of my cubicle; she's on her phone. Treviss stands at her side. She sees me gazing across and gives me one of her quick raised-eyebrow smiles.

"Good morning Delia, this is Detective Salo from LAPD. I wonder if you can help me."

"Surely, Detective, You're my first customer of the day. What can I do for—Hey," she suddenly interrupts herself. "I've seen you in the news lately haven't I? You're the guy that's onto that serial murderer." I'm still looking at Dee and notice she's now holding up a finger and thumb, in the shape of a letter 'C.' I nod as I could really take a coffee.

"Well, Delia, you might be able to help me with that," I say, hoping her interest in the case might loosen her tongue. "I want to speak with a detective who was in charge of another case, a long while ago. He's retired now. He's not at the last known

237

address I have and I was wondering whether you would let me have his current one."

There's silence at the end of the line and I decide to wait it out, knowing it's against the rules to declare any member's contact details over the phone, without authorization. I look up and see that Dee's still in my face, holding up the middle finger of her left hand this time, with an 'up yours' expression on her face. Dee knows I usually have one sugar in my coffee but sometimes two, especially first thing in the morning when I need the sugar boost. I shake my head at Dee, still maintaining my silence with Delia.

There's silence on the phone so I decide to give Delia a prompt.

"I have 458 Bonita Street, Arcadia, but I'm not getting anything for him there."

This was the last address I had for O'Connell and I'm thinking it may still be in Delia's records. This might give her the confidence that I'm a *bona-fide* caller. I start to hear Delia tapping into her keyboard. Result.

Dee's holding up two fingers at me now, so I give her two fingers in return. We both laugh and I put my hand over the mouthpiece as I wait for Delia to respond.

"He moved from that address in ninety-six, Detective," she says, eventually. "That's all I can tell you, without getting his direct permission or authorization." It's Delia's turn to laugh now. "Well, you'll know that … surely, Dee-tec-tive," she adds, emphasizing each syllable.

"Yes, I know that Delia but I need to ascertain where he is now, that's all. It's extremely important."

"I can't tell you that, Detective. I can't reveal a member's contact details unless there's signed and sealed authorization. You knows that, an' I knows that, so why're we going through this little dance of ours?"

I'm starting to lose patience now, not so much with Delia, but with the fucking bureaucracy in this place. I know the confidentiality protocols have been designed to safeguard people's privacy but sometimes they put people's lives in mortal danger. I take a deep breath, thinking about the fish still swimming around the bait.

"Well, Delia, we're also having a little reunion in the department," I lie. "I want to invite him along. I just don't want him to miss out on this because of some silly administrative ruling."

I hear Delia working her keyboard again, so I remain silent. "Whoa. I don't think he'll be coming to your party where he's at."

"Why's that, Delia?"

"Because he's in a hospital or a home of some kind, long-term by all accounts. He's probably severely disabled or ill or something. Some hospice in the sunshine, I'd say."

I try one more push, picking up on Delia's use of the word 'sunshine'.

"Is this the one out on Venice, then?" There's a hearty laugh this time.

"Why you *are* a mighty fine detective, Detective. But you'll not get me to tell you which one … And, anyways, it's not in Venice, it's Long Beach."

I'm immediately on the internet and plug in *'list of hospitals and hospices in Long Beach'* into Google. I find out there are ten to choose from and, thinking that's close enough, I press 'print'.

"Why thank you Delia. You've been mighty helpful."

"And you've been *mighty* inquisitive, De-tec-tive." she says, laughing one more time before closing the line.

Dee arrives carrying two coffees and a pile of papers and sees me smiling as I place the phone back in its cradle. Dee straddles a chair, reminding me of the Chandler pose in that Tomkins' print, and passes across one of the cups.

"Okay, whaddaya got for me?" she asks, good-naturedly.

Now I have the location, I start by asking her to pick up the list of Long Beach hospices from the printer tray and track down O'Connell. I also ask if she'll try and obtain a status report on his health because I don't want to turn up and find he's uncommunicative or in a coma or something. Dee agrees and adds this job to her ever-growing list.

Thinking of the conspiracy angle and because of the sensitivities, I ask Dee to work quietly and look wider for connections between the three murder victims, the lieutenant and the chief. She says she recognizes the danger we're in and manages to convince me she'll take great care and not put up any red flags. The last thing we need now is to have top brass knowing we're sniffing around. Dee needs to thread her way through all of this with great care, knowing her career is on the line.

"What are you getting from the Freephone Team?" I ask next, referring to the staff members who collect information from the general public and sort the legitimate from the time wasters. Switchboards are always jammed by a mixture of would be do-gooders, out-and-out freaks seeking attention and the small percentage with something vital for us. Dee has the charm needed to keep this group of staff on board.

"Nothing interesting has turned up so far," she says. "But we're following up leads with other prostitutes who have phoned in. Treviss and I have started widening the search by going over more of the transcripts. Buttle agreed yesterday to follow up leads on the street but he's not in yet."

Dee sees my concern with Buttle's absence and rocks her head to and fro. She's weighing up the percentages, because it's a little after nine and we both know he should be here by now, but time keeping is not his strong point.

Dee turns a few pages of her notepad. "Interestingly, no one's come forward to claim the body. It's almost as if Chandler was a complete loner. No family. No friends—"

"Apart from Tomkins?"

"Yes. Apart from Tomkins ... and he's not up for that now."

"What about on the street? Any news from the usual band of informers?"

"Yesterday, Buttle and Treviss drew a blank but there's more work to do today. It also appears, from the first trawl, Chandler didn't have a pimp. I'm running that through with Buttle's help today so I'll try and find out if it's really true. He knows the streets better than most and I'll work with him on it."

It's not very common to be a prostitute and not have someone 'look after' your needs. But there are some who slip through the net. They're the ones who end up in a culvert somewhere, or a dumpster, as a warning to all prostitutes that protection is essential in their line of work. If they survive, they remain below the radar, and even LAPD doesn't hear about them. They normally have several discrete clients, like Chandler, and don't trample on the normal prostitute hangouts – hotel bars, street corners and certainly not curbsides.

Dee moves on to say she's been cataloguing Tomkins' stash of photographs, seeking to identify Chandler's group of *bespoke clients*, as she now calls them.

"As you know, in most of the photos, we don't see the clients' faces. We don't know whether they're choosing to remain anonymous or whether Chandler and Tomkins have choreographed it all secretly. Judging by what Tomkins told you, there've been a variety of scenarios. Look at this one," Dee says, opening up a cardboard folder and passing across an eight by ten glossy print.

I see that Chandler is bent over a bed and the client has entered her from behind. He's a muscular guy and I suspect, by the gold hanging off him, that he's a high roller. His face is out of frame but Chandler is looking into the lens with that mischievous grin and familiar pout.

"Maybe that face to camera was the signal to Tomkins to snap the shutter," Dee suggests.

"Have SOCOs found any evidence yet that she used these photos to blackmail clients? Anything found in the apartment?"

"Nothing yet on verbal feedback but I don't think we should rule it out. I've counted fifteen different clients in the whole collection and we think this must cover a period of many months, possibly years. Tomkins did say he'd befriended Chandler over a period of two years, didn't he?"

"You sure she didn't use wigs?"

"Don't think so. Doesn't look like it to me." I know Dee sometimes sports a hairpiece herself so I reckon she knows what she's talking about. "We've started to track down one or two of her clients and we're checking faces on the database. Nothing has shown up so far."

Dee suddenly smiles. "What?"

"Hey, we're knocking on one guy's door this afternoon ... This guy here," she says, pointing at another photograph with a clear enough headshot, making me realize Dee will derive pleasure from confronting these men with their sexual foibles.

"Treviss spotted him from the financial pages of the LA Times, of all places. He's an investment banker working out of Bunker Hill. He's flying in from Singapore today, arriving at LAX this afternoon. Buttle and I are going to surprise him after he lands and jump into his chauffeured Mercedes. He's pretty senior by all accounts ..."

Dee refers to her notes.

"It's a ... Mr. James Parnell, Vice President of the Inter-Group Bank. He'll not take this accusation lying down, I guess." Dee chuckles to herself and passes across the photograph for me to take a closer look.

I see Parnell, lying on a bed whilst Chandler straddles him She's wearing a pink cowboy hat and it looks as if she's going through an act of riding a bucking bronco. She sports a skimpy pink leather waistcoat that just about fits over her shoulders, revealing perfectly shaped silicon-enhanced breasts. She's lifted up her miniscule pink leather skirt as she 'rides' Parnell. Cowboy holsters complete the outfit and she's holding a pair of pink plastic six-shooters. Dee sees me looking closely at the guns because I think I spot smoke coming out of the barrels.

"Yeah, smoke's authentic, but the guns are fake ... You can buy them from sex shops ... Ride 'em cowboy," Dee chortles.

The more I think about this, the more I wonder if blackmail is Chandler's game. Perhaps she became too greedy with one of her rich clients. If this photograph reached the wrong hands, Parnell would almost certainly say goodbye to his long and distinguished career – and also to his wife and family.

Dee eventually stops laughing and holds up the photographs, showing me she's stacked them into two piles, one on each hand.

"With all these clients," Dee says, holding up the smaller pile, "Treviss and I reckon we might be able to identify two, possibly three of the men. Of the others," she says, holding up the larger pile now," there are no headshots but we might be able to cross reference what we have against candidates we bring in by other means. You know, at a later date. We could cross-reference birthmarks, moles and minute scars, and possibly find a match."

I think about this and wonder how such evidence might hold up in court.

"I've put this pile in priority order," Dee adds. "Those at the top have clear, distinguishing features we might be able to work with." Dee looks up and smiles broadly. "Or, you never know, I might just strike it lucky if I go hunk-hunting at one of those high-class gyms," she says, raising her eyebrows towards me. "Fat chance, huh? ... Anyways, the further down this pile we go, the harder it is to identify distinguishing features."

I take the stack from Dee and flick through. The more I look at the prints, the more I realize these are high-quality images. They do indeed reveal the tiniest skin imperfections and markings. Tomkins was clearly an excellent photographer and had all the right kit. The images are so sharp that, in some, I see the smallest of skin colorations and markings.

I notice in the first one, at the top of Dee's 'priority pile', that the guy's still wearing his watch but nothing else. It's a solid gold Daytona, because the diamonds around the dial sparkle under the room lights. I think, under greater magnification, we might persuade Rolex to identify the exact model and possibly the owner.

I look at the next one. There's an extremely fit man cavorting under Chandler – she appears to be modeling herself on Marilyn Munroe in this one. Dee moves round to take a look. "It's clear this guy works out and takes care of himself … and probably what he eats. You could griddle a burger on that belly of his."

I guess he's late forties, early fifties, but it's difficult to tell, because, with all the photographs in this stack, the headshots are missing.

I'm struggling to understand why this print is so high in Dee's priority listing and look at her for an explanation. She's smiling. I look at the print more closely and hold it under a desk light but still can't see anything that might help identify who it is. Dee leans over and points at something on his chest.

"There. Look … It's definitely a tattoo," she says. "Buttle thinks it's army work. First Gulf War. We've sent a copy to the lab for further enhancing. You never know."

I continue working my way through the pile, noticing it does indeed become more difficult the further down the stack I go.

"We're working on these today and we'll keep you posted on developments," Dee says, turning over a page in her notes.

"What's next?" I ask, wanting to keep things moving.

"Hargreaves says the white powdery substance left at the scene of Chandler's murder is sodium thiopental. This news hits me from left field and I'm not sure how to react. "Treviss and I wondered if it was used to anesthetize Chandler, because, strangely, it's the chemical used in one of the lethal cocktails in death chambers; the one injected first, to anesthetize the victim. Not easily obtainable by all accounts – Weird, huh?"

"Could it have been spilt at the scene when used to pull Chandler down?" I ask, more to myself than Dee.

"Maybe, but Emmerson might give us the heads up at eleven, when we go across for the cut."

I'm not concentrating because I'm still thinking about the powder. The fact it's one of the constituent parts of a lethal injection surprises me. Could this be another link to Gargailis? He was, after all, sentenced to death by lethal injection.

I look up to see Dee scouring her list again and, thinking our meeting's about to end, I look at the clock. I suddenly realize that time is pressing and I need to organize things if I'm to extend my trip this afternoon. I know I haven't confided with anyone about what I plan to do overnight because I think the fewer people who know the better. I've been considering how the killer seems to know in advance what I'm about to do, and wonder whether information is leaking out somehow. The evidence for this is thin, I know, but I'm afraid to voice these concerns in case my team start thinking I'm paranoid. After everything that's happened lately, especially with sightings of the 'wraith' last night, I can't help wondering if it's true anyway.

"Let me have the name of the hospice in Long Beach as soon as you can, won't you?" I ask Dee, anxious to have that part of the trip inked into my schedule.

"Yeah. Sure thing. Shouldn't take long," Dee says, continuing to leaf through her notes. Finding nothing, she looks up and drains her coffee cup, preparing to move off.

I look across to Buttle's cubicle. He's still not in and I suddenly remember our meeting.

"Shit. I'm down to meet up with him this afternoon ... At Billy's ... For lunch," I say, raising my eyebrows. "I want to see if I can get more out of him about the Gargailis case. See what he remembers. Son-of-a-bitch ... You know, I did think he'd be in today, having seen him knuckle down yesterday."

I look up to see Dee standing with her stack of papers tucked under her arm but observe she's holding my eyes over something else.

"What?" I ask, as I stand up and grab my sport coat.

"Your coffee."

"My coffee?"

"Yes, your coffee ... You haven't drunk any of it."

I look at my cup and it's still full to the brim. I take a sip. It's no longer hot but I take it with me as I head for the door, checking my pockets as I go. Dee will think I'm stepping outside for a smoke but it's not my cigarettes I'm feeling for. It's my cell phone.

I need to finalize my plans.

41

(Wednesday, 10.56 a.m.)

WHILST DEE AND I finish gowning up in an anteroom, we hear the rasping orders of Emmerson from the autopsy suite next door. When we're ready, we pull up our facemasks in unison and enter through the swing doors. We find him standing there, with his assistant, checking the tools of his trade. The lights are on and he's ready-to-go.

"Good morning, Detectives," he says, without looking up in our direction. "Fine morning for cutting up the dead, don't you think?" It's said as a question but he's not expecting an answer. "I was just saying to my assistant here that you're possibly going to like this one." Emmerson lets his eyes travel across to Dee for a second before returning them to the table. "Although she's ripe, the smell's only rank enough to be considered really grim on my sliding scale from bad to disgusting."

This is Dee's seventh autopsy and I know he remembers the difficulties she's had standing on her feet in the past so his little joke is directed at her.

I believe the smell of dead bodies permeates the fabric of this building and I've often wondered how long it would take for it to leave. I suspect the rank smell would remain, indelibly soaked into the brickwork.

I once worked with a partner who'd convinced me smells are made up of particulates, *'You're breathing these sons-of-bitches,'* he'd often say.

Jane Chandler's body is lying on Emmerson's slab.

It's a slanted, aluminum table with raised sides and has several faucets and drains around the edge. These allow blood and body fluids to drain away during the examination.

The body is face up on the table and a black body block has been placed under the back. This lifts up the rib cage to make the opening of the chest cavity much easier. This also gives the body its macabre look because the victim's large breasts appear to be projecting upwards, quite unnaturally. Emmerson sees me looking and he points to them with the back of a gloved hand.

"Plastic," he says, in his usual matter-of-fact manner.

He looks across at Dee and I see him consider whether to say something else. Both lock eyes for a second. I suspect Emmerson's thinking twice before making his usual reference to this particular victim's 'tools of the trade', as he's called prostitute's silicone implants in the past.

Before starting, Emmerson brings us up to speed on the forensic examination of the victim's clothing – this had been done after the body had been removed from the body bag. He holds up the results on the white substance found at the scene. He'll know I've been informed it was sodium thiopental.

"Toxic stuff. $C_{11}H_{17}N_2NaO_2S$," he quotes. "It causes unconsciousness in thirty seconds if administered intravenously. We'll know if this was the case when the bloods come back."

As Dee walks across to watch Emmerson's assistant lay out more sterilized equipment, Emmerson says quietly that he does have the toxicology results on the substances found under the victim's fingernails. As he says this, he gives me an almost secret cue to look at the nails.

I look down and see Chandler's once carefully manicured fingernails are broken in places. They're damaged in the ways I remember when Emmerson and I crouched next to the body in the early hours of Sunday morning. I look at him, wondering what he particularly wants me to see.

"I'll get to that later," he says, quietly – almost melodramatically building the suspense.

Of course, Dee and I hope what was found under the nails will represent a substantial find, and Emmerson knows this, but it looks as if he wants to be theatrical this morning. For extra effect, he leans across and says he wants to speak to me in private after we've finished up here. Unfortunately, Dee hears him and gives Emmerson one of her *up yours* looks. I'm concerned he's seen this and will shut up shop completely, leaving us to await his report through official channels. That's the last thing I need now, Emmerson in a temperamental huff and Dee retiring to the sidelines with injured pride.

Luckily, it seems, Emmerson hasn't seen anything and, with a slight 'well-here-we-go' rocking of his head, he taps the microphone hanging from the ceiling.

"Testing … Testing … One … Two … Testing," he says, standing on tiptoe and speaking rather too loudly, as if the recording equipment was built in the nineteen-fifties. Satisfied, if for no other reason than he has the full attention of everyone, he makes a start.

He details the date and time and lists those present, using official titles and full names. He goes on to list basic information about the victim. As he talks, I stare at the battered body and think through the sorry end to Chandler's life. But, strange as it may seem, in this state of death she's more alive to me than at any previous stage of the investigation, because her body is about to reveal the secrets which led to her demise.

As I consider the violence of her death, I wonder again why Tomkins didn't hear the sounds of her being attacked in the room, because the wounds look deep and vicious – barbaric even. I remember Tomkins saying he could hear Chandler walk across the floor above, so why not the sounds of her being beaten to death?

Emmerson starts by examining the external wounds. He does this slowly and methodically, measuring the depth of the cuts and the knife's direction. This takes a great deal of time, as he maps them out on a chart with his assistant. There are over forty knife wounds and each one is documented with precision and in a manner of care poignantly in contrast to the frenzy with which they had been delivered.

Whilst he's doing this, I find my eyes traveling back to the victim's fingernails. I wonder what's so special about the damage to make Emmerson signal it the way he did. To my eye, they look to be the defensive wounds of someone seeking to fight off her attacker. Emmerson sees me doing this and holds up his left hand momentarily, wiggling his middle finger.

I move in close and inspect the victim's left hand. The nail on the middle finger is broken in places, like most of the other fingernails on this hand but, on this finger, there's a section not broken away fully left hanging. I look even closer and see a pattern of striation markings and indentations left in the bright red nail lacquer. Is this what all the fuss is about? I look across to Emmerson for an answer but he's too busy completing his inspection of the wounds. I shift uncomfortably on my feet and look at the clock, feeling impatience creep over me.

"If you are going to want me to testify in court and explain my findings, I have to get this bit right and not rush it," Emmerson says, as if reading my mind. "You won't want me to do a 'Kesner' ... will you, dear boy?"

I know what he's referring to.

In 1997 Professor Kesner, one of Emmerson's eminent predecessors, went horribly wrong with an autopsy. The prosecution's case fell apart in front of the jury and the defendant slipped through the net. We had a multiple shooter situation where it became impossible to state categorically which bullet came from which gun. Kesner had done a sloppy job in identifying particular wounds with a particular slug from a particular gun. In the end, the case was thrown out. In his chambers, Judge Andrews referred to it as the 'Leaky Sieve' case because there were so many holes in the victims and so many holes in the medical examiner's evidence. The killer walked free after seven years on good behavior, having received the lesser conviction of actual bodily harm.

After an hour, Emmerson begins his internal examination. He opens the body with a large Y-shaped incision that curves around the bottom of the breasts before meeting at the breastbone.

Over time, I've learned to appreciate Emmerson's craft and see he still has the eye to make incisions with the skill and care he's always said dead bodies deserve. He's neither flippant nor disrespectful about the dead, unlike many of his younger subordinates. I heard him say once, *'It's only a body I grant you, and the spirit's gone, but it still deserves respect'.*

Once he's completed the incision, he takes a scalpel, checks it for sharpness, and uses it to peel back the skin, muscle and soft tissue. The chest flap is then pulled up over the face, exposing the rib cage and neck muscles.

"Pruning shears please," Emmerson barks to his assistant, who passes across what looks to be a large pair of red-handled garden shears.

"I got these last Christmas from my wife," he states, straight-forwardly. "But I didn't have the heart to tell her what I wanted them for. Did you know you can pay over six hundred dollars for shears from official hospital suppliers? My budget's been cut so much I went down this route instead. Works perfectly."

He makes a start on cutting through the rib cage.

"She bought them from a garden-store catalogue," he explains, pausing between each cut. "They cost twenty-five dollars the pair. Not a … bad price if you ask me. What say you, Oskar. What say you? That's what caught my attention … the price!"

Emmerson's exertions are etched into his brow as he cuts – and puffs – his way through the rib cage. His attendant stands nearby, ready to wipe the moisture away from his eyes with a towel.

"The long handles, you see," he continues. "They give me the … leverage I need at my grand age … There, that's that," he says, as he completes the final cut on one side and moves across to the other.

When he's finished cutting, he passes the shears to his attendant and dissects the tissue behind the rib cage. He does this delicately with a small scalpel. Then he lifts the rib cage out of the body, passing it to his assistant in a well-practiced maneuver.

"Ah, the engine room," he announces with relish as he looks into the cavity. "It's what's under the hood that interests me, Oskar," he chortles. "Like my Jaguar."

With the organs exposed, Emmerson makes a series of cuts to detach larynx, esophagus, ligaments and arteries. He separates these from the spinal cord and then from the bladder and rectum. Whilst doing this, he makes sure his assistant is close by. I'm not sure how junior he is but Emmerson identifies every organ, so I suspect he's another new intern, eager to be involved.

Once Emmerson's happy all has been done to his satisfaction, he lifts out the entire set of organs in one piece and takes it across to another work surface. "Now it's your turn to frigging well do something," he says towards his assistant. Emmerson directs the detailed examination of various organs, letting his assistant do much of the work under his direction.

Whilst this is happening, I see Dee lean back against another table, looking dejected, almost pan faced, with her arms folded. I suspect she's having difficulty standing, watching this gory drama unfold.

"Still with us?" I ask quietly, making sure I'm out of earshot of Emmerson. Dee just shrugs and looks up at the clock.

"That's been one hour forty minutes we've been here. I just want to get on now, Oskar. And, anyway, you've got your Old Boys' Club meeting afterwards, haven't you?" I realize what's eating her. "I suggest I get away as soon as I can so that I leave you to wrap things up with your private meeting. What say you, Oskar?" Dee says, a little too loudly for my liking.

"Look, keep your voice down. You know what he's like and you've seen the mood he's in. He obviously thinks it's important so I'll get what I can out of him and phone you back immediately." I lean in close. "What say you, Dee? What say you?" I whisper in her ear. Dee gives me one of her half-smiles and I move back to the table hoping she's placated enough to bide her time – and bite her tongue.

For the next twenty minutes, various organs are examined and weighed and, sometimes, tissue samples are taken in the form of slices so they can be viewed under a microscope later. I can only watch and admire the skills on display.

Emmerson then opens up the stomach and starts examining and weighing the contents. "This can sometimes be extremely helpful in figuring out the exact T.O.D., but it'll take a day or two, I'm afraid," Emmerson says, looking in my direction. I nod, letting him know I can wait for his official time-of-death window. Seemingly satisfied I'm not chasing him, he removes the body block from the victim's back, putting it behind her neck like a pillow. This action lifts up the head.

"Let's get to the hard disk no, shall we?" Emmerson suggests, brushing the skull lightly with the handle of the scalpel.

Leaning over, he makes a cut from behind one ear to the other, taking a path across the forehead. He then makes a second cut around the back of the head, completing the circumnavigation. The cut is divided and, with a look towards his assistant, he pulls away the scalp from the skull in two flaps. One goes over the face and the other over the back of the neck. Satisfied, Emmerson reaches for an electric oscillating saw and starts to cut through the skull, making sure his assistant is by his side, watching his every move.

"I prefer the Stryker. Always have. Always will," he bellows to no one in particular, above the whine of the electric motor.

Once he's made the cut to the depth needed, he removes the top of the skull, revealing the brain. He takes his time, delicately severing the brain's connection to the spinal cord. When he's satisfied, he lifts it out, placing it in a tray supplied by his assistant, on cue.

All the time, Emmerson talks into the microphone, detailing the color and state of the brain's condition.

I look at my watch and realize Dee and I have been here for two hours.

"Am I detaining you, Oskar?" Emmerson asks, ever watchful of what's going on around him. "Nearly finished. Give me five minutes. Max. Promise. Then you and I can have our ... little *tête-à-tête*, eh?" I see him take a look towards Dee, who's backed off to the other side of the room.

"Still on her feet, then ... We're winning. No puke this time, eh?" he chortles, as he indicates to me with his head to look at Dee. I see Dee's sneaked out her cell phone from her pocket and is taking an illicit peak for missed calls and texts.

Emmerson looks between Dee, his assistant and then me.

"They all get there in the end, don't they ... What say you, Oskar ... What say you?"

*

I notice a faint smell of smoke as I enter Emmerson's office and think he's had a quick cigarette whilst I've walked Dee to her car. As I move towards the chair at his desk, Emmerson smiles, waiting for me to sit down and listen to what he has to say.

His desk is a clutter of papers and books and a Scottish tweed jacket is lying over a stack of filing trays and oddments at the far end.

"I don't like this one bit, Oskar," he says by way of making a start. "The whole thing feels wrong. That's why I wanted to speak with you privately. I don't want to set hounds running in the wrong direction at this stage so I apologize if it's caused awkwardness between you and your partner. That's not my intention, I assure you."

Emmerson pauses, sitting back in his chair, looking as though he's trying to find the right words. I remain silent and wait.

"You and I have worked together for nineteen years and we've always trusted each other ... I've counted, by the way. Between 1995 and now we've put nearly seventeen killers away. And I have the greatest respect for the way you've fought tirelessly for the victims. On each and every occasion, Oskar. I really have."

I've had my fill of colleagues pouring out their souls to me lately and I'm starting to wonder where Emmerson's little speech is going.

"When I saw the victim's fingernails on Sunday, in her apartment, I could tell something wasn't right. You'll remember, Oskar. I didn't say anything at the time because I wanted to study her hands carefully, *more* carefully, under my arc lights as it were. And ... I'm still not sure. That's why I want to talk it through with you now. So that you can use your professional judgment accordingly and decide how best to take my anxieties forward into your investigation."

Emmerson's making sure we have his concerns in perspective. These are his 'undocumented', professional concerns so he'll not want me quoting anything that'll be said in here today. That's why he's taking his time to make sure I agree. And more importantly, from a professional rapport point of view, he's ensuring I understand his dilemma. He has his reputation to preserve but he clearly wants to maintain our friendship and help me with my investigation.

"I even brought two of my colleagues into this – confidentially, so to speak," he continues. "You'll know Davis and Serestone. I admire them both tremendously. They didn't see anything untoward ... still don't. But I did ... and still do. They're not convinced that's why I have to find more evidence to back up my hunch if I'm to report it officially." Emmerson sits up higher in his chair now. "You see, I suspect the victim's fingernails were not broken by the act of clawing at the clothing and skin of her attacker, as we first imagined."

I remember seeing Chandler's hands in her apartment on Sunday morning. It seemed as though the fingernails had been cracked and broken from her violent struggle to fend off her attacker. Perhaps this is the reason Tomkins didn't hear a struggle. Maybe she had been brought down by the sodium thiopental and the nails were broken in some other way. On purpose by the killer. As a distraction.

"If the victim had done this herself," Emmerson continues, "the pattern of cracking and breaking of nails would have been quite different, in my view. There would have been indications of multiple attempts to strike out. They're not there in my view, Oskar."

He's still attempting to emphasize this is an opinion and not a fact. "There would have been more evidence of nails bending and more minute samples of material fiber and skin trapped in the small cracks and serrations at the ends. That's what I'd expect to see. Damage caused by her continual clawing at the murderer and his clothing over the prolonged period of the struggle, for example."

Emmerson leans forward.

"Look, based on other murder victims I've examined over my career, the actual amounts of stuff I found under this victim's fingernails suggest there must have been a prolonged struggle ... Okay? ... probably several minutes in length. But the damage to the nails doesn't suggest that – let me explain."

He stands up and goes across to his jacket, lifting it up and revealing what looks to be the mummified remains of a severed arm. He takes out a Leatherman multi-tool from one of his overfilled pockets and places the jacket back down over the arm, before returning to his chair.

"I began to look further. To look for signs of what had actually broken the fingernails. You know, to consider if the damage had been done by some action other than defensive clawing at the murderer."

He holds up his Leatherman, rather in the way he holds up his tools in the autopsy suite before starting a procedure.

"On one finger, I found evidence the nail had possibly been gripped by a vice-like tool of some kind."

I see him open up the multi-tool and I've already started to guess where this is going.

"I found one or two markings that were possibly made by something like this. Particularly on the nail of victim's—"

"Middle finger of the left hand," I say, interrupting his flow.

"Yes, the middle finger of the left hand," he repeats, as he continues to assemble something from his multi-tool. "I'm getting one of Hargreaves' boys to check whether any other nail fragments have been found at the scene, so that a check can be made against these pieces as well."

Emmerson holds up a small pair of miniature pliers, triumphantly, and places one of his own fingernails in the tool's jaws. He squeezes the handles for a few seconds before releasing his grip. He surveys the damage to his own nail and smiles, leaning forward and showing me the small pattern of indentations left on the surface of his nail by the serrations of the teeth. They definitely look similar to the markings I saw on nail hanging off the end of Chandler's middle finger in the autopsy suite.

I nod towards Emmerson, letting him know I'm following his thesis.

"Now, moving to the fabric and tissue samples I found trapped underneath the fingernails," he continues, as he closes up the pliers and starts opening up another tool on his Leatherman. "I'm also surmising that substances we found under her fingernails have been rammed down using a blunt instrument of some kind … Something like this." It's a small screwdriver blade this time. He reaches across and picks up a small petri dish containing pieces of brown wool. "I scraped this little lot off my jacket this morning; I used the saw-blade gadget on this contraption," he explains – as if this would be the normal thing to do to a very expensive Scottish Tweed jacket – and he starts to push small pieces of the wool down behind one of his own fingernails.

I see where this is leading and realize how crucial Emmerson's demonstration might be later on.

"There are further tests I am undertaking and more research I need to do to confirm all this but I thought it only fair to bring it to your attention now. And, hopefully, before you go running off in all directions, it might help you to focus any hypotheses you're forming."

I nod in his direction again and notice he's nodding in mine. This is the sign we're agreeing to move on with our respective jobs, knowing we're both honoring each other's ways of doing things.

42

(Wednesday, 1.57 p.m.)

THE EXPLOSION ROCKS THE early afternoon air as I make my way into the PAB from the smoking shelter. The boom is deafening and I feel the shock wave push me sideways, enabling me to work out where it's come from. It's the underground car park.

I'm the first to arrive on the scene and it doesn't take long to work out what's happened. The fireball has been of such intensity it's started to melt a car in one of the bays, making it almost unrecognizable. But I know what car it is. It's the lieutenant's Oldsmobile, parked up in its usual spot.

A fire is raging and cars either side are beginning to catch alight. Other people arrive and someone starts shouting to me to keep away, fearing other petrol tanks might explode. As I pull back, feeling the acrid air penetrate my lungs, I see the charred remains of the lieutenant through the flames, sitting in the driver's seat. I know it's him because I see the familiar shape of his skull and that solid jaw under the scorched and now blackened skin.

Near the car, I see something lying on the concrete surface and it takes me a moment to comprehend what it is. But, as recognition starts to descend like a lead weight, a feeling of horror grips me. It's a gun, a Beretta, and I suspect it's an ex-issue LAPD gun. As I stand and stare, I feel my arm tugged by someone attempting to pull me back to the safety of the stairwell. But I'm rooted to the spot, unable to move, with Dee's words ringing in my ears – 'Oskar. It's personal' – because I'm thinking the gun will prove to be mine. The spare gun I keep in my desk drawer at home. The gun

I'd managed to keep, back in the nineties, when the department switched to Glocks, following safety scares.

In the mayhem, I hear the sound of approaching fire trucks and, as I make my way up the stairs, two more petrol tanks explode in quick succession. Panic ensues and people make their way even faster towards the exits.

Instead of following others out into the street, I go straight across to the PAB and climb the back stairs, two at a time. I pass many colleagues who come rushing past in the opposite direction and I ignore fire warden colleagues, in yellow bibs, telling me to clear the premises. When I reach the sixth floor I burst through the swing doors, out of breath, and find the squad room completely empty. Everyone has left. All I hear is the fire alarm whining its dramatic message and the *whop, whop,* of a media helicopter outside the window, broadcasting live images of this drama into people's homes.

Not really knowing what danger I'm in, I rehearse in my mind how I'll evacuate the building, deciding the best way out of here will be down the back stairs. It will lead onto a less exposed area, away from the prying eyes of IAD. No doubt their tails will be wagging if they've already heard about the lieutenant and me sparring up with each other this morning. But, when it's reported that I was in the underground car park, immediately after the explosion, they'll want to sink their teeth straight into my ass. How long it will take to tie me to that 'company' gun is anyone's guess. Therefore, I want to slip away unseen, not because I don't want to assist, but because I don't want to be drawn into giving evidence at this stage. I need to maintain momentum because this killer's doing a good job of slowing me down. And, most alarmingly, he's attempting to implicate me in the horror that's just unfolded.

I go straight to the tank and stand at the glass, looking inside for any sign that might lead to an understanding of why the lieutenant would end up being fried. I don't yet know what I'm looking for, so I let my eyes scan the full extent of the room, almost instinctively. I notice his jacket is gone. I don't even know if the lieutenant came back in here today, after our fight, but I suspect he did because everything is tidied away, just as he liked.

I survey the desk and see a single sheet of paper on his blotter. I look over my shoulder and check again that no one is here and then slip on a latex glove and grab hold of the handle, trying to open the door. It's locked. I take out my set of picks and have it open in thirty seconds. I go straight to the desk, making sure I don't touch anything along the way and read from the sheet:

> "One life is all we have. We live it as we believe in living it, but to sacrifice what you are and to live without belief, that is a fate more terrible than dying."

It's printed on our standard white copier paper. There's no signature and nothing to suggest it's a suicide note but I notice it's enclosed in speech marks, as if it's a quote. It's not written in the style of anything I've heard the lieutenant say to me before and I wonder if it ties directly to the lieutenant's inner turmoil.

I'm brought out of my musing by the smell of burnt fuel and a hint of smoke in the air and I suspect the fire is taking hold downstairs. I realize I need to escape from the building so I move out of the lieutenant's office, relocking the door as I go.

As I make my way across to my cubicle, to collect the things I'll need for the next couple of days, my cell phone chirrups. It's a text from Buttle, letting me know he can still meet me as arranged in Billy's if I want to. In the melee and drama of the incident, I'd forgotten about our arrangement. I check my watch and work out I can be there in ten minutes.

Just as I'm about to head off, I realize I'm not alone because I suddenly hear rasping sounds of heavy breathing. I turn to see a six-foot-eight man come through the doorway, wielding an axe. My heart starts thumping at the sight of this giant bearing down on me. My fight or flight options shuttle their way through my head, instinctively, and I brace myself for a decision, feeling my hand go to my gun in its holster.

I suddenly realize he's wearing full body protective gear, including a full-face visor. I work out the reason I can hear his breathing is that he's inhaling and exhaling compressed air from bottles strapped to his back.

"Leave the building, now, sir," he says with urgency, through the din, as he stomps his way towards me. He's a fire officer and he's not taking 'No' for an answer.

I let out an audible sigh of relief, release the hand from my gun and place it on my chest, slipping down in my chair in the process. For some unexplainable reason, I'm reminded of Dee's legendary prank when she crept up on an unsuspecting male colleague and made heavy-breathing Darth Vader noises behind him. It frightened him so much that he fell off his chair.

"Leave now—Sir—Please," the fire officer orders, clearly perturbed by my inaction. He points his axe towards the exit. "Now—Sir—Please," he repeats.

Thankful he's not my killer, I nod my agreement, equally assertively, and make my way out through the swing doors with my things.

43

(Wednesday, 2.30 p.m.)

I STILL HAVE THE smell of gasoline-induced smoke in my nostrils as I go across the street to meet Buttle. As I pass numerous fire trucks along the curb, I hear fire officers shout they have everything under control in the underground car park. I see smoke still billowing out from the entrance and exits, although it's less intense now. It is clear the casualty list could have been higher. Much higher.

On my way down the back stairs just now, I'd shuffled through an array of scenarios to explain the devastation I'd found but none left me confident I'm on the right track. Yes, I'm shocked and stunned by what's happened but my innermost fear is that, if the lieutenant's death is declared a suicide, I'm the one responsible. But, if it's a murder, and that's my illicit Beretta on the floor down there, someone's out to implicate me in his death. Big time.

The nearer I get to Billy's, the more I try to shift my mind from dark thoughts and concentrate on the task at hand. I hope Buttle will recall things from 1993 that will give me something to work on.

As I enter, my thoughts are drowned out by a wall of sound coming from LAPD staff congregating in here rather than out on the sidewalk. They're either waiting for the all-clear signal to go back inside or to hear the news that they can go home. Most are at fever pitch about what's happened on their watch and, literally, *'under their feet'*. I even hear talk of a terrorist bomb plot as I pass between the tables. A few are sitting quietly, almost somber, no doubt surmising that they're the lucky ones to have come out alive. One or two are craning their necks at the windows, giving updates on what's happening outside, despite the fact a large-screen TV on one of the walls is blasting out live coverage. I also hear the incessant sound of the news chopper, still in the sky, adding even more drama to the whole shebang. And, of course, for everyone crammed in here, are always the traumatic memories of 9/11 to feed imaginations.

I look for Buttle in the melee but try not to make a meal of it. Until I know the score on a few things, I want to maintain as low a profile as possible. I expect to find him propping up the bar but can't see him at all, so I take a quick look at my cell phone, thinking he might have texted again. There's nothing. Perhaps he's out looking at the show, live.

I perch on the one remaining stool underneath a TV screen at the far end of the bar. I manage to catch the attention of Alonzo and order a coffee. Waiting for it to arrive, I scour the full extent of the room in the mirrored glass behind the bar, finally deciding Buttle's not here, despite his assurances ten minutes ago that he would be. I immediately punch in his number on my phone, deciding to have it out with him, once and for all. I really thought he'd buried all that grief he said had troubled our relationship in the past. The phone trips to message and I hang up, laying down the phone with a crash. Breathing deeply, trying to stem the anger building inside, I attempt to work out what I should do next. I look at the large clock on the wall and wonder if Buttle has been and gone; I *am* twenty minutes late. As Alonzo puts down my coffee, I have an idea. I slide across a ten-dollar bill, indicating I want to pay for my tab straightaway, but also offer to buy him a drink. "Seen Buttle today?" I ask, as he turns for the till. He just shrugs before continuing on his way to the till, scrunching the ten-dollar bill in his hand.

The unwritten rule in Billy's is that staff will never give the whereabouts of regulars – whoever's doing the asking. Alonzo's annoyed I've put him in the difficult position of offering him a drink first and then asking him that question.

"I haven't seen him in weeks. Nobody has," he says, as he returns with my change. He leans in closer. "But you're not the first person to ask for him today. A guy came in earlier ... Never seen him before ... Just walked in, like you, asks for a drink and puts a twenty on the deck and says, 'Where's Buttle?' I said I didn't know who he was and pushed the bill straight back in his direction ... The sucker just picked it up and walked straight back out. No drink. Nothing."

Thinking he's said enough, Alonzo walks back down the bar to serve another customer, leaving me with an alarm bell ringing inside my head. After what's happened to the lieutenant, I'm suddenly feeling concerned for Buttle. Just as I start considering whether I should ask Cerillo to tease a sketch of this guy out of Alonzo, my concentration is broken by a sarcastic whooping coming from the window. I turn to see someone telling the crowd that the main doors to the PAB have been reopened and everyone can file back inside. There's a mixed chorus of boos and cheers from different groupings around the room. Some people stand up immediately, wanting to return to work straightaway, others turn their attention to Alonzo, hoping there's time for one more drink before they set off. I decide to finish my coffee and stay here to see if Buttle turns up after all.

Whilst waiting, I take out my notebook and start considering my questions for O'Connell later. Suddenly, thinking about Buttle's statement which took me off on this tangent in the first place, I realize my main question for O'Connell will be, 'What was going down?' I just want to know what made Gargailis suddenly confess to a murder I'm sure he didn't commit. O'Connell must have been the closest person to that decision, apart from Gargailis himself.

After five minutes, I close my notebook and finish my coffee, taking one last look for Buttle. He's nowhere to be seen amongst the surreal mix of hardened afternoon drinkers. Most look grateful to have the bar back to themselves. This includes one of the regulars, a timeworn old soak I've known for years, known as Barney. He's sitting on the stool next to me. He's managed to find the TV remote and he's switching channels on the screen above my head. He brings up a program showing the magician, David Copperfield, undertaking his famous illusion with the Statue of Liberty. I have to smile at the incongruity. Dee mentions it one day and it turns up on the TV the next, just because some drunk decides to switch channels. I wonder if Sam's lecture on synchronicity is now credible. I can't help but be drawn to watch it.

The audience, suited-and-booted, is positioned in regular theatre-style seating, looking out through a large opened curtain, across the water, to the Statue of Liberty beyond. Searchlights illuminate the night sky, there's even a helicopter to add a touch of reality to the whole scene. The curtains are closed, removing the Statue from view. Then, moments later, the curtain re-opens to show that the Statue has 'disappeared'. We hear the audience cheer with delight and then we see David Copperfield – with that ridiculous eighties hairstyle of his standing in front of his delighted audience, receiving applause.

Barney gives a sarcastic chuckle and I turn to look into his rheumy eyes.

"The fucker's made us look the other way, that's all," he says, to no one in particular.

I think on this and realize what Barney's saying is right, but I'm not thinking about the Statue.

A charge of electricity races up my spine as I reach for my phone, punching in a number on speed dial.

"The fucker's made us look the other way," I'm saying to myself, as Dee picks up.

"What?" she exclaims.

"Meet me in South Normandie, just down from the junction that's near to Tomkins' apartment," I say.

"When?" she asks. "Now!"

*

I'm in good time and see Dee parked twenty yards from the junction. I pull up behind and alight from my Caprice, expecting Dee to do the same, but she doesn't. She stays put. I go and look in through the driver's side window, assessing the lie of the land. Dee's looking straight ahead, finishing off a cigarette. She looks pale and a bit scared. Sensing this might be another of our make-or-break situations, I tap on the glass.

"Hey, come on, Dee. Trust me on this, will you? We have to maintain momentum. I know what I'm doing—"

Dee looks across and slides down the window, taking her last pull on her cigarette.

"It's not that!" she interrupts, as she tosses the butt onto the sidewalk and starts to collect her jacket and cell phone as if she's about to join me. But she still stays put. Thinking there's more to come, I ease back from the window, to wait her out. After a moment, she looks up before returning her gaze out of the windshield.

"It's just that our lieutenant's got himself fried and you're carrying on as if nothing's happened ... I don't get it, Oskar. You said nothing about it on the phone earlier. Just to meet you here ... And now ... Well ... I don't get it."

What Dee's really saying is, 'I don't get you'

I've experienced the death of a colleague before but Dee hasn't. I know what a difficult lesson it is to learn. If any detective becomes distracted by it, no matter how awful and tragic the circumstances, they can drop into a black hole of despair themselves. I guess Dee's teetering on the edge of that hole right now. Trying to decide whether to carry on living with the fear that someday she might end up being a victim like the lieutenant, or whether she'll leave now and open that boutique on Venice Beach.

I smile as warmly as I can, and take another step back, giving her space to work it out for herself.

Eventually, she looks up, having made her decision. Thankfully, I see that Venice Beach has been put on hold. For the time being, anyway.

I raise my eyebrows and walk back towards my Caprice, moving round to the trunk. As I open and look inside, I hear Dee emerge from her car. I turn around to face her. I'm holding up a crowbar in one hand and two bagged-up pairs of leather work-gloves and a couple of head-torches in the other.

"We're goin' prospectin' ... Part-ner," I say, with my best hillbilly accent.

Dee's smiling but I see she's trying to work out what we're about to do. I maintain the suspense a little longer by going across to the junction, saying nothing. I see the fresh tire marks on the street, remembering the early hours of the morning when I watched Emmerson career his Jaguar around this very corner. I move in tight to the wall and peer down South Normandie. I see Tomkins' bay window in the distance. Cars are parked on both sides of the street, and I think we can gain cover.

I glance over my shoulder to see Dee still standing by her Caprice.

She's smiling, still rooted to the spot.

Thinking on my feet, I turn around quickly and throw her a bag of gloves. Dee catches in one movement and holds it up triumphantly, as if she's just won the game for the Dodgers. I take this as a good sign and hope we're back on track again.

As she joins me at the corner, I explain what we're about to do. When I tell her where we're going, a smile of recognition lights up her face. She reaches into her jacket pocket and asks me to hold out my hand. Then, almost ceremonially, she lays down a set of keys in my outstretched palm. I can't work out why she's done this and look up into her smiling face

"Treviss got these from the agents. They're the keys to the three apartments in the vicinity that are being let. The ones we hadn't visited or searched following the trawl of apartments on Sunday morning. This had been on my to do list before you bust your way in to one of them yesterday."

I suddenly wonder if my 'wraith' had done exactly the same thing. Perhaps he obtained a duplicate set cut from the same keys

I'm holding now. Another charge of electricity races down my spine and, with a quick nod towards Dee, we make our way down South Normandie, using parked vehicles as a screen. As arranged, we talk as we walk, hoping not to draw attention to ourselves.

"The fucker's just made us look the other way," I suddenly say at one point, more to myself than to Dee.

"What?" Dee exclaims, as we shield ourselves from view behind a parked van.

"Nothing ... it's just good to have you on board again," I say in return, looking at Dee's confused expression.

"Okay, Sherlock, tell me once again why're we here?" she asks, infuriatingly over my shoulder as I begin to peer around the back of the van. I'm already planning our next move so I put my finger to my lips and, with another quick glance up to Tomkins' bay window, I make my way across the street and up the front steps to the apartment block opposite.

I push the front door, hoping it's still open, but it isn't this time, and wonder if the killer left it off the latch on purpose the last night. It takes me a few attempts to find the right key on the fob but I soon open up and we enter the lobby. With a quick nod towards Dee, I make my way up the stairs with Dee following. We reach the second floor landing and, although it's quite dark along the corridor, I can see the apartment I'm looking for.

"Well? You haven't answered my question, Sher-lock. What is it you're hoping to find?" Dee whispers as we get to the door.

"Same old, same old ..." I whisper back, attempting to keep things light-hearted, but recognizing she's starting to bug me with her persistent questioning. "I'm looking for evidence the killer holed himself up here before the Chandler killing, and possibly after ... That's why we're here ... Wat-son."

"But what exactly are you expecting us to find? What is this really about?"

I've had enough of her skepticism so I ignore her question and cross to the other side of the door, ducking under the spy hole as I go. I turn to face Dee and put a finger to my lips. I take my gun from its holster and put my ear to the door, listening intently. Thankfully, Dee picks up on this and takes up the same position. I check she's ready, press the doorbell and wait. There's nothing. I try one more time, looking through the letterbox. Still nothing. I use another key from the set and unlock the door. And, with one final look at Dee, I push it open and enter the apartment, gun out front. Dee follows and we spread out, as trained.

"It's the police," I announce. "Please make yourself known." The only sounds I hear are the faint noises of cars passing along the street outside.

Everything appears as it was when we were here in the early hours of this morning. I make my way down the hallway, taking care to cover myself with my gun. Although Dee probably thinks I'm overplaying this maneuver, I see her doing the same – noticing that training can sometimes overcome intuition. Although we've telegraphed we're here, I give hand signals to Dee for us to sweep the apartment in formation. We go from room to room, checking cupboards and wardrobes and any spaces where someone could be hiding. We finally reach the main living room, the one directly opposite Tomkins' apartment. It doesn't take us long to work out it's empty.

I turn and look at Dee as we return our guns to our holsters. Dee's looking piqued and frustrated and doesn't mind showing it.

"Come on, Oskar. What were you hoping to find?" she asks, more petulantly this time. "Tell me, for chrissakes. I *need* to know."

I feel my heart beat faster, and not wanting to fire back a shut-the-fuck-up response, I pause to give myself time to fashion a suitable enough reply. I think Dee deserves this if she's genuinely confused. As I allow my pulse rate settle, I realize it'll be an answer I've been struggling to voice for myself.

Finding Dee's intense stare uncomfortable, I turn away and walk across to the bay window and look out to Tomkins' apartment for inspiration.

"Well ... Dee ... when I went across there last night, I wasn't exactly sure why I was there ... You see, I wasn't sure what made me get up in the middle of the night and bust my way in like that. There was something ... a force pulling me."

I turn to Dee, feeling immediately embarrassed by my choice of the word, *'force'*, knowing her love of Star Wars I'm half expecting her to say something crass. But she doesn't. She just smiles sympathetically, wanting me to continue.

"I just felt drawn to Tomkins' apartment when I read your text, that's all ... And, after I discovered him on that fucking hook, I eventually found myself at his bay window," I say, pointing to the far side of the street. "And, for some unexplainable reason, I looked over here ... to this apartment."

I turn my head towards Dee now, feeling apprehensive about going any further.

"Look, it's weird, I know, but like I said this morning, I thought I saw someone standing in the shadows ... Someone standing more or less where you are now ... He just stood there ... Staring at me ... Just like you are now."

Dee gives me a quick smile but, almost instantaneously, reverts to the same concerned expression she had before.

I turn back to the window.

"He was staring at me through the blackness. You see, Dee, whether I saw something is not really the issue at stake here," I add, thinking about what Sam had mentioned. "I'm even prepared to accept that it's my over-active imagination. But I *am* sure this killer's been here before. In this room. Whilst we've been thinking he went back to the black hole where he resides, he's been watching us. And, do you know what? You're right. It is personal. I think this guy's getting his rocks off with the thought of my demise. At times, I even think he's manipulating me."

The vision of Barney, propping up the bar in Billy's, comes to my mind again.

"The fucker just keeps making me look the other way," I say, quietly.

"What?" Dee asks. "You've said that twice—"

271

"Nothing ... It's ... It's a feeling. No, it's more than a feeling ... I *know* he's been here, He might not have been last night, I grant you, but he *has* been here, I'm sure of that. He just keeps making us look in the wrong direction ... like your fucking David Copperfield."

I look around the room, wishing I could rewind the comings and goings over the last week.

"I think he was here before he murdered Chandler and I think he stayed afterwards, when we all thought he'd disappeared someplace else. I think he likes watching what we're doing and he's getting a kick out of it—so, why don't you help me find this crazy fucker's bolt-hole if it's here," I say, hefting the bar in my hands, as I move away from the window.

"Whoa—whoa, Oskar," Dee exhorts, coming towards me with outstretched arms to grip my shoulders. "Let's do this by the book shall we? Slowdown. I know it's personal but don't let this guy get to you. Let's tread carefully and not be carried away and bust this place apart. Let's do the job properly, by keeping things squeaky clean. If the evidence is here we'll find it. Let's not drop the ball now," Dee says, tossing her leather gloves into the air and catching them cleanly.

Dee's reasoning hits the spot and I see blue start to appear through the red mist.

44

(Wednesday, 4.30 p.m.)

AFTER THE EVENTFUL CONCLUSION to the search, I'm starting to think it was the killer I saw in that apartment last night. And, more importantly, I let him slip away. Of course, I now wish I'd followed my intuitive thoughts at the time and made the intensive search when I first went across. Perhaps I would have caught him red handed, skulking in his lair, and this nightmare would be over. This thought makes me bang the steering wheel with both palms, sending a shockwave of pain up my arms.

I'm heading home, via the Marriott, to pick up Sam, whilst Dee takes a plastic evidence bag with her to the PAB. She'll take Hargreaves and team over there as soon as possible. I need them to find the convincing evidence to confirm what Dee's still calling my 'hunch'.

I also think the killer's murdered the lieutenant to provide the smoke screen he needs to escape detection. He'll have worked out we'd be snagged up dealing with the lieutenant's death and this gave him the chance to slip away. It also reaffirms my resolve to press on and not become distracted by side issues. I owe it to the lieutenant and the other victims. Somebody has to speak for them.

I look in my rear view, wondering if the chief still has Rodriguez following me, but I can't see anybody on my tail. The more I think about this, the more I realize I'm heading for that showdown with the chief. It can't come soon enough. There's the biggest of question marks against his name and it'll stay there until I'm sure I can erase it.

As I approach the Marriott, I see Sam waiting for me on the corner of West 3rd and Figueroa. I'd phoned ahead, instructing her to meet here rather than in the hotel lobby, in case the foyer was being watched. I see she's wearing a large floppy hat, with a long scarf draped over her shoulders. I'd only asked her to employ a little subterfuge by using Raymond's kitchen to make her exit but Sam has taken 'disguise' to a new level.

"Okay, Agent 86, where to next?" she jibes, as she jumps into the passenger seat, lifting the brim of her hat to reveal a big beaming smile.

"Tell me. Reveal all," she instructs as I pull away from the curb. "Well, we pulled the apartment apart, looking behind cupboards, under beds, under floor boards, every-which-way ... anywhere we thought someone could hide. Then, as we were about to give up, Dee spotted impressions in the kitchen floor. And suddenly remembering something she'd seen in her search, Dee fetched a pair of steps from a nearby cupboard and found a perfect match. The feet of the steps fitted the impressions left in the soft kitchen flooring. She climbed up and pushed on the ceiling quite hard because I had to hold the ladder to stop it sliding across the floor. Eventually, the ceiling appeared to lift up a fraction. Then we heard a strong mechanic click."

"Bingo!" Sam says.

"Yes, bingo," I reply. "I went up. I was able to climb into a fairly large void, and it was easily large enough for someone to—"

"Hide."

"Yes, hide," I repeat. "Once up there, on the far wall – an outside wall – I saw rays of light coming in through an old fashioned airbrick. You know, the sort with holes to allow air in and out to keep spaces damp-free. Well, I crawled over and looked through. I could see all the way across to Tomkins' apartment and could even see onto the street below if I raised my head high enough. Anyway, I turned to see Dee had climbed up as well. That's when she spotted something lying on the floor. I couldn't see it at first and had to go across and have a look for myself. It was sweet wrapper. It's on its way to the lab with Dee as we speak. We're hoping to get a decent fingerprint off the waxy surface."

I look at Sam, hoping she's a full believer, but, like Dee, I see the transition is not yet complete.

As I've been relaying this story, I've thought about the other murder sites and the potential for the killer to hide away there as well. On the spur of the moment, I decide to do something about it. If my theory is to work on this occasion, it *has* to work elsewhere.

We're in slow moving traffic on West 5th and I spot a gap in the flow of vehicles coming towards us.

"Pass me the strobe," I ask.

"The what?"

"The bubble, Agent 99. It should be at your feet."

Sam reaches down and fumbles on the floor below her legs, pulling out a magnetic flashing light. I see the gap in the traffic closing fast so I snatch it from her grasp, attaching it to the roof and plugging it into the dash. I drive straight out onto the other side of the street and accelerate towards the oncoming traffic, siren blaring. When I think I've reached a suitable enough speed, I turn the car's steering wheel around in my hands, spinning the rear wheels at the same time and do an extremely tight one eighty. I leave a smell of burnt rubber in the air as I gun the accelerator and we pull away up the street in the opposite direction.

As I'm about to turn left onto South Flower Street, my eyes are drawn to an unmarked cruiser which had been waiting about twenty cars behind us in the traffic. There are two guys inside, who look to be 'official'. IAD official, I'm thinking. They're wearing dark shiny suits with nobody-loves-me expressions on their faces. A complete giveaway in my books – mistake number one.

As I race past, I see the driver can't work out what to do. He's pulled up too close to the car in front and can't maneuver himself out mistake number two. I take the sharp left and see the cruiser attempt a multiple-point turn, trying to come after me. But all he manages is to jam himself up even further, as cars come at him from all directions. Disaster.

I derive pleasure from seeing this and look across at Sam, wondering if she's worked out what's happened. She's caught in the sunlight streaming through the windshield. Her left foot is on the dash and she's gripping hold of the strap handle with her right hand.

"Whoa, cowboy. Steady on, will you? ..." Sam asks good-naturedly, as she puts on dark glasses, "this cowgirl's had a busy day."

We reach Wilshire Boulevard in twelve minutes – without the tail – and I park a hundred yards from the end of the alley where Green was slain.

Without saying a word, we both alight from the car in unison. I pop the trunk and reach in to take out the prospecting equipment I used earlier, but this time I also bring out two nondescript hooded jackets. I pass one to Sam and we put them on, pulling up the hoods around our faces. Sam knows why we're here and I don't have to say anything as we make our way down the sidewalk at a brisk pace.

This is familiar territory to me but Sam hasn't been here before. However, I know she's pored over the video images so it's no surprise that, when we enter the alley, she instinctively steps around where Green had lain in the alley, behind the dumpster, after he had been battered to death. The blood in the dirt surface is still visible but the stain has lost the intensity it had four weeks ago.

I go to the back of the shopping outlet and set to work on the emergency exit doors. They appear to be firmly sealed but I know from experience that these types of doors often become jammed up, making locking them a hit-and-miss affair. I pull out a blade from my penknife and slide it into a gap, hoping this one has not fully engaged, After a few moments of feeling my way around, I disengage the latch, and, with a gentle nudge of the blade, both of the doors swing open towards me.

"Bingo!" Sam says, once again.

We move inside, pulling the doors closed behind us. I bring out a handful of gloves from my pocket and pass a pair to Sam. The percussive snap of latex on our wrists gives us the purpose we need to move straight on with the job. Sam focuses her attention on the cupboards and walls on the far side of the room whilst I start over here.

The shop unit is in the process of being stripped out and refurbished so there's an assortment of wooden planks and boards lying around. There are also tools and pieces of electrical equipment set down in boxes on the floor and I'm guessing these have been left by the shop-fitters. I'm just hoping they've finished for the day.

There's also light coming in through the whitewashed windows at the front. This helps us see around but I'm also pleased this provides us with protection from inquisitive eyes. The last thing we need now is to be snagged up convincing officials we have permission to be here when we don't.

As I make my way along the wall, tapping on partitions and looking for panels which suggest a hollow space behind, I hear Sam doing the same thing along the other side.

After ten minutes, when I'm beginning to think we've drawn a blank, I hear a sharp metallic click from the other side of the room. It's exactly the same sound I heard coming from Dee's ceiling partition in South Normandie, about an hour ago. Sam won't recognize the sound but she'll have guessed its significance.

"Bingo!" she announces, for the third time today.

Hurrying across, I see Sam has hinged down a section of wall. She's looking into a dark void that lies behind. It's near to the corner of the room, up against the back wall which runs along the alley. Perfect, I'm thinking. So, it appears, does Sam. She has the biggest of grins on her face. I put on my head torch and switch on in one movement.

"After you," Sam says, seeing the beam of light, and pulling back from the opening to allow me through – she's definitely looking more like a 'believer' now. I go down on the floor and stick my head inside. After adjusting the focus of the beam, I move my head from side to side, scanning the full extent of the space that lies behind. I quickly work out someone could stand in there and move around easily. I also realize it's large enough for someone to lie down if necessary, thinking someone might have hidden away for a few days, possibly sleeping on the floor.

Thinking about my theory more, I switch off my head torch and look up. I'm immediately greeted by the sight of a small shaft of light coming in through the outside wall, like a beam from a laser. Sam's also managed to squeeze her head through the opening and I'm sure she's seen the shaft of light, so I pull out and stand up, leaving her to inspect everything for herself.

"I'm gonna go round to the other side and check it out from the alley," I say.

"Hold on, partner," Sam responds.

I see Sam reach out fully, trying to grasp at something. After a few moments, she widens her eyes and shuffles back out along the floor. "Now, ain't that a son-of-a-bitch," she says, sitting up and bringing out her latex-gloved hand and opening up her palm.

We both nod slowly.

Sam's definitely a believer now.

I hold out a plastic evidence bag and Sam drops a sweet wrapper inside.

My phone suddenly vibrates. I see from the screen it's a call from Dee so I pick up immediately, wanting to tell her the news.

"The tank's sealed up, Oskar," she exclaims, before I've had a chance to say anything. "So is your desk, they've pulled it apart, Oskar. Shitcreek were just here. In a big hurry to find you." I hear genuine concern and fear etched into her voice. "Are you sure there's nothing I should know?" she asks, inquisitively.

"Why? What do you mean?"

"Well, is there something you're not telling me, Oskar?"

"Why, what else has happened?"

"The word here is that you're in big trouble. There's talk about you and the lieutenant. Talk that you're responsible for his death—I don't like it, Oskar. You need to get—"

Suddenly, the fire doors burst open and Paul Ship and Jason Crick come charging through, almost tumbling to the floor in front of me. I now realize it was these two IAD detectives who had been attempting to follow me just now. They look as though they've put on weight since we last troubled each other and that's why I didn't recognize them on West 5th.

"Good afternoon, gentlemen," I say, as calmly as possible, keeping my phone open, and passing across the evidence bag to Sam, hoping these two IAD goons won't have seen me do this.

"We need to speak with you, Salo—Now," Ship says, with that customary sneer of his, once he regains his breath.

"Why, surely. I'll be right with you, once I've finished up in—"

"Oh no, Salo. We're going straight back to the PAB and up to the tenth floor. Takes priority, I'm afraid. My order trumps anything you might want to do."

I realize the significance of the 'tenth floor' and wonder if my confrontation with the chief is coming sooner than I think.

"As I said, I'll be right along, gentlemen, as soon as I'm finished up in here."

Ship shakes his head like a long-in-the-tooth shop teacher trying to discipline an unruly student.

"Look, tough guy. We can either lay you on the floor, cuff you and haul you back or we take it nice and easy and we all go along peacefully ... your choice."

"Oh, and hear this," Crick chips in. "You choose the hard way and we go the *loooong* way," he drawls, chortling to himself. It's his turn to smile now and I see he's half a toothpick rolling around the inside of his mouth, like some fifties hoodlum. "Yeah, because we'll take you through the squad room first of all," he adds, chuckling some more. He takes what he thinks is a brave confrontational step forward, in my direction. Big mistake. He's closer to me now and easily within striking distance. "I reckon we'll take our time, though," Crick continues. "Because we'll be weaving this way and that, through all those fancy new cubicles of yours. We'll also make sure your detective colleagues know we have you under lock and key. Won't we Paul?" he adds, still keeping his eyes affixed to mine.

"Okay," I say, attempting to stall for time. "If this is to talk about the cases we're investigating, my partner Detective Chance will need to join me. She's back at the PAB so shouldn't be a problem."

Ship and Crick look at each other, attempting the broadest of smiles their tight-lipped mouths will allow.

"No deal, Smartass," Ship says. "Where you're going, you'll not be needing no part-ner."

"No, you'll be needing some cast-iron underpants, though," Crick quips, cracking up at his joke.

I look at him, wanting to wipe that smile off his face with my fist. Sam sees me rising to the bait and puts her hand on my arm.

"Look, you go along, Oskar," Sam says, squeezing my arm a little harder as I feel myself moving in closer to Crick. "I'll take a cab. We'll talk later. You go."

There's another long hard stare between Crick and me whilst I breathe in deeply, realizing Sam's right. I need to remain in control if I'm to find out what's going on.

45

(Wednesday, 5.42 p.m.)

PAUL SHIP DOESN'T READ me my rights but he does ask if this interview can be recorded. I'm seated in a chair in the boardroom, on the tenth floor, opposite him and his IAD sidekick, Jason Crick.

Although the chief's not here, I feel his presence all around. It seems to ooze from all surfaces, like the cigarette smoke in Emmerson's office and the smell of dead bodies in his autopsy suite. As I look down the long conference table, towards the panoramic view of the city through the large window at the far end, I wonder if the vista gives the chief the confidence he needs to undertake his role as a guardian for the city's inhabitants.

After I agree to Ship's request, Crick leans forward and turns on the recorder set out on the table between us. He taps the microphone, checking it's picking up everything to his satisfaction, and sits back, nodding towards Ship, letting him know he can start.

My advice to anyone in this position is always to say nothing and just fetch your lawyer. So, I know it's a risky strategy agreeing to this interview in the first place but I need to find out what's going on around here and what these two goons actually have on me. I want to know what the chief has to do with my investigation. Having this meeting on the tenth floor suggests I might have that chance.

Ship states the date and time and details those present in the room, looking at each of us in turn as if he's presenting to an audience. I wonder if there are people somewhere out of sight.

I look for a hidden camera but can't see one anywhere. I turn my attention to Ship as he opens a spiral notepad, turning the page quite deliberately, showing me he thinks he's in complete control. Jerk. It's a standard ploy used by many detectives to assert authority but it doesn't fool me.

He places a tick against the first thing on his list and leans forward.

"Detective Salo has confirmed his agreement to have this interview recorded. But, just for the record, would you confirm this again, please?"

"That's all okay," I say. "But what's this all about?" I fire back at him.

"Whoa. Easy. We'll get to that," Ship says, leaning into the microphone once again.

"I'd like to ask you the questions if you don't mind. You know the score. We ask. You answer. That's the deal going on here."

"Yeah, but I've come here of my own free will so I think I have a right to know what it's all about. Before I answer anything."

"As I just said, we'll come to that, Detective. It will all become clear. In the end."

"The 'end' being the operative word," Crick adds. "So far as your police career is concerned, that is." He follows this with a low guttural chuckle that seems to emanate from his fat belly and rumble its way around his body before erupting from his mouth.

"Look, I've a killer out there who needs catching and you two amateurs are stopping me getting on with my job."

"Don't you worry about all that, Detective," Ship says. "You've blundered from one catastrophe to the next, haven't you? How many deaths is it now, Jase?" he asks Crick, maintaining direct eye contact with me.

Crick flips through his own notepad, counting, "One ... two, three... four ... it's five, last count, Paul. Five deaths. Not a good score if you ask me," he says.

I'm not sure if Crick's bravado has the better of him or if they've planned it this way to make me lose my temper. All I'm thinking at this point is I want to shove that fucking microphone down his fat neck.

"Where were you between one forty-five and two o'clock this afternoon?" Ship asks, drawing my attention back to him.

"I don't know. You'll need to contact my P.A. for details like that."

"Don't be a smartass, Salo. A dozen or so employees saw you in the vicinity of the basement car park immediately after the explosion. So, how come you were there?"

"Like a *dozen or so other employees,* I heard the explosion and went to investigate and possibly help—why, what are you implying?"

"Like I said, where were you immediately prior to responding to the explosion? Between one forty-five and two o'clock?" he repeats, reading the times from his notebook.

"I was out at the smoking shelter, smoking a cigarette. Two cigarettes, actually."

This seems to take the wind out of his sails.

"Can anyone confirm you were there?" Ship responds, asking a little too quickly.

"No, I was on my own."

Ship and Crick smile at each other, as if they've rescued the situation and caught me in a trap, because I won't have an alibi.

"But I'm sure you can look up the video records if you care to. There's a camera high up which looks down onto the shelter. I would have thought two smart guys like you would have checked that out first, before asking me."

I see this news deflates them instantly.

"Don't you worry. We will. Be sure of that. We'll check," Ship responds, attempting to pump himself up again.

"Good—can I go now?" I ask, speculatively.

"Whoa. Steady. We've a few more questions for you, before I get down to the real business of why we're here."

Both of them lock eyes, exchanging a smirk, suggesting they're fully loaded with something that'll blow me out of the water. Ship leans forward into the microphone again.

"Do you own a handgun?" he asks, thinking he's throwing me a question that'll catch me by surprise. I wonder why it's taken him so long.

"What do you mean, do I own a handgun?"

"Straightforward question, Salo. Deserves a straightforward answer."

I'm determined not to walk into any trap,

"Of course I own a handgun. It's in my holster right now."

"No. Not that gun, Smartass. Do you own another gun? Your own *personal* gun ... a spare gun?"

"Of course not. I don't possess another gun." I'm thinking this might not be a complete lie because I'm sure it's not in my possession any more. "I've already got one here on my hip," I respond, trying to shake him off this line of questioning.

I've also decided I'll not fall into the *liar's trap* by following up with a host of questions, like: *Why are you asking? What's this got to do with me?* I therefore remain silent and stare at Ship, holding his stare until he feels obliged to look away. I think, if this is their best shot at interviewing a suspect who's gun has been used to kill someone, let alone a colleague, they're a discredit to the profession.

"So, you don't possess another gun apart from your government-issue Glock?" Ship says, looking back to me.

"That's what I said, Ship. No. I don't have another gun. How better can I say it for you? Is there anything in the word 'no' that you don't understand?"

"Okay, we'll come back to this later. Let's move on to the death of your suspect Tomkins," Ship now says, looking at his watch.

"Why did you go out to his apartment in the middle of the night and break in the way you did?" he asks, ticking off another item on his list.

"I've said all this before. Haven't you read my report?" "Yes, I have, but we wanna hear it from you."

"Yeah," says Crick. "We want to hear it from the donkey's mouth."

If their strategy is to mix their questions and verbally rough me up at the same time then Crick's definitely starting to piss me off. I look at Ship, desperately trying to remain calm and focused, because I want to be ready for anything he might throw at me. I breathe in deeply.

"I received a text from my partner, Detective Chance. That's why I went to the apartment. She told me the lieutenant had given Tomkins a lift to his place, after he'd been released from custody."

"Yes. We know all that. I just wanna know why you went there in the first place. What gave you cause for concern that you'd get up in the middle of the night – from your sweet, little love-nest – and drive halfway across town? Was it just to make sure that freak Tomkins was safely tucked up in his bed, because I think not?"

"I went to the scene because of my continuing concerns about him. That's all. I'd always had my doubts about his story. I just wanted to see what he might get up to once he was released."

"Yeah, but why bust in the way you did, without your partner?" Crick interjects.

"I didn't bust in. The door was open," I lie. "The lights were on. I called out but no one answered. I pushed open the door and found him hanging from the hook on the wall. I went on my own because it was the middle of the night and I wanted my partner to get a good night's sleep. I didn't think it was worth disturbing her for what I wanted to do. But I did call her as soon as I found Tomkins dead."

Ship seems to accept this response and ticks another thing off his list. There's an expectant look on his face now as he points to his next question, making sure Crick has seen which one it is.

"Tell us about Sam Callan?" he asks, sneeringly, as I hear him roll a boiled sweet along the back of his teeth.

"What do you mean 'tell us about Sam Callan?'" I ask, imitating the same sneer he's used to ask the question.

"Straightforward question, Detective Salo. Tell us about your relationship with her. Says here she spent the night up in that fancy 'cube' of yours. Is that true?"

I pause before answering but hopefully not long enough to suggest I'm trying to hide something.

"Yes. That's true. But it's none of your fucking business what I do in my own time."

"Oh, I think you'll find it is, Salo. You know the rules."

"Yeah," Crick chortles. "You shouldn't get your honey where you get your money."

Crick looks so pleased with himself at the use of this phrase that he glows with pride, looking to Ship for recognition.

"There's a conflict of interest, Detective," Ship continues, ignoring Crick. "We can have your badge for that if we want. But we've got bigger fish to fry, haven't we Jase?"

"Oh baby. We sure have," Crick says, grinning from ear to ear in anticipation, almost salivating. I see his belly bursting its way through his shirt as he attempts to move in closer to the table.

I turn back to Ship. He's telegraphing he's about to ask his 'bombshell' question. But, just as he's about to speak, a side door opens at the end of the room and out walks the chief.

We all turn our heads to face him and I'm guessing he's stepped directly from his office. As he closes the door, I see why I hadn't noticed it before. It's invisible from where we're sitting because it blends in perfectly with the wall and the décor of the room when closed.

The chief glides down the room like the Great White in the Monterey Bay Aquarium – silent and menacing. He looks directly at me the whole time, never taking his unblinking eyes off me. It looks as though he's been in the process of putting on his dress uniform, because his standard work shirt is half undone and out over a pair of dress pants. I see a pair of dark blue elasticated braces hanging down from the waistband.

"Leave us alone for a few minutes will you, gentleman?" Kramer says to Ship and Crick, still with his eyes fixed firmly on mine.

"But, we haven't—"

"Now, if you please," he barks, with a voice that suggests disobedience will result in instant dismissal. Ship and Crick pick up on this instantly, push back their chairs and make their way towards the door. I continue to hold the chief's stare but know I'm not in the alpha position here.

When they're gone, the chief looks down at the table and sees Ship has left his notebook behind. He closes it with a disdainful expression on his face and tosses it aside as if worthless. He sits down and rests both arms on the table, clasping his hands together.

He's in his mid-forties, extremely fit and strong, and clearly works out. There's a controlled, razor-tight, intimidating image about him.

I realize the tape recorder is still on. I also suspect the microphone leads straight to a set of speakers in his office and he's been listening in. So I wonder how many minions he has back there, listening in as well. I glance at the recorder and the chief reads this immediately, turning it off with a swift and exaggerated action.

"This will be off record," he says, pointedly.

I look across to his hidden door and hold my eyes on it for a second, making sure the chief knows. This gesture takes him a little longer to compute, but, when he does, he grabs the microphone from its stand, throws another switch, and shows me it's definitely in the 'off' position.

He sticks the thumb of one hand in the direction of the door Ship and Crick just went through. "These guys have got you by the balls, Detective," he says. "They've shown me the evidence and it doesn't look good."

I think what I have on him doesn't look so good either but decide to keep that to myself.

"They've got nothing on me that'll stick. Nothing they've said stacks—"

"They haven't shown you their full hand," he interrupts, "But they've shown me. And you're up Shit Creek without a fucking paddle. So let's be clear what's going on here. You're not leaving this room with your badge or your gun. You'll not get them back until IAD finish investigating your actions in connection with the death of the lieutenant. But, because of your outstanding record with LAPD, my one and only offer is that, if we can come to a compromise, we might spare you the professional and personal humiliation of being held as a suspect for the lieutenant's murder."

"What do you mean, murder? How was he murdered?"

"They think he was shot with an ex-LAPD service gun and it's being treated as a murder at this stage. IAD suspect this gun belonged to you. Did you own an old gun, from your days as a detective in the nineties? We've always known many guns were never requisitioned from that period."

I continue staring at him, working out how to respond.

"Look, if I need my lawyer here, let's bring him in, Chief. You can't expect me to answer questions like that without having a lawyer present.

"As I've said, this is an off-record conversation, Detective. So we can both speak freely. This is a private conversation between two professional colleagues. Nothing said here will be repeated elsewhere. Unless, of course, you tell me you were involved in the murder of the lieutenant."

I still trust my instincts, suspecting he's people listening in, and look down the board table to the hidden door.

"The lever is under the dado rail if you want to take a look," the chief announces calmly, reading my thoughts.

I stand up, walk down the room and put my hand under the rail, finding the lever easily. The door springs open and I step inside. It is his office. I see his dress uniform laid out on his desk and a pair of gleaming, black shoes positioned neatly on the floor. I take another step inside the room and look around. It's empty.

"Believe me, Detective, no one is listening. It's just you and me here."

"Look, take a seat, will you?" he asks, as he closes the door behind me and he makes his way to the chair behind his large desk. I sit down opposite him, working out what I should do or say next.

"If it's worth anything to you at this stage, I don't think you're guilty," the chief says, as I watch him run his hands across the desk's surface, almost caressing it. "In fact, I think you're completely innocent of the lieutenant's murder. You're also very good at your job but, unfortunately, you've been rather stubborn lately. And, if you don't mind my saying, I think you've been foolish."

I'm wondering why he's so sure I'm innocent when he hardly knows me. "If you think I'm so innocent, why don't you just let me get on with my job?"

"I can't do that just now, Detective. Where you've been going will only lead to problems for LAPD ... for us all." The chief didn't say this would lead to problems for *him* but it was implicit.

"I know you have the greater good to consider, Chief," I say, remembering his use of this phrase at his recent press conference. "But, I can also be trusted with that. I believe there's a better good out there. One that will help solve this murder, make the streets of Los Angeles safe again and maintain the integrity of LAPD. It's all about trusting me with that responsibility as well."

The chief drills his dark eyes into mine, as if he's seriously scrutinizing my offer. He stands up and moves across to his dress jacket, lying at the far end of his desk. He picks it up by the hanger and carries it across the room towards the coat stand on the far wall. I can almost feel the weight of the uniform by the expression on his face and I can also sense the weight of his responsibilities. He lifts the hanger onto a hook and, with the back of his hand, brushes away particles of dust he's seen on an epaulette. When he's satisfied, he turns to look out of his panoramic window, pointing at some distant location.

"Over there, in about an hour's time, I'll shake the hands of the police cadets at their passing-out ceremony. They'll swear their oath of allegiance to this great nation of ours and, of course, to this great city. But they're not going to perform very well if the city's police department is in a state of turmoil, are they? I'm not going to allow that to happen, Detective Salo. I *can't* allow that to happen. That's why you'll have to trust me on this. You'll have to trust I know what I'm doing here ... yes, you're right, there is a greater good to consider but there's not a *better* one on offer from you today, I'm afraid. It's always a delicate balance, making choices between what's acceptable and what's not. And making these choices is the burden of responsibility this office demands. At times, this decision-making process takes precedence over what one particular detective might think is the best course of action—"

"Even if it means a killer goes free?" I ask, bluntly.

The chief pauses momentarily before turning to face me. "Yes... even if it means a killer goes free," he says.

This reply sticks in my gullet like the proverbial fur ball and it takes all my will not to scream out that he's wrong and he's about to degrade the badge of office sewn onto that fucking dress uniform of his.

"I see what you're thinking, Detective, and I understand your position, but things have happened in the past which this department is not proud of. You know what occurred after the Rodney King riots. Much of the city went up in flames and we've had twenty years of backlash to contend with. And we've still got a long way to go to convince whole communities to be law-abiding, to pay their taxes properly and contribute as full members of society. But we are getting there."

He turns to look out of his window again, puffing out his chest this time. He's in full imperious mood now, looking over his kingdom.

He turns around and comes back to face me.

"I can't allow things to develop in ways that might stoke another bout of civil disobedience, Detective Salo. It could possibly take on gargantuan proportions. LAPD couldn't survive another beating like that." The analogy with Rodney King seems to pass him by.

He gives me a slight nod, followed by a look which says he's delivered his message and maintained dignity and integrity throughout, just as he'll do when he makes his fucking speech to the cadets on the parade ground this morning. The chief then looks at his watch and across to his dress uniform. I guess he's thinking about the audience awaiting him.

"Your badge and your gun, if you please Detective Salo, then I'll allow you to leave this room with an untainted record whilst IAD complete their investigations. You'll be on home leave for the time being. But if you choose to fight my decision, I'll feed you to those jokers sitting outside the door. They have more than enough to hold you under lock and key if they wish. It's your choice, Detective, but you must decide before you leave this room. I need to get to those boys and girls, and to their parents and families. They're waiting for me to join their celebrations. How's it going to be, Detective? Are you leaving peacefully, or what?"

The chief bores his cold, dark eyes into mine again, waiting for my answer. I stare back, trying to work out what I'll do next. If I run, do I take the chief down first?

The chief looks at his watch again and goes across to his uniform hanging from the hook, taking off his shirt in the process and dropping it to the floor. He has his back to me now and I think this could be the distraction I'm looking for. But, as I look at his muscled torso, I'm not convinced I could fight my way past him so I consider making a sudden run for the door.

"I'm waiting, Detective," the chief says, still with his back to me.

I watch as the chief takes out his clean shirt, holding it up to the light coming in from the window, inspecting it carefully.

As he's doing this, he turns towards me and I see a small tattoo emblazoned high up on his chest, above his heart.

"What's your answer, Detective? I don't have much time. A decision if you please."

Suddenly, everything falls into place, like the mechanism of a clock about to strike the hour. All the cogs start turning in unison, telling me *my* time has come.

I want to be sure, so I stand up and move across towards the chief to take a closer look. This surprises him and, momentarily, I see him on guard, fearing I might be about to attack, but he relaxes when he realizes all I'm interested in is his tattoo.

"Oh, it's the emblem of the 1st Infantry Division," he says, proudly, looking down at his chest. "The Fighting First."

I see it's been crafted with the customary limited skills and inks found in the desert. But, more importantly, I now understand why the chief has taken such a keen interest in my investigation of the Chandler murder.

I also realize that, if I play this next bit right, I'll be the one walking out of here with my dignity and integrity intact.

Not him.

46

(Wednesday 7.05 p.m.)

I'M ON MY WAY to meet Dee at Chang's, having taken a cab to Wilshire Boulevard to pick up my Caprice. I found the IAD tracker straightaway. It was attached to the underside of my car. I suspected Ship and Crick needed technological help to find Sam and me as they did. I've also bought four pay-as-you-go cell phones because, now the gloves are off, I'm not putting it past Shitcreek to be illegally monitoring our calls as well. I think these throwaways might give us the lifelines to communicate with each other over the next few days. I've phoned ahead to Chang, telling him I'm on my way, but I also added I'd like the help of Sammy – one of his 'techie' cousins – with a technological fix of my own.

Although I'm up against it, my spirits are high after my win with the chief. And I definitely had a lift walking past Ship and Crick the way I did, after I shook hands with the chief at his door. To say they looked gobsmacked would be an understatement. They reminded me of two high school sneaks whose prank had just backfired.

Moments earlier, after confronting the chief with the news I knew about his relationship with Chandler, he slumped – as if I'd punched him in the gut. He looked as though life as he knew it was over. I didn't leave it too long before offering him a way out of his despair because I gave him the opportunity to negotiate a deal, so long as he told me the full story of his relationship and also what he knew about the Gargailis case.

He started by telling me Jane Chandler had been his lover for over two years and that he'd met her, regularly, in a downtown hotel. At one level, he was clearly pleased to purge himself of this *'difficult truth'*, as he called it. He spoke of this relationship being very private and loving and implied he was unaware she had other partners until quite recently. This made me wonder if the intense and exclusive attachment he spoke so fondly about had turned him into the possessive killer we were looking for. Did he kill her when he learned about her infidelity?

His pleadings of complete innocence of anything to do with the Gargailis case seemed real enough to me. He said he'd used the murder book in 1995 to help him complete a reflective diary as part of a career-progression training program, saying he was already attempting to climb his way up the career ladder at the time. He also said he had a copy of the diary in question in his attic if I needed proof.

I asked him why, if he was so innocent, did he go out of his way to try and prevent me reading the Gargailis Murder Book. This was when I saw the first real 'tell' as he attempted to disguise the truth. *'The case is a blind alley, for crying out loud,'* he started by saying. *'I knew the family, I knew the case. It has nothing whatsoever to do with the recent string of murders you're investigating.'* Then came the stroke of his nose and the slight flutter of eyelids. *'When I heard from the lieutenant that you were about to look into John's case ..."* – there was the use of first names again – *"I feared you would go on a wild goose chase and it would slow you down. I needed you to get this case wrapped up quickly. The longer it went on, the more I thought my connection to Jane might come out. I'm running for re-election for chrissakes! I couldn't let your fishing trip interfere with my campaign like that, could I?'* I thought we were approaching the truth but sensed things were heating up too quickly, I decided to back off whilst I was winning. I still needed to strike the deal.

We agreed that, in exchange for doing my best to respect his anonymity, I could continue with my investigation. And on my own terms. I did, after all, have the trump card; the photograph of him having sex with Chandler.

When I questioned the Chief about the part he played in hassling the lieutenant of late, he was at his most contrite. He admitted 'leaning on him', saying his leverage had to do with a skeleton in the lieutenant's cupboard. He wouldn't reveal exactly what that was, and I didn't push it, but he inferred it related to the lieutenant being able to retire with full honors and collect his pension.

He was the one to raise the knotty problem of how he might handle Ship and Crick without drawing attention to the private agreement we'd settled on. I told him not to worry because I had a little plan of my own to deal with them. As if on cue, I see Dee's Caprice parked outside Chang's and think about the part she's about to play in that caper.

I drive round the back and pull up near the back entrance. After leaving my keys on top of the front tire, I make my way inside. I look into the kitchen on my left and one of Chang's sons steps forward to take the bag of phones from me. I continue down the corridor, going past the private room Chang reserves for his discrete gaming sessions, and make my way into the main restaurant.

I see Chang at the checkout.

It's quite remarkable; he's busy reprimanding two members of staff yet is able to smile warmly towards me, communicate that the 'fix' is in and let me know Dee's arrived and is sitting at her favorite table in the corner.

I haven't given Dee full feedback on my tenth-floor experience, and won't, because that's part of the deal I shook hands on but I have my story together. I'll need to deflect any interest she might show in the details and why I've managed to escape censure, summary dismissal or, worse still, detention.

Dee has her head stuck into another of Chang's Americanos. She's characteristically immersing her face right into the brew, whilst trying to read a set of papers on the table. She's also wearing her new glasses and the lenses have steamed up, not making this any easier. But when she sees me through the mist, she gives me a big, beaming smile. I lift up the side of my jacket to show her I'm still carrying and slap my badge on the table, proving my credentials are intact.

"Nice going, Oskar," she says from behind her cup, as we exchange a high five. "But I've got something I need to tell you first," she declares, before I've even had a chance to sit down. "I spoke to Tommy down in ballistics and he said it'll be reported later today that the lieutenant took his own life. Official."

Thoughts shuffle their way through my mind. Then questions: What does this say about the gun? Has the chief put a fix of his own in place to take the heat off me?

"There's more," she says. "Fire damage to the gun cannot verify ownership but it looks to be one of LAPD's old issue handguns, from the nineties. Wife says he kept one hidden in the house somewhere ... a Beretta. And, hear this, according to Tommy, a fluke bullet ricochet took out the fuel tank and that's why the car exploded the way it did."

I look at Dee, checking she's finished. She hasn't. She's holding back on something.

"What is it?"

"Well ... I can't shake off Tomkins' involvement, that's all. Maybe there really is a scam going on we haven't considered yet," she says, putting her cup down and taking off her glasses to clean them.

"Why? What do you mean?"

"Maybe Tomkins was working in partnership with more than one person ... maybe we have him working alongside the murderer as well. I'm thinking about the holes in the walls so maybe Tomkins voyeuristically chronicled the murders, not just for himself, but for some other twisted personality"

'Could this be the chief?' I voice to myself, wondering if I let him off the hook, earlier.

"Who might it be?" I ask, out loud. "Dunno ... have you any ideas?"

"Not sure. My mind is open to any possibility at the moment. Work the idea through with Treviss and let me know what you both think."

My phone starts to rumble in my pocket and I look at the screen before it rings. It's Sam.

"Wassup?" Sam asks into my ear as I pick up.

I take five minutes to give her the run-down on what has happened this morning, leaving out the chief's confession on Chandler at this stage, telling her I'd convinced him I needed to finish the job. But I also run by Sam the same proposition I put to Dee just now, asking her if she'd unpack a personality profile which might fit the thesis that Tomkins was a voyeuristic slave. To two masters.

Discussing this over the phone with Sam, and with Dee sitting opposite, enables me to ensure both of them have all the information I'm prepared to reveal at this point despite the uncomfortable feeling I have that I'm holding back on telling them everything. I'm also keeping my plan for my overnight trip to myself, still thinking the fewer people who know about it the better. But I do discuss in more detail how I'm planning to approach O'Connell when I go to meet him later this evening. As I tell this to Sam, I see Dee sit up and raise her eyebrows at me, with that quirky look. Sam's silence on the end of the line seems to match Dee's look of skepticism. They're both asking '*Is this really the time to go all the way across to Long Beach to interview him?*' Despite all that's happened I've still not convinced them of the relevance of my visit, and this concerns me.

Whilst I hold on to the silence, I bring out the 1993 press photo from the back of my notebook, the one with the picture of Gargailis being escorted through the press pack at the old Parker Center. I lay it down on the table so Dee can see for herself the stark black and white image that captured a moment, twenty years ago.

"Look, Sam, it's a lead which has me worried, that's all ... it's a loose end that needs tidying away. In the picture you sourced for me, we have Kramer, O'Connell, Buttle and, of course, me. And didn't you say every picture tells a story? Well, we have Kramer acting strangely all week and we now have Buttle going AWOL again today. And, heaven knows who it was asking for him in Billy's today. So there's something not right – and don't give me any of your hocus pocus about synchronicity, for chrissakes. I want to find out what all this adds up to. I want to clear it up once and for all. I want to find out what O'Connell knows."

"Yeah, well, I suggest you do that quickly and get back here A-S-A-P because I want to go through aspects of the murderer's profile with you. In the meantime, I'll work on the other angle you mentioned because that's a definite possibility. I'll catch you later?"

"Yeah. I'll be in touch."

I close the phone and see Dee is looking intently at the photograph on the table. Like me, Dee's always been interested in police photos from the past. This one resembles those archive images framed and put on display in trendy restaurants and bars. I've often seen Dee scouring the gangster images in Gerry's, one of our regular post-shift haunts.

Dee's absorption gives me a chance to drink my coffee which has arrived without my noticing. I'm grateful for the injection of caffeine and down it in one.

"This is the chief isn't it?" Dee suddenly asks, pointing at the face of a young Kramer in uniform.

"Yes."

"It's as if he's ... you know ... protecting this guy, Gargailis ... look at his eyes ... he looks to be about eighteen years old, doesn't he? Do you notice he's holding on to Gargailis's arm ... There, see," she says, pointing again. "Almost gently ... even reverently ... yet he's pushing away the press pack with the other arm, quite firmly." Dee turns the photo towards me. "You see. He's also looking at Gargailis as if he's his damn father or something—look at those eyes, will you?"

I hadn't picked up on this before but remain silent, wanting to draw out Dee's intuitive responses. She's on one of her 'visual' rolls and I wonder what other thoughts her synapses are going to connect to.

"Is this you, Oskar?" she asks, pointing at the young face in the background.

"Yeah, that's me."

Dee looks up and smiles.

"Fresh faced kid from around the block, I'd say. You scrubbed up well in those days. No hardened exterior then. Just the young man waiting to burst forth and stun the world with his investigative intellect," she says, maintaining eye contact with the image.

"Whoa, this guy. Who's that?"

"That's O'Connell."

"Whoa, he's old school if I've ever seen one. What was it like working for him? This the guy you're going to see tonight? He looks to be a mean son-of-a-bitch. Did the lieutenant keep him on a leash, or what?"

O'Connell is wearing his trademark light brown, felt fedora. I remember he frequently looked more like a villain than a detective. I recall him saying once, *'You have to meet shmuck with shmuck.'* This was when a team of us waded into a multi-arrest drugs-bust in the middle of the night. *'Not only do we get OT,'* he said to me, *'but we also get to bust some guys' faces as well.'*

"And who's this?" Dee asks, interrupting my memories.

"That's Jardine, O'Connell's partner in crime."

"Where's he now?"

"LAPD records had him 'presumed dead' when I asked because his pension checks went uncollected. They're having problems locating next of kin."

As I say this, I feel a slight electric charge through my body. Dee picks up on this.

"You thinking what I'm thinking?" she asks, lifting her eyes to mine.

"Dunno. Perhaps he's connected into this as well—that's why I want to drill into O'Connell, find out what he knows, what he remembers."

Dee seems to connect to the energy created by this little mystery, and suggests she'll put some time into finding Buttle.

"I'll call at his home on my way back tonight ... to make sure he's okay," she adds.

I take all this as a sign from Dee that my planned visit to O'Connell now has her approval.

Out of the corner of my eye, I see Chang approaching the table. As he arrives, he dumps the plastic bag I brought with me onto the seat and then walks away, without saying a word.

"What the..." Dee says.

I'd forgotten about the cell phones and open the bag and hand two fully charged phones to Dee, keeping two for myself. We take ten minutes working out how and when to use them, confirming, at the same time, the code words and phrases we'll use. Dee is more *au fait* with this sort of thing so I let her set out the ground rules. We both memorize numbers to the phones and switch them off when finished. We also agree to switch off our standard work cell phones should we not want to reveal our position to anyone scanning the airwaves.

Looking up, I see Chang's cousin Sammy arrive through the front door. He goes over to Chang at the checkout and they start haggling. After a minute or two, they come to an agreement and Chang peels off bills and passes them across. Sammy walks through the restaurant and out the back door towards the alley, without making eye contact with me.

Feeling planets are lining up positively and the technology gods are preparing to help me, I make a move. I check with Dee what she'll be doing tomorrow, knowing I won't be around for much of the day. I stand up and walk with Dee to the front door, holding her in conversation until I see Sammy come back inside.

He gives me a quick nod.

"What?" Dee asks, having seen this exchange.

"Nothing" I say, trying to close down a grin. "You better get going. I'll settle up with Chang and then be on my way."

Still not completely satisfied with my explanation, Dee gives me a backward glance as she heads across to her Caprice, parked on the corner.

I watch her settle into her car and drive away.

I move back into the restaurant, in an attempt to keep out of sight of passing motorists. I see Chang at the checkout. He's folding napkins and reading the racing section of a newspaper at the same time. He's seen what I'm doing and is looking out of the window as well. After a few tense minutes when nothing happens, we both see an unmarked cruiser drive past. The two IAD detectives have picked up the signal from the tracker that's now been attached underneath Dee's car.

The 'fix' is in.

47

(Wednesday 8.10 p.m.)

I REACH THE LONG Beach Hospice in good time and park in the street. It's been a beautiful day and the sun has disappeared from view but the heat remains, making it a balmy evening. I check my watch. I'm twenty minutes early and decide turning up ahead of time might shake O'Connell up a bit. I'd phoned ahead asking the receptionist to let him know I was coming but I didn't say what it was about. I'm hoping this will have O'Connell thinking – or possibly worrying – especially if he has something to hide.

This will be the first time I've seen O'Connell since his retirement party fifteen years ago. I remember he had a farewell reception at a local bar and it all ended with a late night poker session. I lost over fifty bucks.

Looking up the path to the front door, I see carefully pruned trees and shrubs surrounding a modern looking building. There are flowerbeds each side of the path, adding color to the scene. The grass along the front is meticulously manicured and everywhere looks peaceful and quiet. And expensive. A beautifully crafted wooden sign announces: *"Long Beach Hospice – Providing Compassionate Care on Life's Journey."*

I check my mirror before opening the door and notice the spider's web is vibrating. A small fruit fly is caught up in the sticky cords. I see the spider curled up in a corner and, as I continue to watch, the spider slowly stretches out its legs and begins to work its way across towards the helpless fly. The spider moves slowly and methodically, seemingly knowing the fly's not going anywhere. Except into his grasp.

I grab my jacket and copy of the Gargailis Murder Book and climb out of the car. As I make my way up the meandering path towards the front door, I see residents sitting on the deck in the late evening sunshine. I wonder if this happens every evening because there seems to be a familiar routine acted out here. Some residents greet me courteously, others look deathly pale and one or two sit trance-like with arms folded around their frail bodies – guarding their memories of happier and healthier times.

As I reach the front door, I see a smiling Asian woman through the glass. She welcomes me from behind the reception desk as I come through. She's dressed impeccably in a smart blue and white uniform. I recognize the voice as the person who took the call when I phoned earlier so I introduce myself and she tells me, in cheery fashion, that O'Connell is awake and ready to meet me.

"It's Room 11, Detective Salo. Straight down the corridor, on your right."

The floor is shining and half way down I see a cleaner. His back is to me and he's working a mop across the tiles, swinging it to and fro mechanically. As he hears me approach, he momentarily stops, allowing me to pass by.

I soon reach Room 11 and look inside, through a small pane of glass in the door. O'Connell is sitting up in bed, reading a book. It looks to be about military campaigns and I remember he used to brag about his collections of army memorabilia.

I knock on the door. O'Connell looks up in surprise and smiles, beckoning me into the room good-naturedly.

"Come in, Oskar. Come in, come in," he says enthusiastically, as I push open the door.

"Thanks for seeing me, Paddy," I say, moving towards the side of his bed.

"No problem, Oskar. No problem ... sit down. Sit down ... here," he says, pointing to a chair set out next to the bed. I sit down and put the murder book onto an adjacent table, placing my jacket over the top.

"Sorry to hear about your problems, Paddy. How's it all going?" I ask by way of an opener.

"Hey, it's a bummer, but that's the deal when you're old and you get sick."

I see O'Connell's skin has a grayish pallor to it and he's much thinner than I recall. I guess his weight loss has been recent by the way his skin sags in places, like a deflated balloon. His breathing is steady but slightly forced, as if it requires conscious effort to suck air into his lungs. I notice a small bottle of oxygen on a trolley nearby and there's a tube and mask within reach.

Once I've settled, he looks at me with a face that demands, *'Come on Oskar, tell me why you're here. Spill the beans, will you, for chrissakes.'*

"It's about an old case, Paddy." "I guessed that, but which one?"

"Gargailis ... John Gargailis. 1993." I look for a tell but see nothing.

He puts a bony finger to his mouth as if having difficulty remembering that far back – and he's certainly not showing me I've struck a raw nerve – but I'm not gonna prompt him. O'Connell's a fine poker player and he'll know how to disguise his hand if he wants to.

"Ah, yes ... Gargailis?" he says finally, still not giving me any indication this is sensitive territory. "I do remember that one now ... a slam dunk wasn't it? Husband confessed. They sent him for the needle but he slipped through the net."

"Yes, he got life."

"What do you want to know?"

"Some recent murders have brought the case back under scrutiny." I continue to study O'Connell's face.

"Whaddaya mean, under scrutiny? The doer's still in jail isn't he?"

"Yes, he is."

"I hear they don't let murderers out with a weekend pass these days, unless they're being chaperoned," O'Connell says, smiling at his joke and attempting to engage me with his humor. This cuts no ice with me and I keep a straight face, continuing to watch him intently.

"But you haven't told me what this is about. How I can help you, Oskar?"

"I want to go through the case with you Paddy, if that's okay."

"My memory isn't so good. It's shot, you see. It doesn't work like it did." He gives a slight rasping cough as if his throat is dry.

"That doesn't matter, Paddy. You can just remember what you remember. That's fine by me."

"Okay, so long as you're aware of my predicament," O'Connell taps his head with his finger, mimicking he's not so smart these days.

I want to move things along so I lean across and pull out the photocopy of the Gargailis Murder Book and lay it on the bed, making sure he's seen the front cover and, possibly, worked out what it is. It's not the same color as the original but I'm banking on him recognizing it, nonetheless.

I spot the tell immediately. It's as if I've laid a straight flush to his full house.

"Look, Oskar. What's going on?"

"I'll get to all that, Paddy. Would you just answer my questions, because everything will become clear? You know the deal, I ask, you answer." I do my best to smile in a way that assertively states I'm leading this discussion. Not him. I'm reminded of Ship's bullying tactics to me earlier today but I'm hoping I've a little more finesse than that jerk.

"What, ain't you gonna read me my rights first?" O'Connell asks sarcastically, chortling slightly and bringing up something from the back of his throat. He takes a tissue from a box on his side table and wipes his mouth.

"Pass me some water please, Oskar?" he asks, gasping through the spasm.

I move across to his bedside table, pick up a glass and pour some water from a pitcher. As I'm doing this, I notice a small 'panic' button on the work surface, attached by a long lead to a box on the wall. When I've filled the glass, O'Connell reaches out with frail-looking hands and takes it from me. As he drinks, I see him look towards the clock on the wall and then at his watch but the bracelet fits too loosely and it keeps slipping round his wrist.

"Look, Paddy. It's an investigation I'm following, that's all. It's no big deal. You know how it goes. I'm looking at potential leads and for some reason questions keep coming back to Gargailis. I need to speak to you about it because you were the lead detective at the time. So relax. Just answer the questions to the best of your ability."

"I know, Oskar, but you were around as well, weren't you? You probably have a better memory about that case than me."

O'Connell's breathing is easier now and he passes the glass back to me. I put it down on his bedside table. As I'm doing this, I see him look at the clock again.

"What's up Paddy, you expecting someone?"

"No ... I mean, yes ... well, my wife usually comes by around this time. I was just wondering when she'll get here. She brings me some food and reading materials and today I've a copy of VFM magazine coming and there's—"

"Look, shall I go to reception and ask that your wife stays there until we're finished here? Then you won't have to worry about her disturbing us."

I need him to know I'll not leave him alone until I obtain what I want. He lets out a long breath, as if considering the offer.

"No. Let's get this over with. I wanna do the best I can for you, Oskar. You were a good kid back then and you did great. They were different times ... The good old days, huh? ... We did things differently then, didn't we? ... Hey, Rodney King, he should think himself fuckin' lucky he didn't have me to face in that alley, 'cause he'd never have gotten off that floor if I'd been dealing out that beating."

He chortles again, smiling at the thought.

I do my best to smile at this weak attempt to justify approaches to policing rife in his 'good old days'. But I also wonder if he's preparing to justify anything I throw at him over Gargailis with the excuse that we worked to a different set of rules in 1993.

I take a deep breath, putting myself into a calmer place. Ready to try again.

"Okay, let's make a start. Why do you think Gargailis came out with his confession when he did, Paddy? Records suggest this came out of the blue, when everyone least expected it. What do you remember about it?"

I pick up the murder book and turn to a section I've marked out with a yellow post-it note.

"Look, you say here that Gargailis *'lawyered up one morning during the trial and just came out with it'.* Can you take me through what happened? How did you see it?"

"Jeez Oskar, d'yer want me to tell you what color shoes I was wearing?"

"No," I say calmly. "I just want to know what you remember about it. You know, when he made his confession."

O'Connell huffs and puffs and goes through a process of smoothing down the bed-sheets he's pulled around his chest. He doesn't look at me. I know he's about to lie.

"Well, Jardine and me arrived at the court to meet the prosecution team ahead of the day's proceedings. We were summoned to the judge to hear him say Gargailis wanted to confess. End of story. The sucker got what he deserved in my opinion ... Hell, Oskar, you were there as well, weren't you?"

"I didn't sit up front like you and Jardine, did I? I wasn't at that particular meeting."

O'Connell keeps looking at the murder book, as if preparing for something that'll come out from the pages and bite him. I've made the point of slipping in more post-its than I actually need, in the hope this will unsettle him. "Tell me what you remember him actually saying when you met him that day. The murder book says he wanted to tell you personally about it, face to face. To you alone. You remember that?" I say, patting the murder book.

O'Connell looks hard at the book again and back to me.

"It's all in there, Oskar. You've seen it. You've read it. Surely."

"Yes, I've read it, Paddy. I just want to hear what you remember of the event. You know ... with hindsight."

"With hindsight? Fuck me, Oskar ... HINDSIGHT?" he suddenly shouts. "Oh, for crying out loud, I don't know, Oskar ... he just came right out with it ... you know, something along the lines of, *"I killed my wife. I killed her in a fit of rage. I'm sorry for what I've done. But she deserved it. Son-of-a-bitch, she deserved it, etcetera, etcetera."*

"He said that? Did he use those words? Did he say 'Son-of-a-bitch', Paddy?"

"I don't know, Oskar. I don't fucking know. It's twenty years for chrissakes. I can't remember it word for word, can I? It's a long time ago ... A long time."

"I know Paddy. I just wondered if there's anything else you can remember that may not be in here."

He remains silent and it's particularly telling he doesn't defend my insinuation that he possibly left something out of the book.

I decide on another tack.

"How did you investigate whether his confession was true or not? The book's a bit thin on this. We go straight from confession to sentence. *'Slam dunk'* is the expression you used earlier. What did you and Jardine do to check his story? To see if he was telling you the truth."

O'Connell is becoming more agitated now because this question has really struck a chord. He suddenly stares at the clock and back to me. He's looking desperate.

"I don't know, Oskar. I can't even remember what I ate yesterday and you're asking me to remember a conversation in nineteen-fucking-ninety-three? You should have a better memory than me. You should know. You knew what was going down, didn't you?"

There it was again. I *knew* what was going down.

"As I said, I wasn't fully involved, especially when the case had gone to trial. Before that, you'd only asked me to follow up some leads. Things you had found in connection with his financial affairs. You had me checking his bank account and his wife's ... you thought Gargailis's estate was being whittled away by her at one point ... *'Follow the money'* you said to me, remember? *'Follow the money.'* That's what I did. I was shut out of other discussions and negotiations behind the scene. That just involved you, the DA and Gargailis, I seem to remember."

"Yes. I do remember all that, now. The lieutenant assigned you and Buttle to me to get the case wrapped up. You did some of the donkeywork, didn't you? But you did good, Oskar. You went on to greater things. I hope your experience working with me helped you up that career ladder."

I ignore his attempt at flattery and press on.

"But you kept me at arm's length, didn't you, Paddy? I've always wondered why you did that. I was never really part of the team."

"You were only a junior—"

"That won't wash either, Paddy, because Buttle was just as much a 'junior' as me and he wasn't shut out, was he? Buttle was on the inside. I was well and truly on the outside. Why was that?"

"Is that what this is about? Your pride, Oskar? For chrissakes, they were different times. Hierarchies were different in those days. The camaraderie between individual detectives was different. You were a rookie then and I was old guard but you had to earn a place at my table if you wanted to get on the *inside*. That was the way it was done. That was the way it was for me when I started out. You had to graft for your position in my day. Not like it is now. No, straight from a mother's breast and guys get a place in the police academy and then a master's degree writing answers to exam questions. And before you know it, they're leading a team on a murder investigation. Fucking sham if you ask me."

Things are heating up. So I do not follow up by asking him again, '*Yes, but why was Buttle part of the team and I was shut out?*' deciding to leave that for another time.

"What if Gargailis was taking the hit on behalf of someone else?" I ask. "What if he really didn't kill his wife? What if he was set up to take the rap?"

"What, you mean he '*took an offer he couldn't refuse?*'" O'Connell says with his best Godfather impersonation, mocking me.

"Yes. What if he really was given an offer he '*couldn't refuse*' Paddy?" I repeat sarcastically, doing my own version of Brando. "Don't talk out of your ass, Oskar. You've been—"

"Up to the point of the confession, the trial had been falling apart," I cut in. "Witnesses refused to go on the stand. Stories changed under oath. He was about to get a not guilty verdict from the jury, so why'd he confess like that? He must have been advised by his lawyers he was about to win his case, so why would he confess all this to you? To you alone?"

O'Connell's agitated now and starts to rub his wrists. The skin is dry and flaky and he brushes particles onto the floor. I see a line of sweat on his top lip and his eyes flickering this way and that, as if he can't settle something in his mind.

I decide to turn on the pressure.

"You see, Paddy, it keeps coming round to the same question and I can't seem to find an answer. Why would Gargailis take the hit for someone else? Because that's what I think happened."

"Look, Oskar, this is water under the bridge. Leave it alone. The guy owned up to it. We got the case together and it looked rock solid. And, yes, it was falling apart at the trial, I agree with you, but the guy had this sudden urge to confess. And, hey presto, we have the jerk back in jail serving the life sentence he deserved. Open and shut case. He seemed happy to take the sentence for chrissakes. And, so far as I know, he's not contested it since he was locked away in 1993."

O'Connell turns to face me as if he suddenly realizes what he's just said. I can see fear in his eyes.

"Why? ... has he? ... what's he saying? Is he saying he was set up? Is he saying he's innocent and that we framed him? ... Is he blaming me? ... THE MOTHERFUCKER!"

O'Connell yells this expletive so loudly I'm worried it will have been heard by the receptionist down the corridor.

"No, that's not what he's said. He's not contesting anything. Just calm down, Paddy, that's not what—"

"Well fuck off, then. Leave me alone, will you?"

O'Connell slumps in his bed, pulling the covers over his shoulders and halfway up his face as if hiding away will help him with his predicament. As he does this, the murder book slides across the bed.

"Leave me alone ... just leave me to die in peace, will you? ... Why did you want to come over here in the first place? ... Just fuck off, Oskar ... leave me alone ... leave me alone," he mumbles under the covers, not looking at me. As he turns his body over, the murder book is caught in the sheets and lifts up so that the front cover is facing him. We both stare at this phenomenon for a moment, before O'Connell sits up with a look of bewilderment, then realization, etched into his face, continuing to stare at the book.

"This is not an official copy is it? ... It's a fucking photocopy!" he blurts out, turning his attention back to me and becoming more agitated in the process. "Where's your fucking partner, Oskar? You're supposed to do these things in pairs, aren't you?" He reaches over and tries to pick up the book. "This is all unofficial, isn't it? ... SON-OF-A-BITCH ... GET OUTTA HERE! ... MOTHERFUCKER!" he screams as he leans across to his bedside table and scrabbles around for the panic button. All he does is knock it further out of reach and, as he pulls his hand back, he tips over his glass of water. It rolls across the surface and falls over the edge, landing with a loud crash on the highly polished floor.

"Hey, steady on, Paddy. Calm down, will you?"

At this point, I hear the door open behind me and turn to see two nurses running in, followed by an elderly woman I take to be O'Connell's wife. The nurses ease O'Connell down against his pillows, uttering soothing noises. One of them gives me a look to scare a witch.

"Please leave immediately, Detective Salo. This will not help him in his condition. Please leave," she demands.

As I reach the door, I turn back to look at O'Connell and see the two nurses fussing around him. He's on his back now, his head on a single pillow, the oxygen mask over his mouth.

"Breathe deeply, Mr. O'Connell," one of the nurses says. "That's it. Nice and steady. Long breaths."

All the while, O'Connell has a bead on me. I think he's more awake and alert than he's making out. I also think his wife knows this, because she's smiling amiably, hands folded together in front of her, waiting by her husband's side. O'Connell continues to hold my eyes, willing me to go away and leave him alone.

I think this has been a big act to deflect attention from what he's holding on to: The truth about what happened to John Gargailis in 1993.

Before I leave, I give O'Connell a look that tells him I'll be back. I move out through the door, nearly bumping into the cleaner.

48

(Wednesday, 8.42 p.m.)

THE REAPER WATCHES DETECTIVE Salo disappear through the front entrance and walk down the path towards his car. He feels a surge of excitement as he realizes he must bring his plans forward. He hadn't expected to but he's not concerned, not in the least. He *always* has contingencies in place.

After watching Detective Salo drive away, the Reaper return to his store cupboard and looks at himself in the mirror above the sink. He stares at his features. He's just come face-to-face with his nemesis. This had been a test, his first *real* test. He had looked Salo in the eye and let nothing slip, he was sure of that. Most importantly, there had been no recognition.

His thoughts are interrupted by the sound of a door opening in the corridor outside. Looking out from his store, he sees a nurse make her way over from Room 11.

"Can you clean up the glass that's dropped onto Mr. O'Connell's floor for me?" she asks. "There's been a little accident with a tumbler of water."

"Yes, of course, I'll do it right away," he replies.

"Thank you," she says, courteously, before returning to Mr.O'Connell's room. She's one of the polite nurses he likes. He remembers how she had stood and watched him whilst he painted the hospice sign out front. *'You have immense talent,'* she'd said on that occasion. *'You're a real credit to this place. Ever since you've arrived, you've smartened this place up, considerably. Thank you.'* The Reaper glows with pride at this thought – because he likes being thanked – and he reaches for his dustpan and brush before making his way to Room 11.

He takes a peek through the window and sees Mr. O'Connell lying in his bed. He moves inside the room quietly, taking care not to disturb the tranquil setting. He smiles at Mrs. O'Connell, who's sitting by her husband's side, patting his hand. She smiles back and mouths a discreet *'Thank you'* to him as he sweeps up the glass from the floor.

He takes care to find every piece because he doesn't want Mr. O'Connell to leave his bed and cut his feet. That's certainly not in his plan. He wouldn't want that.

49

(Wednesday 11.07 p.m.)

THERE'S A CAB DRIVER waiting for me as I come through Arrivals at San Francisco Airport. He's holding a piece of card with my name written across it in felt pen. I'd initially been looking for someone with a long beard, dressed in a cassock and sash and with a large golden cross hanging around his neck, so I'm surprised to find Father Peter has sent a cab instead. The driver is sporting a beard but there's nothing else 'churchy' or orthodox about him, except he's wearing plenty of layers in an anything goes style typical of this city. As I move closer, he transfers a pair of well-worn leather driving gloves to one hand and reaches out with the other.

"Detective Salo, good to meet you. I'm Father Peter," he says as he shakes my hand, warmly. "Welcome to San Francisco."

I must be looking surprised because he smiles broadly, recognizing my embarrassment.

"Why, what did you expect, the full turnout of the Bishopric?"

"N ... No ..." I stammer. "I was just expecting ... someone dressed in official church clothes, that's all."

"I don't wear those unless I'm on duty, Detective. I don't find them very comfortable for driving."

I must still be looking astonished because he imitates holding a car's steering wheel, giving a few turns back and forth before grabbing my case and setting off towards the exit with a smile on his face.

We have to weave our way through other *meeters-and-greeters* but soon reach a short stay multi-story car park. We climb two flights and walk out onto a floor of parked cars. Father Peter indicates he's going to a ticket machine to pay for his parking and points to the far corner where I see a grey Toyota Corolla. I take my overnighter from him and move across to the car. Whilst waiting, I watch Father Peter pump the machine with coins and, after removing his ticket and collecting his change, he walks towards me, holding up a set of keys and pressing a remote at the same time. I hear locks open behind me. Turning back around, I attempt to open the trunk of the Corolla to put in my bag but find it's still locked.

"That's not my car, Detective Salo. This is it," he says, moving past the Corolla towards a small blue and yellow sedan parked behind. It's a low slung, sporty compact, festooned with colored logos and flashes. There's a number 17 emblazoned on one side. He opens up the trunk.

"Here you are, sorry about that. You should have seen the look I got from my archbishop recently when I gave him a lift to a weekend seminary."

I try not to show further embarrassment and throw in my bag as nonchalantly as I can, only to find it sails into the floor-well where I would have expected rear seats.

"You'll be pleased to hear it does have a passenger seat ... you see, it's a road going rally car. A Subaru WRX STI, to be precise," he announces, rather proudly. "It's set up for off road racing but I have a license to drive it on the road so long as the car meets certain conditions and a passenger seat is a must," he says, as he finally closes the trunk.

I move around to the passenger door and climb into the seat he's referring to. It feels snug and is positioned low to the ground. Father Peter slides into the driver's seat effortlessly and shows how to fasten myself into the full body harness. As he's doing this, he sees me looking at the crash helmet attached to a rollover bar.

"Not needed for what we're going to be doing this evening, Detective. Don't worry ... I'll be gentle with you."

We're soon out of the car park and into the late evening traffic. We make our way easily towards the city center. Father Peter drives the car efficiently, expertly maneuvering around slower cars when there's an opportunity. I'm aware of the power under the hood because I hear the gentle but powerful throbbing of the engine the whole time.

As we drive, Father Peter tells me about his history working at the cathedral. He mentions his early life in the army, when he saw service in the first Iraq War. He states it was this experience which gave him the desire to change direction in his life. *'It was the vehemence of the aggression, you see'*, he says, reminding me of Lena's protracted, anti-violence thesis. He said that, when he returned from the Gulf in 1991, he trained to become an ordained priest in the Latvian Orthodox Church. He also mentions that, despite his age, he's never lost his love of rallying. He's forty-five-years old now and still races regularly. His father, a Latvian émigré, was a rally driver in the sixties and Father Peter tells me he has one of his race-built Saabs in a garage in L.A.

"I always travel by car, especially when I go to visit John. I can take detours into the mountains and I'm allowed to use private off-road circuits where I have landowners' permission to open up the throttle."

I realize it wasn't fear of flying that prevented Father Peter traveling up with me this afternoon, it was his passion for driving. Six or seven hours behind the wheel would be a pleasure for him.

He suddenly gives me a sensation of the speed he's referring to, revving the engine and racing towards the next junction. I feel my body thrown into the seat as we accelerate, and, as we stop at a red light, I'm thrown forwards into the harness, the car seemingly coming to rest effortlessly.

Nothing is said but, as I look at Father Peter, I realize he wasn't showing off, he was just giving me an opportunity to share the exhilaration he feels when behind the wheel of this powerful machine. I experienced a similar feeling when Sam spoke about her criminal profiling work. Both just like to express the sheer joy they derive from doing what they do best.

We soon reach the hotel at Fisherman's Wharf, a short hop from the Golden Gate Bridge, for our journey north tomorrow. As I climb out into the cool evening air and look around, I realize this is the first time in two days I haven't been looking for my tail.

Initially, my reason for keeping secret my meeting with Father Peter was to ensure I could do exactly what I wanted, without having to worry about the IAD and the Chief. But I'm now picking up on my heightened sensitivity and fear that the killer knows exactly what I'm doing, what I'm planning, where I'm going, and that's why he appears to be one step ahead of me all the time. I'm even starting to consider whether this information is leaking from my now-extended team, somewhere. Whilst I acknowledge that a little paranoia can keep you sharp, and help you remain focused, too much can stun you into inactivity and lead to a mistrust of the very people you normally rely upon. It's a delicate balance and I'm taking great care to manage it sensibly.

After checking in, we arrange to meet for a drink in the hotel bar in fifteen minutes. I have questions for Father Peter before our onward journey in the morning.

When I reach my room, I realize I switched my cell phone off before setting off for my flight from L.A. I turn to my first throwaway and switch it on and notice I've missed four calls from Dee but there's also a text:

WTFRU?

I call her straightaway. She picks up immediately.

"Where the fuck are you?" she asks, mimicking her text and before I've had a chance to say anything.

"I'm still on the road," I lie. "I've been chasing down O'Connell and a couple of leads."

"Well, I'm at Buttle's *new* apartment."

"New?"

"Yes, new. He moved in a few months back, or so says his wife, or should I say his *estranged* wife. She says he moved out of the matrimonial home after their marriage hit the rocks. I'm sitting outside now. It's a first-floor apartment, above a garage. Has its own external staircase. And Oskar, get this, a neighbor says he hasn't been seen since Monday night ... Monday for chrissakes ... That's two days ago, Oskar. What's he up to? What's going on? Has he got another woman, or what?"

I'm thinking further than this and consider the person who asked for him at Billy's.

"I couldn't see much through the front door when I looked a few minutes ago," Dee continues. "But it looks empty, Oskar. It's got that feel around the place that no one's been here for a few days. You know that feeling, Oskar?

I don't, so remain silent.

"No? Well ... oh ... hold on. Will you look at that?" I almost hear Dee smile.

"What is it?

"It seems as though he's got himself a friend ... She's up on the top step now, giving me that *look* ..."

Again, I've no idea what she's on about. What friend? What look?

"Poor thing, must be starving ... especially if Buttle's not fed her since Monday."

"What are you talking about?"

"It's a cat ... Oh, it's so sweet."

I thought cats were resourceful and went someplace else if you stopped feeding them but, frankly, I haven't time for this.

"Dee, I just want to hear that Buttle is safe and he'll turn up for work. That's all. I certainly don't want you worrying about some cat. Look, let's both go across tomorrow, perhaps we'll know more by then. We'll decide how we'll move forward on the case with or without Buttle's help. I don't want you to waste time looking for him now – or that cat! You hear—"

"What happened with O'Connell?" Dee interjects, having probably decided she'll pop across to a local store for cat food anyway. "Get anything useful out of him?"

"Not much we can work with," I continue. "I'm thinking of going back to have another shot at him in the morning."

Although I have it on my radar to meet him again, I also need an 'alibi' for where I'm really going in the morning.

"Well, you must have got something," Dee says, pushing me further. "Especially if you're wanting to make that trip all the way over to Long Beach to see him again."

She makes a valid point but I wouldn't put it past her to have worked out I'm scheming something anyway. I decide to placate her by giving a full rundown on my meeting with O'Connell. I even tell her of my concerns that he's holding back on revealing his full involvement in the outcome of the trial in 1993. I hope this will satisfy her interest for the time being.

When I've finished, Dee doesn't say anything and we remain silent. I think she's tuning in that 'sixth sense' of hers.

"I spoke with Sam earlier," Dee says, just as I'm contemplating hanging up. "She phoned me because she'd been having difficulty tracking you down all afternoon ... wondered if I knew anything." I continue to remain silent. "Said she'd opened up a *'can of worms'*. You know, related to that Eastern European money gig in the late eighties, early nineties. She said it had to do with property development in the area ... where Gargailis had been living. She also said that local mafia helped with this *'movement of money'*. Both people and their money ... their valuables. And, hear this, gold bullion. So perhaps Sam's been right all along and this really is a gang-related crime. Perhaps your guy Gargailis was more the 'gang-leader' than the 'peace-maker'."

I hear Dee saying all this with sarcasm in her voice, as if she's not convinced.

"What about Tomkins?" I say, changing the subject. "What are you and Treviss concluding?"

"Well, as you know, he's rock solid on those alibis, and there's nothing we can pin on him for the murders themselves, unless he has a double ... an identical twin, a double persona, no less. T-O-Ds and alibis keep him well away from the murder scenes with the time-windows Emmerson's given us now."

There's always some latitude with times of death but I'm sure Dee will have done the math.

"You know what, Oskar? He was a freaky guy and he loved his peeping tom photo-shoots, didn't he? So perhaps the idea he could be working *with* the killer is not so far-fetched after all? Could he and the murderer be working in partnership for some crazy reason? Anyone who secretly photographs the person he loves having sex with other men could get a thrill from photographing the murder scene from a secret lair, couldn't he? It's not that far-fetched, is it?"

Dee fires these questions off, not really expecting any answers, but she makes a good point.

"Yes, Dee. Run with these thoughts overnight and check with Sam for me will you? We'll explore this again tomorrow. Get yourself back home and have some well-earned rest. I'll keep you posted on my whereabouts in the morning. Meantime, watch your back.

"I will ... oh, on that point. I had a couple of rats up my ass all day. After I left you at Chang's this morning, I noticed an IAD cruiser on my tail all the way to Buttle's house. So I think it's a good idea to have these throwaways because I wouldn't put it past them to have our official phones under surveillance as well."

I'd forgotten all about the 'fix' and allow myself a slight smile, deciding not to tell her about my involvement in all this just now.

"Have a good night, Dee."

"You too, Oskar."

50

(Thursday, 10.30 a.m.)

I'M SITTING IN A twelve by ten metal-clad room with Father Peter. The room feels claustrophobic. We're waiting for John Gargailis and he'll be arriving from the even smaller eight by ten cell that's been his home for twenty years.

There's a table bolted to the floor, along with three plastic chairs. A high wattage electric bulb in the ceiling throws bright white light around the room. There are no windows. Fresh air comes from a noisy fan in a duct, high up on one of the walls. We've already waited thirty-five minutes for him to arrive and I'm itching to start.

Father Peter and I have driven across to San Quentin State Penitentiary in his Subaru. Once we arrived, we spent an hour going through the screening process. We filled out forms, had them signed, counter-signed and then had a five minute escorted walk through corridors, eventually ending up in C Block, Interview Room number 17.

As I pace the floor, waiting for Gargailis to appear, Father Peter sits quietly, occasionally looking through his folder. He turns the pages methodically, as if very familiar with the contents. I expect he's rehearsing what he'll be saying to Gargailis later, when the lawyer arrives.

Over drinks last night, I'd taken the opportunity to learn more about Gargailis but I'd also used the time to develop a relationship with Father Peter himself. I want him to trust me fully and tell me everything he knows about the murder case in 1993. But I'm concerned that, if push came to shove in a court, Father Peter

– like Gargailis's lawyer – won't have to reveal anything said between them over the years. Unless, of course, I find a way to make him tell me of his own volition.

I give thought to this and remember an RHD case in 2002. There was an inter-family feud between two competing sons from the same Gordini family; they had been fighting for supremacy as their ageing, gang-leader father, James Gordini, had taken a back seat in old age. A young daughter of one of the villains was kidnapped by the opposing faction and the detective on the case, Jon Bonetti, of Italian descent himself, felt that if he could persuade the villain-in-question's priest to reveal the whereabouts of the hostage, he could bring the feud to a conclusion without bloodshed. Unbeknownst to anyone in the squad room, Bonetti disguised himself as an opposing gang-member and cornered the priest in an alley with a stiletto – the gang's favored assassination weapon. The priest, thinking he was about to be executed, instantly revealed the whereabouts of the girl. We sat in amazement when Bonetti waltzed into the squad room holding her hand.

I know this case is different but wonder what secrets Father Peter is holding and what I might need to do to make him release information to me. He's a page open from his file showing a picture of the ornate casket from St Catherine's Cathedral about which he spoke last night. He'd told me Gargailis crafted the casket shortly before he was imprisoned. It's made of dense, dark grained wood and is slightly larger than a shoebox. I see it's embellished with gold leaf and there are intricate carvings on the faces and around the edges. It's beautiful. Father Peter had been at pains to tell me the casket held something of special significance to the cathedral. I hadn't challenged him to reveal what it was because, at the time, I thought he had been testing how far he could go in revealing things about John Gargailis without answering questions he didn't want to. I'd therefore remained silent and patient, remembering my fishing trips to the Yellowstone and knowing fish would bite in their own time.

Father Peter mentioned this photograph was to be included in Gargailis's parole hearing paperwork because the cathedral planned to return the contents of the casket to their *'rightful place'*, implying it would be a generous gesture by the authorities to allow Gargailis to participate in this ceremony after release from San Quentin. As a free man.

Chewing this over, I think Father Peter wants me to believe there is something more profound at stake here, possibly more important than proving Gargailis's innocence. And, as we await the arrival of John Gargailis, I believe the moment when I find out is about to arrive. Interestingly, Father Peter brought his own wooden box with him today. I carried it from the car for him. It contains the paraphernalia for the communion ceremony he'll be undertaking with Gargailis later the *'Divine Liturgy'* as he called it. I guess his box is about the same size as the one Gargailis crafted, but less ornate. It certainly shows signs of wear and tear. *'This is my travelling set'*, Father Peter had said when he passed it across in the prison's car park.

I was able to see inside the box when prison guards inspected it at the reception center. The communion elements were treated reverently – almost like well-known friends – because they've been inspected every time Father Peter has visited the jail. The guards brought out a small silver chalice, standing eight inches high, and a beautifully engraved plate, no more than three inches in diameter, for the communion wafers. The wafers were stored in a small, wooden box. There were two small glass flasks with glass stoppers, one containing red wine of a deep red color, the other, water. On top of this set was a beautifully embroidered cloth which guards took care to fold up neatly once they'd finished their inspection.

Father Peter said the solid silver chalice and plate dated back to the 14th century, and came as a pair, but the full set of elements had been brought together when Latvian emigrants came to L.A. around the time of Gargailis's trial. I assume the émigrés had somehow managed to smuggle these antiques in their luggage.

Indeed, Father Peter explained last night that, during the 1914–1918 World War, German forces attempted to confiscate all orthodox church property in Latvia and that was why some of the church's treasures – communion elements, religious relics, paintings, icons – had found their way into church members' lofts and cellars. As I reflect on this, I consider whether Father Peter has been telling me these snippets for a good reason. He wants me to decipher their significance for myself, once I manage to put the full story together like a jigsaw. A small charge pulses through me as I grapple with this thought, coinciding with the sound of the door opening in the far wall.

I look up to see two guards enter the room, either side of John Gargailis. It's an incongruous site because the two guards must weigh two hundred and fifty pounds apiece but Gargailis can only weigh eighty – if that. His prison uniform drapes over his bony body, like ill-fitting pajamas. Thankfully, he's not wearing the full security bracelet and anklets because I doubt he would be able to carry them.

The guards treat Gargailis courteously, leading him towards the chair on the other side of the table. As soon as he's seated, they walk back out, closing the door, leaving the three of us alone.

I move to the remaining chair and sit down next to Father Peter, taking my first look at the man I haven't seen for twenty years. He doesn't acknowledge me and sits with head lowered, almost contemplative. His hands are clasped together on his lap, as if in prayer.

Although it's been a long time, I recognize his features but am shocked by his diminutive stature. I remember him standing much taller.

Father Peter leans forward.

"Hello John, thank you for agreeing to meet with us today. May I introduce Detective Salo to you?"

I lift myself out of my chair and lean across with arm outstretched. We shake hands. Interestingly, despite Gargailis's frail appearance, his grip is firm and the skin feels roughened;

325

these are indeed craftsman's hands and I'm immediately reminded of when I first shook his hand, in 1993.

"Good morning, Mr. Gargailis," I say, as I drop back into my chair. "You've probably been told I'm investigating a case in Los Angeles. I want to ask you a few questions."

There's no response.

"Do you remember me, Mr. Gargailis? I was one of the detectives involved in investigating the crime which brought you to San Quentin."

He pushes his glasses higher up his nose and takes a hard look at me this time, as if checking me out.

"Yes," he says, finally. "You're the one ... did a fine job I seem to remember."

There's a long silence, during which I hope he'll say something else, but he doesn't. He just settles back again, head lowered.

Just as I'm feeling this trip will end up being a waste of time, Gargailis looks up, as if he's read my thoughts and sensed my frustration.

"So, Detective Salo, how may I help? What can I do for you?"

I relax slightly and start by telling him why I'm here. But I've also decided to give it to him with 'both barrels', because I think this might be my only chance to extract something from him and it'll be a risk worth taking.

I start by telling him how the recent string of murders has been committed. I omit none of the salient facts and mention the victims have been savagely beaten. I tell him they've had their limbs broken and have bled to death, once their carotid arteries have been severed.

I want him to hear the words, particularly the phrases I've used to describe these macabre rituals in my reports and not the sanitized versions expressed in press releases or newspapers he may have read.

These are stark words about the way innocent victims have been brutally killed. I want him to feel the similarity with the way his wife died twenty years ago. I want him to make the same connections I've made myself so he'll understand why I'm here.

I go on to mention my meeting with Detective O'Connell yesterday and the way this dying man had closed down on me. I tell him about my fears O'Connell knows what really happened to his wife but is holding something back.

I tell him about LAPD's chief of police, David Kramer. I tell him about how the chief has been bearing down on me, especially when I made the connection to his wife's murder and took out the murder book from the archive.

I tell him about the lieutenant's death in the car park and my fears the murders might not stop unless I catch the perpetrator quickly.

I even tell him about the frustrations I've always felt with the outcome of his trial in 1993. I tell him I've never believed he killed his wife and that this has haunted me throughout my career. I tell him I think the person who killed his wife probably killed Eric Green, David Henshaw, Jane Chandler and, possibly, murdered Franklyn Tomkins and the lieutenant.

And, finally, I tell him I'm in relentless pursuit of the truth and that's my main reason – no, my sole purpose – for being here today. When I finish, I sit back in my chair, feeling my pulse quicken and blood thump around my body. I see Gargailis is shocked by my no-holds-barred account.

I wait him out, breathing steadily into the silence. In fact, I want them both to know I'll not let this slide any longer.

After about twenty seconds of waiting, the air-conditioning unit kicks into action, as if it's sensed the heat built up in the room.

I look at Father Peter. Gone is his ecclesiastical and calm exterior. He looks pale and concerned, turning his eyes away from mine. He rubs the soles of his shoes on the floor, nervously, clearly disturbed by what I've just said.

When my pulse has slowed enough, I lean forward to prompt Gargailis into speaking.

327

"I wondered if we could talk about all this, John—may I call you John?" I see a slight nod. "First, can you tell me about your memories of what happened during those last days of the trial?"

Again there's silence as the air-conditioning unit shuts down.

I'm about to ask the question again when Gargailis raises his head. He takes a deep breath and smiles warmly.

"What do you want to know, Detective?"

"Well, I'm interested in why you suddenly confessed. You see, I had you down to receive a not guilty verdict and I'm sure your lawyer would have advised you likewise. So why did you confess like that?"

Gargailis continues holding my eyes for a fraction longer than feels comfortable and then looks across at Father Peter momentarily before returning his gaze to me.

"You like getting to the point, don't you?" he says, smiling good-naturedly. "I remember how you did this back then ... you always got straight to the point ... with everything."

I remain silent, hoping he'll answer my question without being distracted by this memory.

"Well ... the truth is the truth ... isn't it?" he says. "I was responsible for my wife's death so I needed to pay the price. That's why I confessed."

There was the claim of being 'responsible' again, not the claim that he actually murdered her.

"But why did you wait until almost the last day of the trial? Why wait till then?"

There's another pause.

"You see, God moves in mysterious ways, Detective. He always has perfect timing ... it was the right moment. That's all."

I'm not satisfied with his answer so pursue further.

"You had a good defense team and they were doing a great job. They had pulled apart the prosecution's case. Prosecution witnesses had failed to deliver. You were about to walk."

"Is that a statement or a question, Detective Salo?" he says, smiling again.

"It's a statement—can you tell me about the chest you made for St Catherine's Cathedral?" I suddenly say, swerving in another direction, hoping this will throw him off guard. "Tell me how you made it and why it was such an important commission."

Gargailis's eyes dart momentarily to Father Peter and back to me. "Yes, it was a special commission, as you imply. It was a commission I was immensely privileged to pursue, in fact."

Again he looks at Father Peter as if seeking permission to say something else. Gargailis returns his gaze to me.

"It holds ancient relics, Detective. I brought together all my skills and made the casket. I sourced special timber from the east coast, a type of bogwood that comes up to the surface every now and again. It has a dense grain and it's beautiful to work with. I made the casket in my own workshop."

I think these relics came across with the Latvian émigrés Father Peter referred to last night and wonder if they were responsible for inspiring the murder in 1993. I'm also considering if they're the inspiration for the murders now but I can't piece everything together, so decide to come at it from another direction.

"Tell me about your wife. What was she like? Why did you kill—?"

"Is this really fair, Detective?" Father Peter interjects, clearly flabbergasted by my assault. "He's served his sentence and you know he's about to move to a parole hearing in two months. Surely you can't believe it's fair to ask him a question like that? Not now? And, certainly not without having his lawyer—"

"I assure you it won't affect the parole hearing," I say, interrupting, keeping eyes focused on Gargailis. "I'm only here to find answers to questions which help me solve the murders I'm investigating now. That's all. I'm not here to keep this man in prison any longer."

"Then, why are you digging up the past like this? Surely it will only jeopardize his chances of being freed? I thought you believed in his innocence. I thought you—"

"Calm yourself, Peter," Gargailis suddenly interrupts, holding up both hands. "I can answer Detective Salo's questions. He's only doing his job, after all. I have nothing to fear by telling the truth, have I?"

"Yes, but I don't want anything you say here to affect all the hard work you've put into securing your freedom. Not now. You've been in prison for too long, John."

"Don't worry yourself, Peter. Let Detective Salo ask his questions. I want to help him with his investigation. That's why he's here, isn't it? Nothing I say about my wife's murder in 1993 can affect me now. Peter, please, let me answer his questions."

There's silence in the room as things begin to settle down.

Father Peter is clearly angered by my approach, unlike Gargailis, who remains calm and placid. I think he wants to talk and wonder if another golden door is beckoning.

"My wife was a lovely woman," Gargailis continues. "That was why I married her. She was beautiful but we grew apart as time went on. We were not a close family in the end ... After my first wife died, I fell in love with Sylvia, Detective, but that was probably my mistake. She became too interested in money. My money. At first, I think she married me for my money, if the truth be known, but I was blind to that ... she went on to spend it for herself on earthly trifles ... clothes, jewelry, cars ... the usual sorts of things you'll be familiar with in your line of work, Detective Salo. Then things got out of hand, when she found ways to almost make money for herself ... she ... orchestrated ... yes, that's the word, she orchestrated the transfer of wealth to herself."

"Please, John! Don't say any more. It's too—"

"No, Peter. I will. Let me tell Detective Salo the truth. He deserves to know this after what he's been through. I think we can trust him with the truth ... I really do."

Again, there's silence for a few moments, as Gargailis pulls his thoughts together. Father Peter sits back, folding his arms across his chest, sliding his feet back and forth on the floor, agitated and distressed by what's happening. Gargailis lifts his head. My heart's thumping, again.

"It all started because there'd been a member of the congregation at St Catherine's – a woman of Latvian descent – who'd married into an Italian family. Through this connection, the church managed to secretly smuggle the precious relics I told you about, out of Latvia and all the way to L.A. Because of the turmoil with the break-up of the Soviet republic and surrounding states, the clergy over there, quite rightly, thought the relics would end up in criminal hands unless we in St Catherine's intervened. They feared these precious items would be lost forever, perhaps being sold to some Japanese collector. So, we used the channels this Italian family had to transfer the relics to L.A. We knew these channels were being used to launder money and smuggle drugs so it was a difficult decision for the church to take. But a group of us prayed about it and we decided it was the right thing to do."

Gargailis pauses, focusing on this distant past and seemingly remembering the significance of this decision. He lets out a long breath, bringing his eyes back to the present.

"Anyway, the relics made their way over to St Catherine's in Los Angeles and they've remained there ever since. Hidden in a secret location."

I've worked out the significance of the ornate casket now but Gargailis hasn't explained the connection of this to his wife's moneymaking escapade. Again, I know I don't have to ask, because the door has opened now.

"My wife, you see, she found out about this ... this arrangement," Gargailis continues. "She started to make her own connections with the family and, unbeknownst to me and everyone else in the church, managed to smuggle other valuables out of Latvia, for families within the Latvian community. They were small items at first, like jewelry, heirlooms, knick-knacks, until she was making a business out of it. Then she started moving currency, precious gems, diamonds ... I never unpicked the full extent of the dealings before her death; it was only afterwards that I found out what had been happening, when I was in jail. You see, Detective Salo, she had been making a great deal of money. Thousands and thousands of dollars ... I don't really know how much. I found out that she charged a fifty percent commission, based on their value on arrival in L.A. My brother told me when I was awaiting trial in prison. He told me about unceremonious visits in the night when bad people came knocking on the door, demanding money. Money, they said, that was 'owing'. They were polite at first but, when he couldn't pay up, they started sending thugs who threatened him, saying he would be killed unless he complied with their demands. They threatened to kill my thirteen-year-old son, Danil. This was about the time the trial was beginning to collapse and when Detective O'Connell started to investigate the Italian family's connections to the case all over again. I feared the cathedral was going to be drawn into this horrible episode. What could I do? The thugs were clearly not going to take no for an answer. My brother convinced me they had killed my wife."

He pauses at this point as if he's reconnecting with the moment. His face grimaces.

"And now they were coming for my son," he continues. "I had stocks and shares and various properties but I couldn't raise enough money within the timescale demanded and certainly not whilst I was in jail. Things were exacerbated by the renewed police investigation and I saw this as my salvation. Through an intermediary, I managed to negotiate a deal. I agreed that, in exchange for getting the detective team off their backs, once and for all, I would give them the proceeds of the sale of my brother's house out in Beverly Hills, once it was sold. It would take a little longer to obtain the money than they had been expecting but they agreed, because I offered them double the amount demanded."

I start to wonder what O'Connell's role might have been in these negotiations with the mob. There's nothing in the murder book to suggest this line of investigation even took place. So, was O'Connell doing his best to hide this link by eradicating mention of it in the murder book when he took it out of the archive after the trial, in 1994? What about Kramer's role? Was he involved as well? Was he making doubly sure the book had been 'edited' properly when it was his turn to take it out, in 1995?

I come out of my musing and notice Gargailis is looking into my eyes, as if ensuring I've fully understood the significance of what he's just said.

I know my time with Gargailis is limited and want to ask more questions, so I decide to move on. I bring out my copy of the murder book and turn to the section I've marked off with a post-it note.

"Your statement. It says here, John, that you *'went to her side and tried to resuscitate her, but she was gone. I knew she was gone"*. You also said, *'It was hopeless'*. Those are the words you apparently said to Detective O'Connell in your statement to him when he first arrived on the scene. Is this the truth or was the truth what you said to him later, in your confession?"

He smiles as if I've caught him between two truths. "Yes. That is the truth. As I remember it now."

"Thank you. It also says that you found your wife lying on the floor, savagely beaten and lying in a pool of blood. Then you found your son *'cowering in the corner of the kitchen like a frightened child'*. Is that correct? Is that what really happened?"

"Yes, I remember saying all that to one of the detectives at the scene. But, you see, I didn't know the full story then. It was only during the trial ... when your colleagues, Detectives O'Connell and Jardine, started to dig a little deeper into the evidence again, after they started to investigate the link with this Italian family, that I learnt the full story. So, can you see that I fabricated the confession to save the lives of my own family ... and the integrity of the church?"

"Would you tell me about David Kramer?" I ask, remembering Kramer's admission that he'd known the Gargailis family beforehand.

"Yes, you're right, Detective. I did know him. He was a close family friend. He was a fine craftsman, as you may know. He once made a most magnificent rosewood desk."

I suddenly remember the chief's desk in his office, and the way he stroked it with the palms of his hands. I just nod, wanting him to continue.

"I taught him a few things in my workshop and helped him make some beautiful furniture. He really enjoyed working with wood, like me. He went on to greater things, though, didn't he?" he says, smiling broadly. "He's your boss now, I hear."

"Yes, something like that—how long did you know him for?" Gargailis screws his eyes up, as if trying to work this out. "Probably about two years ... I met him when I taught wood craft at an evening class. It was just about the time he was starting out on training to become a police officer. That's when we became friends."

I look across at Father Peter; his head is lowered, as if he's in his own world. The floodgates have definitely opened and he's probably working out what needs to be done to rescue the situation.

"In what way was he close to you and your family?" I ask.

Gargailis smiles, but there's a wry look attached, as if he's thinking I know something else.

"Well, he got to know my family just about the time that things were starting to fall apart with my wife, a few months before her murder," he says, holding my eyes.

I remain silent, wanting him to fill in the gaps to where I think this is leading.

"Yes, he ... got to know my wife very well." There's another pause and I hear Father Peter sit up in his seat, sensing the tension created by this comment.

"What do you mean? Did Kramer and your wife have an affair?" I prompt.

"Yes. That's the right way to express it, I think ... an affair."

Alarm bells ring in my head but I try not to show it, still wanting him to continue telling me in his own words.

"I don't think it was love, Detective ... It was more ... more of a carnal thing. Not love. I don't think my wife was capable of loving anyone, you see."

"How did you know they were having an affair?"

Gargailis coughs slightly and I hear Father Peter's shoes scrape on the floor, once again.

"Well, I found them together on one occasion ... David was embarrassed but my wife wasn't. She seemed to be unashamedly proud of what she was doing but David attempted to assure me his relationship with Sylvia would stop immediately. He tried to apologize but there was nothing to apologize for, my marriage was broken anyway, so I forgave him. He was young. She was beautiful. It was just an opportunity that came his way. A young man like that."

I look across to Father Peter. He looks at me with raised eyebrows, clearly shocked by this news himself and possibly unaware of my own adrenalin-pumping thoughts about a jigsaw coming together.

51

(Thursday, 1.00 p.m.)

I'M SQUEEZED INTO THE passenger seat of Father Peter's Subaru. We're making our way to San Francisco Airport so I can catch my flight to LAX. He's clearly still angry about the way I treated Gargailis this morning and he's not spoken a word since we left San Quentin. He's also not giving me as gentle a ride as yesterday because I've already hit the side of my head on the seat restraint. And I'm sure I've just seen him give another driver the bird after he was cut up.

On one level, his annoyance is justified and down to the way he wants to protect Gargailis from intrusive questions and challenges. He's clearly very attached to this 'peacemaker' and, now it's been confirmed an injustice has been served, I'm sure he wants to ensure Gargailis obtains his release papers in September. I therefore decide I'll let Father Peter stew in his own juice before I attempt reconciliation.

After the interview ended, I was going to leave Father Peter and Gargailis to their communion service, because I wanted to make my way back to the visitors' area and wait there. But, in the end, I joined them, following an invitation from Gargailis himself – *'It would mean a great deal to me if you would join us on this occasion, Detective Salo. It just seems to be the best thing to do in the circumstances.'*

I was slightly embarrassed but soon had the hang of what to do, remembering my days as an altar boy at the local church in my teens. I was surprised how this ritual came back to me after so many years in my own spiritual wilderness.

Although the service was held in the same claustrophobic room we'd used for the interview, the experience somehow felt otherworldly. It was a strangely peaceful experience and I wondered if this had anything to do with Gargailis being referred to as the 'Peacemaker' by guards and fellow inmates.

It was also a strangely incongruous sight. We were following in the wake of a long line of Christians, acting out the most sacred of religious ceremonies, in the middle of California's most oppressive and violent prison. A place where convicts were stripped of their dignity and either executed in a death chamber or left in inhumane conditions, some for the rest of their earthly life.

All in all, the experience was a heady mix, both demanding and uplifting. There weren't any angels singing but I certainly experienced a degree of stillness in that moment. There was also a sense that I had taken part in something significant. I do not show my feelings in public but, at one point, I caught a glimpse of Gargailis acknowledging the impact the service was having on me.

I see the Golden Gate Bridge coming up and this makes me think about my own bridge building.

"I hope your meeting with the lawyer went well?" I ask, genuinely wondering how things had gone after I'd left Father Peter and Gargailis with their counselor

"It went very well, thank you." Father Peter replies courteously.

"Is everything on course for submitting the parole hearing paperwork?"

"Yes. We're nearly there … in fact, we have you to thank for much of that.'

I turn to face him, wondering what I've done.

"Despite your methods to extract information from John, he was in a particularly buoyant and constructive mood. I've experienced it many times before with members of my congregation; once they've given voice to their inner thoughts, they become less constrained. They're freed up, as it were."

"You're unfamiliar with detective questioning methods?" I say, thinking about those 'golden door' moments.

"Yes, I am but John wasn't fazed by your methods was he? Not like me," he smiles. "Anyway, your questions opened up John to some fresh thinking about how to present his case in a few weeks' time. The lawyer seemed grateful and thought it was building into an even stronger case."

I see Father Peter take a deep breath, letting the air out slowly. "Do you have anything further to add which can help me with all this?" I ask, He screws up his face, as if he's pondering whether to say something to me or not, but remains silent.

"What is it?" I prompt.

"It's just ... it's just your methods that concern me. You see, it's the same dilemma I face as a priest. What's said in confidence between a member of the congregation and me is always a sacred matter between the person concerned and Almighty God. Your approach is so different, Detective. It's so much more intrusive ... so much more demanding ... more aggressive. That's all ... it's different ... I just found it difficult to sit and listen to what you were saying to John ... after everything he's gone through. And everything we now know."

I decide to push further.

"Are you saying that, if John had confessed something to you, you wouldn't reveal that to me – to anyone?"

"That's correct ... no one mortal, anyway, Detective," he says, smiling again.

"But what about if another person's life was at risk, Father? What if John had revealed something to you which affected someone else? Someone else's life? Wouldn't you have a responsibility to them?"

"Yes, I would. But that would be just another matter for God to adjudicate on."

"Couldn't you plug yourself into what your God wanted you to say, on his behalf ... once he'd adjudicated?"

"Oh, I do, constantly, Detective Salo. That's my job, you see," he says, smiling even more broadly.

I'm not sure if he's asking me to be patient with him, or if he's justifying the position he's taking over something. Because I'm starting to believe he's holding on to a vital piece of information that will help me solve the murder cases I'm investigating now.

I think he spotted my concern.

"Look, Detective Salo, don't worry. There's nothing I'm not telling you. Please believe me. I want to help you solve these atrocious crimes. It's just the shock of hearing what John said today. Out loud as it were. It ..."

"It what, Father?"

"It just brought many thoughts and emotions to the surface for me and I've been putting them through the wringer. Thoughts, memories, they all came flooding back; memories about the murder scene itself and from those dramatic moments in the courthouse when John was sentenced to death. There'd been the angry crowds outside calling for him to be killed. Did you know we undertook our communion service only a few yards from the actual death chamber itself? Then, there'd been the reprieve, followed by John's cruel incarceration over those years."

He pauses and descends into his thoughts. I decide to give him space to construct what he wants to say next. We're silent for a few minutes, as the road opens in front of us. We're about to approach the Bridge and Father Peter guns the accelerator. I feel a release of inner tension for a moment before he has to pull up behind a slow-moving truck in the outside lane.

"There were also things said today that I've never heard before. Things I'd never even suspected. And now that John has voiced to us both that he was totally innocent of his wife's murder and he's suffered this way for the sakes of others ... well, it makes me angry, that's all ... suffering is an integral part of the Christian story I know but it still makes me angry ... I am human after all."

There's still a smile on his face but it's tinged with sadness and concern. The poignancy is not lost on me and, as we approach the tolls on the far side, Father Peter throws six dollars into the basket and then drifts of into his own thoughts, remaining silent for the rest of the journey.

We eventually reach the airport. As we pull into the drop off zone, I extract a business card from my wallet and scribble the numbers for my throwaways on the reverse. I suspect he might come back to me with information, once he's had a chance to put his thoughts and memories through that 'wringer'. I also write down my address for Geometrix on the back.

"Do not hesitate to contact me anytime, day or night, Father. Believe me, you and your God might just come up with the crucial information to bring this sorry episode to a successful conclusion. There's been too much suffering, don't you think?"

"There's always suffering, Detective, but I take your point. God bless you," he says, as he leans across and shakes my hand.

I attempt to climb out gracefully from his car, pulling my overnight bag with me, but struggle because of the high curb and enveloping fit of the bucket seat. My knee clicks as I push myself up and eventually lift my head into the bright afternoon sunshine.

As I turn and wave at Father Peter, my throwaway cell phone shrills. It's Dee.

"All hell's broken loose, Oskar," she says, sounding really scared and breathless, as if she's been running. "Listen up. This is important. I might only get one chance to say all this. Shitcreek *do* have you by the balls," she says, repeating what the chief said to me yesterday. I make my way quickly into the arrivals concourse, looking for somewhere quieter. "They grilled me for two hours this morning and they've tried to get me to reveal every part of the investigation before—"

"Just tell them what you know, Dee. Don't hold back."

"That's the problem, Oskar, because I obviously don't know everything—just listen, will you? It's the DNA under Chandler's fingernails."

We're both silent now.

"So, what are you're telling me ... partner?" "What are you talking about, Dee? I don't—"

"It's your fucking DNA, Oskar!" she blurts out. "Is that what you and Emmerson were talking about in your old boys' club meeting yesterday?"

"What? You're saying it's my DNA?" I ask, flabbergasted.

"Sure is. There's a BOLO out for you as we speak. My guess is they're working on a warrant right now to search your apartment. I heard Crick discussing it with Ship. That fucker, he's been like an alpha dog with all his bitches on heat. He's mooning around the squad room like he owns the fucking place. Everything's sealed up. All our cubicles. The full works. Don't even think about coming anywhere near the PAB—where are you?"

"Whoa. Slow down. Are you saying I'm accused of Chandler's murder?"

"Yes, I have the docket in front of me—you're wanted in connection with an investigation into Jane Chandlers' murder, it says here. I even had Dick Chesner, a guy on patrol, phone me up to double check. He said a BOLO had been passed to all cars—you're hot, Oskar. Stay clear of this place?"

It sounds as if Dee's still moving quickly. "Where are you now, Dee?" I ask.

"I've come out for a breather. Treviss and I have been ordered to stay away from the case and to stay away from you. I'm on my way to Buttle's apartment 'cause he's still a no-show and I'm worried. I've parked a couple of blocks away and I'm making my way on foot. I'm looking up at his apartment now," she says, in a quieter tone as if she stopped moving. "Hang on, there's a window ... that wasn't open before. He's there. I'll knock on that door and see what's what with that lazy S-O-B."

I hear Dee climb the steps to Buttle's front porch now, breathing heavily again.

"One other thing I need to tell you, Oskar. The chief's gone missing and that's another thing they're laying on you."

"What do you mean gone missing?"

"Exactly that. He's gone missing. I overheard Shitcreek talking and Ship had a hard-on about that, too. Suggested you might have something to do with it. They asked me lots of questions about your recent dealings with him. Took all my files and notes."

"How long has he been missing?"

"He was meant to attend a conference after the cadets' ceremony yesterday. Nothing's been seen of him since. Didn't make it back here. Didn't go home. What's going on, Oskar? What's the deal here? Explain, will you?"

"I'm being set up. That's the deal. I'm being set up, for chrissakes!" There's silence on the phone.

"Dee? ... Dee? ...You still there?"

"Hold on ... this doesn't feel right. The door's open," she says, as she comes back on the line. I hear her snap on a pair of latex gloves and then I hear the creaking of a screen hinge.

"I'm about to push open the front door—Oh ... this doesn't, look—Oh, for pity's sake. It's—Jesus—hold on, Oskar." I hear Dee put her phone down onto a surface.

"It's ... it's the ... what the?" I hear her say, away from her phone. "Dee, take care, pull out and get backup. Dee—DEE!"

There's about thirty seconds of silence interspersed with the sound of opening doors and Dee moving around Buttle's apartment. Eventually, she comes back to the phone.

"The fucker ... the fucker ... Someone's killed the cat, Oskar. It's—I'll have to—"

I suddenly hear the phone go down again and the sound of retching as Dee vomits. These are long heaving sounds from deep inside her belly. Then I hear the sound of running water and start to worry about her contaminating a potential crime scene.

"Sorry Oskar, it's just awful—the cat's been ... it's been butchered, Oskar. There's blood all across the floor. Its legs have been broken and it looks as if it's been beaten ... with something ... yeah, over there. There's a rolling pin ... on the kitchen floor. Oh ... oh ... my ... God. It's ..."

"What about Buttle? Any sign?" I ask. "Have you checked all the rooms?"

"Yes, I've checked. It's a small apartment. There's no sign of anyone in the bedroom or the bathroom."

I think about the other murder scenes now and the evidence we found for a killer's lair and wonder if someone's still there. Hiding. Perhaps watching Dee at this moment. All these thoughts come together quickly and I really start to fear for Dee's safety.

"Dee? Listen. Get yourself outta there, will you? Call for backup." There's silence.

"Dee?"

Still more silence.

"DEE" I shout into the phone.

"Hold on, Oskar," she says.

"Get out of—"

"Hang on, will you?"

I guess Dee's having the same thoughts as me because I hear her moving around the apartment again but, this time, I hear her knocking on walls and panels and opening up cupboards. Eventually, she comes back to the phone.

"Look, Dee. Get out of there and call—"

"It's a flat roof, Oskar. There's no loft. There doesn't seem to be any hiding place in here. I'm sure of that."

I think about the photograph Sam sourced from a newspaper in 1993. I think about Kramer protecting Gargailis from the ravenous press and consider his 'lover', Chandler, brutally murdered, and now he's gone missing. Then, there's Buttle; he's disappeared, and Dee's found his cat ritualistically butchered on the kitchen floor. There's Jardine, missing presumed dead. And, of course, there's O'Connell—

"O'Connell," I say to myself.

"What? What was that you said?"

"Nothing ... nothing. You call it in, Dee. Get people there. I gotta go. Tell IAD if necessary, then let's meet at Chang's." I look at my watch as I race across to a Hertz desk on the far side of the concourse. "Can you get in contact with Sam and Treviss? We'll all meet at Chang's."

"Why—what are you thinking? What's going on? Where are you going?"

"I'll meet you later. I'll set it all down when we meet."

"How can I help, sir?" the woman behind the counter asks as I close my phone on Dee. "I'd like to hire a car after I land at LAX."

52

(Thursday, 7.00 p.m.)

THE SAME NURSE IS on duty as I push through the front door. "I'm here to see Mr. O'Connell," I say, as I walk straight past reception and head towards Room 11.

"Yes he's there. But you can't just—"

"Get me a wheelchair and two nurses in there immediately. We need to move him."

"I don't think—"

"Now, if you please—and get hold of someone senior, so I can explain what we'll be doing," I call back, as I race down the corridor.

I reach the door of Room 11 and look inside. O'Connell looks deathly pale. I suddenly panic, thinking I'm too late, and rush to his side. There's no sign of life so I move in close and rock his head gently.

"Wake up, O'Connell, for chrissakes. Come on, wake up, will you?"

I start to wish I'd phoned ahead when, thankfully, he stirs and his frail-looking lids flutter open to reveal his watery eyes.

He takes a couple of seconds to adjust to what's going on and then screws his face up when he recognizes me.

"What the ... You. Whaddaya want, you fucker?" he says, trying to sit up at the same time.

I reach for another pillow and put it behind his back, just as two nurses come through the door. The same pair as yesterday – the first one's in my face immediately.

"You can't just barge in here and—"

I hold up my badge aggressively, stopping her in her tracks. I'm just hoping news of my BOLO hasn't reached this far yet and the sight of my credentials will silence her. They do.

"Listen up. It's my belief that Mr. O'Connell is in grave danger. I need him to be moved somewhere much safer, somewhere away from this threat. Can you arrange for him to be transferred to another medical center please?"

Both nurses stand completely still, as if I'd suggested flying him to the moon. I'm spared repeating the instruction by the sight of the receptionist, accompanied by someone I take to be the most senior member of staff on duty. I see from her badge she's the Duty Manager, Siobhan Murphy. I move across and explain about the threat to O'Connell, without going into too much detail.

She agrees he can be moved but says she'll need the arrangement approved by her supervisor, whom she'll have to phone. I ask her to do so immediately and to organize a wheelchair ambulance to be made ready.

"Wh—What's this about, Oskar?" O'Connell croaks from behind me. "What threat? Who'd want to threaten me? Who'd want to kill me? I'm dying anyway, for chrissakes. Why would anyone want to murder me?"

"I hope you might be able to help me with that list of questions, O'Connell, because you need to finish what we started yesterday."

"I've got nothing more to say to you about that. You can just go fuck yourself."

"Mr. O'Connell, keep your voice – and your bad language – to a minimum, please. Think of the other patients. And, Detective Salo, you must not excite Mr. O'Connell, he's very frail."

I hear the door open and turn round to see the manager coming towards me, holding a phone. Behind her is an orderly bringing in a wheelchair.

"It's the director of the hospice for you, Detective Salo. Dr. Steven Jamieson."

I take the phone and introduce myself, explaining yet again what we need to do. And why. Jamieson asks me to wait whilst he

346

goes further up the line to seek overall permission from another director, stating that two signatures are required. I'm more frustrated by the minute because of the bureaucracy but I just want to do this quickly so I can head back to L.A.

Whilst I hang on to the phone, hearing Jamieson talking on another line, O'Connell continues to voice his objections, using the same level of expletives and decibels as before. Fearing O'Connell's protests might affect the director's decision, I walk out of the room for some peace and quiet.

Whilst I'm pacing the corridor, waiting for Jamieson, I notice a framed Van Gogh print on the wall and stop to look at it more closely. My eyes are drawn to the golden yellows of the petals and realize this was exactly the same print I used to look at on my classroom wall when I was a small boy. I remember I used to stare at it in lessons. I move in close, bringing my face up to the print, still holding the phone to my ear.

Whilst wondering what mood Van Gogh must have been in when he painted the petals so dramatically, with those daubed brush strokes of his, I'm brought back to reality as the director tells me he has full authorization for O'Connell's transfer. He can be moved to another 'sister' medical center, about five miles away. There are certain conditions and these include taking a specialist nurse on the journey.

By the time we're wheeling O'Connell out to the waiting ambulance, he's looking even greyer than when I arrived. I go in the back with him, after he's ramped up and secured inside. I leave the nurse and driver sitting up front, hoping that, if I sit back here, I might gain privacy and have a chance to extract more from O'Connell on the journey.

I phone through to Dee as soon as the wheels are rolling and ask her to arrange a police guard for O'Connell, once we have him established in his new hospice. She reminds me we're both off limits so far as LAPD is concerned and we scheme a way to do this through Treviss, because he's apparently not on IAD's radar yet.

I see O'Connell listening intently to my call, although he doesn't engage in eye contact with me. I'm sure he's caught the drift of what's going on, but, more importantly, he'll have picked up the danger I think he's in and the lengths I'm going to ensure he's safe. I think it's working to my advantage because he definitely looks worried this time.

I decide to give him a prompt.

"You owe it to yourself, O'Connell," I say. "Look at you here; you might not have much longer to live but you can at least correct this one before it's too late."

He gives me a long, lingering look.

"Do something right, for a change," I add.

"Fuck off, Oskar. You always were the righteous one—it sounds as if you're winging it anyway. What's all this about? IAD?"

"None of your business, O'Connell. Just be grateful I might be giving you a bit longer to live and I'm also giving you a chance to do something right for once."

He grunts another expletive and returns to his thoughts, looking out of the far window. I watch his eyes dart back and forth as we drive through the traffic. Eventually, he turns to face me again.

"You know what Jardine and I used to call you in those days? ... Mr. Clean ... after that detergent shit you could buy in the shops. You weren't prepared to come across to our side of the street, were you? You righteous little fucker."

He looks out of the window again.

"We were the ones dealing with all the dirt bags on a daily basis. You were different. You just came swanning in with a different set of rules ... a different agenda. We'd fought those fuckers on the streets for years. But no, you were the new kid on the block. You wanted to do things your way. The 'right' way ... the righteous way ... the clean way ... Mr. Clean, huh?"

O'Connell turns his head, trying to laugh, but all he manages is to bring up something from the back of his throat. He wipes it away with a Kleenex. I watch as his eyes seem to engage with a distant memory.

"There was so much corruption in those days, Salo. There were murders. We caught the killers. We even cleaned up the streets but it was like a torrent, some days. Clean up one piece of shit and there'd be another a few minutes later. Put away one scumbag and there'd be another in the corridor. Waiting to have a confession hammered out of him if necessary ... it was like an assembly line some days. But to have success we had to work within the system we were given. The system we were brought up with. The system we were schooled in." He looks directly into my eyes, assessing my willingness to understand what he's saying. I show him nothing, so he turns away. "Everyone worked their angle. You know what I mean?" He looks at me again. "The politicians, top brass, all the way down to the lowly patrol officer on his beat ... Even Kramer," he chortles to himself. "He walked-the-beat on our-side-of-the-street," he suddenly says, in a singsong way.

There's a long pause whilst he ponders on something. I think this is about to be another of those golden door moments.

"We took the money to drop the case, Oskar," he blurts out. "That's what you want me to say, isn't it? Once Gargailis had confessed to the crime we took the brown envelopes."

He's staring out of the window now, lips sealed, but I see his eyes are wet.

"Where did the money come from?" I ask, not wanting him to stop now.

"We thought it was from the Orthodox Church at first—can you believe it, the fucking church, for chrissakes? But we soon realized it was twisted up with some Italian mafia family. But we didn't ask too many questions. Believe me, Oskar. Open this one up at your peril." He's staring at me again and I see there's fear behind his eyes. "That's my advice. You'll need to take care with this because the mob have long memories ... And a long reach."

I just nod, willing him to keep his story moving.

"As soon as I knew the mob was involved, I couldn't say no, could I?" he continues, wanting sympathy for his plight. "A little later on, we thought Gargailis might have been covering up for somebody, perhaps taking the hit for someone else. Then we thought he had a terminal illness or something and his stepping in was his way to save someone else from the needle ... you know, if he was about to die anyway ... I didn't know the son-of-a-bitch would get life and still be alive today, did I?"

He looks at me again, still looking for sympathy.

I'm starting to piece together what this means and shift in my seat as ideas connect.

My phone vibrates. It's a text from Dee:

> Forgot to mention. U R right.
> Hargreaves reports same perp, both
> voids.

"You were young, Oskar," O'Connell continues, oblivious to my increased restlessness at what Dee's text is suggesting.

"You had a career in front of you, I realize that. But me and Jardine, we had our pensions to think about. We knew you wouldn't touch it so the share-out went as far as Buttle ... and that little upstart Kramer, who was always sniffing around the edges ... And, anyway, how'd you expect me to pay these fucking hospital bills if I didn't have some cash stashed away somewhere?" he says, smiling towards me. But I'm not really listening. I'm putting thoughts together about the killer's little rituals and what Dee's text seems to be confirming. "Now, Oskar, for chrissakes, tell me what this is all about, will you? Why all the cloak and dagger dramatics?"

Planets suddenly align and, thinking about the photograph I have in my jacket pocket and, now, Dee's text, I realize what I need to do.

Now. Right now!

"STOP THE AMBULANCE!" I shout to the driver. "TURN AROUND. IMMEDIATELY!"

53

(Thursday 7.30 p.m.)

THE REAPER HEARD THE commotion from his storeroom, having just finished cleaning his paintbrushes. He laid them down neatly, next to the sink, to dry, after putting the first coat of paint on Mr. Taylor's bird table – Mr. Taylor likes to sit out front in the morning sunshine, watching the birds amongst the plants and trees. He had looked out of the storeroom and seen Detective Salo running down the corridor, shouting instructions to that nice nurse on reception. He had watched as the duty manager followed down the corridor and ran to her office to make a call. He had even volunteered to collect the wheelchair Detective Salo had been asking for, and he brought it to Room 11 himself, finding the charge of electricity this action gave him thrilling. In the end, he retreated to the safety of his 'lair', to sit and watch from there.

He's still in his lair now. Quietly watching and waiting. And, planning things out, meticulously.

It has been ten minutes since Detective Salo left with Mr. O'Connell in that ambulance and things have changed, quite dramatically. *'But I'm still in control and that's important,'* he tells himself. *'I like my invisibility. I like the dark. It's what makes my life bearable and enjoyable. It makes me feel so powerful ... so invincible'.*

He remembers he was able to study Detective Salo's face this evening. He recalls the shiver of excitement which raced down his spine as he watched Salo look at the detail of the Van Gogh painting from the other side of the wall, only inches away from where he's sitting now.

He's brought out of contemplation by the sound of activity from the direction of the reception area again. He looks through his peephole to see someone running along the corridor. Gradually, he recognizes who it is. It's Mrs. O'Connell. She goes straight into Room 11, followed by a nurse. He watches as she collects a few of her husband's belongings and imagines she's taking them to Mr. O'Connell's new hospice.

The Reaper smiles to himself, thinking of her good fortune. He had been planning to murder her this evening, right where she is standing, next to Mr. O'Connell's bed. It was so important that Mr. O'Connell would watch his wife die, right in front of him, but not be able to do anything about it. The restraints and the chemicals had all been ready.

He smiles to himself a second time, thinking Mrs. O'Connell has to be one of the luckiest women in the world. He really liked Mrs. O'Connell. He thought she was a sweet old thing. Nonetheless, she deserved to die.

He puts his hand inside his pocket and feels for the slim plastic box containing the DVD. It'll soon be time to drive to central L.A. and deliver it because he's decided to bring his whole project to a conclusion without the sacrifice of Mr. O'Connell and his wife.

The countdown has started.

54

(Thursday, 7.55 p.m.)

THE AMBULANCE DRIVER DROPS me off a couple of blocks from the Long Beach hospice. Once he's on his way, I move along the quiet streets, unseen. I am soon within sight of the entrance and immediately see Mrs. O'Connell standing by a cab at the turnaround. She's fussing with the driver about boxes he's lifting into the trunk. Using some flowering shrubs and bushes as a screen, I cut across the front lawn, making my way to the side of the building, looking for a way in. I spot cigarette butts spilling out of a petri dish and go across to find a fire door left open by smokers.

I take out my gun and move inside.

Following my dramatic intervention into the calm order of things, fifteen minutes ago, I'm surprised how quiet it is in the building. Apart from the hushed whir of air-conditioning units and various chill cabinets, everywhere is still. No one is around. The lights are set low and I'm hoping this will work to my advantage.

I'm soon able to move down the main corridor, taking care to keep the sound of footsteps to a minimum. Lights are brighter down the far end, near reception, but there's no sign of any movement there either.

When I reach Room 11, I take a peek through the window panel in the door. Although I see the bed has been stripped, everything is in the same position it was when I left earlier.

I open the door and step inside, gun at the ready, because I'm aware that, if the killer is hiding in this room, he's probably watching me right now, through whatever spyhole he has set up in here. I hold up my gun and turn round a full three sixty degrees, letting him know I have him in my sights. I know I should be doing this by the book – with full police backup – but also know my chance of orchestrating that in my current situation is somewhere between nigh impossible and never. So, if the killer's here somewhere, I'm determined not to let him slip through the net.

First, I go round the room, tapping the walls and listening out for false panels or spaces where I think someone could be hiding. Finding nothing suspicious, I stand up on a chair and push up each ceiling panel in turn, hoping to hear that distinctive click. Again, there's nothing.

Feeling frustrated, I breathe in deeply, trying to settle my mind so that I can work things out logically. I'm thinking the killer would definitely have wanted a good view of O'Connell from his lair, so I go across and sit down on the bed and start looking around the room. My eyes are drawn to the window in the door. I can see a portion of the sunflower painting on the far wall in the corridor, but, when I shift myself further onto the bed, I also see a section of the door leading into the cleaner's cupboard.

I slide my legs around and walk towards the door – almost zen-like – with my gun out front. I open the door and move into the corridor and instantly hear a sharp intake of breath. I turn to see the receptionist standing stock-still, staring in horror at my gun. She has her hand to her mouth as if stifling a scream. Thankfully, she recognizes me, and, as I put my finger to my lips, retreats to the safety of the reception desk around the corner.

With heart pounding, I move across and study the sunflower print again, but this time I'm not looking at Van Gogh's brush strokes, I'm looking for the killer's spy hole. I focus on the dense mix of dark browns at the center of one of the sunflowers and I think I see the distinctive reflection of a small lens, cleverly disguised as one of the seed heads. Feeling energized, I turn my attention to the storeroom and move across to the door, listening for any sign of movement.

Hearing none, I turn the handle. It's unlocked, so I open and move inside, scanning the room quickly. No one is here. I reach across and throw the light switch and hear the fluorescent tube buzz into life, flooding the eight by ten room with a stark, white light.

Looking around, I see an array of plastic containers and boxes on shelves. There's also an assortment of mops in buckets against the far wall and three paintbrushes left out to dry on a wooden draining board. My eyes are drawn to a floor-to-ceiling cupboard on my left, and I notice it abuts the corridor wall outside the room. There's a hasp attached to one of the doors but no padlock, so I'm able to open it easily, using the barrel of my gun.

I look inside.

The top two shelves are crammed with an assortment of cleaning products and various sized tins of paint and varnish. There's also an array of differently colored liquids at the back of one of the shelves. Some have handwritten stickers, presumably displaying their contents. For some reason, I reach all the way in and extract one of the glass jars containing a greenish-yellow colored liquid. Thinking of the chemicals used in the lethal cocktail of drugs in a death chamber, I remove the stopper and smell inside. I regret it instantly and have to pull my nose away, fearing I'm going to choke. I replace the stopper and put it back on the shelf.

Once I have my breath back, I look at the lower three shelves. There's a fine collection of tools, all neatly stored away in racks. I study each of the tools in turn, looking for anything untoward. I try and pull out the racks but they're held securely in place. I wonder what lies behind the back panel because I'm beginning to think these shelves are not as deep as the ones above. I take a step back to make a comparison and estimate there could be at least an eight- or nine-inch difference, possibly more. As I recognize what this might mean, I feel my finger tighten around the trigger of my gun, wondering if a 'magician's' illusion is taking place.

I grab hold of the sides and give the whole cupboard a firm tug, detecting the slightest of movements at the base. I reach up and feel my way along the topmost edge, soon finding what is holding the cupboard to the wall so securely. As I release the latch, there's a discrete metallic click and I feel the cupboard start to swing away from the wall, smoothly and silently, like a large safe door. With my heart beating even faster, I pull the cupboard completely away from the wall and peer behind. I immediately see an ergonomically designed seat built into the space behind the bottom three shelves and into the cavity of the wall itself. The chair is padded for comfort and there's even an adjustable headrest and footrest, allowing the chair to be moved into different positions.

But the killer has gone.

I slip on a pair of latex gloves and climb into the chair, working out it's a brilliantly conceived illusion, because, at first sight, I wouldn't have believed I could have squeezed into this space at all. It reminds me of squeezing into Father Peter's bucket seat in his Subaru, only it's more comfortable.

When I turn my head to the right, I can look out of a small peephole and see all the way across to O'Connell's bed in the distance, and, by adjusting the eyepiece, I can look all the way down the corridor to the front door.

I let out a long sigh and drop my head, recognizing the killer's cunning, and knowing he's one step ahead of me again. That's when I notice the screwed-up sweet wrapper lying on the floor. It's a message – 'his' message – screaming *It's me, it's me!*

55

(Thursday, 9.20 p.m.)

I ARRIVE THROUGH THE back door to see Chang's legs sticking out from under one of the metal cookers in his kitchen. He's lying on the floor with a rudimentary toolbox by his side, barking out orders to three Chinese cooks. They stand to attention, smiling at me in unison, showing me their crooked teeth. Chang senses I'm here and sticks his head out from underneath.

"First left, Mr. Salo," he manages to say whilst he continues to pull on the end of a wrench. "Go behind the screen at the far end. Your friends are there already."

I'd managed to phone ahead and update my team on what O'Connell had finally revealed but I hadn't told them about my go-it-alone trip to San Quentin. I'm going to use this occasion to explain my actions, hopefully convincing them it was all worth it.

I go down the corridor to Chang's private room, open the door and walk in. The room seems to be empty. Four tables are set out with starched white tablecloths and there are enough chairs to seat at least twenty people. I see a large oriental screen in the far corner that Chang referred to and immediately think about Chandler's apartment, only there's a picture of a giant dragon emblazoned on this one. I go across and look behind the screen, expecting to see my team waiting for me to arrive, but no one's there. There's not even a table or any chairs. Thinking I've walked into the wrong room, I turn around but then I hear a door open and turn back to see Dee standing in a doorway I hadn't spotted before.

"I saw you through the peephole, Oskar. Come in," she says, quite solemnly. I walk across, realizing she's standing in a hidden doorway similar to the one in the boardroom on the tenth floor of the PAB. Dee is looking particularly somber and doesn't return my smile as I follow her into the small room that lies behind. Sam and Treviss are both sitting at the only table, huddled round a laptop. They don't smile at me either.

"Shut the door behind you, Oskar?" Dee suggests, as she pulls out a chair for me next to Treviss.

"What's with all the long faces, fellas?" I ask.

Dee's holding up a DVD case.

"This ... Oskar. It came this evening. Just as we were leaving. Front desk. No ID on the sender. Sifonios found it on top of his papers. It's been dusted. No prints."

"What is it?" I ask.

Dee passes the disk across to Treviss, who puts it into the side of his laptop.

"Watch," she says.

I sense the tension as we wait for something to come up on screen.

"What is it?" I ask again, looking across towards Sam this time. She's sitting back in her chair, looking pale. She just shakes her head, remaining silent. I look at Treviss and Dee but they won't look me in the eyes either. I look back to Sam.

"I'm so sorry," she mouths towards me, still shaking her head.

I look back to the laptop and watch the screen fire up. It's very dark at first but, gradually, I see an image come into focus, as if it's the start of a movie. After about thirty seconds, I make out the image of a room that's empty, except for what looks to be a bed or table at the center. As things begin to come into focus, I see someone lying on a bed which I soon work out is a gurney – like the ones you find in a hospital. The person lying on the gurney is dressed in a white gown. I can't recognize who it is because the face is hidden from view but I think it's a woman. I see clearly the person is held down with straps attached around both wrists and ankles.

The realization hits me that we're looking at someone strapped down much in the way convicted murderers are strapped down in a death chamber.

I look across at Dee and Sam for an explanation. Dee keeps her eyes on the screen, hand to her mouth. Sam has moved away to the other side of the room and is looking down at the floor, as if she can't bear to look.

"Who is it? What's going on?" I ask.

I turn back to the screen just as the camera pans around to look at the person's face. I recognize who it is immediately but can't believe what I'm seeing.

"It's Lena," I blurt out. "Jesus, it's Lena."

"It arrived about an hour ago, Oskar. I'm so sorry," Dee says.

I look at the fear in Lena's eyes as the camera zooms in.

"There's more, Oskar." Sam adds, as she nods towards Treviss who freezes the frame. "I'm not sure you'll want to see it."

"Yes, I do—why—what happens?—Does she die? ... Is she dead for chrissakes?"

"No. We don't think she's dead. Not on film anyway," Dee answers. "I'm sorry, Oskar. There's no message. Nothing. Just this thirty-five minute recording."

"Thirty-five minutes?" I ask, incredulously. "What else happens?"

Dee looks towards Sam, as though she's seeking permission to show me the rest. Sam just nods and walks further round the table, away from the screen. Treviss is hovering over the keyboard, looking embarrassed. He won't hold my eyes either.

"What's this about?" I ask. "What's about to happen?—Show me, goddammit—run the film."

Dee nods to Treviss and he clicks the play button.

We see the camera pan away from Lena now and it starts to focus on a TV screen mounted high on the ceiling. It's clear Lena can see it easily from her position strapped to the gurney. Images

359

start to appear on the screen but it's difficult to make out what's happening at first, because of the camera angle, but we soon hear the sound track and then it becomes obvious. It's a recording of Sam and me making love in my apartment, early Wednesday morning.

After about four minutes, the camera pans away from the screen to focus on Lena's face and, agonizingly, I see the distress this is causing. It's excruciatingly painful to watch and, at one point, Treviss leans across to the keyboard and turns down the sound in an attempt to dampen its impact.

"Where's Lena? – where's all this happening?" I blurt out, almost naively.

"These images are professional quality, Oskar," Dee says. "So, we've enhanced some of them using Treviss's know-how and isolated a few pointers to the location that may help us."

I notice Treviss has surreptitiously turned the sound down even further now, making it slightly easier for me to watch. Every now and then, the camera zooms in on Lena's face and, at one point, I see tears rolling down her cheeks. At another, she turns her eyes away from the screen, as if trying to block everything out and hide – but she can't.

"This carries on for twenty more minutes so I suggest we stop here, Oskar, and show you what we've found to help us identify the location. Treviss and I have picked out shots which might give us clues. What do you think, Oskar?"

"Yes, go ahead."

As if on cue, Treviss brings up a freeze-frame image. Sam moves in to watch, squeezing my arm sympathetically in the process.

"Although it's quite dark, this is an internal shot of the room where we think Lena is being held," Dee says. "It captures a moment when the camera pans around. Look, there, we see the corner of a room, showing a section of a central heating radiator below what we think is a curtained window. And, there. Look. Some electric socket points. This makes us think it's possibly a domestic setting, judging by the quality of the fittings, or a

360

hotel somewhere. If we do find a suspect location, we can always check measurements and data against this image ... the color of the carpet, for instance, and the number and positioning of the electric sockets, etcetera. But there's no furniture to work from, apart from the gurney—let's see the next one, Treviss."

Treviss runs a short, five-second sequence which keeps replaying itself on his screen. I see Lena in the foreground, under spotlights, as the camera moves around the gurney. Every time the sequence runs, Dee points out something in the background but I don't see anything at first and keep having to wait for the sequence to replay itself to look again.

"We think it could be someone standing behind a window ... someone standing outside. Or it's possibly a reflection of someone in the glass."

I still can't pick out what Dee's driving at and it must show on my face.

"Look, Oskar. Wait. Here it comes, again—look ... there. See it?"

"No, for chrissakes. Can't you freeze-frame and hold on the image, Treviss?"

When the image comes round again, he manages to halt the sequence but it's extremely fuzzy. I move in closer, adjusting my eyes to focus on what's in the background.

"Look, there. See?" Dee says, tracing her finger around an abstract shape on the laptop's screen. "Can you work on it any more, Treviss – what about the enhanced image you were working on when Oskar arrived?"

Treviss's fingers type in a command and he brings up another image. It's sharper but, in some ways, more abstract. It's almost like an ultrasound photo of a baby in the womb. Dee turns to Treviss.

"No, it doesn't work for me. Go back to the orig—"

"No, leave it," I manage to bark before Treviss changes anything. "Hold on this one. Can you enhance it a little more? In the direction you're going."

Treviss keys in a command and the image distorts even further from the original but the background shape appears to sharpen.

"What is it?" Dee asks.

I ignore her as I concentrate hard on what I'm looking at. The foreground is greyed out, making it easier for me to distinguish the silhouette shape in the background. But it's still difficult to work out exactly what I'm looking at. What I do know, though, is that it's a familiar shape, yet I can't quite lay my finger on it."

"What is it?" Dee asks again, picking up on the tension I'm creating.

"Any more, Treviss? Can you take it any further along this color scale?" Treviss works his magic again and something begins to click into place. There's not enough detail to discern characteristics or discernible features but, as Treviss taps away on his keyboard, adjusting the image even further, a tingle of expectation races up my spine. I move in even closer, crosschecking in my mind what I'm thinking. Before saying anything, I make sure in I have this right. It all comes together in a rush but I know now why the others are having such difficulty working out what it is. It's a person all right but it's a stylized image of a person.

I look at Sam to see if she understands.

"What ... what is it, Oskar?" she asks, impatiently.

"It's at Geometrix, goddammit—the person, this person," I say, pointing at the screen. "It's different to mine. This one's the old guy, dreaming of his death. I've the man looking skyward, contemplating his old age ... The fucker's got Lena in the apartment below mine ... This is not an actual person at all. It's a fucking statue!"

I stand up and race towards the door.

"OSKAR. WAIT!" Sam shouts. "WAIT ... One moment—hear me out. Just for a moment, before you go rushing off."

I pause momentarily, finding it extremely difficult to contain myself. Sam sees this and holds up both hands, imploringly.

"I've been trying to work out what this guy's personality characteristics are saying to us. You know, for how we should approach him, how we should capture him. And I don't like what I'm seeing here. We know this guy's manipulative and he's clever, too clever by half, that's a given, but he's also devious and dangerous ... and needs to be treated with—"

"Don't say 'respect'. For pity's sake, don't say that," Dee implores.

"No, that's not what I was going to say, he needs be treated with ... care. For your own sakes, he *must* be treated with care. I don't think your 'find' here has happened by accident. I really don't. I think he's engineered this recording for you, Oskar, so you'll find these clues. As you have. I believe he's designed them into this 'production' of his so that he'll gain the response he wants. And you rushing off like this is exactly what he wants. I suspect he's waiting for you to show up at Geometrix right now. It wasn't an accident you spotted the window, the statue."

"You must do this properly, Oskar—bring in support," Dee blurts out, supporting Sam.

"I'm not risking Lena's life in a standoff with half of LAPD and our gun-toting deputy chief in full riot gear," I say, emphatically. "I'm going in now ... on my own, if necessary. I can't let him take control of the situation."

"I know that," Sam interjects. "But you'll have to read what you're confronted with very carefully. That's all I'm saying. This is the set-up he's been orchestrating all along. Haven't we said at different times that this case is about *you*? I think it's coming down to a showdown between you and the killer. He's got you in his sights, Oskar. He knows you're coming for him. Just remember that, will you?"

I instinctively pull out my gun – checking it's loaded – and replace it into its holster. I look across at Dee and see she's going through a similar routine – and so is Treviss. They stand up and nod towards me with eager 'what-are-we-waiting-for?' expressions written across their faces. We turn in unison and race towards the door.

56

(Friday, 10.21 a.m.)

THE STREETS ARE EMPTY, so the three of us reach Geometrix in good time. We're in my nondescript hire car and I hope this will be enough of a disguise to keep away prying eyes, especially my 'colleagues' in LAPD.

As I drive past the entrance, I look up to my apartment, noticing no lights have been left on and there are none in the apartment below either. I've discussed with Dee and Treviss how we'll play this. To their credit, both are up for helping me find Lena and continuing with the case despite the personal risks their continued involvement might bring to their future careers. When I'd offered them both an honorable exit, Dee quipped that it's not often she has the chance to work with a lead investigator who's the most wanted man in Los Angeles.

I'd even told them about my trip to San Quentin and my reasons for keeping schtum. I'd worked out that, if the killer had been able to make that sophisticated recording of Sam and me making love, he could just as easily have listened to all my discussions and telephone conversations. It was then that Treviss dropped his bombshell, suggesting the killer might also have hacked into my emails. It was at this point that we all realized my decision to remain so secretive had not been such a bad decision after all...

I park a couple of blocks away and we climb out of the car. It's dark on the streets and we move along the sidewalk without drawing too much attention to ourselves. We're keeping a look out for patrol cars and I'm also watching out for IAD cruisers because Ship will be over here as soon as he can, once he obtains a warrant to search my apartment.

When we reach Geometrix we shimmy over a side gate on the perimeter wall. As agreed, Dee and I take up our positions at the entrance to the stairwell in the lower ground floor car park and Treviss hides behind a wall overlooking the entrance.

I punch in a code on the keypad entry and we proceed up the stairs. We climb steadily, trying not to telegraph our arrival. For once, Dee follows behind and doesn't race ahead.

When I reach the fire door on the second floor, I look out of the window and down the corridor leading to the apartment below mine. I then look the other way and see the atrium with its glass elevator. It's clear no one is around. Everywhere is quiet.

I open the door and step into the corridor. We move swiftly down to the apartment. I have my eyes glued to what's facing me, knowing Dee's watching for anything that might come up from behind. When I reach the front door, I bring out my picks and go to work on the lock. I have it open in two minutes, having practiced on mine on the floor above, many times before. With one final nod towards Dee, I push the door and step inside, gun at the ready. We're greeted by complete darkness. And silence.

Knowing it's an identical apartment to mine, I can lead the way. Using hand signals where needed, we check each room, looking for signs of Lena, the killer or any clues as to their whereabouts. I'm half expecting to see someone running at me, brandishing an axe or a knife, but I dispel these thoughts and focus on the moment, staying alert for anything that might happen. I see that Dee is doing likewise.

We find nothing in the two bedrooms or the bathroom on an initial sweep and we eventually reach the door leading into the main living room where I'm thinking Lena might be held. The door is ajar, so I push it open slowly with the barrel of my gun, and move inside, gun raised, ready to let off a volley of shots if necessary.

When I'm sure no one is here, I lift my hand and throw the light switch, still keeping eyes focused for any sign of movement. I watch as the room is bathed in a soft purplish glow from an array of ceiling and wall lights, very different to my room above. I walk across to the place where I think Lena had been filmed.

"Look, there," Dee says, pointing to the floor. I look down to see an imprint left in the carpet by the gurney's wheels. There's even the faint trail left in the carpet as the killer wheeled her away towards the front door.

Dee looks up and points to a fixing bracket attached to the ceiling, where the screen had been positioned. Bare wires protrude out of a hole nearby, no doubt leading to the camera in my apartment above.

Still remaining alert, I look out of the picture window but have difficulty seeing anything because of the reflection of the lights in the glass. I go across to the door leading to the garden and open it. The smell of orange blossom bombards my senses, reminding me of my time with Sam a few nights ago and the attack on that private moment by the killer. My eyes are drawn to the abstract shape of the wire-framed statue in the distance – the person dreaming of his own death.

"Let's close things down here for the moment and be on our way," Dee asserts suddenly, bringing me out of my trance. "It's not safe for us to remain here for much longer, Oskar. We need to go somewhere else and regroup," she adds, confirming what we both know: Lena's gone. And so has the killer.

I ask Dee to leave me here to finish up, suggesting she waits on the other side of the fire door along the corridor to keep watch. Like Dee, I suspect the full force of the law will be close on my heels.

"Three minutes max," she says, looking at her watch. "I'll check in with Treviss first and see what's what downstairs. Then I'll come grab you, if necessary. But three minutes, Oskar. No more. Please."

As Dee turns to leave, I let my eyes roam the room, doing some thin-slicing myself. My eyes are drawn to a large print at the far end of the room that I hadn't noticed before. It's a print of a picturesque mountain scene, with a forest and lake. In the foreground, there's a farmstead nestling by a stream.

I move in for a closer look. The words, *Big Bear Lake*, are engraved onto a small brass plate attached to the wooden frame.

It's certainly a beautiful photograph and similar to the scenic views I'd seen in Tomkins' apartment. I see a rough road or track running down to the farmstead on the right, as it crosses a slight ridge. It also looks as if the photograph has been taken from a viewpoint – a lookout, perhaps. My mind starts racing and I remember Sam's mention of the killer's ploy to '*haul me in*', as she put it. Is the killer trying to communicate something to me here? With this photograph?

Before heading off, I decide to capture a shot of the print with my iPhone. Just as the shutter clicks, I hear Dee come bustling back into the room behind me – my three minutes clearly up. I put the phone in my pocket and, as I'm about to turn, I feel something dig into the small of my back. I freeze immediately. It's the barrel of a gun. As I try to work out who it is and what to do, a familiar, sweet-sticky smell comes over my shoulder. I hear the clicking sound of a boiled sweet being rolled behind teeth. It's Ship.

"I wouldn't move if I were you, cowboy," Ship says into my ear. "Just drop the gun, very slowly. Then, raise your hands to where I can see them."

I consider my options but realize I have very few. I guess Ship knows this because he pushes the barrel into my back a little harder, as if to emphasize his superior position.

"This is where I'm supposed to say, 'Make my day, punk' isn't it?" he says, letting out one of his customary chuckles. "Because, believe me, Salo, I've dreamt of this moment for more years than I care to remember ... And I'll not blink if I have to pump four or five slugs into your back ... I'll always keep one for the headshot, though, just to have everything neat and tidy. In fact, it's been a fantasy of mine ever since you sank your partner in the dirt and walked away scot free."

Ship had investigated the death of my colleague when a bullet from my gun took him out in a stakeout that went disastrously wrong. "You've got this all wrong, Ship. I'm not the killer, I just need to—"

"Look, Salo, this is the last time I ask you nicely. Drop the gun. Remember, one false move and it's curtains, you hear? Painful way to go ... bullet in your ribcage from this range ... nice for me ... bad for you."

He moves in close again and I receive another waft of his breath. "Now, fuckhead. Decision time. Drop the gun to the floor."

I wonder where Dee is. Surely, she's seen Ship arrive?

"Now, fuckhead!" he demands.

I drop my gun slowly, hearing it clatter onto the floor about three feet away.

"Smart move," Ship says. "Now, raise your hands to where I can see them."

I'm thinking, if I distract Ship in some way I can roll away and grab the gun.

"Hands, cowboy!"

I lift my arms and spread my feet at the same time, taking the opportunity to stand in a position that'll give me the best chance to spring into action – where's Dee, for chrissakes?

"Look, Ship, I'm not the killer. The real killer's been using this apartment to spy on me. That's what I'm doing here. I just need—"

"Save your breath, Salo," he says. "I haven't time for any more of your stories. I just want a confession out of you. That's all." I feel him stick the barrel of his gun a little harder into my ribs. "So, tell me, in your own words, why'd you do it, Salo? Why'd you kill all those people? What was the purpose? What crazy fucked-up brain does that sort of thing? Explain it all to me because I don't understand? Tell me."

"That's funny. I was thinking of asking you those same questions, Ship."

He laughs out loud this time – almost maniacally – and the sound reverberates around the empty room before everything goes silent again and all I hear is his rasping breath at my neck.

"Don't—waste—my—time, Salo," I hear him say through gritted teeth. "We either do this the easy way or the hard way. I just want you to tell me why you did it. That's all. I just wanna hear the words. I don't care if you deny it afterwards because it makes no matter to me. I've all the evidence I need to take you all the way to San Q for the needle. I just wanna hear those words. Why'd you do it?"

"What evidence is that, Ship?" I ask, hoping to keep him talking.

"Huh? The DNA evidence under the fingernails, fuckhead. You murdered Chandler. Semen's yours as well, pal. It's been confirmed. We've had your DNA on file." He moves in close to my ear. "You fuck her first? 'Cause we're thinking you fucked her afterwards, knowing how sick you are in the head. I've also got you down for the lieutenant after you shot and fried him in his car ... all that good enough evidence for you? ... Then, there's the chief. You've got him somewhere. So, how's it gonna be? Will you tell me why you did it or will I have to force it out of you?"

"Look, take me down to the PAB. We can clear it all—"

"WHY DID YOU DO IT?" he suddenly shouts, and I feel his spittle spray the back of my neck.

"Look, Ship. You've got this all—"

"WHY—DID—YOU—DO—IT?"

"I haven't murdered anyone. I'm only—"

There's a flash as Ship's gun explodes behind me. I feel a sudden rush of air around my feet as splinters of wood come up through the carpet from the wooden floor below. I feel a numbing pain and stumble slightly, the bullet has grazed my skin.

"OKAY—OKAY. I'LL CONFESS," I shout back

"There's a good boy ... I was hoping you'd see sense."

Just at that moment, we hear the sound of running along the corridor towards the apartment. I turn my head slightly and, out of the corner of my eye, I see Ship doing the same. I find the energy from somewhere to move on the balls of my feet and roll away, catching Ship by surprise. He fires off another round and misses me completely this time. I hear someone running through the front door and down the hallway, feet sliding on the hardwood floor.

"PAUL. YOU OKAY? ... PAUL?" I hear Crick shout.

Everything seems to go into slow motion. As Ship pauses, I bring my fist round in one sweeping arc. There's a very brief moment when we look at each other, both knowing it's too late for Ship to move out of the way. I see his face crumple as my clenched fist slams into his jaw with a sickening thud. His chin twists around grotesquely as his head snaps back. Ship begins to topple, eventually falling into the outstretched arms of Crick, who's now burst his way in through the door. Both land in a slovenly heap on the floor. I have time to pick up my gun before running past them and into the hallway.

"Hey, Salo. Stop. STOP," Crick bellows, as I hear three more shots come in my direction, but I'm out of sight and they're wasted.

As I'm running down the main corridor, I see Father Peter turn a corner. It's an incongruous sight because he's smiling in greeting, as if I'm just the person he's looking for.

"Detective Salo, why, hello," he says, as I run past. "Have you got a minute? I need to tell you something."

At the same time, I turn to see Crick in full flight coming after me, gun in one hand, walkie-talkie in the other. Despite his size, he's picked up a fair speed. His shirt is out and his fat belly leads him down the corridor towards me.

"MOVE TO THE SIDE, SIR," Crick bellows to Father Peter, who's now standing in his way. "MOVE TO THE SIDE, SIR, IMMEDIATELY."

I continue running, selfishly using Father Peter as a screen, and soon reach the fire door. Glancing back, I assess my chances of escape down the stairs ahead of the ever-advancing Crick. I see

Father Peter still standing in the same place, looking somewhat bemused. I then watch as Crick attempts to sidestep him but I'm sure I see Father Peter stick out a foot because Crick immediately starts to fly through the air, arms flailing, releasing his walkie-talkie in the process. As Crick's two hundred and fifty pound frame falls heavily to the floor, I realize this lucky break gives me a real chance of escaping but, as I hear the dull metallic thud of Crick's head hitting a fire extinguisher, I know it's secured.

Father Peter looks nonplussed and holds up his hands, as if it's nothing to do with him. I turn quickly and make my way down the stairs, hearing Father Peter follow. We exit into the lower ground floor car park together, out of breath.

I spot Treviss hiding in the shadows where Dee and I had left him earlier and we run across to where he's crouching. He looks up with hopeful eyes – they're asking if I've succeeded in my mission of finding Lena. All I can do is shake my head.

"Damn it," he says, as he turns his head to look out front. "They've got Dee in the back of a patrol car. Crick appeared out front with her about ten minutes ago," Treviss says. "He went back up after we all heard the first gunshot—you okay, Oskar?"

"Yeah. Fine," I say, as I look across to the turnaround and spy Dee sitting quietly in the back of a car. She looks across with a hollow-eyed expression on her face which offers me nothing. The one officer who remains on guard is looking pensive, as if he's expecting some action soon.

"You *really* need to go now, Oskar," Treviss demands, as we hear the sirens of approaching squad cars and what looks to be Deputy Chief Eugene Garner in another of those black Lincolns.

"Father Peter, where's your car?" I ask.

"Out on the front on South Grand, a couple of blocks away."

"Can you meet me on the corner with West 6th?" I call back, as I rush off towards the perimeter wall.

"Yes, of course," he replies.

57

(Friday, 11.20 a.m.)

I HEAR THE HOLLOW roar of Father Peter's exhaust before I see his car. I've ducked into a shop doorway to hide from any passing patrol cars and I hear him negotiating the streets as he comes towards me. Whilst waiting in the shadows, I've seen an ever-increasing rash of flashing lights in the sky, as more police vehicles make their way to Geometrix. I hope Father Peter doesn't draw anyone's attention to those pop popping noises from his exhaust.

Whenever a member of LAPD is on the floor, every police officer within a ten-mile radius wants to descend on the scene. They do this in an honorable attempt to offer assistance to 'one-of-their-own' but, unfortunately, this action often provides the perpetrator with the cover he needs to escape detection. I was no exception on this occasion.

Whilst officers' eyes were focused on reaching the crime scene as quickly as they could, they didn't spot me on the streets, ducking behind parked vehicles. I'd even managed to take a slight detour and go via my hire car so that I could pick up my head torch, a few tools and some extra clothes I'd switched from my Caprice at LAX. I'd also managed to grab the 2-shot Cobra Derringer stored under my spare tire and have attached it to my right ankle.

When I see the Subaru come into view, I step from the doorway and raise my hand. Father Peter sees me immediately and pulls over at the curb, opening the passenger door before the car has come to a halt. I move swiftly across the sidewalk and climb into the front seat. I'm able to strap myself into the harness on my own this time, despite my damaged hand swelling quickly after it battered into Ship's jaw.

"Where to?" Father Peter asks, seemingly excited by the drama he's been thrown into.

I don't have an exact location to suggest but I have a vision of the panoramic mountain scene in my mind. "How far is Big Bear Lake?"

"Big Bear Lake?" Father Peter asks, incredulously, as he pulls away from the curb. "I know Big Bear Lake. It's related to one of my reasons for coming to see you tonight. Ever since this morning, when I heard your account, I've been troubled by a distant memory, a distant thought. I couldn't lay my finger on it at the time but it was there, in the background. And I've been chewing it over, ever since. It has to do with the detective team in 1993. I can't remember all their names now but I have a strong visual recollection of what happened. I came across tonight to tell you about it."

I remember the detective team photograph I'm carrying and bring it from my pocket and show it to Father Peter, hoping this might jog his memory.

"Yes, these are the men," he says, almost snatching the photograph from my hands and holding it up against the steering wheel so he can study it as he drives. "I remember seeing this one." He points to Kramer. "The patrol officer – your chief of police I believe visited the house on many occasions but I hadn't known about his relationship with John's wife until today. That's so sad, isn't it? And, this one, the man with the hat?"

"That's O'Connell."

"Yes, O'Connell. He was the lead detective, right?" "Yes, he was."

"And this one?" he asks, pointing to O'Connell's partner. "Jardine," I say.

"Yes, Detective Jardine—and this young one is … ?" "Detective Buttle."

"Yes, Detective Buttle ... well, seeing them like this, all huddled around John, brings back the visual memory I'm referring to. Very clearly indeed."

"Tell me about it? What's it got to do with Big Bear Lake?"

"Well, on one occasion, I caught all four of them discussing things on the front porch at John's house. Voices were raised. I came up on them unnoticed ... they were arguing, I seem to remember."

He pauses again, focusing his eyes as if studying an image in his mind, trying to recall the detail.

"Yes, that was it. I interrupted their discussion ... their argument ... and passed between them on the way to my car. I distinctly remember seeing O'Connell grab Kramer by his jacket. It was something about ... yes, I remember now, something about getting his fair share. That was it. He wanted his fair share."

Father Peter won't know about O'Connell's story of a mafia payout and he also won't know how important his recollection of events might be later on when I have to cross-reference the different accounts against a timeline.

"More importantly, though," he continues, "I'm sure all these men went to John's workshop before he was formally arrested. That's what I came across to tell you. I have this strong image in my mind of seeing them set off in Detective O'Connell's car. I always thought that was a strange thing to do."

"How many of them were in the car?" I ask.

"I can't be sure ... let me think. There are four ... no, there's five.

All five travelled up together to the workshop."

"Who are the people in the car, Father? Can you picture the moment in your mind and remember where they were seated?"

"Let me think ... yes, Detective Jardine is driving and Detective O'Connell and Police Officer Kramer sit each side of John in the back. Yes, I can see O'Connell. He's sitting behind the driver. I can see his hat."

There's a pause now and I fear Father Peter's memory is about to come to a standstill – but I want more.

"You said five. You said all five travelled up together. Who was the fifth person?" I ask, thinking of O'Connell's statement that Buttle was in his inner circle but I wasn't.

"Oh, that was Danil. John's son. He travelled up there with them. He sat in the front next to Detective Jardine."

"What was the purpose of going? Why the workshop?"

"That, I don't know. But it might have been to show them the casket John was working on at the time. I'd been there once to see it myself in construction but why they might have needed to go ... I just don't know. That's the only thing I can think of."

He holds up the photograph again.

"Seeing their faces like this, all huddled round John, brings it all back. It's just ... I thought you ought to know, that's all. That's why I came across to tell you about it this evening." He follows with an almost apologetic smile. "Perhaps it's just the outcome of my shock at hearing everything at San Quentin today that brought all these memories back," Father Peter concludes, shaking his head this time.

He takes one final look at the photograph and passes it back as if he's finished his story.

"So, what's the relevance of Big Bear Lake?" I ask, impatiently, not quite connecting all the dots.

"Because that's where the workshop is. John's workshop is up at Big Bear Lake. In the mountains. In fact, it overlooks the lake. Up one of the mountain tracks from the main road."

I immediately reach for my iPhone and bring up the photograph of the lake and hold it up for Father Peter to see. I point to the farmstead.

"Is this John Gargailis's workshop?"

"Yes, that looks like the place."

"Can you take me to it?"

"I'll give it a try, although it's over twenty years since I was last there."

The further we travel away from central L.A. and Deputy Chief Garner's LAPD army the better. However, it's only as we begin to merge onto the 330 and head towards the mountain resorts that I stop looking over my shoulder so much and start preparing for what might come next. I realize I'm possibly heading for my showdown with the killer and I'm also hoping I can rescue Lena.

This thought sharpens my senses and I take the opportunity to pull out my gun and go through my habitual routine of inspecting it, making sure it's fully loaded and in good working order. I see Father Peter watch as I first unload, then reload, the cartridges, checking the breach and the chamber will work perfectly. I wonder what's going through his mind, remembering his violent past as a combatant in Iraq and his enlightened pacifist views when he returned. When I'm finished, he looks me in the eyes as I replace my gun into its holster, not giving me anything of his views now.

As the road curves round, with the eerie silver reflection of the moon on the mountains in the distance, I notice a patrol car parked on the shoulder. Thankfully, Father Peter has seen it as well and approaches at the same speed, without slowing or hesitating in any way. I slide as low down in my seat as I can and lean my head to one side as if sleeping but this is made difficult by the full body harness that wants to hold me upright.

As we pass the car, Father Peter keeps looking ahead, appearing unperturbed. There are tense seconds as I watch his eyes in his rearview, searching for any sign we're about to be followed and, when they suddenly light up, I know we possibly have trouble.

Father Peter pulls up his driving gloves and secures them in place with poppers at the wrists.

"Sit tight, Father. Don't do anything yet," I say.

The last thing I want is for Father Peter to attempt to outrun them. I'm sure he can but this could be a fool's errand because I know the road will narrow significantly in a few miles and this would be the perfect place for these guys' colleagues to erect a roadblock after radioing ahead. I wonder whether that's already in place and these officers are skillfully coaxing us up the channel and into the net.

"Just keep the same speed and we'll see what they decide to do," I prompt.

It's a tense few miles as we anticipate what might happen next. Fortunately, the patrol car stays put, remaining a constant one hundred yards away as we climb ever upwards.

After forty minutes, just after we pass the junction for Lake Arrowhead and start following signs up to Big Bear Lake, Father Peter releases the poppers on his gloves and I feel the Subaru pull away like an animal taken off its leash. He's telling me the patrol car has pulled off and we can continue along the 303 unimpeded.

Father Peter relaxes and reaches for a bottle of water from a pocket in the door. He takes a long pull as if quenching a deep thirst. After he's finished, he offers me the bottle, just as my cell phone vibrates. I grab the phone and a searing pain screams its way up my arm.

"Hello," I manage to say as I switch the phone to my left hand.

"You okay, partner?" Sam asks.

"Yes. I'm fine," I say, stretching out the fingers of my right hand to ease the pain.

"Doesn't sound like it to me—I've spoken with Treviss and he's told me what he knows," Sam says, straight to her point.

"Which is what?" I ask.

"You've raced off with Father Peter, Dee's being questioned by Deputy Chief Garner as I speak and Shitcreek are laid up in hospital. Ship's having emergency reconstructive surgery and Crick's head is the size of a balloon. And, to top it all, Kramer's still missing, feared dead. TV reports suggest you're the murderer—so, where are you?"

I spend the next ten minutes updating her on how I ended up driving into the mountains with Father Peter. I give her a resume of what happened in *Geometrix* and my inability to find Lena or the killer. I mention I think he's been listening in to my telephone conversations and possibly reading my emails. And I tell her what Father Peter revealed to me in the car about O'Connell, Jardine and Kramer travelling up to Gargailis's workshop in the mountains in 1993. Realizing this in itself is no reason to make the journey, I go on to explain about the print. I hear sharp intake of breath because Sam knows – like me – this is another of the killer's signs to draw me to his 'lair'.

"Is this really the right way to do it, Oskar?" she eventually says. "Shouldn't you bring in a SWAT team or something?"

"I can't wait for that, Sam. It'll be too late. You know that. Yes, he's drawing me in for a faceoff but I reckon it's the best chance I've got to rescue Lena. I have the momentum and think I can use this to my advantage. I can surprise him and catch him off-guard and hopefully snatch Lena before he has a chance to do anything."

"But listen, Oskar. If he's as meticulous and cunning as we think, he'll have worked this through himself. He'll be waiting for you up there," Sam asserts, chillingly. "I think he knows you inside out. And possibly better than most of us," she adds. "He's been watching you and listening to you. And, as you know, he's always been one step ahead throughout your investigation. He knows you're coming, Oskar. He's waiting. It's what he wants. It's what he's been planning all the time."

"I know this, Sam. But I don't think there's a better option at the moment."

"Well, listen to me on this. I've been studying the video recording.

I've uncovered something."

"What have you found?"

"Well, one good sign is he's probably not killed Lena yet. She's the bait in this. If she weren't the bait you'd probably listen to common sense and not go in single-handed. You *would* go in with a SWAT team and do this properly. Our killer knows this. That's how he's brought you to his door. On your own. It *is* personal, Oskar. It *is* about you. It has been all along. He's choreographed everything so don't be taken in by the amateur dramatics and flatter yourself too much that you've worked it all out for yourself. Don't be fooled by that 'mistake' of his when we thought he'd accidentally showed us the garden sculpture. He planned it that way, sure as houses. He knew you'd work it out. That was the point. He orchestrated it that way, so you'd end up in that apartment. He positioned that print so that you'd see it. He knew you'd work out what it was saying to you. But, and it's a big 'but', he's also playing out his own 'drama' in all this, and that, my friend, is possibly his only weakness. And perhaps you can use this to your advantage in this one-man mission. It's the one area where I think you might find the opportunity to take him down."

"What do you mean?"

"Well, I think he's working to a script, crafted with utmost care. He's fastidious. A perfectionist. This weakness could be your one opportunity to pull him down. He wants you alive for some reason. And I think he wants you to witness something before he kills you. There's a drama playing out here and you have the starring role."

There's silence as we think about this.

"The other thing, Sam, now I've had a chance to think it through more, is we know he's hurting people in ritualistic ways before he kills them. All three murders are similar to the way Sylvia Gargailis was killed but I think there's a replay button. He's replaying that experience with the victims he's choosing now. And it looks to be the complete detective team—"

"Or one of them is the killer," Sam interrupts, chillingly.

"Or one of them is the killer," I reply.

Again, there's silence whilst we ponder. I go straight to my new theory and run it past Sam.

"Hear me out before you say anything, Sam but, for the sake of this argument, let's assume the entire detective team is about to be murdered. Okay?"

"Okay."

"Well, I think our killer derives sadistic pleasure from knowing they'll suffer first, before he turns his attention to them. He wants them to suffer by experiencing the death of a loved one before he kills them. For Kramer, it was Chandler, for Buttle it was his cat and for me it'll be Lena. And, of course, I'm sure he was about to do the same to O'Connell and it was probably gonna be his wife first if I hadn't bust in. I know it doesn't explain the Green and Henshaw murders ... but it doesn't always fit together that neatly, does it Sam?"

Father Peter looks across as I say this and, although he's negotiating the twists and turns in the mountain road, he has time to nod in agreement. I notice a road sign saying Big Bear Lake and estimate we're only ten minutes away.

"Yes, it's messy," Sam says, thoughtfully. "But don't forget serial killers learn on the job as well as planning things out to their advantage. They'll often 'learn' their way through by getting a greater understanding of who they are and what they can do as they move forward. As they progress ... they'll improvise. They'll sometimes find distorted pleasure in repeating things that surprise them. I've studied countless examples of serial killers who treat their mission as one big learning curve about themselves. They find new things which thrill them, often by accident, and repeat them the next time around. Satiating their lust for power, revenge, sexual gratification or whatever it is turns them on. This guy has possibly a basic script that he's working on but it's a script in progress, if you will. That's what makes serial killers dangerous and difficult to predict. That's what makes them difficult to apprehend. They're predictable with some things and that's a weakness. That's often their undoing, enabling them to be caught ... eventually."

There's silence again and I almost hear Sam's brain working something through.

"What, Sam?"

"You know, I've come across serial murderers who are sane on the one hand and insane on the other. They often have opposing personalities driving them forward – two forces. I had a professor once who said you have to feel sorry for these son-of-a-bitches, because they have the capacity for good and evil. Both ends of the spectrum, as it were."

Father Peter slows down and looks intently at the side of the road.

"Hold on, Sam," I say as I turn to Father Peter, holding my hand over the cell phone.

"What's up?"

"You want to go to John's workshop up in the mountains, right?" "Yes."

"Well, I'm trying to find that dirt track that leads up there. It's along here somewhere—and, look. We've company again," he says, looking in his mirror. I turn in my seat and look down the road to see two patrol cars gaining on us, rapidly.

I go back to my phone.

"Look, Sam. I've got to go now. Things are starting to heat up."

"One last thing, Oskar. Take real care here. Don't underestimate his cunning. He may be the least likely person you're expecting."

I close the phone immediately because I see two more patrol cars come thundering round a bend towards us, lights flashing, sirens blaring, These two are side by side and they're taking up both lanes of the road. When they see us, they veer round and come to a screeching stop, blocking the road in both directions. At the same time, the patrol cars behind switch on their lights and blare their own sirens as they sweep us up into their trap.

In the commotion, Father Peter appears remarkably calm. I watch his eyes dart this way and that, looking for a means of escape. I turn my eyes back to the road and, in the darkness, see a track off to the left.

"There!" I shout.

"Yes, that's it. That's the track I've been looking for. It will take us up that hill," he says, pointing to the mass of rock to my left.

Father Peter suddenly accelerates towards the roadblock at an alarming speed. Then, with a skillful turn of the steering wheel, the car veers to the left, sending a shower of gravel in the direction of the two patrol cars and races off up the track. With the engine screaming at maximum power, the Subaru claws its way up the hill. This first stretch is a straight-line uphill climb of about half a mile and I am held firmly back in my seat as we accelerate at a breath-taking speed towards the first bend. As I look to my left, I realize this hill is more of a mountain. Father Peter seems to be in his element as I watch him snatch at the gear lever and expertly maneuver the car around loose boulders strewn across the track as we race away.

Suddenly, I hear and feel two bullets thud into the car in quick succession—then, a third smashes its way through the rear screen with a loud crack. The bullet must have passed between Father Peter and me, because I see a hole about the size of a dime in the windshield Deputy Chief Garner has clearly given orders to shoot to kill.

All this doesn't faze Father Peter, in fact it seems to spur him on. He presses even harder on the throttle in an attempt to move us out of sharpshooter range. When we approach the first bend, I look out of the shattered rear window to see the first of the patrol cars, as we disappear from sight.

It's a bumpy ride and I am thrown about in the seat despite the harness. At one point, Father Peter has to steer around a fallen branch and, in the process, I rap my head, rather painfully, against the door.

"Try this for size," Father Peter says, smiling broadly as he reaches back for the crash helmet I'd first seen when I'd entered the car at San Francisco Airport. "You might need it this time."

We start to zigzag our way around hairpin bends as we climb even higher. At points along the way, I look down and see the progress of our pursuers. Although the engines in the patrol cars are powerful, it's clear they're no match in overall performance for this thoroughbred racing machine.

"I know this track goes on for twenty miles," Father Peter shouts across the sound of the screaming engine. "I'm not expecting to meet anyone coming the other way, so hold on tight."

After about fifteen minutes, we reach the very top of this mountain and, in the moonlight, I see all the way across to the other peaks in this beautiful part of California.

"How far now, do you think?" I ask.

"I'm not sure but I seem to remember that, as this track descends, there's a path off to the left—yes, here it is," he says, pointing out into the darkness. "I think this is it."

I look to where Father Peter is pointing and barely discern a rough overgrown path.

"Yes. This is it. I'm sure," he says.

"How far to the farmstead?"

"About a mile, mile and a half, I guess. It's all downhill from here." "Can you drive without headlights?" I ask.

Father Peter thinks about this for a moment, then not only turns off the lights but the ignition as well.

With moonlight showing us the way, Father Peter releases the handbrake and the Subaru rolls forward, picking up speed gently. As he steers the car down the incline and away from the main track, the only sound comes from the plants and grasses brushing the underside of the car. At one point, the car picks up too much speed and Father Peter engages the handbrake, not wanting to flare his lights and give away our position to anyone.

I smile at Father Peter because he knows what he's doing.

After a few minutes freewheeling down the path and seeing the main track behind us disappear from view, Big Bear Lake looms out of the darkness, glistening under the moonlight. I have in mind the print on the wall and switch on my iPhone. I stare at the image on the screen and then out of the window, comparing both views.

"A little further please, but slowly," I say. "We're almost there."

We coast gently down the path for a few hundred yards and I see a passing place ahead.

"Look," I say, pointing. "Pull up there."

Father Peter stops the car and we climb out together, moving across to a small bluff overlooking the panoramic scene in front of us.

In the foreground, there's a farmstead with barns nestling by a small river and, in the background, the moonlight plays on the surface of Big Bear Lake, sending up shimmers of silver light.

"This is it," I declare.

"You're right," Father Peter says, as he looks at the image on my phone and then out across the panorama. "This is it."

58

(Saturday 2.45 a.m.)

IN THE DARKNESS, I gaze upon the panoramic scene, assessing my chances of descending the mountain without being noticed. Clearly, the easiest route would be to continue along the curving path to the farmstead but I'm tempted to go in a straight line, traversing the open country between where I'm standing now and where I think the killer's holed up with Lena. Fortuitously, the moon suddenly shines through a gap in the clouds and I'm able to study the terrain more carefully. I see trees and boulders clinging to the slope and I spot small gullies gouged out of the rock by water, over time. I decide these features will give me the cover I'll need to escape detection because I know the killer will be watching for me.

Thinking the farmstead might be out of view for most of the climb, I quickly plot a course, dividing the route into three sections. As I collect my head torch and a few tools I think I'll need, I instruct Father Peter to wait for me here. I also ask him to make sure his car is ready for a quick getaway when I return. With eyes focused on my first marker, a fallen tree about five hundred yards away, I drop over the edge of the path and begin my scramble down the side of the mountain.

I clamber my way around old tree roots and loose boulders at first, knowing that one false move could send rocks tumbling down the slope – or, worse still, me. At one point, my foot disappears into an unseen hole and I come to a stop, making me realize just how dangerous this journey might be. Nonetheless, I eventually reach the tree, out of breath, but without further mishap.

Whilst I regain breath I take the opportunity to look back up the incline to where I'd left Father Peter, at the viewpoint. It takes a few seconds to find the Subaru in the shadows but I also catch sight of the faint burn of police lights in the sky, fast disappearing into the distance.

Feeling relieved about this, I turn and look for my second marker a small cliff with a rocky outcrop – about two hundred yards away. I soon realize this second section is also fraught with danger because I have to step through small, slippery rivulets and jump deep gullies. I even have to traverse slabs of rock set at such perilous angles that I have to feel my way across on all fours. On one, I reach out with my damaged right hand to stop myself toppling over the edge. I instantly feel a sharp pain up my arm and have to pull back my hand, dislodging a small boulder in the process. All I can do is watch it clatter noisily down the slope before it comes to rest fifty yards away. Once silence returns, I take a deep breath and continue but slide across on my butt this time, using only my left hand to steady myself.

Arriving at the second marker, I peer around the bluff and see the farmstead straight ahead, closer than expected. Everywhere looks to be quiet but I don't want to be fooled into believing the killer isn't there somewhere looking out for me from his own hiding place. Waiting for me to arrive.

The ground levels off from here and I move at a brisk pace using trees as a screen, eventually climbing into the farmstead through a perimeter fence. I then move up alongside the first of the wood-paneled barns, with the sound of my heart pounding in my chest. I have to brush away cobwebs as I work my way towards the corner and peer around the side, preparing for the assault I'm about to make. A rank smell hits me – the unmistakable stench of death and decay. It's a toxic, heavy odor which clings to my nasal passages like cloying glue. My heart sinks as I think about Lena, wondering if I'm too late.

I reach for my gun, instinctively, feeling my pulse quicken as the adrenalin fuels me for the chase. I pull up my buff to cover my mouth and work out what to do.

From here, I'm able to look onto the main farmyard and across to the other buildings which make up the farmstead. I see the three barns I counted in Tomkins' photograph and see also the farmhouse itself. Everywhere appears deserted. There are no lights. No signs of movement. There's silence.

I turn back and look up the mountain, seeing more flashing lights this time. They're still in the distance but I realize there's no time to spare because I think Deputy Garner will guess the significance of the print of Big Bear Lake and soon come over the horizon with his 'troops'.

I move out and look inside the first barn. It's open sided and I spot it's full of old vehicles and what looks to be redundant farm machinery. There are tractors, trailers and wooden carts. I see also the remains of a stripped-down truck, parked in one corner. I move inside and look around more closely, checking to see if Lena could be hidden. Thinking about the killer's other lairs, I take care to look in all corners. I even look on the floor for signs of a trap door that may lead down to an underground cellar. Finding nothing, I make my way back outside and move across to the next barn.

This one is slightly larger and I enter through a set of double doors, left wide open. I see a pickup parked inside and move in for a closer look. It's a silver Toyota Hilux and I think back to the Eric Green murder and the tire track evidence we found at the scene. I place my hand on the hood and feel the engine is still warm. Next to the Toyota is a flatbed truck, with a heavy-duty winch attached on the back. I nearly trip up on the long cable draped over the side. Once again, I move around the barn, checking out every nook and cranny for any sign of Lena. Just as I'm about to leave, I see a vehicle under a dustsheet in the far corner. I move across, knowing what's underneath before I've arrived there. It has the distinctive shape of Lena's precious Alfa.

I come out into the moonlight running, with my heart beating faster, and move swiftly across the yard in the direction of the final barn. The smell of death is stronger with every step I take. The double doors are firmly closed and secured. From the inside. I hear a strange buzzing noise. A bluebottle lands on my face and then scuttles away as I work out what the noise is. Looking down to the bottom of the set of doors, I see swarms of flies moving back and forth, like bees at an entrance to a hive.

My instincts tell me to bust my way in, Rambo-style, but Sam's warning rings true in my ears, reminding me that Lena's the 'bait' here, and no doubt the killer will be waiting for me on the other side. I therefore make my way around the barn to see if there's another way in. I still want to use the element of surprise to gain an advantage.

I move quietly and carefully, looking for strategically placed traps or alarms which might signal to the killer that I'm outside. But, as I'm doing this, I think he knows this already and has been charting my progress ever since I left L.A. There are no cobwebs brushing against my face this time, making me think I'm walking a well-trodden route, so I'm not surprised to find a single door around the back. It's sited alongside a roofed wood store, where I can see long planks of rough sawn timber seasoning in the racks.

With my gun raised and primed, I lean across and gently turn the handle. The door opens easily on well-oiled hinges. A sudden rush of flies greets me, seemingly seeking a means of escape from this house of horrors.

I take a deep breath and step inside.

59

(Saturday 3.30 a.m.)

IT'S PITCH BLACK INSIDE the barn but the infrared image on the screen gives the Reaper the real-time visual information he wants.

He can see everything. Perfectly.

Just as planned.

He watches Salo, gun in hand, roll across the barn floor and position himself behind a workbench. Then, pressing a key on his console, the barn fills with the sonorous opening of Lauridsen's *O Magnum Mysterium*, creating the thrilling effect he is wanting for this moment. He knows Salo will have recognized the meaning immediately.

"We're so pleased you've made it down the mountain safely, Detective Salo? Why don't you come right inside?" he says into a microphone, as he fades in a series of spotlights positioned high in the rafters, sending down cones of light onto the floor below.

With a sense of triumph, the Reaper watches Salo peer over the top of the bench, trying to comprehend the grotesque sight confronting him.

Seated in a row of chairs are six people. They are in front of the Reaper's pride and joy, the metal-clad chamber, about twenty feet away in the shadows. All are held securely to their seats by a mixture of ties and restraints. The dead only need rudimentary fixing to hold them in place but the two alive are held securely at their wrists and ankles, to stop them escaping.

The first chair on the extreme left is empty. In the second sits Kramer, mouth agape, barely conscious. He stares out with a wild fear in his eyes, jerking his head back and forth as he tries to ascertain what is about to happen next. An inch wide metal band around his throat glints under the spotlight. The Reaper hopes Salo has seen this because it has a major part to play in his drama that's about to unfold. A stepper motor attached to the adjusting bracket allows him the opportunity to either tighten or loosen the strap remotely.

"Chief. You okay?" Salo calls out but all Kramer can do is let out a long, bitter cry of anguish, like a wounded animal.

"Save your breath, Detective," the Reaper announces. "His brain-to-mouth coordination is not as it should be. It's the chemicals, you see. He's fully awake but he knows what's happening and he also knows what I'll do to him should you decide to try anything foolish," he adds, as he positions his finger over a two-way toggle switch.

Next to Kramer sits Buttle. He is held in his seat, much in the same way, but is barely conscious and clearly not going anywhere in a hurry. Then comes the first of the dead bodies. Flies swarm on this more bloated of corpses but the body at the far end is almost skeletal where there's skin, it's blackened and stretched tight like a drum.

"Chief, it's me, Detective Salo. Where's Lena?" Salo calls out.

Kramer tries to speak but his mouth can't form the words and everything comes out in a garble. The Reaper sees Salo tense at this so he takes the initiative by throwing the switch forward. The metal band around Kramer's throat begins to tighten, like a tourniquet.

"This is no time for heroics, Detective Salo. No time at all."

Kramer starts to splutter and choke as his windpipe closes in on itself.

"Okay—okay—what do you want?" Salo calls out.

"That's better. You see you'll have to do exactly as you're told if you want to save your Chief ... And let's not forget about Lena, shall we?"

The Reaper smiles to himself, knowing he now has Salo's complete attention. He throws the switch the other way and the band around Kramer's neck begins to loosen off around his throat. There's a sharp intake of breath as Kramer sucks air back into his lungs.

"Where's Lena? Release everybody and we can clear all this up."

"It's too late for that, Detective Salo. In your heart I think you know that as well. So save your speech for someone more gullible ... Look, come over here and everything will become clear. I've reserved a seat for you."

The infrared camera gives the Reaper a clear image of Salo and he watches him stand up and walk towards the row of chairs.

"That's it. Nice and easy. And before you sit down, drop the gun to the floor."

Salo hesitates slightly at this command, so the Reaper gently nudges the switch and the stepper motor whirrs into action for a second or two.

"Okay, okay," Salo says as he hears this, dropping the gun at the same time.

"That's it. Now, as you sit down, position your wrists and ankles in those shackles on the legs and arms of the chair."

The Reaper sees everything clearly on his screens and, when he's satisfied Salo is in the correct position, he throws another switch and hasps snap shut around Salo's wrists and ankles with a resounding click.

Perfect.

*

I hear the waves of sonorous music stop, throwing the barn into eerie silence. Even Kramer's whimpering ceases as he looks around, anxiously. From my position under the spotlights I can't see much apart from the horrific sight of the dead and dying, sitting in their chairs. The rank smell of rotting flesh has embedded itself in my nasal passages and it's all I can do to stop gagging. Flies swarm everywhere. Even Kramer can do nothing to stop them sucking at the gaping wounds where the cuffs have cut into his wrists. Through the glare of the spotlights, I can just about make out the large, looming shape of a metal container which dominates the center of the barn. Is this the control room where the killer is playing out his twisted, sadistic drama?

"LENA. IT'S OSKAR, WHERE ARE YOU?" I shout out, wondering if she can hear me inside.

There's nothing.

I pull on the shackles at my wrists, noticing they're modeled on police cuffs. I see an array of electronic components and wires showing how the killer has been able to snap them shut, remotely.

Suddenly, out of the corner of my eye, I see a flash of moonlight. I turn my head just in time to catch the fleeting glimpse of someone coming in through one of the barn doors at the far end. I can't work out who it is because the figure glided in so quickly, like some ethereal ghost.

Trying to think rationally, I wonder if backup has arrived. Perhaps it's Father Peter? Has he come down the mountain to assist? Was the white vision just the reflection of the moonlight on his clothes?

A minute goes by, then another. There's no sign of anybody. No sounds, no movements at all. Nothing. Just as I'm convincing myself it was another of my imaginary 'wraiths', I see a ghost-like image, clothed in white, come out of the darkness and walk towards me. As he comes in closer, nearer to the light, the realization suddenly hits me. The reason he's looking so ghostly is because he's wearing white protective clothing, like SOCOs wear at crime scenes, complete with white hood, mask and white bootees. But, more menacingly still, he's wielding a wrecking bar in his hands.

As he moves ever nearer, another recognition hits me but this time it's like an express train. Things start to fall into place and a cloak of dread and fear wraps around me, like a wet shower curtain. I immediately wonder why I've been so blind. Why have I failed to see what was staring me in the face all along?

It *is* Father Peter.

I never did work out why he managed to find me on the second floor of *Geometrix* when I lived on the third. And it really was his foot that tripped over Ship in the corridor. He's the person who has masterminded this whole caper. He organized everything to bring the detective team from 1993 to this hellhole in the mountains.

As he moves in closer and steps into a cone of light, we lock eyes for a moment. I see him challenge me to piece everything together because he's picked up that I've spotted something else. His smile broadens under the mask as recognition dawns on me. The eyes. I've connected with them before. Just like this. And then I have it. I'm wrong. It's not Father Peter. I stared at this person twenty years ago. Across the courtroom in 1993. On the day John Gargailis was sentenced to death by lethal injection.

He picks up on my recognition, continuing to stare, seemingly relishing this moment. The control.

It's Danil. John Gargailis's son.

After a minute, he takes out a small remote from his pocket and raises it high into the air, pressing a button.

The barn is thrown into complete darkness this time.

"I like the dark, Detective Salo," he says, menacingly. "In fact, I thrive in dark places ... that's where I belong, really. In the dark."

Another set of illuminations comes on. But, this time, light shines out from a window running the full length of the metal container.

It takes me a few seconds to adjust to the glare but I soon work out what it is. The inside is built as a replica of the death chamber at San Quentin, complete with clock on the wall. And, strapped to the gurney center stage, is Lena. My heart sinks. She lifts her head and I see utter despair etched into her eyes.

"Now you understand why you're here, don't you, Detective—?"

"Let her go. She's done nothing wrong. I'm the one you want. You have me now. Let her go."

"No deal, Detective Salo. She's written into the script, I'm afraid. A minor player I grant you but an important one nonetheless."

"Look, Danil, we can work this—"

"I'm not Danil. I'm the Reaper," he says, through gritted teeth, wielding the bar once again."Danil is the person who let things ride, just like you. He did nothing about the injustices ... just like you and your detective cronies."

"But she's done nothing wrong—"

"That *is* the point, don't you see?" he says, followed by a maniacal laugh. "You must feel the pain of knowing she's about to die ... just like I had to endure the pain of knowing my father was going to die in San Quentin."

He looks across to the chamber.

"You see the clock in there? When I press this button, the second hand will start its ten-minute countdown. Then, the poisons will start pumping their way into her body. Firstly, sodium thiopental to render her unconscious – you remember that clue I left you – then pancuronium bromide to stop her breathing. And, finally, potassium chloride ... that'll freeze her heart. Full stop."

He says all this without emotion, as if reciting an objective fact for clarity.

"You see I realized you were particularly responsible for my suffering, Detective Salo, because you knew my father was innocent, didn't you? But you did nothing about it? That's been the real crime, Detective Salo. My father – my *Master* – had to spend three years preparing to be put to death in a chamber like this. And at one point, he said his goodbyes to me and was strapped to the gurney. Can you imagine? And then, after receiving a reprieve, he's now spent twenty years in prison for a crime he didn't commit. Now it's time for all of you to pay your dues ..."

Danil turns to Kramer, with hate in his eyes.

"Even this hypocrite sitting here, he's going to die soon. He didn't witness seeing his whore mistress being put to death, I grant you, but I know he suffered and that's good enough for me. He preaches about righteous behavior, as if he's a god, but he's no better than the dregs of society he has responsibility for locking away."

He leans in closer and I'm sure I see the beginnings of pain in his eyes, as if he's remembering some deep hurt.

"Do you know I had to sit in my bed at home as a small boy and listen to him having sex with my stepmother, whilst my father was up here in his workshop. Can you imagine that, Detective Salo?"

He looks further down the line.

"Then, there are the other detectives. They couldn't care less, could they? They were prepared to fabricate evidence to secure a conviction. And we know now they took bribes, as I suspected all along ... that's Jardine down there, second from the end. I got to him quite early in my campaign. He was a test run, really."

"What about the others?" I ask, wanting to continue stalling him.

"The others? They're just people who've upset me along the way. That shriveled up corpse at the far end was one of my teachers. He was the first."

"What about Eric Green and David Henshaw? Why them?"

"Clever, wasn't it? By hacking into your computer whilst you were asleep, I could read your emails and I found out ten weeks ago that you were next up on the roster for a case, so I chose Green at random.

You see I knew your lieutenant would send you out to investigate and we could get to know each other. Henshaw, on the other hand, was more complicated. I'd had him in my sights for many years. He was a school-friend who ended up being just another mindless bully in the schoolyard."

He lifts the remote, once again, pointing it towards the chamber this time.

"But, first, your turn to suffer—"

"Look, we can do something about all this, now" I interrupt. "We can prove your father's innocence and—"

"Save your breath. It's too late," he says, as he presses a button and the second hand starts ticking.

He puts the remote in his pocket and lifts up the bar.

"Did you know, my stepmother used to beat me with a broom handle to keep me quiet as a small boy?" he says, advancing towards me. I can only watch, helplessly, as he lifts the bar high into the air. There's a pause as he drills his eyes into mine, before swinging the bar down in a long, curving arc. Bones crack under the impact and I see sparks fly up from the shackle as he smashes into that as well. A sharp and intense pain races up my arm as I close my eyes and let out a long, piercing scream.

Danil moves in close and I feel his breath on my face. I open my eyes to see him glaring into mine with a ferocious and maniacal anger. He's holding a craft knife now, showing me what his twisted and warped mind is about to do next.

He grabs hold of my head and yanks it to one side, viciously.

"You see, I was the one who killed my stepmother, Detective Salo. The Reaper. Not Danil. He wouldn't say boo to a goose, that boy ... he couldn't ... he can't! In fact, I'm the man he isn't," he blurts out, as if it's the first time he's ever put it together like that. The pause continues as he looks into the distance – a distant memory. His demeanor suddenly changes and the intensity of his grip slackens slightly as a childlike face begins to emerge from behind the mask.

"You see I'd had enough ... all the abuse ... the beatings ... the pain ... did you know she used to hit me until I cried?"

It's the voice I heard when I spoke to the thirteen-year-old boy in 1993.

"I could only stand so much ... can you feel that pain in your arm?" he asks, almost sympathetically. "She beat me so hard that she once broke my arm with an iron bar like this one." I see him physically wince at the thought and then he looks directly into my eyes, almost pleadingly.

"Help ... me ... Detective," he says, looking deep into my eyes.

"Look—Danil—stop the clock—release Lena now. We can sort this out and save the situation, before it goes too far."

As I say this, I feel his grip around my head tighten, once again, as if a switch has been thrown. All I can do is look on helplessly as the 'little boy' disappears and the Reaper returns. He yanks my head to one side as the blade of a knife reappears.

I pull at my wrists and excruciating pain runs up my broken arm. Through the pain, I have the sensation my right wrist has broken free from its shackle. I'm able to reach down the side of my right leg and grasp the derringer at my ankle. I pull my hand back up with it held firmly between my fingers.

As I feel the blade of the knife cut into my neck, there's an ear splitting explosion from my derringer. I see a bullet rip away the Reaper's mask, leaving a deep channel in his cheek. The second bullet sinks into his jaw and exits at the top of his skull, snapping his head back, viciously, spraying blood and brain matter over my face. He slumps on top of me, sliding towards the floor. As his contorted face passes mine I see, momentarily, the boy-like expression return for the last time. It's Danil. He seems to look at me with gratitude before dropping to my feet, finally released from the monster within.

I look at the clock in the chamber. Four minutes to go.

I reach for the wrecking bar with my damaged right arm and manage to scoop it up with my bloodied fingers, ignoring the intense pain. I place the chiseled end into the shackle at my left wrist and lever it open, using all the weight I can muster from my right shoulder. I do the same with the shackles at my ankles and rush to the window of the chamber, taking the wrecking bar with me.

I look around for a way in and find a door but there's no obvious way to open it. I see no handles or locks. I find a small gap and try to force it open with the bar but nothing gives, nothing moves. I realize the outside of the chamber is encased in steel. It's impenetrable.

Father Peter arrives, having heard the gunfire and immediately works out what's happening. He picks up a sledgehammer from one of the racks and starts to smash away at the glass but the head of the sledge just bounces off, hardly leaving a mark.

Realizing something else is needed, I rush through the barn doors and come into the fresh air, looking for inspiration. My eyes are drawn to three helicopters coming over the horizon but I ignore this and go straight into the barn opposite, where I'd seen the Toyota Hilux, thinking I might use it to ram the chamber. As I rush inside, I almost hit my head on the jib of the winch on the back of the flatbed. That's when I work out a plan.

The truck fires up at the first attempt and I drive it out of the barn towards the workshop. I back the truck against a large boulder at the center of the yard. From this position, I see directly in through the barn doors and into the chamber itself.

I jump out of the truck and run in with the cable. With Father Peter's help, we wrap it completely around the chamber, securing the stout hook back onto the cable itself. I then race back out and, with the truck's engine revving, pull on the lever that starts to wind in the cable. The winch begins to steadily pull in the slack and we both rush around, making sure nothing catches on the cable. It's agonizingly slow but, with a minute left on the clock, a moment comes when the chamber seems to strain under the pull. Then, at a critical moment, when I hear the winch begin to scream, the truck itself starts to slide across the dirt floor, finally coming to a halt against the boulder with a thud. Sensing this is, literally, the make or break moment, I go across to where Danil's body is lying and take the small craft knife from his grasp. As I'm doing this, I hear a sudden crack from the chamber and rush back to see the far side of the chamber lift up from its foundations. It's only a small gap but it continues to rise, inch by inch. I wait until there's a space big enough for me to slide underneath and rush to Lena's side, cutting the tube at her wrist. I pull it away from her body as the second hand finishes its countdown and I hear the pumps kick into action. As I slump to the ground with the tube in my hands, I watch the first of the lethal poisons spew out onto the floor beside me.

As if in a dream, I watch black clad members of LAPD's SWAT team descend on the scene. They point their attack rifles at me and yell out well-rehearsed instructions. Above the noise, I just about hear Lena's sobbing. It's not in despair this time but in relief that she's finally freed from her nightmare.

I see Deputy Chief Garner in full protective gear look into the chamber, through the window, as he tries to work out what the hell's happened. He stares at me with a disbelieving look as officers cuff me on the floor and medics swarm around Lena.

Epilogue

(Two months later)

FATHER PETER COMES INTO the departure lounge at LAX. It's impossible to miss him this time because he's wearing his official orthodox church regalia – long black cassock, sash around his waist, traditional gold cross hanging from a chain at his neck. Next to him is the diminutive figure of John Gargailis. He's walking between two airport security guards as he carries the casket in his hands.

The sight of them makes me think about the unintended consequences of my actions in 1993, which I've been wrestling with these past months. I still rue my decision to have done nothing about the injustices which took place at the time. I think also that Gargailis must be contemplating what might have happened had he chosen a different path. By initially confessing to a murder he didn't commit, Gargailis thought he was saving his family from further harm but now he knows the truth about his son. Even Father Peter must be struggling with his god as he tries to deal with his own list of 'what-ifs'.

Hindsight can be a cruel master on occasions like these.

Thankfully, Lena survived her ordeal but it will take many months, possibly years, for her to return to any semblance of normality. After leaving hospital, she went to recuperate at her parents' home in San Francisco. We spoke on the phone a few times but these conversations became stilted once we tried to discuss our own relationship.

Fortunately, Dee and Treviss were not disciplined over their decision to disobey the order to stay away from me once I'd become the most wanted man in California. Dee's not spoken any more about seeking a transfer but, occasionally, she'll give me one of those long, hard stares over the top of her 5-shot coffee cup. With that twinkle in her eye, she lets me know I'm still on borrowed time.

Buttle and Kramer survived their ordeal but Buttle's still on sick leave, having told me privately he's gonna bail out when he's struck a deal over his pension. However, Kramer's back on the tenth floor after winning his pissing contest with Eugene Garner. Nothing's been said about the deal we'd initially struck, with a handshake, and I'm happy to leave it at that.

Sam is in Denver, having left for home immediately after the showdown in the mountains. I've been in touch with her since then, arranging all the ducks in line for my official report. We learnt a bit more about Danil Gargailis but why his metamorphosis into the Reaper took the form it did remains a mystery.

With the help of Hargreaves and his team, I eventually found the Reaper's lair up at Big Bear Lake, about half a mile from the farmstead, buried into the hillside. It was clear that, had he succeeded in killing us all in the barn, he intended to hide himself away – for weeks if necessary – watching over the scene of death from afar and masterminding his eventual escape, remotely.

I'm brought out of this dark musing by the sight of Father Peter and Gargailis walking towards me, smiling warmly. I do my best to smile back and hold out my hand in greeting but we're immediately steered towards the departure gate by one of the security guards – he's keen to load the precious cargo safely on board. He directs us along a jetway, where we're met by the pilot and crew. A photographer is there to capture the moment and we all look towards camera. A steward then leads us into business class seating for our seventeen hour flight to Riga, where we will 'return the relics to their rightful home', as the LA Times had reported this morning.

We watch in silence as the security guards carefully place the casket inside a specially prepared and padded overhead locker and, as Gargailis moves past me to sit down, he puts a hand on my shoulder and grips it firmly. This makes me look into his eyes. I've seen him focus them on me like this once before. In the courtroom in 1993.

"Don't worry, Detective Salo," he says, as if he's recognized my own misgivings about the part I've played in this whole drama. "Trust me on this, everything will be all right in the end."

I do my best to smile, feeling moved by this man's sensitivity, and then we both sit down to strap ourselves in for the long flight.

I feel my cell phone vibrate and look at the screen. It's from Sam. I'd texted her this morning, suggesting I could reroute to Denver on my return.

It reads:

Sure thing Partner!